P9-DFK-682

## BOOKS BY ELMORE LEONARD

The Bounty Hunters
The Law at Randado
Escape from Five
    Shadows
Last Stand at Saber
    River
Hombre
The Big Bounce
The Moonshine War
Valdez Is Coming
Forty Lashes Less
    One
Mr. Majestyk
Fifty-two Pickup
Swag
Unknown Man No. 89
The Hunted
The Switch
Gunsights
Gold Coast

City Primeval
Split Images
Cat Chaser
Stick
LaBrava
Glitz
Bandits
Touch
Freaky Deaky
Killshot
Get Shorty
Maximum Bob
Rum Punch
Pronto
Riding the Rap
Out of Sight
Cuba Libre
The Tonto Woman
    and Other Western
    Stories

# ELMORE LEONARD

# CUBA LIBRE

A Dell Book

Published by
**DELL PUBLISHING**
a division of
Random House, Inc.
1540 Broadway
New York, New York 10036

ISBN: 0-440-22559-0

Reprinted by arrangement with Delacorte Press

Printed in the United States of America

Published simultaneously in Canada

Design by Virginia Norey

January 1999

10  9  8  7  6  5  4  3  2  1

OPM

*For my old friend Allan Hayes*

# 1

TYLER ARRIVED WITH THE HORSES February eighteenth, three days after the battleship *Maine* blew up in Havana harbor. He saw buzzards floating in the sky the way they do but couldn't make out what they were after. This was off Morro Castle, the cattle boat streaming black smoke as it came through the narrows.

But then pretty soon he saw a ship's mast and a tangle of metal sticking out of the water, gulls resting on it. One of the Mexican deckhands called to the pilot tug bringing them in, wanting to know what the wreckage was. The pilot yelled back it was the *Maine*.

Yeah? The main what? Tyler's border Spanish failed to serve, trying to make out voices raised against the wind. The deckhand told him it was a *buque de guerra,* a warship.

Earlier that month he had left Sweetmary in the Arizona Territory by rail: loaded thirty-one mares aboard Southern Pacific stock cars and rode them all the way to Galveston on the Gulf of Mexico. Here he was met by his partner in this deal, Charlie Burke, Tyler's foreman at one time, years ago. Charlie Burke introduced him to a little Cuban mulatto—"Ben Tyler, Victor Fuentes"—the man appearing to be a good sixty years old, though it was hard to tell, his skin the color of mahogany.

Fuentes inspected the mares, none more than six years old or bigger than fifteen hands, checked each one's conformation and teeth, Fuentes wiping his hands on the pants of his white suit, picked twenty-five out of the bunch, all bays, browns and sorrels, and said he was sure they could sell the rest for the same money, one hundred fifty dollars each. He said Mr. Boudreaux was going to like these girls and would give them a check for thirty-seven hundred fifty dollars drawn on the Banco de Comercio before they left Havana. Fuentes said he would expect only five hundred of it for his services.

Tyler said to Charlie Burke, later, the deal sounded different than the way he'd originally explained it.

Charlie Burke said the way you did business in Cuba was the same as it worked in Mexico, everybody getting their cut. Tyler said, what he meant, he thought they were going directly from here to Matanzas, where Boudreaux's sugar estate was located. Charlie Burke said he thought so too; but Boudreaux happened to be in Havana this week and next. It meant they'd take the string off the boat, put the horses in stock pens for the man to look at, reload them and go on to Matanzas. What Tyler wanted to know, and Charlie Burke didn't have the answer: "Who pays for stopping in Havana?"

That evening Charlie Burke and Mr. Fuentes left on a Ward Line steamer bound for Havana.

It was late the next day Tyler watched his mares brought aboard the cattle boat, the name *Vamoose* barely readable on its rusted hull. Next came bales of hay and some oats, one of the stock handlers saying you didn't want a horse to eat much out at sea. Tyler stepped aboard with his saddle and gear to mind the animals himself. That was fine with the stock handlers; they had the cattle to tend. They said the trip would take five days.

IT WAS BACK toward the end of December Charlie Burke had wired: FOUND WAY TO GET RICH WITH HORSES.

He came out on the train from East Texas and was waiting for Tyler the first day of the new year, 1898, on the porch of the Congress Hotel in Sweetmary, a town named for a copper mine, LaSalle Street empty going on 10:00 A.M., the mine shut down and the town sleeping off last night.

Charlie Burke came out of the rocking chair to

watch Tyler walking his dun mare this way past the
Gold Dollar, past I.S. Weiss Mercantile, past the
Maricopa Bank—Charlie Burke watching him look-
ing hard at the bank as he came along. Tyler
brought the dun up to the porch railing and said,
"You know what horses are going for in Kansas
City?"

"Tell me," Charlie Burke said.

"Twenty-five cents a head."

They hadn't seen each other in almost four
years.

Charlie Burke said, "Then we don't want to go
to Kansas City, do we?"

He watched Tyler chew on that as he stepped
down from the dun and came up on the porch. They
took time now to hug each other, Charlie Burke's
mind going back to the boy who'd come out here
dying to work for a cattle outfit and ride horses for
pay. Ben Tyler, sixteen years old and done with
school, St. Simeon something or other for Boys, in
New Orleans, this one quicker than the farm kids
who wandered out from Missouri and Tennessee.
Charlie Burke, foreman of the Circle-Eye at the
time, as many as thirty riders under him spring
through fall, put the boy to work chasing mustangs
and company stock that had quit the bunch, and
watched this kid gentle the green ones with a
patience you didn't find in most hands. Watched him
trail-boss herds they brought down in Old Mexico
and drove to graze. Watched him quit the big spread

after seven years to work for a mustanger named Dana Moon, supplying horses to mine companies and stage lines and remounts to the U.S. cavalry. Watched him take over the business after Moon was made Indian agent at White Tanks, a Mimbreño Apache subagency north of town. The next thing he saw of Ben Tyler was his face on a wanted poster above the notice:

$500 REWARD
DEAD OR ALIVE

What happened, Tyler's business fell on hard times and he took to robbing banks. So then the next time Charlie Burke actually saw him was out in the far reaches of the territory at Yuma Prison: convicts and their visitors sitting across from one another at tables placed end to end down the center of the mess hall. Mothers, wives, sweethearts all wondering how their loved ones would fare in this stone prison known as the Hell Hole on the Bluff; Charlie Burke wondering why, if Tyler had made up his mind to rob banks, he chose the Maricopa branch in Sweetmary, where he was known.

He said on account of it was the closest one.

Charlie Burke said, "I come all the way out here to watch you stare past me at the wall?"

So then Tyler said, all right, because it was where LaSalle Mining did their banking and LaSalle Mining owed him nine hundred dollars. "Four times

I went up the hill to collect," Tyler said in his prison stripes and haircut, looking hard and half starved. "Try and find anybody in charge can cut a check. I went to the Maricopa Bank, showed the teller a .44 and withdrew the nine hundred from the mine company's account."

"That's how you do business, huh?"

"Hatch and Hodges owed me twelve hundred the day they shut down their line. They said don't worry, you'll get your money. I waited another four months, the same as I did with LaSalle, and drew it out of their bank over in Benson."

"Who else owed you money?"

"Nobody."

"But you robbed another bank."

"Yeah, well, once we had the hang of it . . . I'm kidding. It wasn't like Red and I got drunk and went out and robbed a bank. Red worked for Dana Moon before he came with me, had all that experience, so I offered him a share, but he'd only work for wages. After we did the two banks I paid Red what he had coming and he bought a suit of clothes cost him ten dollars, and wanted to put the rest in the bank. We're in St. David at the time. We go to the bank to open a savings account and the bank refused him. I asked the manager, was it on account of Red being Warm Springs Apache? The manager become snotty and one thing led to another. . . ."

"You robbed the bank to teach him manners."

"Red was about to shoot him."

"Speaking of shooting people," Charlie Burke said, prompting his friend the convict.

"We were on the dodge by then," Tyler said, "wanted posters out on us. To some people that five hundred reward looked like a year's wages. These fellas I *know* were horse thieves—they ran my stock more than once—they got after us for the reward, followed our tracks all the way to Nogales and threw down on us in a cantina—smoky place, had a real low ceiling."

"The story going around," Charlie Burke said, "they pulled, Ben Tyler pulled and shot all three of them dead."

"Maybe, though I doubt it. All the guns going off in there and the smoke, it was hard to tell. We came back across the border, the deputies were waiting there to run us down."

"Have you learned anything?"

"Always have fresh horses with you."

"You've become a smart aleck, huh?"

"Not around here. They put you in leg irons."

"What do you need I can get you?"

"Some books, magazines. Dana Moon sends me the Chicago *Times* he gets from some fella he knows."

"You don't seem to be doing too bad."

"Considering I live in a cell with five hot-headed morons and bust rocks into gravel all day. I've started teaching Mr. Rinning's children how to ride the horsey and they like me. Mr. Rinning's the superintendent; he says to me, 'You're no outlaw, you're just stupid—a big educated fella like you robbing banks?' He says if I'm done being stupid I'll be out as soon as I do three years."

Charlie Burke said to him that day in the Yuma mess hall, "Are you done?"

"I was mad is all, those people owing me money I'd worked hard for. Yeah, I got it out of my system," Tyler said. "But you know what? There ain't nothing to robbing a bank."

He was back at the Circle-Eye riding the winter range, looking for late calves or ones that had dodged the roundup.

Giving each other that hug, Charlie Burke felt the shape of a revolver beneath Tyler's sheepskin hanging open. Stepping back, he pulled the coat open a little more, enough to see the .44 revolver hanging in a shoulder rig.

"You have somebody mad at you?" Charlie Burke speaking, as usual, through his big mustache and a wad of Mail Pouch.

"You don't ever want to win fame as an outlaw," Tyler said, "unless everybody knows you've done your time. There're people who save wanted dodgers and keep an eye out. They see me riding up the street and think, Why, there's five hundred dollars going by. Next thing I know, I'm trying to explain the situation to these men holding Winchesters on me. I've been shot at twice out on the graze, long range. Another time I'm in a line shack, a fella rode right into my camp and pulled on me."

"You shot him?"

"I had to. Now I got his relatives looking for me. It's the kind of thing never ends."

"Well," Charlie Burke said, "you should never've robbed those banks."

Tyler said, "Thanks for telling me."


THEY SAT in rocking chairs on the shaded hotel porch, the day warming up, Charlie Burke in town clothes, a dark suit and necktie, his hat off now to show his pure white forehead, thin hair plastered across his scalp. In no hurry. He said, "If the market ain't Kansas City, where you suppose it is?"

"I'm trying to think," Tyler said, sounding tired from a life of scratching by and those years busting rocks, his long legs stretched out, run-down boots resting on the porch rail. A saddle tramp, if Charlie Burke didn't know better. The boy had weathered to appear older than his thirty or so years, his light tan J. B. Stetson favoring one eye as he turned his head to look at Charlie Burke, the hat stained and shaped forever with a gentle curl to the brim.

"You've been reading about the gold fields," Tyler said. "Take a string up to Skagway, not a soul around last year, now there're three thousand miners, a dozen saloons and a couple whorehouses on the site. I suppose put the horses on a boat, it's too far to trail drive. I've thought about it myself," Tyler said, though he didn't sound fond of the idea.

That pleased Charlie Burke, his plans already laid. He said, "You could do that. But if you're gonna take a boat ride, where'd you rather go, to a town where people live in tents stiff with the cold, or one that's been there since Columbus, four hundred years?" He saw Tyler smile; he knew. "Has palm trees and pretty little dark-eyed girls and you don't freeze to death you step outside."

"So we're talking about Cuba," Tyler said, "and you thought of me because I've been there."

"I thought of you 'cause horses do what you tell 'em. I recall though," Charlie Burke said, still in no hurry, "your daddy ran a sugar mill down there, when you were a kid."

"The mill," Tyler said, "what they call a sugar plantation. The mill itself they call the *central*. Yeah, I was nine years old the summer we went to visit."

"I thought you lived there awhile."

"One summer's all. My dad wanted us with him, but my mother said she'd lay across the railroad tracks if he didn't book us passage home. My mother generally had her way. She was afraid if we stayed through the rainy season we'd all die of yellow fever. Seven years later her and both my sisters died of influenza. And my dad, he came back to New Orleans to run a sugarhouse out in the parish, the old Belle Alliance, and was killed in an accident out there."

Charlie Burke took time to suck on his chewing tobacco, raise up the chair and spit a stream of juice at the hard-packed street.

"You recall much of Cuba?"

"I remember it being green and humid, nothing like this hardscrabble land. Cuba, you can always find shade when you want some. The only thing ugly are the sugar mills, black smoke pouring out the chimneys. . . ."

"You have a feeling for that place, don't you?"

"Sixteen years old, I was either going back to Cuba or come out here, and hopping a freight was cheaper than taking a boat."

"Well, this trip won't cost you a cent, and you'll make a pile of money before you're through."

Tyler said, "What about the war going on down there? It was in the paper the whole time I was at Yuma, the Cubans fighting for their independence."

They were getting to it now.

"It isn't anything like a real war," Charlie Burke said. "The two sides line up and shoot at each other. It's more hit and run. The Cuban insurgents blow up railroad tracks, raid the big estates, burn down sugar mills, and the Spanish army, the dons, chase after 'em. You understand that's what gives us our market, replacing the stock they run off or kill. Once I'd made a few trips for a Texas outfit ships cattle down there, it dawned on me, hell, I can run this kind of business. No time at all I'm living in railroad hotels and drinking red wine with my supper."

"Speaking of hotels," Tyler said, "I spent Christmas in Benson."

"You visit Miz Inez?"

"I stopped in."

"Camille still there?"

"She married a railroad dick, man hangs around freight yards with a ball bat."

"You wanted, you could've married her."

"I would've, she knew how to walk down a mustang. Listen, what I did for two days, I sat in the lobby of the Charles Crooker and read newspapers as far back as they had any. All the news, I swear, was about Cuba and how the Spanish are mistreating the people there. A correspondent named Richard Harding Davis saw whole villages of people taken from their homes and put in prison camps, where he says they starve to death or die of sickness. Another one, Neely Tucker, saw Cubans lined up against a wall and shot in the back, their hands tied behind them. At La Cabaña, the fort right there in Havana harbor. This Neely Tucker said the wall had blood all over it and what must've been a thousand Mauser bullet holes."

Charlie Burke said, "You read for two days, huh?"

"Any time now we could be going to war with Spain."

"We do, it'll be a popular cause, won't it? Help the Cubans win their independence? You see nothing wrong with that?"

"Not a thing," Tyler said. "Only I read the main reason we'd go to war'd be to protect American business down there."

"And I hear the newspapers are the ones want war," Charlie Burke said. "Print casualty lists and increase their circulation." He sat up in his chair to spit a brown stream, some of it hitting the porch rail this time. "I guess we'll have to wait and see what McKinley wants to do. There's a war, you'll be back selling remounts, 'less you volunteer and ride off with the troops. Get sent to Cuba to shoot at people you never saw before, some Spanish kids with no idea what they're doing there. In the meantime, partner, what's wrong with taking a string down to Cuba? The buyer's an American, Mr. Roland Boudreaux. You ever hear of him? From your old hometown, New Orleans, rich as sin." He watched Tyler shake his head. "Owns a sugar estate near Matanzas. You know where that is?" Now Tyler was nodding and Charlie Burke knew he had him.

"The sugarhouse my dad ran was south of there, near a place called Limonar."

"You'll be right at home then, won't you? How many mares can you put on the train by the end of the month, say around fifty?"

"Be more like half that, even with help. Hire

some trackers out of White Tanks. You want 'em by the end of the month, huh?"

"How about Galveston the middle of February the latest?" Charlie Burke brought out a billfold from inside his coat. "You sign the passport application—I brought one along—I'll have it by the time you come to Galveston." He handed Tyler a packet of U.S. scrip with a bank strap around it, the price of doing business already calculated. "That'll cover your expenses, get you a couple of mustangers and put the horses on the train, you'll have enough left to buy yourself some town clothes and a new hat. You aren't a poor workaday ranny no more, Mr. Tyler, you're a horse trader."

Looking at the money, Tyler said, "What's this man paying for range stock?"

"Hundred and fifty a head."

"You serious?"

"The man wants cutting horses to use for polo; he's a famous polo player."

"Who pays expenses?"

"We do."

"What's it come to?"

"Let's see, freight costs? Train and boat would run close to thirty-six dollars a head plus feed, wharfage, loading, veterinary inspection. Get to Cuba there's an eighty-five-dollar-a-head duty the Spanish make on horses. What's that come to?" Charlie Burke said, looking right at Tyler, wanting to see if he was as smart as he used to be.

It took him maybe four seconds.

"You aren't selling horses."

"What am I doing?"

"I wouldn't be surprised you're running guns," Tyler said. He watched Charlie Burke turn his head to spit a stream. "You are, aren't you? Jesus Christ, you're filibustering, and that's against the law."

Now Charlie Burke was shaking his head. "I'm not joining the fight or stirring up insurrection, that's filibustering. I'm delivering merchandise, that's all, as a business. This trip, a hundred and fifty shotguns. Two hundred Smith & Wesson .44s, both the regular model and the Russian. Like the one you have if I'm not mistaken, except these are copies made in Spain and shipped to Mexico. I'm also delivering a couple hundred Krag-Jorgensen carbines, five hundred rounds for each weapon, and we're throwing in a pile of machetes picked up used."

"You bankroll all that?"

"Their man in Mexico buys the arms. What'd you pay for your .44 Russian?"

"Fifteen dollars, like new. I bought it off a fella use to be in the cavalry."

"Their man in Mexico picked up two hundred brand-new for ten apiece, still had factory oil on them."

"Stolen."

"I imagine. All the weapons are bought in Mexico and shipped out of Matamoros. See, what happened, this particular Cuban sees me delivering cows, he asks me what side I favor in the revolution. I said well, if I had to pick one it wouldn't be Spain. He says what're the chances of bringing his friend Máximo some guns?"

"Máximo Gómez?"

"Head of insurgents. How would I like to run guns for the rebels? But as a business, without taking sides or contributing to the cause. There's no outlay of money either. This delivery coming up will cost the insurgents about twelve thousand. So what they can do, they send a message to one of the sugar planters: 'Give us twelve thousand pesos or see your mill burned to the ground.' The peso being worth ninety-two cents on the dollar right now. They raise the money that way or get it from people supporting the movement—Cuban cigar rollers in Tampa and Key West. Two-thirds of the money goes for the purchase of weapons, covers expenses and pays the crew of the cattle boat, the *Vamoose;* and the rest we get for risking our necks. It's against the law; yeah, you can go to jail, but that ain't as bad as if the dons catch you. You either get stood against a wall or they use the garrote on you: strangle you to death."

Tyler watched him rub the back of his neck, like he was feeling to see if he needed a haircut.

"Half the crew of the *Vamoose* are Mexicans and half are Cubans, the kind of fellas you don't have to worry about. They load the weapons aboard off a lighter and come up to Galveston for the cows and horses. There isn't much of a duty on beef, they're so glad to get it, so we ship fifty or so head and make a few dollars there. By the time the *Vamoose* gets to Matanzas the guns are underneath a deck covered with manure. We bring the horses and cows ashore, the Cuban custom inspector takes a quick look below and leaves with a few pesos but without getting anything on his shoes. So now the *Vamoose* heads east along the coast to where it's been arranged to drop the weapons. A Spanish gunboat stops them beforehand, they can show they've been inspected and cleared customs."

"You've done this already," Tyler said.

"One trip with guns. The next one after this, the fella in Mexico is lining up a Hotchkiss 12-pounder and that Sims-Dudley dynamite gun. Artillery's what the insurgents want more'n anything. Or machine guns. Get your hands on some machine guns, you can ask anything you want."

Tyler said, "I don't see what you need me for."

"The horses."

"You can get all the horses you want in Texas."

"I'd have to pay for 'em."

"Come on—why me?"

"This business makes me edgy and you have nerve."

"You think I've done it?"

"No, but you've rode the high country and had a price on your head. I feel if I'm gonna break the law I ought to have a partner knows what it's like," Charlie Burke said, "somebody that's et the cake."

# 2

THEY BROUGHT THE HORSES ASHORE at Regla, across the harbor from Havana: led them out of dim confinement into sunlight and down a ramp to the wharf, the horses poky, disoriented after five days at sea. Tyler and the Mexican stock handlers from the *Vamoose* brought the animals single file through rows of cargo stacked high and covered with tarps—hogsheads of sugar and molasses, stalks of bananas—the smell of coffee taking Ben Tyler back to the summer he spent here. It reminded him some of New Orleans, too, that same coffee aroma on the wharves along the river. Negro dockhands stood to look at the parade of horses, some of them smiling, reaching out. There were merchants and officials in town clothes and all kinds of hats—straw boaters among them—who took their time moving out of the way. Tyler came to a Spanish soldier, an officer in a pale gray uniform that seemed familiar: red facings on the collar, a white shirt and loosely knotted black necktie beneath the jacket, his hat a preshaped military straw set squarely on his head.

Tyler held the dun by a hackamore. He said, "Excuse me." Willing to say it once.

Now they were eye to eye, each with his own measure of curiosity, the man's hat shading a tired expression, tired or bored; or it was his mustache, the way it drooped over the corners of his mouth, that gave him that look. He turned and walked away, showing no interest in the horses, a man armed with a sword, his hand resting on the hilt.

Tyler felt himself waking up from what had been his life among cowhands and convicts, neighbor to reservation people once nomads, on occasion visiting bartenders and whores who passed for old friends. It seemed a thinly populated life to what he saw here, this mix of people and sounds and colors in a place he imagined Africa might be like: familiar smells, like the coffee, and customs that never changed. It was a country run by soldiers from another land and worked by people bought and sold only a dozen years ago, slavery not abolished here until '86—a fact he'd forgot until reading *Harper's* at the Charles Crooker reminded him, made him realize all those people working at his father's sugarhouse and in the fields had been slaves. These dockhands too.

There was Charlie Burke up the road.

And Fuentes in his white suit, arm raised, waving his hat, near the customhouse on the road that approached the wharf. Fuentes was pointing now to feed lots just up the road. The stock handlers were nodding, they knew where to take the horses.

Tyler left them, went back to the cattle boat for his gear, this time looking around at all the different kinds of straw hats there were, boaters, big raggedy ones, lightweight panamas with black bands that looked pretty good. A couple of soldiers in seersucker uniforms, blue pinstriping, wore straw hats with red badges pinned to the turned-up brim. Some of the convicts at Yuma wore straw hats, but no stockmen Tyler had ever seen, except in Mexico and down here. Later on he might look for a hat and a suit of clothes. Not a white one; he couldn't see himself in a white suit.

This time he came off the cattle boat with his saddle and most of what he owned in the world rolled up in a poncho. He stepped to the open harbor-side of the wharf and looked across at Havana in the late afternoon sun, a familiar view, an old colonial city in the same bright colors as the picture postcards his dad used to send and he'd saved for a time in a cigar box that bore the portrait of a Spanish general with full muttonchops that curved into his mustache, the man's chest loaded with medals. In Galveston he had mentioned the cigar box to Mr. Fuentes and the little mulatto knew exactly who it was. "Yes, of course, Captain-General Valeriano Weyler, recalled to Spain only last year. Spanish, despite his name, more often called the Butcher, the one who put thousands of people—no, hundreds of thousands in concentration camps to die. A terrible man," Fuentes said, "but not a bad smoke."

Tyler looked at the wreckage, what was left of some warship, gulls still perched out there, the scavengers circling. . . . His gaze moved to a trail of smoke, a steam launch coming away from a warship anchored not far from the wreck. He could make out the Spanish flag and sailors on deck in white. The launch reached the end of the wharf and now officers in dress uniforms were up the ladder, three of them coming this way along the wharf. Looking him over now, the *yanqui*—he heard one of them say it and another one use the word *vaquero*. As they passed, Tyler turned to see the nearest one looking back and he nodded, saying, "How're you today?" not giving it much and not getting anything in return, not a word. He saw Charlie Burke now beyond them, coming this way, Charlie Burke in his town clothes giving them a nod and saying something as he passed, and they ignored him, kept looking straight ahead.

Tyler dropped the saddle, still watching the officers. He was pretty sure they were army: triplets dressed in the same short red tunics with gold buttons and braid, light blue trousers with yellow stripes and kepis a darker shade of blue. They marched along in polished black boots, holding their sabers almost under their arms to point in the direction they were going.

As Charlie Burke reached him Tyler said, "You can't miss those fellas, can you?"

Charlie Burke glanced back at them but didn't say anything.

"They come off that ship. I guess visiting, 'cause they look army to me, cavalry."

"The ship's the *Alfonso XII*," Charlie Burke said.

He kept staring at it while Tyler waited for him to say something about the horses, still a little wobbly but all were safe and sound; or to tell him he looked like a grub-line rider and ask how come he hadn't bought any town clothes. But it didn't seem to be on his mind.

No, as his gaze moved he said, "That steamship yonder's the *City of Washington*. And that pile of scrap out there—you know what it is?"

"I was told a warship," Tyler said.

Charlie Burke looked at him now. "You don't know, do you? You were at sea. That's the USS *Maine*."

"One of ours?"

"What's left of her. Three nights ago, nine-forty on the dot," Charlie Burke said, "she blew up."

Tyler said, "Jesus," staring at the twisted metal sticking out of the water. "What about the crew?"

"Over two hundred fifty dead so far, out of three hundred seventy officers and men."

"What caused it, a fire?"

"That's what every American by now wants to know. What or *who* caused it, if you get my meaning."

"You were here when it happened?"

"We got in about six on the fifteenth, checked into the hotel. Nine-thirty that evening we went to supper—people here don't eat till it's time to go to bed. There was two explosions, actually, one and then a pause and then another one. The glass doors of the café blew in, the lights went out—I think every light in the city. Everybody in the place ran outside. It's pitch-dark in the street, but the sky's all lit up and you could hear explosions out there and see what looked like fireworks, Roman candles going off." Charlie Burke shook his head, more solemn than Tyler had ever seen him. "Yesterday I spoke to a deckhand off the *City of Washington* who saw the whole thing from close by. He said the first explosion pitched the bow of the *Maine* right up out of the water. With the second explosion the mid part of the ship burst into flames and blew apart. This deckhand was right there. He said you could hear men screaming, 'Lord God, help me!' Sailors out in the water, some hurt pretty bad, some drowning. The *City of Washington* and the *Alfonso XII* sent lifeboats over, and the *Diva*, a British ship tied up here at Regla, it sent boats. The wounded they managed to find were taken to hospitals; men missing arms and legs, some burned so bad, the deckhand said, you couldn't tell if they was man or beast."

"Jesus," Tyler said.

Except for the crow's nest sticking straight up, the wreckage barely looked like a ship. Tyler's gaze rose to the buzzards circling in a sky beginning to lose its light.

"Waiting for bodies or parts of 'em to rise up," Charlie Burke said. "They buried nineteen at Colón Cemetery yesterday and dragged forty more bodies out of the water today. Some of 'em in the hospital, they say, aren't gonna make it. The captain of the *Maine*, man named Sigsbee, wants to send divers down to look for bodies, but the dons won't let 'em near it."

"How come?"

"Because they might find out the explosion came from *under* the ship and not from inside it. If the keel's buckled inward, then it was a mine or torpedo blew her up. If the bottom's shoved outward, then it could've been a fire that started in one of the coal bunkers and spread to a magazine, where the high explosives are stored, and she blew. That's what everybody in Havana's talking about, what way did it happen. Fella at the hotel, one of the newspaper correspondents, had a copy of the New York *Journal,* just come by boat from Key West. The headline said, 'Destruction of the Warship Maine Was the Work of an Enemy,' not making any bones about it. Who's the enemy, but Spain? They're saying the Spanish arranged to have the ship anchored over a harbor mine, then they exploded it from the shore using an electric current. Or they shot a torpedo at her."

They were quiet for a time, staring at the wreckage, Tyler thinking of the men down inside in the dark, underwater. "Is there talk about us going to war?"

Charlie Burke said, "You bet there is. The newspaper fellas at the hotel say it won't be long now. And the dons seem for it. They're passing out circulars in town that say 'Long live Spain' and 'Death to the Americans.' "

They were quiet again, looking at Havana and hearing ships' bells and the *chug-chug* of steam launches out on the water. Charlie Burke said, "You know how much tobacco they grow on this island?"

"No," Tyler said. "How much?"

"A whole lot. But they don't put one bit of it aside for chewing tobacco."

Tyler slung his saddle over his shoulder by the horn. Charlie Burke picked up the rolled poncho, saying they'd meet Fuentes by the customhouse.

BUT THERE HE WAS across the road and up a piece at the stock pens, arm raised, waving at them. With him were the three officers in dress uniforms who'd come off the Spanish ship, and a few strides away, the officer in the familiar gray uniform Tyler had run into earlier, this time smoking a tailor-made cigarette.

Fuentes, Tyler noticed, had cut out the five horses he didn't want and put them in the same lot with the dun; and now Fuentes was coming out to the road to meet them, Charlie Burke saying, "Like he don't want us getting too close to the dons."

Maybe. Fuentes had an anxious look on his face. He said, "I think you can sell a horse today. Lieutenant Teo Barbón wants to know how old is the dun."

Tyler did a half turn, swinging the saddle from his shoulder. "Teo—that's his name?"

"For Teobaldo."

"Which one is he?"

Fuentes glanced over. "The hussar, the one with his hand on the fence rail."

In the red tunic and blue kepi, one of those, with their swords; all three intent on the horses while the one in gray was looking this way. Tyler said, "I remember that gray uniform from a long time ago. Or one like it."

Without looking around Fuentes said, "Guardia Civil. His name is Lionel Tavalera, a major; he's very . . . he makes himself known."

That was it, the Guardia, Tyler remembering

them as a kind of rural police, known to be hard-headed and mean. He said to Fuentes, "These fellas speak English?"

Fuentes shrugged. "I believe enough. Try them."

Tyler called out, "Hey, Teo?" And as the officers turned this way, Teo Barbón looking surprised to hear his name, Tyler said, "I'd put the dun's age at ten years old, no more'n that, but she ain't for sale. Pick another one, she's yours."

He saw Teo wore a neat little mustache waxed to needle points. The young man seemed to be studying him now, like he was wondering who this cowboy thought he was.

Teo said, "Why is that, you don't want to sell her?"

"I'd miss her. She and I get along, never have any arguments."

"Oh, the two of you are lovers?"

Teo's fellow officers were already grinning as he turned his head and said something to them in Spanish. Now they were laughing.

Tyler looked at Fuentes. "What'd he just say?"

"He said he thought *vaqueros* only fucked heifers."

Now one of the others was making a kissing sound toward the mares. The three boys having fun and Tyler realized that's what they were, boys, all in their early twenties—except for the Guardia Civil officer, Lionel Tavalera, who had a good ten years on them, or more. These boys were young and frisky, no different than cavalry officers Tyler had seen at Whipple Barracks and Fort Thomas their first time out, on frontier station with the "Dandy Fifth" and had that same strut and pose, feeling themselves above poor civilians and common soldiers. Tyler said to Fuentes, "What do these boys do all dressed up like that?"

They heard him, all of them looking over.

Fuentes said, "They're hussars," sounding surprised. "Lieutenant Barbón and his companions are of the Pavia Hussars, with the regiment here I believe six months."

Tyler said to Teo, "You're with a cavalry outfit, uh?"

"Hussars, *caballería*," Teo said, "the same as you have in your country to kill *indios*, yes? We kill *insurrectos*."

"Well, I was way off," Tyler said. "I thought the circus was in town and you boys played in the band."

They heard him, the three hussars giving Tyler a dead-eyed look now. Lionel Tavalera, the Guardia Civil officer, seemed to appreciate it, he was grinning. And so was Fuentes, his back to the officers, Fuentes with kind of a surprised expression in his eyes, like he was seeing the real Ben Tyler for the first time. Charlie Burke turned his head to say,

"What's wrong with you?" And then, to the officers: "Fellas, don't mind my partner, we're all friends here. Pick out a mount and we'll make you a deal."

Fuentes, turning to them, said, "Yes, please, while you have the opportunity." He said, "Lieutenant Barbón," and began speaking to him in Spanish as he walked back to the stock pens, now and again nodding at the horses. Now Teo was speaking to Fuentes in Spanish, Tyler getting some of it. It sounded like Teo wanted to ride one of the horses.

Lionel Tavalera, standing apart, said to Tyler, "You don't think I play in a circus band, do you?"

He had kind of a sissified way of holding his cigarette, Tyler thought, up in front of him and between the tips of two fingers. Tyler said, "I know who you are, you're Guardia Civil, you're a policeman."

"You pronounce it pretty good," Tavalera said, "but the Guardia are not police during time of war. We're like those people, the *caballería*, except we don't stay in Havana and go sightseeing, we hunt *insurrectos*. We the first to go to war, the front line always." He said, "You saw the ship that was destroyed?" nodding toward the harbor. "They say a fire began in the coal and spread to the munitions. It's too bad, uh, all those men dying. Tell me, you bring the horses from where, Texas?"

"Arizona," Tyler said.

"That's a long way. Your family live there?"

"I don't have a family, not anymore."

Tavalera looked at the stock pens and then at Tyler again. "May I ask how much you sell the horses for?"

Charlie Burke stepped in. "Hundred and fifty pesos, any horse you want."

Tavalera was nodding. "But with the duty tax, how do you make money? Or you don't pay so much of the duty. Listen, I don't care, it's your business."

"We're delivering this string," Charlie Burke said, "to Mr. Roland Boudreaux in Matanzas, along with some beef cows. Giving him a special deal."

"I know Mr. Roland Boudreaux," Tavalera said, and looked at Tyler again. "I visit in Mexico when I was young. At that time I want to be a cow*boy* like you. But I return home and they accept me to attend the *Colegio Real Militar*. You know what that is? Like your West Point. I was honored to be assigned to the Guardia Civil when I was in Spanish Africa, then they send me here at the beginning of the second Cuban insurrection, February 1895, again assigned to the Guardia Civil." Tavalera was saying, "In these three years . . ." as Fuentes called to them:

"Lieutenant Barbón ask how much for all five horses."

Charlie Burke answered him. "You know what we're asking."

Tyler watched the Guardia officer's expression turn hard, not caring for this interruption.

He waited another moment before saying, "In these three years I've come to love this country," telling it in a flat voice with an accent, cold, stating a fact. "After the war I intend to stay here to live in Matanzas, the most beautiful city in Cuba." He glanced at Charlie Burke. "Where he say you going to deliver these horses."

And now Fuentes was calling to them again.

"Lieutenant Barbón will give you four hundred pesos for the five horses. Right now, cash money."

Tavalera said to Tyler, "They're not worth it, the horses are too small," as Charlie Burke called back to Fuentes:

"Tell him a hundred and a half each, seven fifty. Pesos, escudos or double eagles, we don't care."

"Teo's worried," Tavalera said, "they won't be able to procure horses."

Tyler turned to him. "Why's that?"

Tavalera said, "The war," sounding surprised that he had to explain this. "Not the War of Insurrection, but the one that's coming soon. You blame us for blowing up your battleship and your government will use it to declare war on Spain. Avenge the blowing up of the ship and help the poor Cuban people, so oppressed. But the true reason will be so you can have Cuba for yourself, a place for American business to make money."

Tyler said to him, "Did you blow up the *Maine*?"

Tavalera shrugged and said, "Perhaps."

Sounding to Tyler as though he didn't care one way or the other.

Now Fuentes was calling to them, saying, "He's attracted to the bay with the star, but he says it's too small to be worth a hundred and fifty pesos."

"Tell him," Charlie Burke said, "we don't sell 'em by the pound. That's a saddle-broke cutting horse, can turn on a dime and leave you five centavos change. Ask him if he plays polo. That's what Boudreaux's buying his string for."

Tavalera said, "Rollie thinks he's going to be playing polo?" as Fuentes was saying:

"The lieutenant wants the saddle put on the bay with the star, so he can ride her, see what he thinks."

Tyler said, "He wants it put on?"

"He wants us to, yes."

Tyler looked across at Teo Barbón. "You say you're with a cavalry outfit?"

The officer turned to face him. "Pavia Hussars. You heard your man."

"Well, if you know how to ride, you ought to know how to saddle a horse."

Teo said, "Yes?"

He didn't get it.

"What I mean," Tyler said, "if you're not helpless, you can saddle it yourself. I'm not your *mozo*."

He understood that, staring at Tyler as if he couldn't believe anyone would speak to him this way. Now he was talking a mile a minute to the other hussar officers and to Tavalera, including him; Tyler seeing how a spoiled kid from Spain acted when the help talked back and he didn't get his way —no different than spoiled kids Tyler had seen at home. Now Fuentes was hurrying over, stooping to pick up the saddle.

Tyler placed a boot on it.

"Who's putting it on, you or him?"

"I can do it; it's nothing to saddle a horse."

"We don't work for him," Tyler said.

Fuentes shook his head. "You take it too far."

Teo was yelling, gesturing to Lionel Tavalera, who was listening to him, nodding, and seemed interested. But then he shrugged, shaking his head, and said to Tyler, "He wants me to give you my sword. Teo believes you insulted him."

Tyler said, "He wants me to *sword* fight with him?" Grinning, because it sounded funny, like he was talking about playing a kids' game.

"That's enough," Fuentes said. "All right? Please, let's go, we finished here."

"Go on with your business," Tavalera said. "I can speak to him, tell him to behave as a gentleman."

Fuentes said, "We have to go to the customhouse before they close."

Tavalera said, "Yes, go. I can take care of this, it's nothing."

All Charlie Burke said to Tyler was "You're some horse trader. Pick up your chair and let's go."

Tyler swung the saddle to his shoulder and stood there looking at Lionel Tavalera and the hussar officers. He said to Fuentes, "They won't bother the horses, will they?"

"They don't want any horses today, they change their mind," Fuentes said. He hurried Tyler and Charlie Burke away from there, out of the field and along the road to the customhouse, telling them he would speak to the custom people and to leave the filling in of the declaration to him. "We finish and take the ferry to Havana. Mr. Boudreaux say he can see you tonight at the hotel. He look at the horses tomorrow, pay you, we put the horses aboard the ship again and go to Matanzas. Is not very far." He said to Tyler, "You been there, uh?"

"A long time ago."

"But you know people there?"

"I was a boy then."

"Perhaps someone will remember you. Sure, you never know. See over there? The sugar warehouses, biggest in the world. That building? The electric lighting plant. And there? The Plaza de Toros, the Regla bullring. The famous Gentleman Matador from Spain, Mazzantini, will perform there Sunday, again. Last Sunday twice they gave him both ears. It's too bad you won't be here. Maybe when you come back. Let me ask you something," Fuentes said. "Do you have a pistol?"

Tyler looked at him. "In my poke."

"Keep it on you after we go to customs. Don't tell them you have one or you have to give it up."

Tyler said, "You're worried about Teo, that dandy? The Guardia, Tavalera, said he'd speak to him."

Fuentes said, "Yes, but what is he going to tell him?"

LIONEL TAVALERA WATCHED the two Americans and the mulatto as they walked off toward the customhouse. He had seen the mulatto before in Matanzas and knew of him, an employee of Rollie Boudreaux, the polo player, but had not decided yet if he should trust him, or if it mattered whether he did or not. Now he looked at the three hussar officers lounging against the rails of the stock pen, their kepis cocked over bored expressions, the way they were known to pose. Walking toward them, Tavalera said, "Teobaldo?"

The hussar straightened to stand half turned, looking along his shoulder at Tavalera, waiting as the Guardia officer stopped only a few feet from him.

"Let me ask you, did you think the cowboy was going to fight you with a sword?"

"If he was a man," Teo said.

"You think, out on the western plain of his country, a primitive place to live, he learned to fence? Use the épée, the saber?"

Teo shrugged.

"Don't you realize," Tavalera said, "if you drew your sword the cowboy would have shot you?"

"He had a pistol? Where was it?"

"Somewhere, you can be sure. Where he lives they all carry pistols and use them to settle their differences." He paused and said, "You wanted to kill him?"

"I want to cut him," Teo said, drawing a finger across his cheek. "Give him a scar to remember this day."

"But who is he? Do you know?"

"A *yanqui*. You saw him."

"And I say again, who is he? Does he have friends here, a connection with wealthy Americans? He delivers the horses to one. It isn't possible to bring horses to Cuba and make a profit, but he brings horses. As a favor to the wealthy American? The other American, the old one, tells me they have cows, too, they ship to Matanzas. Yes, and what do they do then, turn around and go home? What else is on that boat, the *Vamoose*, that rusting corruption? Do you think you should know more about this cowboy before you scar his face?"

Tavalera waited.

Teo said, "I don't care if he knows someone here or not, he insulted me."

"By not saddling the horse for you?"

"By his manner, the way he spoke to me."

"Where are you from, Madrid?"

"Of course. And you are from where, Africa?" His companions grinned.

"Be careful," Tavalera said.

"Oh? You aren't from Africa? I heard you were born there."

Tavalera said, "Look, I know what they say about you. You have a reputation and it gives you confidence. So the next time you see the cowboy you offer him pistols, uh? Here, take your pick."

"If I feel like it."

"If you feel like it," Tavalera said, knowing this young man as he had known dozens before him. "You say about me for your companions to hear, He's from Africa. The same as saying, What does he know of anything? I admit it, I was born there— why not?—in the penal colony at Velez de la Gomera, where my father was superintendent. And I returned to Africa with the Guardia, to Melilla during the war with the Iqar'ayen Rifs. Of course you know of that war. But let me ask you something. Can you imagine what it's like to cut off a man's hands?" He paused. "To put out his eyes with a bayonet?" Again he paused. "To bury a man alive in the sand?"

His gaze held on Teo, now with the feeling he was wasting his time, Teo waiting for this to be over.

"You don't say to me," Tavalera said, "you'll do something if you feel like it. You only do what you feel like if I say it's all right. You understand?" He waited until Teo gave him a nod. There. "But listen," Tavalera said, "I can be a sympathetic person. Ask my permission first. That's all you have to do."

# 3

VIRGIL WEBSTER HEARD A VOICE with an accent speaking English telling somebody this man was in shock. Talking about *him*. Blown senseless by the explosion, fished out of the water for dead and taken aboard the *City of Washington*. Brought to San Ambrosio early the following morning. Virgil knew that. He knew he'd been in this hospital staring at a ceiling that was flaking and needed paint two days now. What he didn't know was why he couldn't move or speak, or why he didn't blink his eyes when a hand passed back and forth in front of his face. Lying here like he was made of stone. Every once in a while seeing a face looking down at him. A face that was usually an American. With a hat on. A correspondent—that was it—with a tablet, writing things down as the voice with the accent told the correspondent this man was in shock due to a severe head injury. Or he may have suffered a stroke. Though from his appearance, the voice said, this one seemed in reasonably good shape.

Oh, was that right? Then how come he couldn't move?

Virgil heard men screaming.

He heard a man moaning, calling for his mother.

He heard a voice fairly close by saying, "I can't move my legs."

And a voice saying, "I can't see. Will somebody help me? I can't *see*."

The screaming and moaning went on and on, not close by but somewhere else in the room or ward or wherever he was.

A hand touched his face, moved back and forth in front of his eyes. A woman's voice without an accent said, "Can you hear me?"

She wasn't one of the nurses; they talked in Spanish or had accents. He wanted to ask her what she thought he was doing, sleeping with his eyes open?

The woman's voice said to somebody else, "There is so little we can do."

A man's voice said, "Miss Barton?" and then said something to her Virgil couldn't make out.

The woman's voice said, "I've been able to identify only twelve so far. Many are so horribly burned." Virgil heard her sigh. "And the rest—I'm told as many as two hundred are still in the ship."

Virgil was sure he wasn't burned or he'd feel it.

He heard the woman say she'd been in the provinces distributing food to the *reconcentrados*, Cubans the dons locked up in camps to starve to death. The woman sounded kind of old. Then, close to him, he heard her say, "Dear, can you tell me your name?"

He was Private Virgil Webster, a seagoing marine off the USS *Maine*, but for some reason couldn't form the words to tell her. He wanted to. Christ, yes. Virgil Webster. Home: Okmulgee, Indian Territory. Left there to become a fighting marine. Look at my tattoos. *Semper Fi* on one arm, with the Marine Corps insignia. *In Memory of Mother* on the other, though it didn't mean his ma was dead, he just liked the looks of it, the flower and the gravestone cross. But somebody better tell her he wasn't dead either, else she'd see a newspaper or hear about the *Maine* and be worried to death. His ma was part northern Cheyenne.

Virgil Webster, twenty-four years old and into his second five-year enlistment. Joined when he was sixteen, inspired by stories his uncle Hartley Webster told. Uncle Hartley a marine who'd fought in Korea in the spring of '71: steamed up the Han River aboard a gunboat and beat hell out of the Koreans for mistreating American merchant seamen, killed two hundred fifty of them and lost only two marines. Virgil joined up looking for action: guarded a quarantine camp at Sandy Hook, New Jersey, for people who'd come off ships immigrating here and were found to have cholera. He guarded Southern Pacific railroad yards during a strike and marched in the dedication ceremony of Grant's Tomb. He got in trouble once in Venezuela, there protecting a consulate, part of a marine detachment off the USS *Chicago*. They all got drunk and the captain was court-martialed. Guayra, Venezuela . . . Reupped in Norfolk.

Assigned to the USS *Maine* November the tenth of last year at Newport News, Virginia, where she was taking on coal. January the eighteenth she was coaled again at Key West. January the twenty-fourth, with the North Atlantic Squadron sixty miles off Key West, the torpedo boat *Dumont* came alongside to deliver a message from the Navy Department. By 11:00 P.M. the *Maine* had her steam up and was bound for Havana. Twelve hours later a Spanish pilot was bringing her into the harbor. A rumor had gone around they'd be in New Orleans for Mardi Gras, representing the fleet. Well, they were supposed to have pretty much the same kind of carnival here, so Havana didn't sound too bad. Except, as it turned out, none of the crew was allowed ashore, just officers. Virgil asked Captain Sigsbee's orderly, twenty-eight years in the military, with the army out west half of it and now a career marine, "How come just the officers?"

Sigsbee's orderly said, "Because the dons don't like it we're here to begin with, and you smart alecks'd be sure to make trouble."

Virgil asked the career marine, who heard things

on the bridge and standing outside the captain's quarters, "How come we *are* here?"

"Making a friendly call on the dons."

"We got here and sat out in the stream till it was good and light so as not to surprise them coming in."

"Is that a question?"

"When did we become friends with them?"

"Would you understand the situation if I explained it to you?"

"Well, I been to school."

"How far?"

"The sixth grade."

"We're here to protect American citizens and their property."

"Protect them from what?"

"Unenlightened people with anti-American aims. Or," the career marine said, "you could say we're here in case it looks like the Cubans are gonna take over their own country before we get a chance to do it ourselves. But don't tell nobody. That's between Captain Sigsbee, the Secretary of the Navy and Bill McKinley."

So Virgil never got to go ashore. One of the midshipmen who did, delivering messages to the consulate, said the city was full of beggars and Spanish soldiers; he said people walked in the middle of the street, rode horses holding umbrellas over their heads, and the women wore so much white face powder they looked like they were dead. Virgil said

he'd like to see them anyway. The midshipman said
don't step in the gutters; some places there was poop
in the gutters. He said hey, he bet that's why everybody walked in the middle of the street.

Tuesday, February the fifteenth, the sun set at
5:36 P.M. There it was hanging over the outskirts of
Havana and the next minute gone for the day, the
way it did in the tropics, disappeared on you as you
watched. The sky became overcast and pretty soon
it was pitch-dark.

That afternoon they had set up targets to practice with their new Lee magazine rifles. Before long,
though, there was the *Alfonso XII* in the background
and rifle practice was halted in case the dons became
nervous. Without anyone noticing it right away, the
*Maine* had drifted on her anchor to a northwest
heading, putting her starboard 10-inch battery on
Morro Castle, on the old La Cabaña fortress next to
it and on the Spanish warship. The *Maine*'s port batteries were now bearing on the city. Virgil knew it
was the wind and tide had put the ship in this heading—one they'd take if they were going to shell the
city and its forts—but it had never happened before
tonight. Strange. Officers and men were all talking
about it.

At 8:00 P.M. the Officer of the Deck reported the
ship secure, all hands aboard except four officers
who'd gone ashore on overnight liberty.

At 9:00 P.M., two bells, the bosun piped the ship
down for the night: all hands not on watch lay below

and turn in. Ten minutes later the marine bugler sounded taps. This night being hot and muggy they had permission to sling their hammocks topside if they wanted, go to sleep breathing fresh air.

Virgil picked a spot by the after turret on the port side, swung his hammock from the forward side of the turret to an engine-room skylight he managed to hook on to. He was ready to climb in the sack when he realized he was missing something important: the three-foot notched board he'd wedge across one end of the hammock, where he'd lay his head, to keep it spread open. Otherwise it was like sleeping in a cocoon. Virgil slipped below to the crew's berth, forward, but couldn't find his board anywhere, god-damn it; he was pretty sure some swabbie, trying to be funny, had hidden it. And it was too late now to go to the ship's carpenter shop, find the right piece of board, cut it to size and notch it. Shit. He had in mind to look for a swabbie already asleep and swipe his board. But it could end in trouble, and he'd already done 10 days' bread and water this cruise for fighting. As he went back topside three bells sounded. It was 9:30.

Two officers at the rail, aft of the turret, were watching a steam launch as it swung wide around the stern and headed for the Havana docks. Both officers were smoking cigars. Virgil remembered this, the smell of tobacco and their comments, wondering who the launch belonged to and where it had come from. There were boats out there all day long:

bumboats coming alongside to sell different kinds of fruit and sweets; gigs and lighters chasing around the harbor like taxis with cargo or passengers; but hardly any this late.

When Virgil finally rolled into the sack the canvas curled around him and there was nothing he could do about it. Again he considered looking for a board, but then thought, hell, count the stars and go to sleep. Except there weren't any stars, not with that layer of clouds up there. Christ, but he wished he had a board. You didn't have one, there was no way to sleep on your side in a hammock without suffocating to death. Virgil told himself to quit complaining. He closed his eyes, hearing very faintly rumba music coming across the water from Havana, three hundred yards to port. . . .

The explosion—the way it came there was no getting ready for it. It was like it burst in his head, deafened him, in that moment shattering all sense of where he was until he felt the ship heave and shudder beneath him and saw the bow rise from the water like it was climbing out of the trough of a storm wave. He could *see* it, the bow a good three hundred feet from him in the air, in smoke rising so thick the bow was hidden now, though he could see pieces of the ship bursting in the smoke, flying into the night sky like rockets, and bodies. Christ, *men*, blown out of the fo'c'sle, and he felt the ship heave again as the bow came down to settle in the water, listing to port and swinging his hammock close to the rail. He heard screams now of men in pain and screams for help, the sound of the screams clear and then dying out, fading, a quiet settling, and he became aware of a faint whistling-hissing sound, air being forced out of the ship by the water rising inside her. Virgil breathed to calm himself, thinking, you have to get out of here, out of the goddamn hammock and over the side, swim for that steamship only about a hundred yards away, the *City of Washington*. . . . And the second explosion rocked the *Maine* amidships, the towering twin smokestacks vanishing from Virgil's sight, gone, the superstructure gone, in that moment erupting in a blaze of light, the ship bursting, ripped apart, and Virgil felt himself lifted from the deck, hammock still around him, blown into the cloud of smoke, stunned, his head ringing so loud it was all he heard, blown into the hot sky, an oven, and then falling through smoke to hit the water, the surface on fire, Virgil still wrapped in his canvas shroud.

HE WAS PICKED UP a good fifty yards from the ship, taken from his scorched hammock, both ends burned away, and laid in the bottom of a lifeboat among bodies gathered from the water. He knew this. He could smell burnt flesh. He was on his side, close to a lifeless face without hair or eyebrows staring at him, a fireman he believed he recognized, a fireman or one of the coal passers. He'd seen him in the head washing, the same one who'd been playing an accordion that evening in the starboard gangway. Virgil tried to move but couldn't, wedged in among the dead, below him and on both sides. He could hear voices, the sailors aboard the lifeboat talking to each other. He wanted to yell to one of them, Hey, mate, I ain't dead. But, Christ, he couldn't speak. Couldn't move or speak.

They hauled him up a ladder, not too gentle about it, and laid him out with the dead bodies on a varnished wood deck, close by a row of chairs with leg rests, and left him. He could hear voices and wanted to call out, Sweet Jesus, somebody, look at me, will you? Don't slide me over the side blowing taps till you take a look at me. Feel my goddamn pulse. Finally—how much later he wasn't sure, it was still dark—he felt the toe of a shoe nudge him and heard a voice say, "I think this one's still alive."

THE EVENING OF THE SECOND DAY he closed his eyes and opened them and closed them again sighing with relief, saying, "Thank you, Jesus," and in the morning when he woke up he was able to move his head, his hands, his feet. . . . He cleared his throat, pretty sure he could talk, and the nurse ran out before he could say anything and returned with the doctor who had said yesterday he'd been blown senseless. So the first words Virgil spoke after his experience were to the doctor. He said, "I think somebody set off a mine," and told about the launch running full-out away from the ship just before the explosion. After that he asked how many were killed and if Captain Sigsbee was all right. The nurse told him Clara Barton stopped by his bed to see him and asked him his name.

Virgil said, "Oh, is that right?" trying to think of who Clara Barton was.

They got him up on his feet. Virgil walked to the end of the ward and back past empty beds, seeing not one of his shipmates here. The nurse, holding on to him, said he was the only one in this ward who had survived. Virgil had to lie down again, dizzy from the exertion. The doctor told him to be patient, he was lucky to be alive.

That night a man in a light gray military uniform came to see him, sat at his bedside in the dark and smoked cigarettes as he asked Virgil questions, never taking off his hat. Virgil didn't know if he was Spanish or Cuban. The man asked Virgil about his experience and listened with a grave manner, saying, "Oh, that must have been terrible." . . . "Oh, you are so brave." . . . "Oh, you were fortunate to sleep on deck." Finally asking about the launch Virgil saw before the explosion.

"Did you get a good look at it?"

"I've seen plenty like it," Virgil said. The harbor was full of them. "What do you call those boats, *falucas?*"

"Yes, but this particular one—if you saw it again, could you identify it?"

Virgil hesitated. "Are you investigating the explosion?"

"Assisting with it, yes."

"Are Americans investigating too?"

"Oh yes, we both are. What we like to know, if you saw a person on the boat you believe you can identify."

Virgil barely saw the launch, much less anyone aboard. Still, he didn't like this guy asking him questions in the dark and he said, "Since I'm American, I better wait and talk to the Americans investigating it."

"What's the difference? We all want to find out what happen."

The man speaking with a strained sound to his voice now, Virgil sensing the guy would like to scream at him and shake him and was holding on to his temper.

"I'll talk to the Americans," Virgil said.

The man in the dark said, "You want to make this difficult, uh? Is that what you want?"

Virgil said, "You want to know what you can do with your questions?"

His mysterious visitor got up and left.

When the nurse came to check on him, Virgil asked her who that guy in the uniform was. She said he didn't tell her his name and probably wouldn't if she asked him. She said, "They have an ugly disposition, those people. They like to make your life miserable."

Virgil asked her who she was talking about. Who's *they*?

The nurse said, "The Guardia Civil. They're like police, only worse."

Later that night Virgil woke up as two guys in uniform were pulling him out of bed. He said, "Hey, what's going on?" smelling ether. One of them said something in Spanish and a third one stepped in and pressed a cloth to Virgil's face. This was all he'd remember of his last night in San Ambrosio.

# 4

ANDRES PALENZUELA, chief of municipal police for the city of Havana, received a telephone call informing him of an American named Tyler who arrived today at Regla with horses and cattle. Palenzuela assigned an investigator by the name of Rudi Calvo to follow the American, see if he was here for a reason other than the livestock. This Ben Tyler appeared to be a drover, he told Rudi Calvo, but who knows? He could be an agent of the United States government. Rudi Calvo asked who it was wanted to know about the American. His chief said, "Guardia Civil, Lionel Tavalera."

"Him?" Rudi Calvo said. "Why doesn't he use his own people?"

"Who knows? Maybe they're busy somewhere torturing children."

"But why is it his business?"

"The American brought thirty horses to sell," Palenzuela said, "but according to the custom declaration paid duty on only ten, eight hundred fifty pesos instead of twenty-five hundred."

"So?" Rudi Calvo said. "Why is that his business?"

"Whatever his reason," Palenzuela said, "he's Guardia Civil. You must know it's their business to know everyone's business."

AT 9:00 P.M. Rudi Calvo came to the home in the Vedado suburb of Havana where Palenzuela kept his American mistress—her name was Lorraine—and entertained close friends. Rudi sat with his chief in the front courtyard of the house to give his report.

"From the ferry dock the subject went directly to the Hotel Inglaterra, where he registered and left his belongings, a bedroll and a saddle. He spent almost two hours in the bar among the newspaper correspondents before going out again. His associate, the one named Burke, remained."

He had caught Palenzuela getting dressed for the evening, suspenders hanging, buttoning his shirt, a collar not yet attached, the chief's mind apparently on something else, the reason he said, "Who?"

"Charlie Burke," Rudi said, always patient with his chief, and explained that they already had a file on Burke, a dealer in cattle who had been here several times before. "The subject went out again accompanied by Victor Fuentes and proceeded to la Habana Vieja, where they dined in a café and then visited stores, selecting new clothes for the subject. Shirts, trousers, a suit coat, good boots and a very fine panama."

"He bought a suit?" Palenzuela said.

"Only the coat, a black one."

"Expensive?"

"I believe alpaca."

"Where did he go for the boots?"

"Naranjo y Vazquez."

"They're all right, but not the best."

"He removed his spurs from the old boots and put them on the new ones."

"Why? If he wasn't riding?"

"No, I think because he's used to wearing them. Or he likes to hear himself walk."

"A cowboy," Palenzuela said. "And where did he buy his hat?"

"Viadero's."

"Of course."

"He put on the clothes, the black suit coat and pants the color of sand, or perhaps more of a cinnamon shade."

"How did it look?"

"Elegant, with a white shirt and a kerchief of a light blue shade, the kerchief his own."

Palenzuela said, "Hmmmm," nodding. "I like a kerchief sometimes."

"He had something he brought with him

wrapped in newspaper," Rudi Calvo said. "I had been wondering, what is that he's carrying? Well, he unwrapped it now in the store. It was a revolver, I believe a Smith & Wesson .44, the one with the spur beneath the trigger guard for the second finger."

"The .44 Russian," Palenzuela said, "originally designed for a grand duke. I have a pair."

"He carried it," Rudi said, "in a shoulder holster."

"If he isn't a spy," Palenzuela said, "he could be an assassin."

"He put on the holstered pistol beneath the suit coat and stood in front of a mirror to look at himself this way and that, pausing to adjust the hat, getting a slight but very smart curve to the brim. He stood there it seemed for several minutes."

"Admiring himself."

"Perhaps, though it seemed more as if he was surprised at his appearance, not used to seeing himself dressed this way."

"Or to see if the revolver was noticeable," Palenzuela said. "I can't believe the customhouse would allow him to have it."

"I'm sure he didn't declare it," Rudi said, "and because he was with Fuentes they didn't search him."

"Yes, Fuentes would handle it," Palenzuela said. "Then what?"

"The subject returned with Fuentes to the Inglaterra, to the hotel bar where the other one,

Burke, was drinking with one of the newspaper correspondents."

"Which one?"

"Neely Tucker, of Chicago."

"Is he an important one?"

"Not as important as the ones with the New York papers. If you aren't certain how important they are, ask them. This Neely Tucker has gone into the country a few times. He wrote about visiting General Gómez, but I don't believe he's a spy."

"Is he the one who said Gómez looks like an Egyptian mummy?"

"I believe that was the correspondent who wrote *Facts and Fakes about Cuba,* a very popular book in America. Did you read it?"

"Why would I?"

"It's very good. It tells how much of the war news is made up in Tampa and Key West, the correspondents too lazy to come here."

"Or afraid," Palenzuela said.

"Yes, and write stories from communiqués they receive. Skirmishes become battles."

"Well, soon we won't have to worry about the correspondents, the ones here will be going home."

"Why is that?"

"*Why?* Because we'll be at war. The Americans have an excuse now, the ship blowing up."

"Did we do it?" Rudi said.

"Who do you mean *we?* We can be *we* with the

Spanish when it suits us, but not when they blow up an American battleship."

"Did they?"

"How do I know? They don't tell me things like that and I don't ask."

"It could have been accidental, a fire."

"If you want to believe that. Anyway," Palenzuela said, "perhaps the horses are the only business of this Ben Tyler. The customhouse said his bill of sale is to Señor Boudreaux."

The American planter, the same Señor Roland Boudreaux who had presented Andres Palenzuela with a matched pair of palominos for his carriage and had been to this house with his own American mistress, who was a good friend of the police chief's American mistress.

"And the other one, Burke," Rudi said, "has sold cattle to Señor Boudreaux. I believe livestock is their only business." Rudi paused. "At least it would seem to be so."

Palenzuela had learned to listen to Rudi Calvo and trust him, since it was necessary to trust at least someone.

"But what?"

"Several times I noticed the same individual, an officer of the regular army, lingering in the vicinity, on one street and then another, twice in the same shop we were in but trying not to show himself in a conspicuous way."

"Lingering," Palenzuela said. "Not simply loitering, passing the time."

"I could be mistaken," Rudi said, "but I was given the feeling, from his manner, we were both observing the same subject."

"He was following the American?"

"I believe so."

"Do you know this officer?"

"He's with a hussar regiment, one of those peacocks in the bright uniform, Lieutenant Teobaldo Barbón."

"Why is that name familiar?"

A woman's voice came from somewhere in the house, in English. "Will you be much longer?"

Rudi watched Palenzuela look up at the ceiling. "We are nearly finished."

"We don't want to be late."

"No, we won't be."

Rudi waited to see if the woman kept here was satisfied with that reply from the chief of the municipal police of the city of Havana. She seemed to be, having nothing else to say, so Rudi said, "You want to know why the name Teobaldo Barbón is familiar. He's the officer who enjoys fighting duels."

Palenzuela nodded. "I remember now, easily insulted."

"And from what I understand," Rudi said, "it's difficult not to insult him. Barbón is Madrileño, from a good family. In the time he's been here he's called out three men to satisfy his honor."

"Other officers?"

"Cubans of class, not military. He didn't hesitate to shoot each one through the heart."

"On the beach at dawn?"

"On the Prado at dawn, before the statue of Queen Isabella."

"God protect us from patriots," Palenzuela said.

Again the woman's voice: "Andres, are you ready?"

"Am I ready," the chief said, not to Rudi Calvo, maybe to himself.

# 5

THE WHORES IN HAVANA, Fuentes said to Tyler, won't take money from the common Spanish soldier, the *soldado raso,* who's paid next to nothing. What they do, they charge one hundred Mauser cartridges to go to bed with them, which to the soldier is like getting it for nothing. Fuentes said the whores gave the cartridges to the *insurrectos* and this was one of the ways they got bullets for their Mausers, the rifles they took from Spanish soldiers they killed.

Tyler said, "You know it for a fact?"

"Maybe not asking so many bullets," Fuentes said, "but it happens, yes."

The soldiers were in every street, in groups or pairs, boys in blue-striped seersucker and straw hats with regimental badges, like tourists taking in the sights of the city. Many of these boys, Fuentes said, from Andalusia and the Canary Islands. The somewhat older men in light gray uniforms were Guardia Civil. They stood about with thumbs hooked in their black leather belts waiting to be noticed, or daring you to look them in the face. That was the feeling Tyler got seeing them again on the street and remembering how they would ride into the mill looking for a fugitive—a man who might have committed only a minor crime—ransack the workers' living quarters, chase down suspects and sympathizers and beat them. They threatened to shoot his dad one time, when he tried to keep them off the mill property.

They walked past a pair of Guardia posing on a street corner and Tyler said to Fuentes, "My dad called them barbarians, thugs, I forgot what else. What do you call them?"

"Usually," Fuentes said, "I call them sir. The Guardia are known for their loyalty, devotion to duty and lack of feelings. Imagine an insensitive brute having absolute power over people he considers his inferiors. Since they see themselves as infallible, I have no reason to antagonize them."

"I've been trying to figure out," Tyler said, "what side you're on, for Spanish rule or a free Cuba."

Fuentes grinned, his mahogany face shining in the lights of an open-air café. "And what side do you think?"

"The landowners, even Americans," Tyler said, "are for Spanish rule, happy with the way things are. If you're sitting on top, why change it? And since you work for one of the biggest landowners in Cuba . . ."

"Also a man of influence," Fuentes said.

"It's in your best interest to agree with him."

"Yes, if I want to be paid."

"Or at least appear to agree with him."

"So what side am I on?"

"I think you're for Cuba and to hell with Spain."

"If I tell you yes, you're right, would you believe me?"

Tyler hesitated. "Yeah, but I'd keep an eye on you."

"That's the way to be," Fuentes said. "Don't trust anyone. Or look around when I tell you we're being followed."

Tyler half turned to look over his shoulder, then up at the decorative tiled facade of a building, at people in windows and doorways talking, girls in white dresses looking out at the street from behind grillwork.

"The first thing you do is what I tell you not to," Fuentes said. "It's all right. The one following is from the police; he wants to know if you are who you say you are. Maybe someone else is following, but I'm not sure, so don't worry about it."

They walked back to the hotel, Tyler in his new duds and carrying packages, shirts and underwear and his old hat he couldn't part with wrapped in newspaper and tied with string. Everything else had been left at stores to be thrown away or offered to beggars. He kept touching his panama, not trusting the airy feel of it. When Fuentes told him he looked splendid, Tyler grinned. He liked Fuentes and liked Havana. The old part, la Habana Vieja, made him think of New Orleans: a look he remembered of shaded galleries and shutters closed against the heat, old government buildings and banana trees and broad esplanades, cannons, monuments. Havana had Morro Castle and La Cabaña fortress; New Orleans had Fort Pike on the Rigolets, Fort Jackson in Plaquemines Parish, another fort down on Grand Terre you could count. The narrow streets here were like streets in the Quarter, St. Philip, where they lived before moving to Terpsichore and he went to St. Simeon's Select on Annunciation, there two years when his mother and sisters took sick and died and he left to go west and work for a cattle out-fit. The lobby of the Inglaterra, all lit up, could be the St. Charles and the dining room in there could be any number of restaurants in New Orleans, tile floor, white tablecloths, and mirrors on the walls. All kinds of things here reminded him of a home-town he'd been away from half his life. It was strange to feel at home here.

Fuentes gave the packages to a bellboy to put in Tyler's room. He took a breath and said, "All right, now I see about Mr. Boudreaux and come and get you when he's ready."

Tyler said fine and headed for the bar.

"I SEE YOU COME IN," Charlie Burke said, acting puzzled, "I was about to say to Neely, 'Do I know that fella?' My Lord, stand there and let me look at you." Charlie Burke with his hat on, a cigar stuck in his jaw, enjoying his evening at the Inglaterra. Men at the next table, correspondents, looked over and Neely Tucker had a grin on his face.

He said to Tyler, "Join us, please," in his eager way, rising, pulling out a chair for him, then got the waiter to bring a rye whiskey with ice. Neely seemed anxious for people to like him, younger than the other correspondents and didn't seem full of himself like some Tyler had overheard, here and in the lobby, talking in loud voices to each other, ordering the help around, complaining to waiters, asking them where they'd been hiding. This bar, with its formal garden in the middle of the room, its gold statue of a woman flamenco dancer, was the correspondents' hangout. "Where rumors and fabrications are created to justify hotel bills," Neely had said when they'd met in here earlier. "Some can stir up sentiment against Spain with mordant diatribes, recount eyewitness scenes of atrocity without leaving this room. That's not to say, you understand, atrocities aren't committed. Lots of them are, all the time."

Tyler had seen correspondents using their typewriting machines in here, smoking cigars, drinking, typing away.

On that earlier occasion Neely Tucker had said, "You don't remember, but we met one time before."

Tyler said no, he didn't recall, though he'd read enough of Neely's stories to feel like he knew him. The Chicago *Times* was the newspaper Dana Moon used to send him when he was at Yuma—editions of the paper, it turned out, Neely had sent Moon.

"We met in Sweetmary five years ago," Neely said, "when LaSalle Mining was trying to run those squatters off the mountain and Dana Moon stood up to the company and its gun thugs. It was in the Gold Dollar. All us correspondents were in there trying to decide what to call the situation, a war, a bloody feud, or what. Everyone felt we needed a catchy label, like the Rincon Mountain War was one, the Sweetmary War another. You were at the bar right next to me. You recall what you said?"

Tyler shook his head. "I must've been drinking."

"You said, quote, 'You people come out here not knowing mesquite beans from goat shit and become the authority on whatever catches your eye.' "

"Yeah, I was drinking." Tyler nodded, thinking of the time. "But it didn't make what I said less true, did it?"

"Ben Tyler went to the tenth grade," Charlie Burke said. "He can be quite the authority his ownself."

Sounding to Tyler like Charlie Burke was still

smarting over the incident at the stock pens, missing the chance to sell a horse.

Neely was grinning again. He said, "I would have quoted your remark in a dispatch had it not been indelicate to do so."

"He was in a period of his life," Charlie Burke said, "where he made up his own rules of behavior. I thought he'd worked it out of his system busting rocks, but now I'm not so sure."

This was earlier in the evening.

Charlie Burke's mood had mellowed now with the rye whiskey. He said, "I saw you come in, I thought for a moment you were Richard Harding Davis, but Neely says he's over in France. I saw him a time before. There's a man knows how to dress."

"He knows how to write too," Neely said. "Richard Harding Davis and this young fellow Stephen Crane. Their ability to produce a feeling of verisimilitude is scary. Stephen Crane wrote *The Red Badge of Courage* when he was only twenty-four. Have you read it?"

"I've heard of it," Tyler said, looking around the room at all the correspondents.

"Last year," Neely said, "Crane wrote 'The Open Boat' about a shipwreck; it's based on an experience that actually happened on one of his trips here to Cuba. 'The Open Boat' offers some of the most vivid writing I've ever read. It isn't flowery, if you know what I mean; it's stark, you might say, without a single wasted word. I say that, not taking anything away from Harding Davis. The *Journal* pays him three thousand a month—not a year, a *month*. *Harper's Monthly* paid him six hundred for a single story and he's worth every penny. Read 'The Death of Rodriguez' that ran last month, about the execution of a young rebel. The boy falls dead before the firing squad and Harding Davis wrote that at that moment the sun 'shot up suddenly from behind them in all the splendor of the tropics, a fierce red disc of heat, and filled the air with warmth and light. . . . The whole world of Santa Clara seemed to stir and stretch itself and to wake to welcome the day just begun.' "

"That's writing," Charlie Burke said.

"Wait," Neely said. "The way Harding Davis ends it, he looks back as he walks away"—Neely looking off as he said it—"and in this tragic moment sees the young Cuban as if, quote, 'asleep in the wet grass, his motionless arms still bound tightly behind him, the scapular awry across his face, and the blood from his breast sinking into the soil he had tried to free.' "

"Gives you a chill," Charlie Burke said. "You say this was in Santa Clara?"

Neely's gaze came back to the table, his expression reverent, the neat little correspondent touching his bow tie and nodding as he said, "Santa Clara has long been a hotbed of insurgent activity, a soil that seems to nourish a love of freedom."

It amazed Tyler, people actually spoke like that.

He saw Fuentes looking for them as he came in from the lobby and around the garden, coming over now and pausing as he reached the table, making sure he wasn't interrupting their conversation.

Charlie Burke looked up. "Boudreaux's ready for us?"

"He's with business associates and his lady friend, but he say okay," Fuentes said, and looked at Tyler. "Lionel Tavalera, the Guardia Civil officer? Is in the lobby."

Neely seemed surprised. "Spanish military don't often frequent this hotel."

"It's true," Fuentes said. They were getting up from the table as he said, "Who knows why he's here." And to Tyler, "But, listen, you don't have to speak to him. All right?"

THE MUNICIPAL POLICE INVESTIGATOR, Rudi Calvo, had noticed him too: the Guardia Civil officer in civilian clothes, a dark suit this evening, seated in one of the wicker chairs smoking a cigarette. Lionel Tavalera, who wanted to know about the American and was here perhaps to get a look at him. Or he could be waiting for one of the American newspaperwomen, popular with officers because as a rule they drank spirits, some of them smoked and none required a chaperone. So Lionel Tavalera's presence didn't give Rudi the same uneasy feeling he had experienced seeing that other one, Teo Barbón, lingering in the streets of the Old City. There . . .

Tyler was coming out of the bar now with his associate and Fuentes, crossing the lobby to the dining room, Fuentes leading the parade, this Ben Tyler looking very smart in his new clothes, very fly, as the Americans would say. Tyler knew how to wear that hat.

By this time Rudi had forgotten about Lionel Tavalera and didn't see him get up from his chair.

TYLER DID. He saw the Guardia officer coming toward them and raised his hand. "Lionel, how're you this evening?"

"A moment," Tavalera said. "I need to tell you something."

"Can't do it right now, got business to tend to."

Now Charlie Burke looked around as Tavalera was saying, "Listen to me. The man you insulted is outside, Teobaldo. He wants to speak to you."

Tyler gave him a shrug, not caring for the Guardia's tone of voice, and said to Charlie Burke, "I doubt he still wants the horse, but I'll see him later if he's around," and followed his partner to this private dining room in a corner of the lobby, the door closed. He had noticed the regular dining room over next to the bar, people in there were having supper this late. Fuentes, about to knock, paused and turned to them.

"The one who opens the door," Fuentes said, barely above a whisper, "is Novis, Mr. Boudreaux's bodyguard, Novis Crowe. He looks at you as if you must be guilty of something or you want to harm his boss." Fuentes said, "I'm telling you so you know who it is," turned now and rapped twice on the door.

It opened right away and now the bodyguard, Novis, stood looking them over the way Fuentes said he would as Fuentes asked if Mr. Boudreaux would see them now. Novis didn't answer, his gaze holding on Tyler now, Tyler seeing Novis as a workingman in a town suit, reddish hair combed flat and parted in the middle; or he could be a strike-breaker, that type, with a pick handle and a mean disposition. He turned now and brought them into the private dining room one behind the other, leading a procession along the banquet table covered in white linen, cleared of dinner plates, to approach four men in evening dress with cigars grouped about one end: prosperous-looking gents in their middle years, beards showing gray, though the one Tyler took to be Roland Boudreaux, seated in the center with a map spread open in front of him, was clean shaven and somewhat younger looking, a wave in his full head of dark hair. All of them seemed intent on following a course Boudreaux was slowly tracing across the map with the tip of a table knife.

Fuentes peeked around Novis, waited, and then finally said, "Sir, when you are ready."

Tyler waited for Boudreaux to look up and acknowledge them. The men with him, Americans, all appeared well-to-do, patient, content to follow Boudreaux's plan for a road or maybe a rail line that would extend across half of Cuba.

They waited, Charlie Burke and Fuentes behind Novis, holding their hats in front of them. Waiting for an audience with the king. To ask a favor. Tyler remained a few steps behind them, wondering now what would happen if he were to say, Excuse me. How long are we supposed to stand here? Or give this important man one more minute. If he didn't look up and say something by then, walk out. The trouble was, Tyler didn't have a watch to time the man with.

He turned enough to take in the room, the crystal chandelier, a bottle of cognac, snifters, a coffee service and cups on the tablecloth . . . and a *girl* —he couldn't believe it, not ten feet away from him —sitting by herself at the other end of the table, a girl with reddish-brown hair piled and swirled in a way that showed her slender neck, her hair shining in the light from the chandelier, the girl looking right at him, already looking at him when he turned and saw her. In one hand she held a demitasse raised almost to her lips, and in the other a perfectly round cigarette, no question about it, a tailor-made. She said to Tyler, "I like your hat," and kept looking at him—not smiling or anything, like she was giving him the eye, no, just looking him over.

Tyler touched the brim to her realizing this must be Boudreaux's mistress. Fuentes had mentioned his boss's lady friend being here and Tyler had imagined an older, more mature woman with rouge on her face, not anyone like this girl. She was a beauty and looked rich, even smoking the cigarette. Camille had smoked, but she was a whore.

Fuentes was saying, "Mr. Boudreaux, you know Mr. Charlie Burke from when he was here, and this is Ben Tyler, the one brought the horses."

Tyler turned as Fuentes said his name, heard the girl say "Ben?" and saw Boudreaux looking this way, at the girl and then at him. From his expression he seemed pleasant enough, a man who could be as old as fifty, had that wave in his hair and was called Rollie, the only one at the table without whiskers or a mustache.

He said to Tyler, "You're the horse breaker," telling him who he was, "the *jinete*."

Tyler said, "That's right. And I understand you're the horse buyer."

He wanted to look at the girl again, but kept his eyes on Boudreaux, the man not saying yes or no, though he did maintain his pleasant expression. He said, "I'm told you've delivered a fair string. Take them to Matanzas tomorrow and you can go on home." Sounding like that was it, you're dismissed. And now he was looking at his girlfriend again.

"Amelia?"

Tyler glanced around to see the girl raise her eyebrows.

"Yes?"

"Why don't you go on upstairs. I won't be much longer here." The man speaking to her with that soft New Orleans sound to his voice.

She said, "I haven't finished my coffee."

"Honey, the waiter will bring you some, all you want."

Boudreaux waited.

Tyler waited.

All the men in the room waited while Amelia sat there and appeared to be thinking about it.

Boudreaux said, "Amelia?" His tone not as soft this time. "You want Novis to see you to the room?"

Tyler saw the bodyguard turn to face Amelia.

She said, "I think I can find it," and rose from the table, taking her time then to pick up a little beaded purse.

Boudreaux said, "Honey, leave the cigarette."

Tyler watched her look at an ashtray on the table and then seem to change her mind and dab the cigarette into her demitasse. Now she placed it in the ashtray. She came toward the door, her eyes held his and she said, "Nice meeting you, Ben." He held the door open and she walked past, out to the lobby.

Tyler turned to see Boudreaux watching him.

Now Fuentes stood up straight and said to his boss, "Excuse me, but you don't want to see the horses?"

"I'll take your word," Boudreaux said, "they're what I want."

Fuentes nodded. He said, "Well, all right," and said, "I told these gentlemen you would write a draft on the bank for three thousand seven hundred fifty dollars, if you would, please."

Boudreaux looked puzzled. "For twenty-five head? That's . . . a hundred fifty each." He said to his associates, "Gentlemen, can you imagine paying a hundred and a half for western range stock?"

Tyler watched them shake their heads and blow cigar smoke at the ceiling. Indeed they could not.

"I believe what I agreed to was a hundred dollars a head," Boudreaux said, and to his associates, "I don't ask how they avoid paying duty, but they must to make a profit, even if they stole the horses to begin with. I didn't ask if these fellas are horse thieves, and I won't."

This got a chuckle.

"Sir?" Fuentes said. "You agree to one hundred fifty when I told you the price they ask."

"Now my *segundo*'s calling me a liar," Boudreaux said. "Or he's getting old on me, losing his memory. Victor, is that it, you're becoming forgetful?"

"I don't think so," Fuentes said, standing up to him, and it surprised Tyler.

"Tell me, Victor," Boudreaux was saying now, "what's your cut on this deal?"

It got sly grins from his friends as Fuentes shook his head.

"No, I don't take nothing for myself."

"I'll tell you what, Victor, you forget your commission and I'll buy all the horses they brought. What'd you tell me, thirty mares? I'll pay a hundred each and these boys'll make within two hundred dollars of what you're saying was the original deal. Soon as they deliver and I like what I see, they get my check for three thousand dollars."

Tyler saw Charlie Burke turn to glance at him, the old ranny appearing to be mystified, as Fuentes was saying, "They have deliver already, the horses are at Regla."

"When they deliver to the estate," Boudreaux said. "Having horses at Regla in these times—an American battleship blown to hell, insurgents getting cockier by the day—having horses over there is no guarantee I'd ever see them."

"Is what I promise these men," Fuentes said, "when I tell them we stop first in Havana."

Boudreaux said, "Are you listening to me?" Still with his pleasant expression and tone. "They get paid when the horses are in Matanzas. The delivery is their job and their risk, not mine."

There was a silence. Boudreaux waiting, his associates puffing on their cigars waiting, all of them patient about this business.

Finally Charlie Burke said, "Sir, will you be there when we come, at your estate?"

"Most likely, yes. If I'm not, I'll see you get your money. Now you can take my word on that," Boudreaux said, still with the nice tone, "or you can put your horses on the boat and take them home. I'll leave it up to you, all right?"

Tyler watched Charlie Burke accept this with a shrug, twenty years ramrod of a big cow outfit, a man who never took an ugly word off any of his hands, here he was backing down from this man in evening clothes, a wave in his hair.

Tyler said to Boudreaux, "We took your man's word we'd be paid when we got to Havana."

"Yes, well, you have to know whose word you can take," Boudreaux said, "and whose you can't, don't you? Now if you'll excuse us . . ."

Tyler said to him, "Stopping here wasn't in the deal. You'll have to pay for wharfage and feed."

Boudreaux looked up from his map and stared at Tyler, taking his time. "Wharfage and feed. What are you saying that will cost me?"

"Dollar and a half a head."

"And that comes to?"

The man waiting to see if Tyler knew how to do his figures.

"Forty-five dollars," Tyler said.

And Boudreaux said, "You sure?"

Tyler stared, keeping his mouth shut with an effort.

Finally Boudreaux said, "Very well. Now will you excuse us?"

Tyler touched Charlie Burke's shoulder, saying, "Let's go," wanting to leave before he did something dumb. It was the man's reasonable tone that made you want to climb over the table and hit him, mess up his goddamn hair. The man sounded like he was stating a simple fact, take his word or take the horses and go home. Wasn't that reasonable? Or saying you had to know whose word to take. How can you argue with that? It was true, wasn't it?

Novis was holding the door open.

Once they were in the lobby again, the door closed behind them, Tyler took his time saying, "He wants you to lose your temper and carry on, act like a fool while he stays calm and pretends to be surprised, raises his eyebrows—you see him do that?— the son of a bitch."

Charlie Burke still seemed mystified. He didn't say a word.

Tyler said, "Once we get the string to Matanzas the man is gonna pay the price we agreed on, a hundred fifty a head times thirty plus forty-five for wharfage and feed. That's forty-five hundred and forty-five dollars." He said to Fuentes, "And you get your cut out of it, that was the deal."

"You know why he did that?" Fuentes said. "He knows what he suppose to pay, but now he sees the war coming he can sell the horses to the Spanish for twice what he pays. You understand? Do it before there is a war. As soon as it starts they take the horses from him. Also, I think because his lady friend spoke to you, Amelia, and he saw the way she acted."

Tyler said, "It looked to me like she was being polite's all she was doing."

"Is that what you think? Listen," Fuentes said, "Mr. Boudreaux makes sure she belongs to him and no one else. You don't believe me, ask her. She's over there with the journalist. You see her? I think she's waiting for you to look at her again."

# 6

THE FIRST TIME Neely Tucker and Amelia met—it happened to be right here at the hotel cigar counter—Neely said, "I have never bought a lady a cigar before, but if I may . . . ?" Amelia said, "You're sweet, but I prefer cigarettes." And Neely said, "Whatever pleases you gives me pleasure."

This evening when Neely, leaning on the glass counter, said he'd never bought a lady cigarettes before, Amelia turned to him saying, "You were waiting for me, weren't you?" giving him her famous smile. *Eyes twinkling mischievously, her countenance aglow,* would be the way he'd write it, rather than say her smile showed in her eyes and made her seem so, well, alive. Amelia, when she wanted, could express all sorts of emotions with her eyes. Neely told her one time she could've been an actress, caught himself right away and said, "What am I talking about, *could* have been."

He watched her turn to the young man behind the cigar counter.

"You know what I like, Tony, Sweet Caporals, *por favor*."

Neely struck a match and held it ready as she tore open the pack of cigarettes.

"Rollie sees me smoking in public he has a fit."

Neely watched her light the cigarette now, puffing away, her delicate little nostrils dilating, her pile of auburn hair shining in the lobby's electric lights.

"You do everything he tells you?"

"Just about. He's in there with his sugar buddies."

"What're they up to now?"

"The usual, making money."

"You must know Rollie's not your type."

"But I'm his, and that's what counts, isn't it?"

Neely and Amelia Brown were good friends from the moment they'd started talking early last fall and would meet whenever both were in Havana at the same time. Neely loved Amelia. He thought of her as the most adorable, the most unusual—bizarre, really—and intelligent girl he'd ever met in his life. Talking to her wasn't like talking to a girl. She knew things, what was going on in the world. You could say anything you wanted to her, even slip and use curse words and she never acted shocked. Hell, she used them herself. It rankled him a little that the time he spent with her didn't seem to bother Boudreaux. The way Amelia explained it, "Well, he knows I'm discreet, and he doesn't see you otherwise as a threat."

Neely said, "Why not?" Naturally a little hurt.

She said, "I don't know. Maybe if you were taller."

This evening he was curious to know what she thought of Ben Tyler.

"Did you meet the cowboy?"

"Ben? Yes, indeed."

"Rollie introduced you?"

"Hardly. I spoke to him though."

"Uh-oh."

"I have a new theory," Amelia said. "It isn't that Rollie gets jealous if he thinks I'm flirting . . . Well, he does, yeah. But he also likes to see people grovel, and if I acknowledge them, even by saying a few words, it raises their status so to speak, puts us all on the same level and then Rollie has trouble feeling superior."

Neely loved her theories.

"I've never seen you grovel."

"No, that's why he respects me." Amelia paused as though she might explain this, but said, "You know what I mean."

She had always been candid with Neely about her role as Boudreaux's mistress, saying it was like a free lunch, she could have anything she wanted as long as it was Cuban. Amelia lived here year-round, on the sugar estate or at the summerhouse, on the beach not far from Matanzas. They'd met on a steamer, Amelia coming to Havana on holiday with her friend Lorraine. . . . What Neely couldn't understand was why a girl from a respectable New Orleans family, good-looking, convent-educated, would ever consider being a kept woman. Amelia told him respectability was not an issue here, not with a mother who lived on cocaine toothache drops and Koca-Nola and a daddy who practically lived with his quadroon when he wasn't at the Cotton Exchange. She said, "I'm less kept than if I were married to Rollie; I can walk away anytime I want."

Neely said, "Are you sure?" Another time he said, "But you don't love him. Do you?"

She said, "Rollie's fun."

"Oh, come on."

"I mean fun to watch, the way nothing seems to bother him. And nothing does, because whatever he *believes*, he considers fact, and what he doesn't believe isn't worth talking about. He speaks, Neely, and no one questions or interrupts him. But is he confident because he's rich or because he's also kind of dumb, unaware? Would you ask him that, Neely?"

He did try to interview the man one time.

"Mr. Boudreaux, sir, how can you sympathize with a regime that puts entire villages in concentration camps and is responsible for the annihilation of several hundred thousand innocent people?"

Boudreaux's answer: he asked Neely if he was aware of the raw sewage in the residential streets of Havana; if he realized there was no ordinance requiring a householder to empty his privy vault. "No, they use it until it overflows and then hire a night-scavenger to dip the filth into barrels. But then the honey wagon bumps along the street, the plugs in the underside of the barrels come out, and before the wagon's gone a block the street's full of raw sewage."

Amelia's interpretation: "He's saying this indicates the Cuban people are lazy and irresponsible, therefore harsh measures are sometimes required to govern them."

Neely tried another approach. "Mr. Boudreaux, you represent the main reason the United States could shortly be at war with Spain, and that is to protect American interests here in Cuba." It was meant as a question even though it didn't sound like one.

Boudreaux said, "Mr. Tucker," in that soft way he spoke, "if what you say is true and you were a soldier in the army of the United States, you think I would expect you to be willing to give your life for my personal interests?"

Amelia's comment: "You bet he would. Except Rollie wouldn't care who wins, Spain or us. Either way he'll still be sitting on top. Rollie's fear is the Cubans will end up running their own country, the

Creoles and all those black people who used to be slaves. He knows they wouldn't put up with him."

Neely had interviewed people on both sides of the insurrection. Máximo Gómez, the leader of the insurgents, the "chocolate-colored, withered old man" the New York *Herald* said looked like an Egyptian mummy. During the two months Neely spent with Gómez's troops his camera, his razor and a pair of lace-up boots disappeared.

He had interviewed Calixto Garcia, the insurgent field commander with the bullet hole in the middle of his forehead, put there years ago when he shot himself in an attempt to avoid capture. A Spanish surgeon saved his life and Garcia wore the wound stuffed with cotton.

He had interviewed a British military observer, a young subaltern named Churchill who had high praise for Cuban cigars but not much to say about the tactics of this war: "If the Cubans wish to convince the world that they have a real army, they must fight a real battle."

Neely had interviewed Spanish generals and naval officers. Most recently he'd interviewed Captain Sigsbee and survivors of the *Maine* disaster and had told Amelia about the marine at San Ambrosio who stared without moving or speaking, in total shock from the blast. He was arranging to have a chat with Clara Barton, here representing the American Red Cross on behalf of the *reconcentrados*. But the person he'd rather talk to than Bill McKinley or the queen regent of Spain was Amelia Brown.

She'd say, "Why? I'm not news."

No, but she had met just about everyone in Cuba who *was* and her air of insouciance talking about them was fascinating. He asked her, "What do you think of Fitz?"

General Fitzhugh Lee, American consul here in Havana, former Civil War hero and nephew of Robert E.

"He's fat," Amelia said.

"That's all?"

"He told me he thinks the *Maine* was blown up by a mine that was the work of a few, quote, 'malicious individuals.' Interesting? Not unlike saying some naughty boys did it. He also believes that nearly every person born on this island is instilled with a dislike of the Spaniards and their methods. Even, he said, those born of Spanish parents."

Interesting.

Another one. What about the former captain-general, Weyler, known to one and all as "the Butcher"?

"He has rather soft blue eyes for a Spaniard."

"Really."

"He asked me to leave Rollie and go to Madrid with him. I thought about it—I've never been to Europe."

"Amelia, the man's a monster, the most blood-thirsty military leader in recent history."

"I didn't go, did I?"

Neely would tell her that one of these days she actually would become tired of Rollie and leave him. "Then what will you do?"

"I haven't thought about it."

"When you were a girl, what did you want to be when you grew up?"

"I'm still a girl, Neely. I'm only twenty."

"How old?"

"Does it matter? What you're trying to say is, didn't I dream of becoming something more respectable than a courtesan, a rich man's girlfriend? Well, yes, I could see myself married to someone like him, but would I be better off?"

"Could you see yourself married to an ordinary workingman?"

"Well, not if he's just ordinary. What would be wrong with his having money? The question is, do I want to marry someday and have babies? I don't know. I guess I've never thought about it."

The feeling Neely had, he wouldn't be surprised to see Amelia step out of some type of cause-célèbre incident and become world famous overnight.

"In the company of a visiting dignitary," Amelia said, "when he's assassinated, shot through the heart by an anarchist, and in the photograph you see his blood all over my white organdy tea dress."

Neely said he had in mind something more on the order of what Mr. William Randolph Hearst did with Evangelina Cisneros in the *Journal*.

"Invented her," Amelia said.

"Well, she did exist," Neely said. "They found her in prison awaiting trial for rebellious actions against the state."

"Or was it for not going to bed with the *alcalde*?"

"Amelia, there was a worldwide petition to get her out, 'the beautiful seventeen-year-old daughter of the revolution languishing in Death's Shadow,' Casa de Recogidas, the vilest prison in all Cuba. Julia Ward Howe said, 'How can we think of this pure flower of maidenhood condemned to live with felons and outcasts, without succor, without protection' . . . something about 'under a torrid sky, suffering privation, indignity. . . .' "

"How do you remember all that?"

"It didn't do Evangelina any good at all. Spain wanted to send her to an even worse prison, in Africa. So one of Mr. Hearst's boys helped her escape."

"You mean," Amelia said, "he paid off the guards and she walked out."

"They made it look like an escape—it's the same thing. The beautiful Evangelina was escorted to Washington, where she was received by President McKinley. . . ."

"Julia Ward Howe singing 'The Battle Hymn of the Republic'?"

"Possibly. The president, anyway, and one hundred thousand cheering Americans."

Amelia said she never thought Evangelina Cisneros was that good-looking. Neely said, well, she wasn't bad.

This evening at the hotel cigar counter Neely said, "You know something? I would rather write about you than Julia Ward Howe."

"And Clara Barton?"

"Even Clara Barton, and there's a good story there. The Red Cross has brought in so much condensed milk for the starving children, some of the Cubans are selling it to buy cigars. Oh, and before too long I want to interview that insurgent leader they call Islero, I'm told a very colorful character."

"Colorful meaning colored?"

"That's right, Islero is pure Negro, a slave at one time, before he ran away to become a bloodthirsty bandit and evolved, finally, into a moderately famous insurrectionist. He's known as the Black Death. Or it might be the Black Plague; now I'm not sure."

"What about the cowboy? He might be interesting," Amelia said. She turned from the cigar counter. "He's right over there as we speak."

By the dining room talking to his partner and Rollie's man, Victor Fuentes, the cowboy looking this way as Fuentes said something to him. Amelia smiled and watched him touch his new panama.

"I already know a few things about him," Neely said. "One, he was born and raised in your hometown, New Orleans."

"You made that up."

"Lives in Arizona now. He's been to prison."

"Really. What did he do?"

"Robbed banks."

Amelia said, "Oh my," her eyes shining.

It wasn't more than moments later Lionel Tavalera, in civilian clothes, a black suit, walked past them from the hotel entrance and started across the lobby. Neely saw him first. He said, "Well, look who's here," fairly sure Boudreaux knew him, and maybe Amelia did too.

She said, "The major himself," sounding surprised.

Because of the way he was dressed, or being in this hotel, or what? They watched Tavalera walk up to Ben Tyler and begin talking to him.

Neely said, "You do know Lionel, I take it."

Amelia, staring across the lobby, said, "I watched him kill two men."

"My God—where was this?"

"I'll tell you about it sometime."

"Lionel and some hussar officers," Neely said, "had a set-to with the cowboy this afternoon. According to Charlie Burke, one of them was interested in buying a horse. He asked the cowboy to saddle it for him and Tyler refused. What he said was 'I'm not your *mozo.*' "

Amelia drew on her cigarette, inhaled and blew out a slow stream of smoke. She said, " 'I'm not your *mozo,*' huh?" watching Lionel Tavalera coming back this way now with a set expression, walking past them toward the street entrance.

"It doesn't appear," Amelia said, "anything was settled, does it?"

"Meanwhile," Neely said, "Tyler and his friends are repairing to the bar. Did I notice him looking this way? Certainly not at me. I'm going to San Ambrosio tomorrow to check on the marine, see if he's regained his speech. If you'd like to come . . ." He let it hang and said, "You're right, it's not settled," as Tavalera came back past them accompanied now by a young man with a pointy mustache, also in a black business suit. They crossed the lobby toward the bar.

When Amelia didn't comment, Neely said, "That, speak of the devil, is the hussar officer, Lieutenant Teobaldo Barbón, who asked Tyler to saddle the horse for him. Tyler is said to have replied, 'What's the matter, you helpless?' "

"Well, naturally," Amelia said, "since he isn't his *mozo*."

"You like that, don't you? Remember last month I did an essay, 'For Honor's Sake: The Rites of Duello'?"

"I recall your working on it."

"That's what I mean; it hasn't run yet. But Teo Barbón was my main source. I asked him what it was like to call a man out, point pistols at each other and, under quite formal conditions, shoot the man through the heart."

Amelia said, "Why don't you accompany me into the bar."


THERE WAS NO QUESTION in Neely's mind, Teo Barbón was going to walk up to Tyler and demand satisfaction, lay down the challenge to meet him in the morning with pistols. It was what this young hussar officer had done successfully three times since arriving in Cuba. There was a story told about a New York correspondent who offended or insulted Teo in some way. When Teo's second presented the challenge the correspondent said, "I'll fight the don if he can prove he's white and has at least two clean shirts." But when Teo sought out the correspondent he was told the gentleman had been called back to America.

Teo did have the shirts and was obviously white. He could be French, for that matter, or even English. His appearance was not what the correspondents considered typically Spanish. Tavalera, on the other hand, was dark, no doubt from Andalusia in the south of Spain and was, they said, very likely part Gypsy.

Teo, in his dark suit and vest, slender, poised, standing now at the bar with Tavalera, removed his gloves as he stared at Tyler. Tyler and Charlie Burke at the same table they'd occupied earlier with Neely. Victor Fuentes did not appear eager to join them; he stood by the table telling them something. But what?

Leave? It was too late for that. Lionel Tavalera, a few minutes ago in the lobby, had evidently asked Tyler to step outside to meet with Teo, and Tyler, it seemed, had refused. Why wouldn't he? If Teo had something to say to him . . . Sure, let him put his prejudices aside—the Spaniard's reluctance to enter this hotel and associate with so many Americans in one place—come in here and say it.

Which seemed about to happen.

Neely's view was from the entrance, standing with Amelia Brown, who was getting looks from all over the room. The correspondents openly appraised Amelia whenever she made an appearance and were free with their comments. That's Rollie Boudreaux's baby doll. Isn't she a dish? Imagine taking that to bed whenever you feel like it. But she looked so sweet and innocent. Oh, is that so?

What they needed was a table. They couldn't stand at the bar with Teo and Lionel Tavalera. Ladies didn't stand at the bar. And they couldn't very well join Tyler and his partner. What if Boudreaux came in looking for her? The only available tables were here by the door, away from what was about to happen. If words were exchanged they wouldn't be able to hear what was said. Neely turned to Amelia.

"There aren't any good seats left."

Amelia said, "What are you talking about?" and led the way to center stage, where else but to the table where Tyler and Charlie Burke rose to their feet, surprised, naturally, but immediately asked the two to join them, please. Amelia said, "Are you sure we won't be in the way?" taking the chair Neely pulled out for her.

Tyler said, "In the way of what?"

At this moment Amelia looked away from him to see the Guardia, Tavalera, coming over to the table and that seemed to answer the question. Tyler was now the only one still on his feet. He said, "Lionel, I thought you were gonna have a talk with the boy."

Neely took that to mean with Teo, still at the bar waiting, looking this way.

Tavalera said, "My name is not Ly-nel, what you call me. It's Leyo-nel."

Tyler said, "I'll try to remember that, Lionel."

"You just call me that again."

Neely noticed that something about Tyler had changed, along with his tone as he said, "Why don't we get to it? Tell me what's on your mind."

"All right. Teo wants to speak to you. At the bar."

"Tell me why I'm suppose to go to him."

"Man, he isn't ordering you."

"I hope to tell you he isn't."

"It's for privacy. No one else's business."

"He has something to say, Lionel, he can come over here. We're all friends."

Neely watched Tavalera hesitate, trying to decide—it looked like—if he wanted to make any more out of the way Tyler pronounced his name,

Neely wondering if Tyler was doing it on purpose, to be irksome. Tavalera made up his mind, evidently not to say any more about it. He turned in kind of a military about-face and went back to the bar, exchanged a few words with Teo and now Teo was on his way over.

He brought a card from his vest pocket with the tips of two fingers, a calling card, it looked like, and with a very solemn expression on his face offered it to Tyler—Tyler, still on his feet, one might say waiting for him. Neely noticed Teo holding his black kid gloves in his left hand. He also noticed Tyler was the taller of the two and possibly ten years older. He'd have to check on that, Neely pretty sure he had a story here he'd be writing as a feature. He watched Tyler look at the card and then at the young hussar officer, more a dandy than a fop, with his neat little waxed mustache. Tyler said, "Teobaldo," and glanced at the card again. "*Teniente*. What can I do for you?" As easy about it as you please.

It surprised Neely that Teo didn't acknowledge Amelia first, ask her pardon for interrupting, walking up to the table unannounced. Amelia's eyes were glued to the two men facing each other, Teo saying now in a very formal manner, "I request that you meet me tomorrow . . ." with an accent but the words clear enough: that Tyler meet him in the morning at first light in the Prado by the statue of Her Majesty Queen Isabella, Teo saying his second, Major Lionel Tavalera, would bring the pistols and

Tyler would be given his choice of which one he would prefer to use.

Look at Amelia's eyes, big as saucers, the sweet thing hanging on every word.

Tyler said, "I thought you wanted to sword-fight."

She loved it, looking at Tyler almost adoringly, her new hero, her lips slightly parted.

Tyler saying, "Now you want to shoot me. 'Cause I wouldn't saddle a horse for you?"

Neely would tell her later her mouth was open and it distracted him, made it hard to concentrate on details, and he didn't want to take out his notebook —how would that look? He'd have to remember what was said.

Teo was saying now, "You insult me."

Tyler asking him, "How do I do that?"

"The way you speak. You show no respect."

"Why should I respect you?"

"There. You see?"

"What you need to do," Tyler said, "is get over your touchiness. You understand what I mean? You're too sensitive, got a thin skin on you. I'm not gonna stand out there by a statue and let you aim your pistol at me, not over something as piddling as you wanting your own way."

There was no missing the hussar officer's expression of hostility. Neely noted the narrowing of his eyes to slits; he glanced at Amelia to see the adorable creature completely absorbed.

Spellbound.

Tyler saying now to Teo, "You have a war going on. Doesn't it give you enough people to kill?"

Teo didn't waste a moment. Neely watched him shift his gloves from his left to his right hand and crack Tyler across the face, stinging him good with those kid gloves—harder in fact than need be, only the formality of a slap required and ordinarily accepted as a challenge. What was in no way part of duello rites was Tyler cocking his left fist and driving it hard into Teo's wide-eyed expression, sending him stumbling back off-balance all the way to the bar, where Lionel Tavalera caught him around the shoulders and kept him on his feet. Neely could see that Teo, now the center of attention, wanted no help from anyone. He used his elbows to free himself of Tavalera, and Neely thought, Now what? Rant and rave? Promise the American he'll kill him for sure on the morrow?

No, what Teo did, he drew a short-barrel pistol from inside his suit—a .32, it looked like—extended the weapon in what must be a classic dueling pose in the direction of Tyler, barely more than six paces away, and while he was taking deliberate aim, intent on an immediate finish to this business, Tyler pulled a big .44 revolver from inside his new alpaca coat and shot Teo Barbón in the middle of his forehead. My Lord, the sound it made! And *there,* you could see the bullet hole like a small black spot, just for a moment before Teo fell to the floor.

Neely thought of Amelia.

In that moment, the sound of the shot still ringing in his head, he actually thought of Amelia.

Not a sound came from her. All eyes, her pretty mouth still open, her expression one of awe in the silence that followed, gun smoke hanging in the air . . . No, wait.

Neely got out his notebook, his pencil inside where he'd made his last entry, the one about Charlie Burke not able to find any chewing tobacco.

There.

*Charlie Burke, old-time cowpoke who liked nothing better than a good "chaw," couldn't believe it. All the tobacco that was grown in Cuba, famous the world over for its fine cigars, not one pinch of it goes into the production of chewing tobacco, scrap or plug. Idea for a heading: See a Spittoon Anywhere?*

Neely began to write:

*As gun smoke hung heavily in the air and a young man lay dead (presumably) in the bar of the Hotel Inglaterra, on a sultry evening only three days following the destruction of the United States battleship* Maine *in Havana harbor . . .* Or how about: *As gun smoke hung heavily in the air and a young Spanish officer lay dead . . . ?*

He wished Teo had been smoking a cigarette. Like in "The Death of Rodriguez," the boy appears before the firing squad smoking his last cigarette. How did Harding Davis put it? "Not arrogantly nor with bravado," something about being nonchalant and so "shockingly young for such a sacrifice."

That idea, get some emotion into it, but not so the reader sympathizes with Teo, a Spaniard.

Remember the scene, Neely told himself, the tableau.

Tyler kneeling over Teo's prostrate form, Teo obviously gone from this world.

Tavalera standing, looking down.

Amelia not moving a muscle, her expression, though, fairly calm.

Tavalera looking toward the entrance. Nodding.

And now uniformed Guardia Civil, armed with carbines, were coming into the bar.

# 7

THIS TIME THEY SAT in the inner courtyard of the home in Vedado, each with a glass of dark sherry while Rudi Calvo gave his report. As before, earlier this evening, Palenzuela's collar was off and his suspenders hung below his hips, this time the chief of municipal police preparing for bed when Rudi arrived. It was almost two A.M. and Palenzuela sat with his legs stretched out, now and then yawning.

"There were witnesses?"

"More than we need," Rudi said. "All the regulars in there, the correspondents, all professional observers. They were attentive because Amelia Brown entered and took a seat with the Americans."

"Alone?" The police chief sounding surprised.

"Mr. Boudreaux was still in the dining room, with his partners in the railroad venture."

"How do you know this?"

"Fuentes."

"What would you do without him?"

"He was in the bar and witnessed the shooting, but was gone when I looked for him after. And of course I was a witness, no more than a few steps from Barbón when he drew his pistol."

"After the American struck him."

"Which was after Barbón struck the American."

"The slap, that was a formality."

"Does the American know that?"

"Everyone knows it."

"But it was a hard slap, more an act of aggression than a formality."

"Why does this have to be complicated?"

"It isn't," Rudi said. "Barbón struck the American and the American struck him back. Barbón drew a pistol to shoot the American and the American drew a pistol and shot Barbón first. To me that doesn't seem complicated."

"You know what I mean, with the fucking Guardia Civil. Why did they have to be there?"

"Tavalera was acting as Barbón's second."

"With a squad outside?"

"He said they were waiting to report to him about the ship that brought the horses, and came in when they heard the shot. Tavalera took the pistol from Barbón's hand, a Smith & Wesson .32, the one with the very short barrel, and also disarmed the American, taking his revolver in the name of the law."

"The .44 Russian you mentioned. I have a matched pair," Palenzuela said, "made in Spain by Obea Brothers and presented to me by the Butcher himself, Weyler." Palenzuela paused. "I don't remember the occasion."

"Perhaps one of your anniversaries in office."

"Yes, I suppose."

Rudi Calvo saw his boss as a member of the establishment who took advantage of his position and would be crazy if he didn't. Still, in his years here he had come to sound more Cuban than what he actually was, of the Spanish-born elite, a *peninsulare*. Rudi was sure that if his boss was careful and continued to appear harmless, he could become a member of whatever establishment came after the present one. Naturally Andres was nervous—the Spanish still in power but hanging on by their fingernails.

"We don't want it to be complicated," Rudi said, "but it serves the purpose of the Guardia to confuse us. I identified myself to Lionel Tavalera and requested that he give me both weapons. I explained they would be introduced at a judicial hearing to determine exactly what happened here. Tavalera said, 'You saw this man shoot and kill Lieutenant Barbón. That's what happened.' He said, 'Concern yourself with city ordinances and the inspection of buildings, what you're paid to do; this is a military matter.'"

His chief frowned, not wanting to hear this

Guardia opinion of his office, but he didn't comment on it. No, what he said was "Don't tell me the American turns out to be a spy."

"The Guardia wants to believe he is, either a spy or he's giving aid to the enemy. So both the Americans will be held while the Guardia hopes to find evidence to bring them before a military tribunal."

"What kind of evidence?"

"Contraband, arms. They believe they'll find guns aboard the ship that brought the horses; but when they went to search it, the ship had already left. So now they go to Matanzas and hope to board the ship there."

"Because they didn't pay the tax on all the livestock," Palenzuela said. "Remember, you asked why was it the business of the Guardia? All right, now we know."

"What?" Rudi said. "The custom man accepted a bribe to believe there were ten horses instead of thirty. In fact, Tavalera said it was what made him suspicious. Why ship horses if you can't make a profit on them? But that doesn't mean the ship was carrying contraband."

"They'll find out. They'll question the custom man, see what he knows about it."

"And the man is never seen again," Rudi said. "Locked in a Morro dungeon and forgotten."

His chief shrugged. "He shouldn't have taken the bribe. But listen, the part I don't understand—if they believe the Americans are delivering contraband, why wait until the one shoots the hussar officer before they arrest him?"

Rudi said, "Well," taking his time, "if the duel took place and Barbón killed the American, they wouldn't have to bother dealing with him. Or perhaps Tavalera has his own reason, something personal between him and the American we don't know about."

"Do we care?" Palenzuela said, looking at Rudi, who didn't answer. "Where will they put them," the chief said now, "the Morro or La Cabaña, one or the other, uh?"

"The Morro for political prisoners," Rudi said. "It's full of people no one has heard from—some since the time of the Ten Years War or even before that. How old is the Morro, three, four hundred years old?"

Palenzuela said it again, "Do we care what happens to the two Americans?"

This time Rudi said, "They may be friends of Mr. Boudreaux."

"Ask your source, Fuentes," Palenzuela said.

He looked up as a woman's voice said, "Andres?" but waited until she called his name again before he said, "Yes?"

"Are you coming to bed?"

"In a moment."

The woman's voice said, "You were going to bring me a glass of sherry." It was his mistress, Lorraine. She said, "I'm waiting."

Now the chief of police waited, but that was all she said. He saw his expert investigator, a man he trusted, looking at him.

"What's the matter?"

Rudi shook his head. "Nothing."

"They become like wives," Palenzuela said. "In time it's hard to tell the difference. You don't know what I mean, do you?"

"I know one was enough for me," Rudi said.

Palenzuela smiled, looking very tired.

"Keep your life simple."

"I try to."

"Do you know where I am this evening? Cárdenas, attending a political function. I tell my wife I'll be back on the morning train and she says, 'Oh, you're going to function tonight.' She knows. She says, 'You must function somewhere, because you don't function at home.'"

Rudi wasn't sure if he should smile, so he didn't give it much. His chief smiled, appearing more tired now than he did before, yawning.

Looking at Rudi again he said, "Do you think of us as friends?"

"Not on a social level," Rudi said, "but yes, I think of you as a friend."

"Do you ever talk about me to others? I mean in regard to my personal life?"

"No, of course not."

"That was a foolish question. What else are you going to say."

"No, your personal life," Rudi said, "that's what it is. I can swear I never speak of you except with respect."

"Thank you. And I don't talk about you or your private activities," Palenzuela said, and held Rudi's gaze for several moments, Rudi making himself look back at his chief with the same serious intent, all the while trying quickly to think of something to say.

When it came to him he said, "All the correspondents in the hotel bar this evening will write about what happened. If they don't pass the story through the military censor in the morning, send it over the wire, it will go by boat to Key West and in a few days everyone in America will read about their two countrymen being held in a dungeon in the Morro."

"Unless the Guardia find contraband aboard the ship and they shoot the Americans right away," Palenzuela said. "I don't know about you, but I'm going to bed. It's been a long day."

# 8

"YOU ARE NOW ENTERING the presidio, the prison gallery of the famous Castillo de los Tres Reyes del Morro, completed in 1610 to protect the city from hostile forces, marauders, invaders. . . . The lamps along the wall burn coal oil. The soldiers asleep on the floor? They arrived today from a penal settlement in Africa—where you two could be going, if you aren't taken out and shot one morning at sunrise. You see, what I'm thinking," the lieutenant—who gave his name as Molina—said in English, slurring his words a little, but with only the trace of an accent, "is to remain here after the war and give tours of the Morro. There will be a war, of course, soon, and America will win. Our ships are rusting, fouled, our army can't subdue even these peasants. The Morro will become a place for American tourists to visit and I can tell them in the proper

English I learned in your country what notables were here, like a guest list, and show them the wall where thousands of prisoners were lined up and shot."

Tyler and Charlie Burke, following Lieutenant Molina along this corridor that resembled a tunnel cut through stone, looked at one another. The two guards following behind gave them each a shove to keep moving. Tyler believed Lieutenant Molina was drunk.

He was saying now, "By the way, what did you do to be brought here?"

"Nothing I know of," Tyler said.

"That's everyone's answer."

Tyler said, "What did you do?"

And the lieutenant looked over his shoulder with raised eyebrows. "Oh, so you don't think this is a reward, uh, to serve here? I was on the staff of our legation in Washington, where I made many friends, aide to the military attaché when I quite literally fucked myself out of a job. Perhaps I also drank too much of your bourbon."

He came to a cell door, a grating of steel bars, and stopped. While one of the guards unlocked the door and pulled it open, the lieutenant looked at Charlie Burke and said, "You go in here, please."

Light from the corridor showed the beginning of a row of canvas hammocks, sagging and rounded with the weight of men sleeping, in a cell that looked as wide as a road and with a vaulted ceiling, but too dark in there to tell how far it extended.

Tyler said to the lieutenant, "Wait. Can't we stay together?"

"I was told to separate you. I suppose so you won't be able to make up a story."

Tyler said, "You don't care, do you?"

"Listen," Molina said, "I could have been assigned to Africa. I can tell you the Morro is a hotel, the Inglaterra, compared to prison settlements over there. That Guardia officer who brought you, Lionel Tavalera? He wants to see you go to Ceuta, Melilla, one of those places where they send anarchists and assassins of the lowest class, men sentenced to hard labor or reclusion for life. Prisoners work in chains on a public road, beaten unmercifully by *cabos,* the prisoners they use as guards. Or they weld your fetters on permanently and drop you into a dungeon with a small hole in the ceiling, so that light comes to you only at midday. The food is a scrap of meat, usually infested with maggots, and some kind of pulse. The vermin eat you alive and you don't come out until they finish and you're dead." Lieutenant Molina looked at Charlie Burke then and said, "Please go in there. Here, not doing what you're told will be met with blows and imprecations."

Tyler put his hand on Charlie Burke's shoulder and Charlie Burke shook his head saying, "I'm sorry I got you into this, partner, but I don't imagine we'll

be here too long." He didn't sound at all sure of it
and added, "Do you?"

"Once it's in the newspapers and everybody
knows about it," Tyler said, "Neely's pretty sure
it'll get some action from the consulate. They'll
demand a hearing right away."

The worry was in Charlie Burke's eyes, watery
and shining in the lamplight.

He said, "Once they get hold of the
*Vamoose* . . ."

Now he was starting to say too much.

"We don't have to go into that, Charlie."

He said, "Well . . ."

And that was all as one of the guards shoved him
into the cell and slammed the grating closed. Molina
said to him through the grille, "If you can, find a
hammock not occupied."

Tyler asked, "Who's he in there with?"

"Revolutionaries," Molina said. "From their
point of view, patriots."

Moving along the corridor again, their shadows
accompanying them on the wall, he said, "You get
food twice a day, eleven o'clock and I believe five,
stew made from some kind of meat and rancho
bread. It can make you sick, give you the shits, so
don't eat it if you have money. Pay one of the
guards to bring you food from the cantina. It's bad,
but not as bad as the food they serve you. Let me see
—you can buy coffee and fix your own, otherwise I
don't think you get any."

Tyler said, "You're not in charge here?"

"I'm told what to do."

Tyler let it go. They had come to another cell and the guard with the key was pulling open the door in the steel grating.

Time to ask one more question.

"How soon will we get a hearing?"

Molina seemed to think about what he was going to say. Then: "If you're transferred to La Cabaña—you know the other prison? It's right here, so close it appears to be part of the Morro. Prisoners are usually transferred there before they go to a hearing. But then, more executions take place in La Cabaña than here. They have a procession, the priest accompanying the condemned man, who usually acts quite brave while he must be frightened to death. He'll cry out, *'Viva Cuba Libre!'* in the moment before the firing squad shoots him. The officer then uses his pistol to give the victim the *tiro de gracia,* a bullet in the brain. The executions take place in the *foso* over there, the moat; it's always dry. You see papaya trees growing there, the soil rich with the blood of martyrs to the cause."

It sounded to Tyler like something Neely Tucker had said in the hotel bar. Molina, though, expressed the idea in a melancholy tone of voice that he changed immediately, adding, "That is, if you think of those people as martyrs."

Tyler said, "And if we're kept here?"

"In the Morro? The best I can tell you," Molina
said, "to give you hope . . ."

Tyler waited.

"Is to say, Who knows?"

# 9

VIRGIL HEARD THE NEW ONE put in here during the night, heard him bumping into hammocks and heard words in Spanish among the chorus of snores—louder snores than you heard in the crew's quarters aboard the *Maine,* these men here being much older than fleet marines—but Virgil made no effort to have a look at the new one. What for? Virgil was new himself, put in here the night before and spent the next day discussing the possibility of America declaring war on Spain with his sixteen cellmates; most of them skinny old guys losing their teeth who'd been locked up here the past two years, some of them locked up other places before coming here, stuck in cells the whole time, not let outside even once. They were excited to have Virgil, a United States marine; he was like a messenger from heaven, as good as the Angel Gabriel come to tell them Uncle Sam was on their side now, so there was nothing to worry about. They made coffee for Virgil and served him some pretty tasty black beans and rice; and they let him hang his hammock down by the outside grating that looked out on the prison yard. The cell, with its oval ceiling, was about fifteen feet wide by forty feet deep, the grating at one end being the door to the corridor, the grating at the other end serving as a barred window. Hammocks hung from hooks in the wall and extended to posts that ran down the center of the room. The floor was flagstone and a few of the geezers preferred it to trying to climb into a goddamn hammock every night. They'd bed down on the floor with straw mats and blankets.

It was Lieutenant Molina who saw to Virgil's need for something to wear, having arrived drugged from the hospital in his drawers. Molina gave him one of his own cotton shirts and blue uniform trousers with yellow stripes down the sides. They fit snug—dons as a rule being smaller than Americans —and were shiny in the seat, but fine with Virgil. This was after the lieutenant told Virgil about his Washington duty and that he'd visited various points of interest along the eastern seaboard. It turned out both Virgil and Lieutenant Molina had attended the dedication of Grant's Tomb. Imagine that. Virgil didn't mind not having shoes, the flagstone in here cool on his feet. He asked the lieutenant just what he was in jail for. Molina said he didn't know but would try to find out.

As soon as Virgil woke up he saw the new man by the grating that looked out at the yard. Virgil thought at first glance he was U.S. Army, the dark coat and tan-colored pants, except there was no insignia on the coat. Right then the new man turned around and walked away and Virgil noticed the light blue neckerchief and heard that *ching . . . ching* and looked down to see the man was wearing high-heeled boots and spurs with big wheels that made that *ching*ing sound. It looked like the new man was pacing. When he came back this way Virgil said from the hammock:

"Mister, are you a cowpuncher by any chance?"

"Yes, I am," Tyler said, locating Virgil in the hammock. "Ben Tyler, from around Sweetmary, Arizona."

Now Virgil rolled out of the hammock and hit the floor in a pair of drawers, to Tyler a young guy with a full head of hair on top but none around the ears, a haircut that would last him a good while.

"I could tell," Virgil said. "You have that look of a cowpuncher."

"I had a panama hat might've thrown you off," Tyler said, "but a guard swiped it right off my head, grabbed it as he shoved me in here."

"Well, least you have your own clothes."

"I just bought 'em yesterday; they're brand-new."

"What'd you do to be in here?"

"I thought it was for shooting a don, but now I don't think so. And you're . . . ?" Tyler said. "I'm gonna say you're in the military from your haircut, but I can't tell which one from your drawers."

Virgil stuck out his hand. "Virgil Webster, one time from Okmulgee, Indian Territory. Most recently Private Webster, a seagoing marine off what used to be the USS *Maine*. God help the boys still aboard her."

"Jesus," Tyler said, shaking Virgil's hand, "you survived that terrible explosion."

"Barely," Virgil said.

Tyler squinted, studying him. "Well, what's a hero of the *Maine* doing in this flophouse?"

"I find out I'll let you know," Virgil said. "How about yourself? An honest-to-God cowpuncher, what I always thought I'd grow up to be when I was little."

"I know what you mean," Tyler said.

This was how they began talking that first day.


ON THE FIFTH DAY, February twenty-third, two guards brought Tyler along the corridor to the lieutenant's office, a large room with bare walls, a swept stone floor and a feeling of having been left abandoned until a desk and file cabinets were moved in. Molina looked up. He said in Spanish to the man sitting across the desk from him, "I'll leave you. Take as much time as you like."

The lieutenant got up and came this way, giving Tyler's shoulder a pat as he walked past him. He paused in the doorway and said something to the two guards. They turned and followed him out.

The man at the desk, one of those little Cuban guys with a big mustache, gestured for Tyler to come over, saying in English with the usual accent, "I like to ask you some questions."

There was something familiar about him. Tyler approached the desk and stood there, a few feet from it.

"Please, sit down."

The only chair was the one Molina had left, behind the desk, a wooden swivel chair with a leather pad on the seat.

"Here?"

"Yes, why not. It's all right." The man, in a rigid-looking straight chair, waited until Tyler was seated. "My name is Rudi Calvo. I'm an investigator with the municipal police for the city of Havana."

Tyler remembered him now.

"You were at the Inglaterra the other night."

"Yes, I was present." He smiled then. "You notice me, uh?"

"I did, and you saw why I shot him. You were a witness, you and a barful of correspondents. It must've been in their newspapers."

"The ones I saw," Rudi said, "they say it was

self-defense. So they want to know why you're here
if it's not for the shooting. Also why do they arrest
your partner. The Guardia Civil say you're held on
suspicion of being spies while they look for the boat,
the *Vámanos,* you came here with the horses."

"What do they want with the boat?"

"It's Lionel Tavalera. He believe you brought
guns for the *insurrectos.* They waited at Matanzas,
but the boat never came there."

"What if they don't find it?"

Rudi shrugged. "Yes? What if they don't?"

"I could be here the rest of my life?"

"Well, it isn't something new, is it? You were in
prison one time before."

"How do you know that, from the newspapers?"

"Someone told me."

"You talk to Charlie Burke?"

"Not yet."

Tyler stared at Rudi Calvo. When the police
investigator looked away, Tyler said, "You know
they're holding a U.S. marine here?" He watched
Rudi Calvo's gaze return, eyes full of interest. "Private Virgil Webster, off the *Maine.* You don't know
about him?"

Rudi shook his head.

"Blown into the water. Picked up and taken to a
hospital. The night before last the Guards dragged
him out of bed and brought him here. They think he
saw something the night the ship blew up."

"Did he?"

"Not that he knows of."

Tyler watched the municipal police investigator taking time to think about this, staring at one of the bare stone walls.

"You're police, the Guardia are police—they don't tell you what they're doing?"

Rudi took his time. "They have their own way of doing things."

"You knew I was in prison. Did you know I was here before, in Cuba? That my father ran a mill?"

"I heard that, yes."

"Do the Guardia know I was in prison back home?"

Rudi again took his time. "I don't think so."

"It was Fuentes told you about me," Tyler said. He waited, and Rudi waited, not saying a word. "You followed us when he took me to buy clothes. I'm guessing, but I'm pretty sure about it. We're on the street, Fuentes says, 'Don't look now . . .' No, he said, 'Don't look around when I tell you we're being followed.' But I did, I looked around. You know why? Because Fuentes wasn't worried about it. He said, 'It's okay, it's the police.' See, but before that he wouldn't say much talking about the Guardia or what side he was on; he was careful. I asked him if he was for Spain or a free Cuba. He said, 'If I told you I was for Cuba, would you believe me?' I said, 'Yes, but I'd keep an eye on you.' And he said that's the way to be, don't trust anybody."

"But you believe he wants Cuba to be free," Rudi said. "Is that right?"

Tyler said, "Do you care what I think? What difference does it make? You said you wanted to ask me some questions. Is that it? What I think about Fuentes?"

This man made you wait while he thought things over.

"I want to ask you about your boat, the *Vámanos*."

"The *Vamoose*. If she isn't in Matanzas, I don't know where she is. Are there guns aboard? I haven't seen any. If I tell anyone what I believe about Victor Fuentes, should I say what I believe about you?"

Rudi said, "I don't know what you think." When Tyler didn't tell him he said, "Why would you talk about me?" And when Tyler didn't answer, Rudi said, "It's best not to say anything if you don't have to," and left.

TWICE A DAY criminal convicts from another part of the Morro brought fresh water and carried away the slop buckets. Three times a day one of the guards handed in a broom and the men took turns sweeping the flagstone floor. The guards didn't bother them much: half the men in here sick with fever and diarrhea, and there were always two or three moaning in their hammocks all day with stomach pains. The doctor was supposed to come twice a week, but they rarely saw him, told by the guards the doctor himself was sick or he was drunk. When he did come and look at them, he would attribute their ills to worms, or vermin. So these men in here accused of committing treason would bang the filthy metal food pans against the grating, demanding aspirin and quinine and once in a while they were given some. When cases of cholera or yellow fever were diagnosed, the sick ones were removed from the cell, Tyler was told, and never seen again. There was a leper among them from Santa Clara who was beginning to acquire the facial look of a lion, but had not yet lost any of his fingers or toes.

After a few days their cellmates had asked all the questions they could think of and left the Americans in peace to sit by the grating, the one that looked out on the yard.

"That's cannister stacked out there," Virgil said, "what used to be called grapeshot. It looks like they're getting ready to load it onto Spanish warships. You know what one of their problems is? Their coal ain't worth shit. We got 'em beat a mile in the grade of coal our ships burn. The *Maine* carried eight hundred and twenty-five ton, enough to steam seven thousand miles at a speed of ten knots. Our 10-inch guns—there was a pair mounted fore and aft. Each one could throw a five-hundred-pound shell a good nine miles, mister. We had 6-inch guns, 6-pounders, rapid-fire 1-pounders, four Gatlings and a stock of Whitehead torpedos. Man, if we had known what was coming . . ."

He said, "I've been in the brig aboard ship, but it was nothing like this, nothing to eat, everybody sick. . . ."

Tyler said, "Yuma was worse'n this. You know why? You lived with convicts there, not political prisoners."


ON THE TENTH OF MARCH, Tyler's twentieth day in the Morro, Victor Fuentes came to visit. He sat in the swivel chair behind Lieutenant Molina's desk, waiting. Tyler was brought in and took the straight chair that was too small to offer comfort. He said to Fuentes, "Your friend the policeman was here."

Fuentes hesitated, then nodded. "He told me."

"Can anyone visit?"

"If you pay. It cost a bottle of dark rum for an hour or so. A bottle of bourbon whiskey you can stay as long as you want. The lieutenant drinks it and goes to sleep." Fuentes shoved his hands into the pockets of his suit coat, came out with a half-pint bottle of quinine in each hand and placed them on the desk. From a vest pocket he drew two double eagles, worth twenty dollars each, and reached across the desk to put them in Tyler's hand.

"For whatever you need."

"We appreciate it, all of us, but who is it from?"

"What do you mean, who? Is from me."

"Can you afford it?"

"Don't insult me."

"Sorry." Tyler thought of Virgil and said, "I imagine the policeman told you about the marine."

Fuentes said, "The rumor that he's here? I heard that."

"He *is* here. We're in the same cell."

Fuentes said, "Listen, we took the horses to Matanzas. All of them, yours too, on the train. I didn't want to leave your horse in Regla."

"And you don't want to talk about the marine," Tyler said.

"I have no reason to."

"Or the policeman, Rudi Calvo?"

"I know him, that's all. So, I took the horses to Matanzas. Boudreaux went, but now he's in Havana again. Also Amelia Brown, she's here. She wants to visit you."

"She wants to come here?"

"That's what she say."

"What for?"

"If she comes you can ask her."

Tyler pushed the image of the girl out of his mind and said, "Have you seen Charlie?"

"A little while ago. He looks worse than you."

"What's wrong with him?"

"He has the shits, what else? Listen, I have to get him some medicine and come back. What I want to tell you, they haven't found the ship yet, the *Vamoose*, and they won't find it. Don't ask me where it is, all right? Or ask me anything about it. I say this because they going to come and ask you where it is, and if you don't know you can't tell them. That's all I'm going to say to you," Fuentes said.

As he rose from the desk Tyler said, "When she say she's coming?"

"Who, Amelia?"

"Who else we talking about?"


HE TOLD VIRGIL, the two of them sitting by the outside grating, wild studs loved gentle mares; they'd get hold of some that'd wandered away from the home graze and run off with these nice girls, whether the mares wanted to go or not.

Virgil said, "Man, the studs, huh?"

Tyler told him the way to go after a big herd, put about a hundred and fifty gentle horses out there and drive the wild bunch into them. "See, then the gentle horses that were already with the wild ones, they'd stop, and some of the colts and yearlings'd get separated and stay with the gentle bunch. So then the hands shake out their ropes . . ."

"That's how, huh?" Virgil ate it up.

Tyler told him you had to be a big cow outfit to do it like that, be able to put twenty riders out there for the drive. He told Virgil the way you worked it by yourself, or with Red and a couple of Mimbres along, you had to walk down the wild herd, slip up on them gradually, the wild ones likely never having seen a mounted man before, the bunch of them wondering what in the hell kind of horse is that?

Virgil said, "Man," shaking his head. He told Tyler he'd bought a horse for five dollars when he was fifteen—worked at the F.B. Severs Cash Store in Okmulgee, stocking shelves and sweeping floors to earn the money—and his stepfather, the son of a bitch, a Church of the Most Holy Word missionary who didn't know shit about anything except Scripture, took the horse away from him and sold it and kept the money.

Tyler told him if he ever worked for a big cow outfit he'd have ten of his own horses on a trail drive. Ride two or three a day and turn them back into the remuda for three days' rest. You had a special horse you rode at night. Green broncos were saved for winter.

"The first thing I learned about horses," Virgil said, "living where we did, was Indins like horse meat."

"Apaches," Tyler said, "prefer mule. Did you ever see Geronimo?"

"One time in '94 I was home on leave, I went over to Fort Sill to get a look at him, but he was off traveling with Pawnee Bill's Wild West Circus."

"I saw him and Nachez at Bowie in '86," Tyler said, "the day they shipped 'em off to Florida. The army gave 'em little hats to put on looked foolish, like flower pots, and they still scared the shit out of anybody was present. I think it was General Nelson

Miles said the only man he ever knew with eyes as dark and piercing as Geronimo's was William Tecumseh Sherman. They had the kind of eyes could look right through you."

WHEN TAVALERA CAME TO VISIT he sat in Lieutenant Molina's chair and swiveled back and forth while Tyler stood facing him across the desk.

"You don't look so good."

"It's the food," Tyler said.

"You don't like it? You can leave anytime—once you tell me where the ship is."

"I don't know."

"You tell me it was going to Matanzas."

"That's right."

"But it didn't come there."

"Maybe it's still on its way."

"It doesn't take thirty days, Havana to Matanzas."

"I can't help you, Lionel," Tyler said, pronouncing the name "Lynel" the way he did in the hotel bar. Tavalera stared at him and Tyler said, "I mean Leo-nel. I bet the ship went back home, partner. Can you check?"

"We did. Is not in Key West or Tampa or Galveston, Texas. Is still here somewhere. I believe from the beginning it has contraband aboard. Now I'm more sure than before. You refuse to tell me and your friend refuse when I talk to him. What am I going to do with you? . . . You think you helping these people to have freedom. I'll tell you something. If they do succeed, have their own government, you think it will be different for poor people than it is now? They talk about the ones in power as moved by greed, always wanting more. You think the Cubans, they get in power they won't be moved by greed? Anyone can learn how if they don't know. All right, what about the Negroes? Pretty soon half the people here are going to be black. You want some of them in power? These people were slaves only a few years ago. Listen, your own people in business here, they don't want Cubans or Negroes making laws, telling them what to do. Of course not. So what is it to you? Why don't you give up this game you play? Tell me where the boat is and you can go home. What do you say?"

RED WAS WARM SPRINGS APACHE, he couldn't stand to be locked up like that, then taken out to work shackled, the way he was at Yuma the whole first year, to bust rocks. He couldn't eat the food either. The first day his leg irons are off after a year, we're working a section of road up on a high bank where you look down and there's the Colorado River, say a mile from the road to the other side. Red dropped his pick, not even checking the guards first, dropped his pick and ran. They chased him. . . . Red was in the river, halfway to California, when they shot him."

"How was the chow at Yuma?"

"Terrible. Sometimes you couldn't tell what you were eating."

"That ain't all that's wrong with this shit; it's got bugs in it."

"Least they're cooked."

Virgil picked a maggot out of his meat. "This one ain't. Bread and water's the best, less the bread's moldy. Otherwise you can't mess up bread and water."

A FEW DAYS LATER, Tyler's thirty-fourth day in the Morro, guards kept him in the cell while they brought everybody else out single file and marched them down the corridor, Virgil the last one out, looking back.

Tyler waited.

Now Tavalera appeared and entered the cell followed by two Guardia Civil privates armed with Mauser carbines. Tavalera said, "Come here," motioning Tyler down to the grating at the other end of the cell. When they got there and both were looking out at the empty yard in sunlight, Tavalera said, *"Listo,"* in a loud voice.

Within a minute or so two Guardias came out of a doorway to the yard with Charlie Burke between them. They brought him all the way across the yard to the wall opposite the cell grating and faced him this way, head uncovered, hands fastened behind his back, a chew showing in his jaw.

Now six Guardia with carbines and an officer came out in a line to stand facing Charlie Burke.

"Five years ago in Spanish Africa," Tavalera said to Tyler, "the Iqar'ayen declared war on us for desecrating their mosque. Some soldiers, they said, pissed on it. The Iqar'ayen are Rifs, a Berber tribe." Tavalera began to smile. "Everyone in Spain loved that war. For that war twenty-nine generals came to Africa, hastened to Africa, for here was a pure war without economic rewards. The only thing we fought for that time was the honor of Spain. There was not even territory to be gained, only national pride and honor.

"It appears much different here, a great deal to be gained, this island a source of wealth, a cow that's been giving us milk for four hundred years. Still, the inspiration to keep this island is not economic but a matter of honor. You understand? You can be willing to give your life for honor, but not for the price of sugar. In Africa I tortured and mutilated my enemy for the sake of honor, to learn things from him or as punishment. I could do that here, but I respect you. So when I say to tell me where the boat is, you tell me. You don't tell me, we shoot your friend. Out there, look. The officer is telling him now the way it is, so you see him looking this way. Would you like to say something to your friend?"

Tyler, staring through the bars, didn't answer.

"All right then," Tavalera said. "Ready? I ask you once, where is the boat you call the *Vamoose?*"

"Believe me," Tyler said, staring at Charlie Burke, "if I knew I'd tell you."

"That's all you going to say?"

"I don't *know* where the goddamn boat is."

Tavalera, raising his voice, said, "*¡Mátanle!*"

VIRGIL SAID, "And they shot him?"

"They shot him. Just before—Charlie had a wad of scrap in his cheek. He'd brought some from home, plug and scrap, and I know he had chewed up the plug. He said 'Wait' as they were about to shoot and he turned his head to spit off to the side. They shot him and then the officer went over to Charlie lying on the ground and shot him in the head."

"Jesus," Virgil said, "you watched your partner get killed. I imagine they had you covered good, in case you went crazy on them and tried something."

"The officer, Lionel, had his pistol in his hand. When I didn't raise a rumpus or even say a word he kept staring at me."

"Like the old man, when he turned his head to spit," Virgil said, "was accepting what was about to happen?"

Tyler nodded. "He wasn't much for show. Then Lionel said maybe he was wrong and we weren't bringing guns after all."

"He said that?"

"He said if he was wrong, well, that was too bad. He said, but he'd never know for sure, would he?"

"What did you say to him?"

"I didn't say anything."

Virgil said, "Well, you're sure better behaved than I am."

THE DAY AMELIA BROWN CAME to visit was Tyler's forty-fifth day in the Morro. She was already seated when he entered the office, Amelia smiling beneath a big sun hat, then frowning as Tyler took the lieutenant's swivel chair and she saw him up close.

"You don't look good. How are you?" She went right on, not giving Tyler a chance to answer, telling him Neely Tucker was here too, Neely wanting to talk to the marine who was blown off the *Maine* and then abducted from the hospital. "Neely told Lieutenant Molina, well, since everyone knows he's here and it's going to be in all the newspapers anyway . . . Neely then produced a bottle of bourbon. He's with the marine now, in another office. Would you like a cigarette?"

Tyler nodded.

She brought a pack out of her bag, but then dropped it in again, saying, "Oh. Did you hear? It's official, the Spanish blew up the *Maine*. It took the Naval Court of Inquiry over a month to figure out that the destruction of an American warship in a hostile if not enemy harbor did not happen by accident; it must have been a submerged mine or some such explosive device. They sent divers down in forty feet of nasty murky water to take a look and get the evidence. I think what they found, the hull was blown inward from the keel. Now, according to every paper I've seen, enthusiasm for war is sweeping the country. Buffalo Bill said thirty thousand Indian fighters could run the dons out of Cuba in sixty days. Jesse James's brother Frank wants to bring over a bunch of cowboys and settle the matter, and six thousand Sioux braves are more than ready to take Spanish scalps. The Sioux, of all people."

There was a silence.

She said, "I would have come to visit before this, but Rollie made me go to Matanzas with him. He and his sugar buddies want to add a rail line from Santa Clara all the way to Santiago de Cuba, at the far eastern end of the island." She waited a moment and said, "No, you don't look well at all."

"They stood my partner in front of a firing squad," Tyler said, "out in the yard and killed him."

Amelia said, "Oh." And in a different voice than before, a quiet tone, she said, "And you saw it, didn't you? They made you watch."

"Tavalera," Tyler said, "the Guardia Civil officer who was at the hotel—"

"Yes, I know him."

"He thinks Charlie Burke and I were bringing in guns, but he can't prove it 'cause he can't locate the boat. He said I had to tell him where it is or he'd have them shoot Charlie."

"But you don't know where it is."

Tyler said, "No," shaking his head.

"Or if the guns are still aboard."

There was a silence again, Amelia waiting for him.

"I said he *thought* we brought guns, not that we actually did."

"Two hundred revolvers," Amelia said, "two hundred Krag carbines, the machetes . . . What else?"

Tyler stared at her. He said, "Jesus," in a hushed voice.

And Amelia said, "Our Savior. The guns were put ashore near Sagua la Grande and the ship returned to Mexico. Where's your hat? Do you still have it?"

He said, "One of the guards took it," staring at her, not able to take his eyes from her face so pure and clean, her eyes full of life.

She said, "That kind of panama is called a *jipi-japa*. Did you know that?"

He shook his head.

She said, "We'll have to find you another one." She said, "And we'll have to think of a way to get you out of here. Pretty soon there's going to be a war. A real one."

THERE WERE DIFFERENT REACTIONS from Tyler's cellmates when he told them what the Naval Court of Inquiry had found. Some cheered, seeing American soldiers busting in here to free them. But there were revolutionists here, old patriots, some near death, who'd been fighting most of their lives and believed they were close to driving the dons out of Cuba, winning their own independence. They saw America taking the place of Spain and little change in their lives.

Virgil said, "I can't cheer the loss of so many of my shipmates, but if this means war, then okay, good. Let's get her done."

"You talked to Neely Tucker," Tyler said.

"With the lieutenant sitting there drunk."

"You tell him your story?"

"I did and he said, 'This will ice the cake, a hero of the *Maine* moldering in an El Morro dungeon.' What's moldering mean?"

"I guess what it sounds like. What else did he say?"

"He said America's gonna break off diplomatic relations with Spain and in about a week the consulate here will shut down and all the Americans living and working in Cuba will have to go home. He said we'd have to get out, too, or we'd become prisoners of war and be stuck here till it's over."

"How'd he know you were here?"

"He never said."

"I told Rudi Calvo, the policeman," Tyler said.

"It must've been Rudi told Fuentes, Fuentes told Amelia and she told Neely. She's living with this wavy-haired snake owes me forty-five hundred and forty-five dollars, but she's working, it looks like, for the revolution. Even though she's American. I haven't figured her out yet." Tyler paused.

Virgil said, "Yeah?"

"I think she's gonna make something happen."

"Like what?"

"I don't know, but it must be why she brought Neely to talk to you. It'll get in the newspapers you're here, a hero of the *Maine,* and then something will happen."

# 10

MARCH THE FOURTH A YEAR AGO, the same day President McKinley was inaugurated, Amelia Brown was introduced to a gentleman by the name of Roland Boudreaux in the saloon of the Morgan Line steamer's first evening out of New Orleans. The way it came about:

Amelia's dear friend Lorraine Regal had met a man named Andres Palenzuela at a reception given by her boss, a New Orleans sugar broker. Andres turned out to be the chief of police for the city of Havana. When he asked Lorraine to come for a visit she saw promise in his soft brown eyes, said yes, got hold of Amelia and told her to quick pack a few summer things and a bottle of Ayer's pills, she *had* to come along. Not as a chaperone, or even to give the impression of two young ladies on holiday. Uh-unh, it was so Amelia could meet the police chief's good friend, Roland Boudreaux.

Amelia told everyone March fourth was her birthday, her twentieth, and watched Lorraine roll her eyes as the gentlemen raised their glasses of champagne. Boudreaux said to call him Rollie, please. He told Amelia he'd always suspected he was inordinately lucky and meeting her like this confirmed it. He told her he owned a sugar estate, a railroad, polo grounds and a lot of horses and a summerhome on the Gulf coast of Cuba. Amelia said she loved to ride, asked if revolutionaries or anarchists interfered with his way of life. Rollie said no, he had his own army. By the end of the first evening aboard, the couples had paired off and were settled in for the short voyage.

A few days later at the Inglaterra, Lorraine said to Amelia, "Well, I won't be going back to the counting room, thank God. A police chief down here does all right; I'll have my own house." She said going to Soulé Business College and getting a job was finally paying off.

Amelia said she could look at her prospects much the same way. If she hadn't quit going to Newcomb after a couple of years and spent her time horseback riding and being available to people, she wouldn't have been available for this trip.

"Rollie wants me to stay," Amelia said.

"As what?"

"His sweetie pie, what else? His wife won't set

foot in Cuba, scared to death of yellow fever. They don't have children."

"What do you think?"

"Well, it isn't like the others."

She had been quite fond of a gentleman by the name of Avery Wild who was in coffee and kept rooms on Julia Street, where they'd meet Mondays and Thursdays in the late afternoon. It went on for most of a year. An executive with Maison Blanche she'd met at a Carnival ball was fun; he'd take her along on his buying trips to New York. Another gentleman had taken her to Saratoga by train during the racing season, and she accompanied still another gent to Tampa on his yacht. Amelia might have been in love with Avery Wild. Or she might not. She most definitely fell in love with Dr. Walter Guidry. He taught at Tulane Medical, had the bluest eyes Amelia had ever seen, and set her arm when she broke it in a fall from her horse. He was handsome. He was kind. He was patient. He was the most dedicated man she had ever known. Walter Guidry spent a week each month at the Louisiana Leprosy Home near Carville, a good seventy miles upriver from New Orleans. Took the train there every month. She said, "Walter, is it awful?" He told her they had close to fifty patients now, up from the five men and two women delivered there two years ago on a coal barge, the home's first patients. Now they came on a special train with the windows covered and sealed; once there, the patients couldn't leave. "It must be horrible," Amelia said. No, what it was, Walter Guidry said, it was frustrating, trying to get the public to understand that leprosy was not evidence of God's wrath, inflicted as punishment for a sinful life. Walter told Amelia that nuns, the Daughters of Charity, were taking care of the lepers, but the sisters were few in number and more patients were arriving daily. It came to Amelia all at once as she looked into his blue eyes, she'd go with Walter and help the sisters. She touched Walter's face. "I'll wash the lepers' wounds, their sores, I'll change their dressings, empty chamber pots." She kissed him tenderly. "You're a saint, Walter. You were sent to me, weren't you? That I might see a purpose in life and dedicate myself to its end."

Amelia said to Lorraine, "Do you remember my doctor lover, Walter Guidry?"

"Ah," Lorraine said, "do I. You'll never find another one like Walter."

"Rollie's better-looking."

"Some might say that."

"I had to think of a way to hold him off," Amelia said, "while I make up my mind. So I told him I'm still a virgin."

"Well, if he believes you're only twenty . . ."

"He treats me like I'm recovering from diphtheria or tuberculosis. He's considerate . . . but he's so sure of himself and that's one of the things I wonder about. Is he confident because he knows what he's doing, or because he's rich and everyone agrees with him? He talks a lot, in that quiet way he has. He doesn't laugh much. Did you notice? He's fairly clever with words, but doesn't have much of a sense of humor. Does he? I can't imagine why he has a bodyguard. Not if he has an army."

They switched from tea to sherry.

"I could do without Novis hanging around. He's so serious, he's creepy. I was out on deck—Novis came up to me and said, 'Mr. Boudreaux wants to see you inside,' and motioned with his thumb, like he's telling me to get in there. I said to tell Mr. Boudreaux if he wants to see me I'm out here. Novis didn't know what to do. Go in and tell his highness I wasn't coming? He wants me to go with him to visit his estate, Rollie does, I think to impress me. Look at how rich I am, girl. What're you saving you're so proud of when you can have *me*? Take the train to Matanzas to look at the estate, then go up to Varadero to see his summer place. Lots of horses to ride. I've decided I have to be myself with Rollie, not some poor little girl awed by his attention. What would I be giving up if I exiled myself to this island? Well, living with Mama and Daddy, for one thing. Mama taking laudanum and whatever else she can get her hands on. Daddy coming home with another woman's scent on him, what does he care, all the money he's made selling cotton abroad, he can do anything he wants. What I'd be giving up is boredom. Now, what I'd gain . . . If Boudreaux's wealth doesn't impress me, what would be my reward, living on a sugar plantation with the poor and deprived? Not a happy bunch, I'll bet, out in those cane fields."

Amelia paused to sip her sherry in the lobby of the Inglaterra Hotel with Lorraine, Lorraine quiet, no doubt thinking about her police chief, no longer giving Amelia her full attention. Or she didn't know what Amelia was getting at and wasn't interested enough to care.

"We had a housemaid when I was a little girl," Amelia said, "who was from the south of Spain, Jerez de la Frontera, where they make sherry. I loved to say her name, Altagracia. . . . Are you listening?"

"Of course I am."

"She used to tell me bedtime stories about anarchists. I was eight or nine years old. How the anarchists got the vineyard workers to stand together and demand justice and higher wages. In her stories the landowners are all bad, but the real villains are the Civil Guards. They arrest and torture the anarchists and accuse them of forming a secret society called the Black Hand. They said its purpose was to assassinate all the landowners in the district."

Amelia paused again to sip her sherry.

"He's showing me the house tomorrow," Lorraine said. "It's in Vedado, a suburb. Just like a *placé* on Rampart Street. Where gentlemen kept their mistresses in days gone by." She said to Amelia, "Are we living in the past?"

"Or we're ahead of our time," Amelia said. "I'm not sure which."

ON THE TRAIN to Matanzas, seventy miles east of Havana, Amelia would see people working in cane fields they passed and she would think of Altagracia's anarchists and vineyard laborers. She asked Rollie Boudreaux if he'd ever heard of the Black Hand.

He said, "Of course. It's a secret society of assassins."

"Altagracia said the only people they assassinated were informers. In fact, she said there was no such organization as the Black Hand. The Civil Guard made up the story so they could persecute the anarchists."

"You mean prosecute."

"I mean persecute."

"And who is Altagracia, please?"

"Our maid when I was a little girl."

She watched him laugh out loud for the first time and dab at his eyes with a hankie he kept in his sleeve.

He told Amelia as she looked out the window of the first-class compartment at palm trees and wooded hills, huts with thatched roofs, cultivated fields, "That's corn. That's yucca. That, of course, is cane." She asked if this was his railroad. No, this line was the Ferro Carriles Unidos, owned by a

Havana bank heavy with British and German capital. His sugar railroad ran north and south, from the *central* below a place called Benavides to the Matanzas docks and a few miles up the coast. He told her he was talking to American investors about building a major line from Santa Clara to Santiago de Cuba, at the eastern end of the island.

She asked him, "Why not Cuban investors?"

"There aren't any."

She asked why he believed Cubans were unable to govern themselves, a view he had expressed on the boat.

"Read *Cuban Sketches*," Boudreaux said. "I'll give you my copy. The book's observer characterizes Cubans as a people of 'smiles, easy talk and time-killing dilettante-ism.' "

Amelia said, "Yes? What's wrong with that?"

"You're kidding, of course." He said, "The book's observer comes to the conclusion that laziness is as natural to the Cuban as foppery is common."

She said, "Do you believe that?"

"Well, the book exaggerates, yes, to make a point, but no more than Cubans themselves, who exaggerate with an ease that's appalling. They deplore manual labor and reserve it for the Negroes, of which there are plenty on the island." He said, "Just past Benavides we come to a main road, where horses will be waiting." He said, "You weren't kidding me, you do like to ride."

"I love to."

"Because if you were kidding, what I'll do is send someone down from Benavides on a handcar and bring a carriage of some kind, a small barouche."

"Believe me," Amelia said, "I ride."

He told her this was considered quite a fast train, though you wouldn't know it, would you, with all the stops it made. Regla station to Matanzas would take about seven hours.

He told her Cubans loved ornamentation and bright colors, though young ladies applied an astonishing amount of rice powder to their faces.

He told her both men and women in Cuba prided themselves on having small feet.

He told her that while Cubans were basically honest, they tended to become homicidal when jealous.

"Wait till you read *Cuban Sketches*."

Amelia dozed off.

She opened her eyes to find the train sliding past a facing of stone buildings, a water tower, soldiers tending a dozen or more saddled horses in a barn lot, and now the compartment window came to a station platform, the train barely moving, slowing to a stop in the shade, opposite the center of the platform crowded with soldiers in pale gray uniforms and military straws, some of them looking this way now, at the train, Amelia in the window. "Guardia

Civil," Boudreaux said. He rose to open the window and sat down again in the seat facing Amelia.

"They've got a couple of prisoners. See? The two wearing filthy clothes. I don't understand why dirt doesn't bother these people. You'd think they'd wear something darker, in a heavy denim."

They were farm workers and looked to Amelia like all the Cuban laborers she had seen in the past few days. If they weren't black they were small men, like these two, with big mustaches, yes, in heavily soiled clothes and shapeless straw hats. These two were bareheaded, hands tied behind them, ropes around their necks, the ropes looped over beams that supported the platform's wooden awning. The two stood less than twenty feet from the compartment window, staring back at Amelia, while about them the Guardia seemed to be arguing among themselves.

Boudreaux turned his head and called out, "Victor!"

The compartment door opened and Fuentes and Novis were standing in the aisle looking in.

"What's going on out there?"

"You want me to, I find out."

"Yes, I want you to. Go on." Boudreaux said to Amelia, "Why does he think I called him?"

Novis, still in the doorway, said, "You don't mind my saying, it's 'cause they're stupid, all of 'em."

Now, as Amelia watched, Fuentes appeared on

the platform and approached one of the soldiers, an officer. "That's Lionel Tavalera," Boudreaux said. "He fought the Berbers in North Africa before coming here. You want someone to tell you something and he refuses, you hand him over to Tavalera." Amelia was looking at Boudreaux now. "They say he hates Americans, but he and I get along just dandy. What it comes down to, despite political differences, is mutual respect. They can be mean, those Guardia Civil—some say barbaric—but they get it done."

Amelia turned her head to watch Fuentes in his white suit talking to the Guardia officer towering over him. Earlier, when they were waiting to board the train, Boudreaux called Fuentes over and said to Amelia, "This is Victor, he's supposed to be my *segundo,* but all he does is argue with me. Victor, I'm putting Miss Brown in your care. You understand? Miss Brown wants something, you make sure she gets it." They looked at each other as Boudreaux spoke, Amelia sensing that Victor was sizing her up, curious, wanting to know who she was rather than waste his time fawning, trying to make an impression. Amelia smiled and Victor seemed surprised.

Now, as Fuentes spoke to him, the Guardia officer was looking this way. Boudreaux said in the open window, "Major," giving him kind of a salute and called to his man, "Victor, if you'll come over here, please."

Fuentes glanced over but continued talking to

Tavalera, gesturing, telling him something in earnest.

Novis said, "I'll get the squirt."

But now Boudreaux raised his voice to Victor: "Goddamn it, get over here." And this time he came, concerned, though, glancing back at the two prisoners.

"The Guardia officer say they insurgents, but I don't think so."

Amelia watched Boudreaux as he asked Fuentes if he knew them.

"I know they work for you and live on the mill. They cut cane, both of them." He looked at Amelia and for a moment held her gaze. "I tell this Guardia, but he doesn't believe me."

Boudreaux said, "You're sure?"

"Yes, I'm sure."

Amelia waited for Rollie to call to the officer now and put in a word for the two men, clear up an apparent misunderstanding. But he didn't. He said, "They could still be mambises, couldn't they?"

Amelia's gaze moved to Victor, close to the open window. He said, "How can I see them in the field fighting the cane every day if they someplace else fighting these people?"

Boudreaux nodded, thinking about it. He said to Novis, "You ever see those two before?"

"I may have, but how can you tell?" Novis said. "All these squirts look alike to me."

Boudreaux turned to Fuentes again. "What're they arguing about?"

"They need the two men to stand on something," Fuentes said, "they can pull out from under their feet when they hang them. One of the soldiers say a baggage cart. No, too high. Somebody say lay a hogshead on its side. No, much too high. A trunk, the kind you put clothes in. No, too high standing up, too low on its side. Whatever they say is that way, either too high or too low. Now somebody say put them on horses. But the horses, running from under them, whose horses you want to use?"

Novis said, "Hell, yank on the ropes and pull 'em up by hand."

Amelia watched Boudreaux look past Victor to Tavalera standing by the two prisoners, Amelia certain Rollie would now straighten out what appeared to be a misunderstanding. Yes, calling to Tavalera, "Major, if I could have a word with you . . ."

The Guardia officer came over to the window, touching the brim of his hat and smiling as he noticed Amelia. He said to Boudreaux, "Yes, how can I be of service?"

"Victor says these two work for me."

"Oh, is that so? I'm sorry, because we pretty sure these are bad people who fight us."

"But you're not sure."

"No, I say we pretty sure. What's the same as pretty sure? Quite sure? Very sure? Let's say I'm as sure as I have to be."

Boudreaux said, "Well, if you're that sure . . ."
and smiled slightly.

Tavalera started to turn, but stopped as Amelia
said, "Wait a minute," amazed that Rollie was letting it go. "Victor's just as sure they're *not* insurgents. There must be a way to resolve this kind of
situation. Isn't there?"

"Yes, of course," Tavalera said. "What we say
is, why take a chance of making a mistake?" He
turned from the window, motioned his men out of
the way as he approached the two prisoners,
removed the ropes from around their necks and
placed the men one in front of the other, as though
to march them off the platform. Now he drew his
revolver and shot each one, *bam bam,* like that, in
the right temple.

Tavalera did not look at the train window again.
His men did when he said something to them in
Spanish, but Tavalera walked away without looking
back.

Fuentes watched him, then turned to the window
as Boudreaux said, "Well." And said, "I guess that's
that."

Fuentes looked at Amelia. In the moment she
was looking back at him with no expression, nothing, her face drained of color, and yet each knew
what the other was thinking.

Before they came to the road where the horses
were waiting, Amelia used another compartment to
change into boots and a riding skirt. It was the mid-

dle of the afternoon. Fuentes knocked on the door for her luggage, which would follow the horses in a wagon.

She said to him, "Tell me something about Mr. Boudreaux. What side is he on?"

Fuentes said, "Excuse me?"

"You know what I mean."

Fuentes looked at her directly and said, "The government or the *insurrectos*, the insurgents?"

Amelia nodded. "Which?"

"The wrong side," Fuentes said.

"What kind of man is he?"

"Like the rest of them. He knows only his own kind."


THE TEA THIS TIME was served in the inner courtyard of Lorraine's home in Vedado, jade plants in pots, decorative blue tile on the walls, pillars that gave the courtyard the look of a cloister.

"For supper," Amelia said, "we might have soup, rice, eggs, plantain, a crab salad, roast peacock, guava, cheese and some kind of pudding."

"Peacock?" Lorraine said.

"Peacock. Like the Romans."

"What does it taste like, chicken?"

"Turkey. Then for breakfast we might have soup, rice, eggs, plantain, fried crabs, guava, cheese and coffee. Breakfast is really dinner, the midday meal. The cook's name is Cimbana, she's from the

Congo and keeps cigar butts in her turban, among other things."

"It's different here, isn't it?"

"Very different."

"What about the house?"

"There's the sugarhouse," Amelia said, "full of machinery they shove the cane into to make sugar. . . ." She paused. "If the mill doesn't have a centrifuge it can only make brown sugar. Did you know that? And there's the *vivienda,* the residence, built in 1848. It has a red tile roof, verandas on three sides of both floors—kind of like old plantation homes but not as Greek Revival–looking. More austere, and without trees close around it. The living quarters are upstairs—dining room, sitting room, everything—offices and the servants' quarters downstairs, and a hall full of saddles, bridles and guns locked in cabinets. The kitchen's in back."

Amelia looked up at the courtyard's high ceiling and the second-floor balcony.

"I like your house better. It's warmer."

Lorraine said, "Can I ask you something?"

Amelia was still looking around. "Rollie's house has glass panes in the windows and doors, but they're always open; flies come in and out as they please. There're a few shrubs, tropical plants, a lot of banana trees, a few mango, vegetable plots and twenty thousand acres of sugarcane, three estates Rollie bought and combined into one. They call them estates, but what they are really are little towns with the main house in the center, the sugarhouse with its big ugly smokestacks, and streets of stone houses for the workers, a Negro quarter, a Creole quarter, a street that's all Chinese and a nicer area where the higher-ups, the people in charge, have their homes: the estate manager, another man who's a chemist and runs the sugarhouse—I think he's the one they call the sugarmaster—and a few others who work directly under him, engineers, machinists. . . . Rollie has over a million and a half in just the land, and spent another hundred thousand to modernize the sugarhouse, put in all the newest machinery. If it's a good year, you know how much sugar he'll produce and ship?"

"Amelia?"

"I've forgotten now how much, but it's an awful lot." She paused and said, "What?"

"Have you slept with him?"

"I have, yes," Amelia said, and had to smile at the way Lorraine was staring at her so intently.

"So you're staying?"

"For a while anyway."

"Where're you going to live?"

"I guess wherever he wants me to."

Lorraine continued to stare.

"There's something you're not telling me."

"What do you want, intimate details?"

"You sound different."

"Well," Amelia said, "nothing happened until we got to the summerhouse. It's smaller than the one on the estate but more comfortable, with a veranda and a view of the Gulf rather than cane fields. The first night we were there, finally, after not saying a word to each other for hours, he took me into the bedroom. Mine; he has his own. And kissed me for the first time. I'm quite sure he thinks he seduced me. He was serious to the point of being grim, sort of ritualistic about it, first you do this and then you do that. It's funny, when we're alone—and this was true of other times, too, on the train or riding horses together—he doesn't seem as confident as he does when he's with people, an audience agreeing with him. It might be me," Amelia said, "or he's just not that comfortable with women. Anyway, Rollie finished, he got off and said, as he stepped into his underwear, 'That wasn't entirely unpleasant, was it?' "

"He said that?"

"He wasn't kidding, either."

"When I said there's something you're not telling me. Remember, before? I wasn't referring to what you did in bed. It was a feeling I had."

"About what?"

"That something happened you're not telling me about."

THEY CAME THROUGH ROLLING HILLS aboard the sugar train to Matanzas, Boudreaux telling Amelia there were more sugar estates here than in any province in

Cuba. "How many, Victor? Four hundred and seventy-eight, if I'm not mistaken?"

"Not anymore," Fuentes said. "Maybe three hundred something. Many of them in the past year burn down, or the owner has enough—wake up in the morning and see black smoke in the sky, over his fields."

"I ask you a question," Boudreaux said, "I like a simple answer, whatever is the fact, not your opinion."

"You want to know exactly how many burn down?"

"That's enough, Victor."

The train was creeping through the outskirts of the city, pale stone and steeples and red tile roofs, and now Boudreaux was pointing out to Amelia the villas of the wealthy, the old cathedral, the domed railway station, the ornate bridge that linked the city to the fortress of San Severino on the bay. "The second largest city in Cuba," Boudreaux said, "and some say the most beautiful."

"It's true," Fuentes said, "even though the word *matanzas* means slaughtering place."

"That's enough," Boudreaux said. He turned, shaking his head, to give Amelia a weary look.

"For the slaughter of livestock," Fuentes said, "cows to make *biftec* for here and for Havana. I don't mean the slaughter of the Indians who lived here—"

"Victor?"

"Or the twenty-three thousand last year, the *reconcentrados* who were made to starve to death, kept in filthy sheds along the Punta Gorda."

"I said that's enough," Boudreaux said. "Are you becoming restless, Victor, you want to move on?" He said to Amelia, "Victor, at one time, was a reader in a cigar factory. Which one was it, Victor?"

"La Corona."

"Victor read to the employees while they rolled cigars. He'd read every word of the newspaper including the advertisements while they sat there rolling away. He even read a book once. Wasn't it Martí, Victor, the poet who's become you-all's hero?"

"They wouldn't let me read Martí."

"I can understand why. But Victor did read a book by Martí. *A* book. Beware, Amelia, of anyone who's read a book and, hence, believes he knows everything."

Amelia watched Fuentes, the way he stood stoop-shouldered, swaying on his feet, as he gazed out the window of this private parlor car, the man not appearing bothered by Boudreaux's remarks. Fuentes even seemed to smile as he shrugged and said to Amelia, "Maybe you like to read Martí some-time. He say a country with only a few rich men is not rich."

"You see," Boudreaux said to her, sounding weary of it, "what I have to put up with?"

He told Amelia they were coming to a village

called Varadero and showed her on a map how his
rail line went past Matanzas, circled the east side of
the harbor and ran along the shore to a peninsula, a
finger of land pointing into the Gulf, the Bay of
Matanzas on one side, the Bay of Cárdenas on the
other. Varadero was situated at the neck of the peninsula, where Boudreaux's rail line ended and he
kept a stable of horses and a squad of his private
army he called Boudreaux's Guerrillas—a name, he
told Amelia, he'd thought of himself, Boudreaux's
Guerrillas—to patrol the finger of land and protect
his summerhouse, about six miles from Varadero.
Several homes along the beach, he said, had been
destroyed by insurgents. And for no reason, perfectly good summerhomes burned to the ground.

At Varadero the horses were brought to them as
they stepped from the train into afternoon sunlight.
Amelia found Victor staying close to her while Boudreaux rode off at the head of his guerrilla column
with Novis Crowe—the bodyguard holding on to
the saddle horn with both hands—and the officer in
charge of the squad. "A young man by the name of
Rafi Vasquez," Fuentes told Amelia, "a wealthy
*peninsulare* from Havana."

He said, "*Peninsulares* are the Spaniards living
here. All the rest of us, no matter our color, are
Cuban. We go to war with the Spanish government
and thousands of *peninsulares* take up arms against
us, calling themselves Volunteers. And I can tell
you, the Volunteers are as barbaric as the Guardia,

or even worse. Thirty years ago in Havana—January 22, 1869, I know, because I was there—they surround a theatre, the Villanueva, and while the audience is watching the play, the Volunteers fire into them, killing dozens of men, women and children. Only weeks later, Easter Sunday, the assassins perform the same criminal act at the Café del Louvre, again killing unarm people. You want to hear about the Volunteers, I can tell you. There was a captain-general name Valmaseda who turned their foul passions loose on the countryside, allowing them to kill whoever they want, without fear of punishment. The Butcher Weyler, during this Ten Years War, was a student of the Butcher Valmaseda. Weyler went home last fall and the new captain-general, Blanco, the loyalists consider a joke. What else do you want to know? Listen, in a military trial thirty-eight students, young boys, were accused of defacing a Spaniard's grave; they wrote something on the stone. Eight were executed and the rest sent to prison for life. You know what the Volunteers say? 'Suffer the little children to come unto me that I may strangle their precious young lives.' What else? I keep in my head a list of indiscriminate mass murders, rapes, molestations of all kinds and obscene mutilations.

"These men," Fuentes said, indicating Boudreaux's column, his private army, "are known as guerrillas, but they come from the Volunteers. Just as Tavalera the Guardia is a peasant by birth, the son of a prison guard, Rafi Vasquez the Volunteer is a gentleman, the son of wealth. And both are criminal assassins.

"Now then, on the side of liberty," Fuentes said, "the revolutionists are insurgents or *insurrectos*, or you heard them called mambís or mambíses."

"Rollie," Amelia said, "calls them that sometimes."

"Yes, because he believes he knows everything. He says it's an African word brought here from the Congo by slaves and is from the word *mambíli*. I tell him, well, I was a slave at one time and use the word, but it didn't come from Africa."

"Really? You were a slave?"

"Until I was sixteen and became a *cimarron*, what you call a runaway. Before that, part of me was Masungo, related by blood to the Bantu. Now I'm Cuban. I tell Mr. Boudreaux the word *mambí* came from Santo Domingo. Fifty years ago the people there fighting for their independence had a leader called Eutimio Mambí. So the Spanish soldiers called them the men of Mambí. Then when they came here the Spanish began to call Cuban revolutionists mambís and mambíses. I tell Mr. Boudreaux some of this history; he doesn't listen. I ask him has he read the words of José Martí, patriot and martyr, first president of the Cuban Revolutionary Party? No, of course not. I leave the essays of Martí in English where Mr. Boudreaux can find them, learn something about human rights. He throws them in the fire. What is right to him is the way things are."

"I believe it," Amelia said.

"Mr. Boudreaux looks at me. . . . What do I know of anything?"

They kept to high ground along the finger of land, following a road cut through dense thickets, a road that looked down on mangrove and lagoons, a stretch of white sand, a chimney rising out of brick and stone rubble. Fuentes pointed.

"You think they burn it down for no reason? Your Mr. Boudreaux, his head up there in a cloud, he think so."

"When did he become my Mr. Boudreaux?"

"Anytime you want him, he's yours."

"Why would I, because he's rich?"

"That's a good reason."

"Give me a better one."

"You meet famous people with him."

"On a sugar estate?"

"Sure, or here. You know who came to this house where we going? General Weyler himself, the man who made the twenty-three thousand people he sent to Matanzas starve to death. The Butcher came here to visit on someone's yacht. He meets you, he want to come back. Sure, you meet generals and admirals and envoys from Spain, the most important people. Also you hear Mr. Boudreaux talk to his friends, all those rich men who want to invest money with him. You see what they're doing, what the Spanish are doing. . . ."

She could hear the horses ahead of them and the clink of metal. She said, "You're asking me to spy for the mambís."

Fuentes turned his head to look at her. "You like that name?"

"Aren't you?"

"I see you not very busy, so I wonder, what is the point of you?"

A good question.

"I haven't yet decided." And then right away she said, "You stay close to Rollie. You hear him talking to people, don't you?"

"I don't get as close as you."

"But you talk about the crimes of the Spanish— you annoy him with it. Isn't he suspicious?"

"Perhaps in a way he is, yes, but it doesn't worry him. He believe he smarter than I am. He believe he smarter than everybody, and I think is important he continue to believe it." Fuentes looked off at the Gulf and said, "Do you see that ship, what's left of it? A wreck now, but it was once a coastal vessel from Nueva Gerona, on the Isle of Pines, a ship with two masts and two sails, big ones. They carry yucca and tobacco from the Isle of Pines to Havana and sometime to Matanzas and Cárdenas, so they know the coast and places to hide. Oh, they smuggle goods too. But on this day two years ago they came from Key West, the ship full of rifles and cases of bullets and they get caught in the open by a gunboat that chase the ship and it run aground and break up on that sandbar. You can't see it, but is there. Two years ago to this day, March the seventeenth, 1895. There was seven of them aboard. And now come a company of Volunteers to wait for them on the sand. The men of the ship have no choice but to wade ashore and surrender. When they do this, half the Volunteers continue to aim their Mausers at them, while the others draw machetes and hack the unarmed men to death. Rafi Vasquez was the officer, the one who order it to happen. Your Mr. Boudreaux was also here, to watch."

"And you were here," Amelia said.

"Yes, I was here. And you see two men shot in the head. You see how easy it is for the Guardia to do it. I watched you. You don't close your eyes or turn your head to look away. You don't say oh, how can they do that. You accept what you see with your own eyes and you think about it. A crime is committed, the execution without giving it a thought of two innocent men. You don't say oh, no, is none of your business. You see they don't care, they can kill anybody they want, and you begin to wonder is there something you can do about it."

For several minutes they rode in silence, until Fuentes said, "How do you think about that?"

"Last year," Amelia said, "or was it the year before, it doesn't matter, I took work to help the sisters in a home for lepers."

As she spoke, Fuentes turned in his saddle, stirred. He said, "There is a leper home in Las Villas, San Lázaro," and gestured, "That way, in Santa Clara, the next province east of here. I was there once to visit a woman I know and I see the devotion of the people working there, the most dedicated people in the world to do that. And you are one of those people?"

"I didn't do much," Amelia said. "I wrote letters for them, I played checkers, I gave them their medicine, two hundred drops of chaulmoogra oil a day. For fever we gave them Fowler's solution. Powdered mangrove bark was given for something, I don't remember what."

"For nausea," Fuentes said, "sure, mangrove. Look at it down there, in the swamp. So, you know how to prepare it as medicine."

"I lasted five days," Amelia said, "less than a week among the lepers and I ran out of dedication. What it means is, I can believe in something, I can want to throw myself into a cause and see myself tireless in my devotion—look at her, a saint—but it turns out I don't have enough of a sense of . . . I don't know."

Fuentes said, "Duty?"

"Yes, I suppose, duty or a sense of purpose. Five days and I gave up."

"No, I think the reason you left there," Fuentes said, "is because if you stay at the leper home then you don't come here. You understand? Then this would not become what you want to do most. But it must be what you want to do because you came here, didn't you?"

"Is it that simple?"

"What, to know what you want to do? Go by what you feel and don't think so much."

"It takes energy," Amelia said, "and a strong will."

"Yes, of course."

"And hatred."

"Hating can help, but it isn't necessary."

"You asked me, 'What is the point of you?' " Amelia said, and smiled a little hearing herself. "Tell me what's the point of you, Victor. Are you an anarchist, a communist of some kind, a collectivist?"

His face brightened as he said, "More of you comes out. You prepare yourself for this."

"At the knees of my maid," Amelia said. "Are you one of those, an anarchist?"

"It's enough at this time," Fuentes said, "to be Cuban."

# 11

ONE OF THE OLD MEN in the cell had been an ordained priest before he unfrocked himself and joined the revolution; he had promised the others that tomorrow, Easter Sunday, he would say Mass for them.

Today was April the ninth, Tyler's fiftieth day in the Morro, and he believed they were getting ready to hang him.

They brought him out of the cell from darkness into the dull lamplight of the corridor, where soldiers were waiting with a man in clean white clothes, a burlap sack over his head and his hands manacled. Now they were bringing out Virgil Webster and that was all Tyler saw before the sack came over his head. They tied it closed with a rope around his neck—giving him the reason to think he was going to be hanged—and clamped his wrists in iron.

He said, "Virgil?" with the soldiers close around him talking to each other. Virgil answered, "Aye," and Tyler asked if he had a sack over his head and Virgil said he did. So it looked like they were getting ready to hang both of them, along with the man in white who was protesting in Spanish in a voice that was somehow familiar. The guards were laughing. The three were being marched along the corridor now, Tyler pushed from behind to keep up without seeing. He raised his voice to say, "Lieutenant Molina, is that you?" A guard swatted him across the back of the head, using his knuckles, as a voice said in English, "Yes, it's I," with the barest hint of an accent.

"What happened to you?"

Tyler was swatted again for an answer.

Once outside the building they were given over to a different squad of guards who pulled Tyler into the back end of an ambulance wagon, canvas covering the frame over the bed, and forced him down on the board floor. He heard Virgil say, "Goddamn it," and felt the marine fall against him. Then Molina was brought aboard. Tyler said his name. When he wasn't struck this time he asked, "You know where we're going?"

"To another prison," Molina's voice said close to Tyler, "or a place of execution."

"What did you do?"

"Offended the sensitive Guardia, allowed visitors, refused to permit torture, forgot to say my morning prayers. They resent not being taken seriously. Or for whatever reason, here we are, carried off in the dead of night. I asked Tavalera where he's sending us; he wouldn't tell me. I said, 'The Americans will be missed, you know.' He said, 'How can that be? They were never here.' "

AMELIA COULD SEE THE MORRO and La Cabaña from the hotel suite's bedroom window: bleak walls in sunlight, way over there beyond the red tile roofs of the Old City and across the channel to the Gulf. Ironclad Spanish warships were now anchored in the harbor, with the U.S. Navy supply ship *Fern* among them. It would sail this evening with Fitzhugh Lee, the American members of the consulate staff, most of the correspondents and Amelia's friend Lorraine Regal. By tomorrow, Rollie had said earlier, everyone who was going would be gone, including Miss Amelia Brown. He said, "I'll miss you, *cher*." Indicating that he wasn't leaving just yet. Amelia didn't tell him she wasn't either. There would be no reason to tell him anything; when the time came she'd simply vanish.

Boudreaux, stretched out on the bedspread fully clothed except for his suit jacket, was catching up on the latest American newspapers to reach the island. The New York paper he held in front of him displayed the headline WAR SEEMS CLOSE AT HAND.

The paper lying next to him announced
HOSTILITIES NOT FAR OFF.

She heard him say from behind the newspaper,
"What it comes down to, the limited form of
autonomy Spain offered is not acceptable to the
Cubans, or to the Spanish either, the ones living
here. This writer has it on good authority that
sometime this week McKinley will ask Congress to
allow him to use military force to bring about a
peaceful settlement. Don't you love the way that's
worded? The next step will be a declaration of war
against Spain, I'll say within two weeks, and that
will be that. Anyone still here had better get out
quick."

"Unless," Amelia said, "one has his own
army."

"I'll get by. I'll hold off the mambís or pay trib-
ute to them if I have to, until the United States
Army comes storming ashore. I have a hunch it will
be near Havana. I hope close enough I can see the
show from here. Watch the cannonade with a glass
of the house tinto and a good cigar. I'll send you a
wire when it's safe to return."

"Neely hasn't left," Amelia said.

"Still sniffing around my lady friend?"

"He went off to interview one of the insurgent
generals, Islero."

"He's crazy. I meant Neely, but they both are,
for that matter. Islero's an animal, he'll make
gumbo out of Neely and have him for supper. He's a

perfect example of the kind of terrorist we'll have running things if we let the Cubans gain control. Weyler's a saint compared to that ferocious nigger."

Amelia, arms folded in her white satin robe, turned from the window. "The Chicago *Times* arrived with Neely's story about the marine being held and the military censor burned every copy. They're saying no such person is in El Morro, La Cabaña or anywhere else. The marine left San Ambrosio weeks ago on his own and they had no reason to stop him. Except Neely *saw* Virgil Webster at the Morro and spoke to him for more than an hour. It cost him a bottle of bourbon."

"He isn't there," Rollie said, eyes holding straight ahead on the newspaper page.

"Neely *saw* him."

"Yes, but that was the other day. You were there, didn't you see the marine?"

Amelia hesitated. How did he know that?

"The officer would only allow Neely to talk to him."

Still behind the newspaper Rollie said, "I wondered why you didn't tell me you went there."

"I thought I should wait till Neely wrote his story," Amelia said, "before I started talking about it, risk some other correspondent filing the story first."

He seemed to accept that.

"You waited, huh? Didn't see anyone?"

She said, "No, I didn't," without hesitation this

time. She came over to the bed, a big four-poster, and stretched out next to Rollie, there in profile behind his newspaper.

"Do you know where he is now?"

Amelia waited.

It took Boudreaux several moments to say, "Who?"

"The marine."

"If this suite were across the hall and you were looking out the window," Boudreaux said, "you'd see an old star-shaped fortress at the south end of the harbor, and I mean old. It even has a drawbridge. The place is called Atarés, and that's where they're holding him."

"Why?" Amelia said.

She watched him concentrating on a news item to make her wait—something he'd been doing almost the entire year they'd been together. She wondered what the satisfaction was in making her repeat herself.

"Rollie?"

"What?"

"Why is he being held?"

"The marine? They believe he's a spy."

"That's impossible. He didn't leave the ship till he was blown off the deck."

"*Cher*, I'm not saying he's a spy, they are."

"How'd you find out where he is?"

"I was asking about the two that brought the

horses. Remember? Charlie Burke and the other one?"

"Ben Tyler," Amelia said.

"That's right, Tyler," Boudreaux said, turning his head to look right at her for the first time, "the cowboy. I asked Lionel Tavalera—you remember Lionel, that Civil Guard officer? Tall for a Spaniard and fairly good-looking if you don't mind them more than a bit swarthy."

"The way I remember him," Amelia said, "is on the station platform at Benavides."

"That's right, when he shot those two boys. My Lord, but that must've been an awful shock to your system; you'd only left New Orleans a few days before. That's why I want to get you away from here, before there's a chance of your being exposed to any more violence. Anyway, I asked Lionel if they were still holding the cowboy and the old man, as I'd been out in the country awhile and had lost track. I remember they were in all the papers when the cowboy shot that officer and they were under investigation of aiding the enemy, running guns or some such activity. We came back from the estate and I don't recall reading any more about them; it was all the Naval Court of Inquiry and how their investigation was coming along. I said to Lionel, 'We're in the middle of negotiating for a string of mustangs and you throw the horse traders in prison. What am I suppose to do now, I have the horses?' He got a kick out of that. He said, 'Keep the horses if you want them.' By the way, that dun you were riding last week, in the country? That's the cowboy's; I didn't buy that one, but I guess it's mine now."

He turned back to the newspaper he was still holding upright in front of him.

"Rollie?"

He made her wait a few moments before finally saying, "What?"

"You haven't answered my question," Amelia said, in no hurry, never letting her irritation show. "I asked how you found out about the marine, where he is."

"And I told you, he's in Atarés, that old fort."

"You found out from the Civil Guard officer?"

"Yeah, Tavalera."

"Well, what happened to the cowboy and his partner? You said you were asking about the two that brought the horses?"

"Charlie Burke, the old man," Boudreaux said, looking at the paper as he spoke, "came down with a serious case of dysentery, if you'll pardon my saying so, and wore himself out sitting on the bucket. Lionel says he's buried in the Colón cemetery."

"And what happened to the cowboy?"

Boudreaux turned his head for the second time to look right at her.

"Tyler? He's hanging on."

"Where do they have him?"

"In Atarés, with the marine. Lionel says he'll be there till they locate the shipment of guns he brought, and then he'll be in La Cabaña the rest of his life." Boudreaux turned to the paper, but then turned back again to Amelia. "Lionel says that's if they don't send him to Africa or shoot him."

Amelia lay there for several minutes staring at the ceiling, until Boudreaux said, "*Cher,* bring me one of my cigars, if you'd be so kind?"

She got one out of his humidor, nipped the end off with her front teeth before Rollie, calling her name, could stop her. "You know I like it cut with my penknife." Amelia paid no attention. She found a match to light the cigar, got it going good, handed it to Rollie and crossed to the armoire, where she took off the robe and hung it up. She stood there naked deciding what to wear this afternoon, fairly sure Rollie was watching.

"You going out?"

He was watching.

But wouldn't ever hint about having sex unless she showed an inclination first, touching, kissing or looking at him a certain way. He would never risk appearing to be in heat and come off as having natural inclinations. Not that much passion was ever expressed in this union. When they did go to bed he'd begin kissing and fondling and Amelia would wonder if they were ever going to get to it. He seemed experienced enough, but too self-conscious to bring any real fun to the bed. He never ever perspired.

She slipped on a kimono and walked to the window again to see, three floors below, the coaches lining the street, the beggars, the children with swollen bellies, mounted soldiers passing by. Across the street rows of folding chairs faced the center of the park and the statue of a queen where, several nights a week, military bands played on and on in the brilliant glow of electric streetlights. Amelia raised her gaze to twin spires on the far edge of the Old City.

"I thought I'd drop by the cathedral."

"You've seen Columbus's tomb, haven't you?"

"It's Easter Sunday. I thought I might go to Mass."

"You're thinking about it, or yes, you're going?"

"I'm going."

"Won't you have to go to Confession?"

"I won't have to, but I may."

He had lowered the paper and was staring at her now. He said, "Your Church allows you to fuck all week and then go to Mass on Sunday?" in that quiet, condescending tone of his.

She said, "Rollie, when have you ever wanted to fuck all week?"

She watched him raise his eyebrows.

"I don't believe I've ever heard a woman use that word."

"It must be you've lived a sheltered life," Amelia said, not caring what he thought, "you only know your own kind." She said, "After Mass I'll go say good-bye to Lorraine. She's leaving tonight."

"What do you mean by my own kind?"

"People who have everything they want." She returned to the armoire and stood looking in. "Don't bother calling Novis, all right? I'd rather have Victor take me."

"Novis isn't your kind, uh?"

"I don't have anything I want to say to him."

"You get back," Boudreaux said, "I want to hear more about my sheltered life." He disappeared behind his newspaper.

THEY RODE TO ATARÉS in an open coach. "A twenty-cent ride," Fuentes said, "from the hotel and the gardens of the Parque Central to the most depressing sight in Havana. And there it is, the field called the Death Hole."

Amelia was aware of shod hooves on paving stones and the sound of iron tires and the squeak of springs as they approached the walls of the Castillo de Atarés.

"Last year," Fuentes said, "the bodies of people that Weyler killed with famine and disease were brought here, thousands of them during those months, and left for the carrion to mutilate and devour."

He had wanted to open an umbrella to protect Amelia from the sun, but she said no and held the brim of her sun hat, staring at the desolate field, a wide depression off the left side of the road, the field stretching all the way to the scarred stone-and-mortar walls of the fortress.

"It was always a place of death. Forty-seven years ago, when I was sixteen," Fuentes said, "a patriot by the name of Narciso Lopez came with four hundred men to join with insurgents already fighting the Spanish." He said to Amelia, "You've heard of an American patriot by the name of Crittenden?" She said she wasn't sure and Fuentes said, "He came with Narciso Lopez as the second in command, as half the men with them were Americans. But they had very bad luck. They landed at Mariel during a storm, so all their powder was wet when the Spanish attack them and Crittenden and fifty of his men were brought here. You see the drawbridge? Crittenden was crossing it to enter the fort and the Spanish soldiers couldn't wait any longer, they shot him down on the bridge. His men were taken to the field, chained together in three groups and they were shot down. I was sixteen years old."

Amelia turned to Fuentes, an old man in a white suit holding the umbrella between his knees.

"You were here?"

"I was with Narciso Lopez. Not on the boat, but with the ones already here, and I was with them when the Spanish came and we had no dry powder to use. Narciso Lopez was taken to the Morro and made to perish by the garrote, strangle to death, God rest his soul. One hundred were sent to Spanish dungeons in Africa and some of us were kept here to wait to be tortured. I think of it that way, because to wait makes it worse. The Spanish hung us on a wall, the iron ring twelve feet from the floor, sometime upside down, and beat us with cane, our wrists bound so tight our hands swell to twice their size," Fuentes said, showing Amelia his hands with their yellowed, cracked nails. "Others were seated in the chair with the iron collar, the garrote; a single turn of the screw from behind will strangle the person, crushing his neck. They like to break legs, too, and leave the person to perish from starvation. I was taken to the parade ground, all open, and put in stocks. You know what I mean by stocks? They hold you by the neck and the wrists, like in the old pictures you see of your Puritans. But this one they put you in face-up to the sun and leave you there all day. They said it was worse than the garrote, looking at the sun like that, and always the person couldn't stand it and became blind and insane. I shut my eyes as tight as I could squeeze them shut and still I could see the brightness of the sun through my eyelids. So I prayed to St. Francis of Assisi, because I remember from when I was a boy, a priest telling me St. Francis was a friend of Brother Sun, he called it, and Sister Moon. He liked all the animals, birds rested on his shoulders and he never stepped on insects. You know of St. Francis?" Amelia told him yes, of course, and Fuentes said, "I prayed to him, asking if he had any friends that were clouds, and you know what happened?"

"It rained," Amelia said.

"Listen, it rained for six days and six nights," Fuentes told her, "in the spring, before the big season of rain. It rained so much they put me in a cell and forgot about me for three years, when they said that was enough and gave me a pardon."

They were approaching the drawbridge now. It was down and the sally port was open to show the parade grounds inside and a Guardia with a carbine slung from his shoulder.

"In there, straight across the grounds," Fuentes said, "are the torture rooms. To the right, past an outside stairway, is the entrance to the dungeons they use. Rudi Calvo say the Guardias released some people, *reconcentrados*, and told him now they the only ones, a squad of Guardias. Rudi Calvo thinks eight of them on duty to guard the three prisoners; Tyler, the United States marine and the officer from El Morro, Lieutenant Molina. They took his uniform away from him."

"I liked him," Amelia said. "Maybe that's why I'm not surprised he's here."

"Rudi Calvo thinks they'll send him to Africa."

Amelia said, "Victor," and then waited as she heard him speaking to the coachman, who brought the team around in the cobblestone road to start back to Havana. "Do you still pray to St. Francis?"

"I don't believe in God anymore," Fuentes said. "Well, sometimes, but not always. I do believe in St. Francis, but I don't use him anytime I want or for small favors. No, I pray to him only when it becomes life or death."

"Do you remember a year ago," Amelia said, "the train station at Benavides, the Guardia and the two men on the platform?"

Fuentes began to nod. "Wanting to hang the two cane cutters, but could find nothing for them to stand on. Yes, of course I remember. So the Guardia shot them."

"That time, did you pray to St. Francis?"

Fuentes said, "No, I didn't," and seemed surprised. "I didn't think of it and I don't know why." He seemed to be thinking about it now, squinting his eyes to look back on that time at Benavides. "No, I believe what I imagined doing was shooting Tavalera and then seeing his men shoot me to pieces. All that instead of praying for the two men to be saved. But there you are. If there is no prayer to answer, what's St. Francis suppose to do?"

WHEN THE *VIZCAYA* ARRIVED," Palenzuela said to Rudi Calvo, "I was in the party that went out to greet the ship. There were small boats everywhere, people shouting 'Long live Spain! Long live our navy!' People on the wharf shouting it, people on the ferry from Regla, everyone taking pride in who we are, and not offering one word of anti-American sentiment. The launch passed within ten meters of what can be seen of the *Maine* and there were no cheers, as I've heard before, or expressions of approval. Aboard the *Vizcaya*, an armored cruiser heavy with guns, I heard nothing discussed that would resemble a feeling of hostility."

They rode in the chief's personal carriage, two bodyguards up on the box acting as coachmen, his matched pair of palominos in harness. The route they took from police headquarters, near the channel, followed San Lázaro along the north shore to the outskirts of Vedado and the home occupied by Palenzuela's mistress, Lorraine.

"It doesn't matter," Rudi Calvo said, "what you feel or what you want or don't want, there's going to be a war. All you have to do is read the American newspapers."

"Yes, but everything they write is inflammatory."

"Of course, because they want war."

Rudi speaking bluntly to his boss, without choosing his words, something he had never done before.

"Did you see," Palenzuela said, "Pope Leo is thinking of requesting an armistice?"

Rudi felt like suggesting to his boss, Oh, for God's sake, use your head. But he resumed his place again and what he said was "Excuse me, but do you think an American president is going to follow the wishes of the Catholic Church?"

They rode past soldiers in summer uniforms along the avenue, Rudi seeing them as boys away from home for the first time, enjoying themselves for now, having adventures in a strange city, experiencing the offer of exotic sins. In a few months some of them would be dead, some would be in hospitals burning with fever. But if you told them this they wouldn't believe you. Their mothers would. Rudi Calvo had one child left out of four, a boy who had survived his mother's death at his birth and made it through early childhood, the boy now ten, a gift Rudi was determined not to lose. His sister took care of the boy when he was absent, away on police business. He gave his sister money and told her, "If you don't see me again, please take care of the boy as you would your own." His sister didn't say anything, but he could see in her eyes she understood. Later, when she would have time to be herself, she would allow herself to cry.

"It crept up on us during the forty days of Lent," the police chief said, "when we weren't looking." He said, "What can hold back the tide of war?"

He might have made that up, or thought he did.

"Nothing can," Rudi said.

"I told Lorraine it won't last long. I told her if she remained in Vedado she might not even notice the war. Still, being an American citizen she would be viewed by some as an enemy of this land and her life here could be made intolerable, subject to vile insults, if not placed in grave danger."

Perhaps. Though it was Rudi's belief his chief

was sending Lorraine home because he was tired of her, because a mistress had to be worth the trouble of leading a double life. Once the trouble exceeded the pleasure and the mistress became as familiar as the wife, what was the point?

Palenzuela would say good-bye to her and in an hour or so Rudi would escort Lorraine to the wharf where a launch would take her out to the naval supply ship *Fern* at anchor, and that would be that. He doubted he would ever see her again, and that was too bad. In the past months he had escorted Lorraine to places out of the city to meet the police chief and he could tell she was beginning to enjoy his company. She told him one time, "I can relax with you, Rudi, not have to worry about who sees us." He had been thinking lately of taking her to bed, but now . . .

"I'm afraid you can't accompany her in this coach," the police chief said.

"No, I'll arrange to hire one."

"The last day of this," the police chief said.

This *what*, he didn't say.

"I have to tell you something," Rudi said. "This is also my last day. I mean with the police."

His chief said, "Of course, I saw it coming and have been thinking about it. But I won't ask what you plan to do."

So Rudi kept quiet and seemed interested in something out the window, looking up the street they were passing to see the Gulf of Mexico a block away.

"When you turn in your badge," the police chief said, "they'll ask you the reason and what you're going to do."

Rudi said, "Oh," not concerned, because he had no intention of turning his badge in; he was going to use it for something.

"Your pistol, of course, is your own."

"Yes."

Rudi listened to the horses' hooves, the sound one sound to him, continuous, never varying.

His chief said, "Well, I imagine you'll be leaving the city."

"I think so," Rudi said.

"You don't know?"

"Do you want me to tell you exactly what I'm going to do?" Again speaking to his superior in a way he never had before.

The police chief said, "Certainly not."

"No, you don't want that responsibility," Rudi said, and was silent until they reached the house in Vedado and saw the carriage standing by the entrance, Fuentes and the young woman, Amelia Brown, waiting for them.

"Your friend Victor," Palenzuela said as they were about to get out of the coach. "Is this also his last day?"

It wasn't a question Rudi had to answer. It wasn't a question at all, it was the chief reminding him he knew what was going on. Or believed he did. Once they were out of the coach, Palenzuela greeted the young woman, Amelia Brown, and gestured for them all to come in the house. In the first courtyard, the outer one, he said to Rudi, "I'll have a servant bring you and your friend a refreshment."

"You know Victor Fuentes, but you've never met him," Rudi said.

Palenzuela shook his head. Not once did he look at Fuentes, but took the young woman by the arm into another part of the house, leaving Rudi and Fuentes alone.

Rudi shrugged and Fuentes said, "It's just as well. Sometime later if he has to he can say no, we never met. Did you tell him?"

"Yes, and he asked if this was also your last day."

"You're not concerned about him?"

"Why? What he knows actually is that he doesn't know anything."

A servant brought them cups of coffee and they sat down. Rudi Calvo raised his cup and Fuentes raised his. "Tomorrow," Rudi said. "Or is there a reason to wait?"

"Tomorrow is good," Fuentes said. He sipped his coffee and said, "Amelia Brown wants to go with us. She told me today, in the coach."

Rudi frowned, because it didn't make sense to him, a rich man's woman.

"She says she helped us. We wouldn't know things that we know without her."

Rudi said, "Yes?" and waited. It was true, but what did telling them things she heard have to do with going with them tomorrow?

"She wants to be known for something," Fuentes said, "she wants to fulfill herself, become involved in a celebrated cause, perhaps in the manner of Evangelina Cisneros."

Rudi frowned again. "What did Evangelina Cisneros do? Nothing. The newspapers did it."

"She lived, as they say, 'in Death's Shadow,' confined to a dungeon in Recogidas. She became 'the daughter of the revolution' and touched people's hearts when she escaped from the prison. Don't forget that."

"Evangelina was there," Rudi said, "so they used her. But she was never a revolutionist. How many women are there who take up arms and fight?"

"There were the Amazons of the Ten Years War."

"Yes, you're right, those women."

"Paulina Gonzales," Fuentes said, "in this war. Her passion was to carry the flag in battle and lead machete charges. I saw her with my own eyes kill Volunteers, this young woman twenty-one years old. I met her when I was with Gómez in Santa Clara."

"But Paulina Gonzales," Rudi said, "is the only woman I know of who's made a name for herself."

"There were *amazonas* during her time and I believe Amelia Brown will be another one," Fuentes said. "Listen, we go riding, she sits astride the horse wearing trousers beneath a skirt only to her knees. I said to her, 'That's a good idea.' You know what she said? 'Yes, it's the way Paulina Gonzales dressed.' How does she know that? The correspondent, her friend Neely Tucker, told her. She knows about the war and she knows how to shoot with the pistol or the rifle. I watched her, at the mill."

"Yes," Rudi said, "but what does she want?"

"She wants to be famous."

"Is that enough?"

"For us, I think yes. It costs us nothing and she knows fame isn't given to you unless you earn it, risk your life."

"And sometimes doesn't come until you're dead," Rudi said. "Does she know that?"

IN THE CARRIAGE on the way back to the hotel Amelia said, "You spoke to Rudi?"

"He say it's up to you."

"But he doesn't like the idea."

Fuentes shook his head. "No, he's not going to judge you. He knows you have intelligence. . . . But did you tell your friend Lorraine?"

"No."

"You didn't even hint you could be risking your life?"

"She wouldn't understand if I told her," Amelia said, "and there wasn't time to explain. All she's thinking about now is leaving."

"You could too."

"Yes, I have a choice." She looked at the sky losing its light, the sun fading behind them, shod hooves on paving stones the only sound. "I want you to tell me the truth," Amelia said, "when I ask you a question. Will you?"

"I promise. What is it?"

"Do you think Rollie loves me?"

"What a question. Of course he does."

"Do you think he loves me enough, that if I were held as a hostage . . ." She saw Fuentes begin to smile. "He'd pay fifty thousand dollars to get me back?"

Watching Fuentes smiling, Amelia began to smile.


EASTER SUNDAY EVENING Amelia and Rollie dined in their suite on the top floor of the three-story Gran Hotel Inglaterra. Rollie began:

"Did you have an interesting day?"

"It was all right."

"You go to church?"

"I changed my mind."

"Oh? Where were you all afternoon?"

"Saying good-bye to Lorraine. Remember?"

"Is she sad she's leaving?"

"In some ways."

"She'll miss Andres, won't she?"

"She'll miss the servants."

"When you leave, will you miss me?"

"I suppose."

"What do you mean, you suppose?"

"I was kidding."

"Why did you say I've lived a sheltered life?"

"Have you ever been to prison?"

"Is that a criterion?"

"Have you?"

"Of course not."

"Have you ever not had enough to eat?"

"The portions here aren't exactly generous."

"You know what I mean."

"It's strictly American, the cooking here."

"Northern American. Have you ever killed any-one?"

"If I haven't, I've lived a sheltered life?"

"Have you? Ever killed anyone?"

"I've never had to."

"What does that mean?"

"People do what I want."

"I'm going riding tomorrow."

"Take Novis with you."

"He doesn't know how to ride."

"Teach him."

"Rollie, do you love me?"

"Of course I do."

"Victor's going with me."

"And Novis," Rollie said. "Tell Victor to find him a gentle horse."

# 12

VIRGIL SAID WHAT IF THEY WERE hauled around town a few times in the wagon and brought right back to El Morro? And that's why they put the sacks over their heads.

Tyler believed this place smelled different and wasn't as close to the open sea, though it was damp and moldy and had more spiders and rats than the Morro because, Tyler believed, there weren't as many prisoners here. He had the feeling they might be the only ones. He asked Virgil if he'd heard voices last night, any screams. They had been placed in separate cells, but now were together with one water bucket and one waste bucket between them. It was as if the Guardia were saying to them: You can talk and scheme all you want, you aren't going anyplace. Look at it another way, together they'd be easier to mind.

Virgil said what was there to scheme about? They were in a cell with big goddamn iron rings on the stone walls they could be chained to and iron bars crisscrossing the door. Virgil was talkative this morning.

He said he hoped to God this *was* a different place and not the Morro. The day war was declared the whole goddamn Atlantic Squadron would be out there. You'd have the *Indiana* and the *Massachusetts*, first-class twin-screw battlewagons with four 13-inch guns each. You'd have the *Iowa* with her four 12-inchers, the *Texas*, the *Montgomery* and the *New York*, an armored cruiser that could go twenty-one knots. And you'd have the *Terror*, a double-turret twin-screw monitor, like a raft with four 10-inch rifles on her. Virgil told Tyler the *Maine* was a second-class battleship, but had twelve inches of armor around her hull and eight to twelve inches protecting her turrets and barbettes. If the *Maine* had been unarmored the explosion would've crushed her like an eggshell and probably everybody aboard would have been killed.

Anyway, Virgil said, if they were still in the Morro and there was a war, they'd be goners. The squadron could sit out in the stream, turn their batteries on this old place. Shit, a couple of salvos and it would be gone, a pile of rubble.

Something else he told Tyler: "I said I'd never been in jail before? It's 'cause I never got caught." The horse his stepfather the preacher took from him and sold? Virgil stole back. Then, he told Tyler, there were some men from Fort Gibson had insulted his mother, saying she was a whore and offering her twenty-five cents each to fuck them. Virgil stole a pistol from the place where he worked, then right after he got his horse back, he held up these men who'd insulted his mother as they were playing poker in the back room of the feed store in Fort Gibson, a bandanna hiding his face. Robbed them and hit 'em over the head with his gun barrel, the dirty-mouth sons of bitches. The funds got him clear to Port Tampa, where he went to bed with a whore the first time in his life, sixteen years old, and lied about his age to join the United States Marines.

Tyler had mentioned the forty-five hundred dollars he had coming from Boudreaux. Virgil said he believed you could live a long time on forty-five hundred, Jesus, years and years. He said to Tyler it was too bad he didn't have it on him, he could bribe his way out of here. Tyler said if he'd had it he sure wouldn't have it now.

"This is a country of banditry," he told Virgil, "or for anyone bent on scalawaggery." He had learned from Fuentes that bandits here put up signs on the road that said MONEY OR MUTILATION. Take your pick. He said to Virgil there seemed to be mostly road agents in Cuba, highwaymen, Fuentes called them, something Tyler said he didn't understand, banks being so easy to rob.

———

LIONEL TAVALERA ENTERED THE CELL unarmed. A guard came in behind him to place a canvas chair on the dirt floor for the major, and now he sat facing Tyler and Virgil, the two sitting on the ground with their legs stretched out, their backs against the old scarred stone blocks of the wall. They were together in the cell this morning so he could address them at the same time. He began by saying he was going to the captain-general's palace, where they were having a meeting about the war he believed would be declared any day now. They would discuss America's ability to raise an army. How long would that take, a few months? It was thirty-three years since Americans had the war among themselves. Then when the army was ready they would board the troop ships in Port Tampa and perhaps Key West and sail here to Cuba.

"But where will they land? Excuse me," Tavalera said, "where will this army try to come ashore?" He looked at Virgil. "Marine Virgil Webster, from a place called Indian Territory. Are you Indian?"

"That's correct," Virgil said. "And the first thing I do when I get out of here, Don, is track you down and lift your scalp, you son of a bitch."

"That's the spirit to have," Tavalera said. "If there many like you it could be a good war. But you don't answer the question. Where do you think your army will come ashore?"

"Downtown Havana with John Philip Sousa's band leading the parade," Virgil said, "once our guns flatten the Morro and all your puny harbor defenses."

Tavalera liked this marine; he wouldn't mind having about four hundred just like him to bring his 2d Corps up to strength. He had arrived with 750 men under his command, one of six Guardia Civil corps sent to Cuba, and in three years had lost more than half of them fighting in the province of Matanzas. He believed more insurgents were recruited from there than from any other province. Maybe because so many were shot in the Plaza de las Armas and showed how to die bravely.

He said, "Our fleet will be here, in the harbor."

Virgil said, "You mean at the bottom of the harbor. Any ship still afloat we'll board."

Tyler said, "You come to tell us something?"

"No, nothing in particular," Tavalera said. "I thought we could talk for a few minutes, see what you think about the war that's coming." He said this because he believed he had much in common with these two.

But all they did was stare at him until the marine said, "I just told you, we're gonna give you a whipping. Now, when're you letting us out of here?"

Maybe they had nothing in common after all, or this was not a time to talk. Tavalera said to the marine, "When your country declares war you become a prisoner of war and will be sent to

Africa." He said to Tyler, "And when that happens
you will be taken outside and shot as a spy. If that's
all you want to know, there it is."

Deciding their fate almost as he said it.

He got up and left the cell, now to see if the
drunken Lieutenant Molina would like to talk.

# 13

NOVIS CROWE ASKED FUENTES if he could count. If there was three of them going riding, how come he brought four horses from the stable? They were in front of the hotel, 9:00 A.M., ready to mount.

Fuentes believed he could tell Novis almost anything. He could say, "Mr. Boudreaux's orders," and Novis would have to accept it and shut up. What Fuentes told him, the horse was green and they were getting it used to the saddle and bridle. Novis said well, what was in that pack tied to the saddle? Fuentes said it was their lunch, they were going to have a picnic. He saw Amelia looked at him with no expression on her lovely face.

Having Novis along, Fuentes had told her, wasn't going to change the plan. No, in fact, he saw a way to use Novis. Early this morning he had contacted the people he needed to make it work.

Amelia set off on the avenue heading east, the two following her past old buildings with Greek columns, past decorative stucco facades, gray ones, yellow ones, Fuentes leading the horse with the canvas pack, Novis telling them there weren't any horses to speak of where he came from, the bottom end of Lake Okeechobee in Florida; it was all swamp, no place for a horse. Telling them he believed, though, gators would like horse as much as they liked dog. Telling them he fished the lake till he went to work for the railroad up to Port of Tampa, took part in strikebreaking for the railroad anyplace him and his bunch was needed and came to Newerleans where he worked on the docks and took up prizefighting, what he was doing when he was hired by Mr. Boudreaux after Mr. Boudreaux saw him knock a man out across the river in Algiers, hired him as his personal bodyguard. By this time they were riding past warehouses over by the Central railroad yards, coming past an oxcart full of coffee sacks being unloaded. Fuentes said good day to the Negro standing in the cart and nodded toward Novis, now most of a length ahead of him, Novis telling how he had won a hundred prizefights before he retired, beating opponents who came in all sizes, many of them bigger than him, as the Negro in the wagon swung a fifty-pound sack of coffee beans at Novis, caught him across the shoulders and swept him out of the saddle. Finally, to Amelia's relief, shutting him up. The Negro and another man dragged Novis into the warehouse and Fuentes dismounted to follow them inside. Amelia waited with the horses.

When Fuentes came out he said, "They going to take him to a place south of here, Puentes Grandes with a sack over his head and hide him there until you write a letter to your Mr. Boudreaux, tell him you been taken hostage. We don't have time now, so you write it tonight. He wants to see you again he has to pay fifty thousand dollars. And you tell him in the letter how he must send the money."

Amelia nodded. "Good, but how does he?"

"We have to think about it. Tomorrow morning a man comes to where we are and we give him the letter. They give it to Novis to deliver and release him. Still Novis hasn't seen them, who they are. He finds himself on a street somewhere in Havana."

Amelia said, "What about you?"

"What?"

"How much for your release?"

"He won't pay for me. Novis tells him he gets me back at no cost."

"I've been thinking," Amelia said. "I might be worth more than that."

Fuentes, looking up at Amelia dressed for her new role, this girl astride the saddle in her skirt and trousers and polished riding boots, this lovely girl in one of Boudreaux's starched white shirts, a blue scarf tied pirate-fashion beneath her panama, silver earrings with the scarf, very nice, he said, "Yes, indeed, you worth more than that, but how much?"

"Eighty thousand," Amelia said.

"You pick that from the air?"

"Rollie has close to twenty thousand acres of sugarcane worth eighty dollars an acre. His gross income per acre is forty dollars. Operating costs, thirty-two dollars. He sells on the average at three and a half cents a pound, the rum and molasses at a much lower rate, of course; but it gives him a net income of eight dollars an acre times twenty thousand, or, one hundred and sixty thousand dollars. I think I'm worth at least half that. Don't you?"

Fuentes, grinning at her, said, "You been looking at his books."

"You're the one made me a spy."

"Is it all right," Fuentes said, "I tell you I love you?"

SHE DIDN'T SEE RUDI CALVO join them. It happened in the vicinity of the Atarés piers and coaling station; one minute she was alone with Fuentes leading two horses now, the next minute there was Rudi Calvo riding along on the other side of Fuentes. He nodded to her and touched his hat.

They were on the road now that approached the fortress, gray walls against a clear sky, and a rider on a gray horse approaching, walking his mount; the rider, like Fuentes and Rudi Calvo, wearing a dark suit and necktie, a straw hat. He reined in as they reached him and began speaking Spanish in a quiet

tone of voice, addressing Rudi. Fuentes waited until
he finished before saying to Amelia, "This is Yaro
Ruiz; he was a policeman like Rudi, but also quit. He
say Tavalera left there this morning and hasn't
return. That's fine with us. He believe there are only
eight Guardia inside. They leave the gate open in
the sally port like they saying to anybody comes by,
look, there is little of importance here; we have this
duty of guarding these old stones to give us something to do. He ask them if there are any prisoners,
saying one of the inspectors of buildings is coming
and will be here soon. Rudi Calvo is the inspector. If
you remember," Fuentes said, "when Ben Tyler
shot the hussar officer Rudi Calvo was there. He
asked for the pistols and Tavalera said to him, 'Concern yourself with city ordinances and the inspection
of buildings.' Meaning it to insult him. So it's the
reason Rudi is here. They told Yaro Ruiz no, there
are no prisoners at this time. Yaro told the Guardia
they heard the *reconcentrados* had been expelled and
it was why the inspector was coming, the place
being empty. Atarés was to be renovated because of
its historic value and the inspector would determine
the amount of work to be done."

Amelia said, "What's our reason for being
here?"

"We meet Rudi Calvo on the road, he ask why
don't we come along, visit the famous Castillo de
Atarés."

"But will they let us in?"

"The Guardia usually don't speak to you," Yaro said, "unless they give an order, tell you what to do. You ask a question, they may not bother to answer. If they do, it will be in a bored way of speaking, saying no more than they have to. I've been waiting for this day," Yaro said.

He seemed in control but anxious. His English was good. Amelia saw a pleasant-looking young man in his mid-twenties, no doubt educated. A machete hung in a scabbard from his saddle.

"There is one sentry at the gate, inside," Yaro said, "in the sally port that's like a tunnel through the wall. Most of the time he sits in there in the shade, between the bridge and the inside door. And most of the time the door is open, so you can see the parade grounds in there. If the sentry stops us, stay in the sally port, even if he shouts at you to get out, and let me speak to him."

Rudi led now, taking them along the street to the fortress, the wooden drawbridge hanging by a pair of iron chains: Rudi, Fuentes, Amelia, and Yaro leading the two riderless horses. They clattered over the drawbridge and were in the sally port, got this far before the sentry stepped into the dim enclosure, came through a door in the inner gate and began swatting at the horses and shouting at them to get out, leave this place or he'd throw them into dungeons. Now Rudi was trying to talk to him, explain why they were here. Only Yaro dismounted.

Amelia, from her horse, looked down at Yaro
and then at the sentry, the Guardia taller than Yaro,
heavier, his face flushed, a Mauser carbine slung
from his shoulder, the sentry turning then to slam
the inner door of the sally port closed. And now
Amelia watched Yaro step away from his horse and
saw the machete in his hand, though she didn't see
him draw it from the scabbard, Yaro holding it
against his leg as he moved through the horses
toward the sentry who was still shouting, waving his
arms and slapping at the horses, not looking at Yaro,
not seeing him raise the machete, Yaro taking it
across his body in two hands and now the Guardia
saw him and tried to turn away and snatch the Mauser from his shoulder, use it to block the machete,
but he was too late. Yaro swung the blade at the side
of the man away from the Mauser and Amelia saw it
bite into the man's shoulder and saw blood, saw the
blade hack at the man's neck and continue hacking,
the man going down and Yaro over him working
hard, hacking until the man on the ground didn't
move and all noise in the dim sally port seemed to
stop. No shouting, no one speaking, until Amelia
heard Fuentes say, *"Listo?"* And heard him say,
"Girl, are you ready? Get down." Fuentes and
Calvo had dismounted and were handing their reins
to Yaro. Fuentes said to her now, "You want to save
the cowboy and the marine?" His voice calm. "Isn't
it why we came?"

Amelia said, "I'm scared to death."

Fuentes nodded. "Of course."

She said, "I've never been so scared in my life."

"You become more afraid when you think you going to die," Fuentes said. "Listen, you want to go home, is all right, go. This doesn't have to be your war."

She said, "How do you keep from shaking?"

"Hold a gun in your hand, the pistol I put in your saddlebag. Listen, you see people killed before. In the hotel, the one who tried to shoot the cowboy, and the two at Benavides, the two innocent men Tavalera shot. Remember those two if you don't want to shake so much. Use what you have already seen to hold your anger where you can feel it and that way you don't become so scared. You want to be in this war, come with us."

Amelia stepped out of the saddle and got the pistol from the saddlebag, a Smith & Wesson .44, the kind Ben Tyler had pulled out of his coat in the hotel bar, pointed it at the hussar officer and shot him dead, the scene in her mind with the one on the station platform at Benavides, the two frightened-to-death innocent men who were part of the reason she was here.

Fuentes turned to open the door in the inner gate, then turned back to her to say, "Hold the pistol beneath your skirt."

RUDI CROSSED THE PARADE GROUNDS with purpose while Fuentes and Amelia took their time, sightseers looking up at the walls of weathered gray stone, parts of it worn black with age; tourists on a visit to Atarés. Yaro remained with the horses. They watched Rudi step into an open doorway and stand there. Approaching now, they heard him speaking in Spanish, Amelia understanding some of what she could hear. Fuentes said to her, "Telling them what he wants, to inspect the entire fortress. He asks is it all right with them, the ones he's talking to."

They would see them in a moment: four Guardia sitting at a table playing dominoes.

Rudi stepped through the doorway. Fuentes nudged Amelia to follow and there they were, only a few paces away, the four at the table with their blank expressions and big mustaches, three in shirtsleeves, one shirtless, suspenders over bare white skin, dark hair on his chest, another one wearing his hat, his military straw cocked down on his eyes, and the fourth one smoking a cigarette, holding it in the corner of his mouth as he stared at the visitors. Not one of the Guardia said a word.

Amelia glanced around the room: a good size but bare except for a stove, a pile of wood, a rack of Mauser carbines on one wall, a cupboard and the table where the Guardia sat. Fuentes was saying in Spanish, "Forgive us for intruding. I like to show my friend from America where I was a guest forty-seven years ago, when I was a boy." And now Amelia wanted to say something, be part of this, say in a casual way she'd read about Atarés, the history of the place, and had always wanted to see it. With a smile. Wouldn't a sightseer be very polite and smile? Fuentes was telling now how he had been placed in stocks, the four Guardia looking at Amelia as they listened.

"On my back," Fuentes said, "locked in facing the sun and unable to move, not even to turn my head an inch." He looked past them into the room. "They used to keep the stocks in here, also fetters, balls and chains. Do you still use balls and chains?"

Not one of them answered him, maybe accepting what he was saying, maybe not.

"I was placed in the stocks out there," Fuentes said, turning his back to them to look out the door, "at midday. They told me by evening the sun would have burned through my eyes and I would be blind and out of my head. But you know what?" Fuentes said, starting to turn, "I was saved by a miracle." He came around to face the men at the table bringing his revolver, an old-model Colt six-shooter, out of his suit coat.

The one with his chest bare said, "Old man, what are you thinking to do with that?"

Fuentes said, "I'm going to kill you with it," extended the revolver and shot the man in the middle of his chest, moved the gun and shot the one smoking a cigarette and the next one to him as this one tried to lunge away from the table. Rudi had his pistol in his hand and shot the one lunging and the fourth one also, the one wearing his hat who was directly in front of Rudi, Rudi touching his gun to the man's hat and shooting him, the straw catching fire, smoking; and it was done.

Amelia stood rigid, the gunfire ringing in her head, her hand through a slit in her skirt gripping the revolver. She heard Fuentes say, "What were you waiting for?"

She breathed in and out and said, "I didn't know you were going to shoot them."

"Oh?" Fuentes said. "You didn't? Listen to me. When you see the chance to kill Guardia, you don't stop and think about it, you kill them. Get your pistol out, little girl, or go home." Fuentes the insurgent speaking, no longer Fuentes the *segundo*.

Amelia watched him turn to the doorway, where Rudi was looking out at the yard. She brought the big pistol out of her skirt.

"Three left," Rudi said. He waved to Yaro, over there in the door in the sally port gate. Yaro waved back, pushed the gate open and started across the parade grounds with the horses.

"Now I lead," Fuentes was saying, looking out the door and gesturing. "That direction. The archway there, the big doors open like an entrance to a church? We go in there and follow the first corridor we come to. It leads to the guardrooms, torture rooms and dungeons. All right? I think the three Guardia we have left will be in there, somewhere. Maybe two sleeping, the ones on duty last night, and another one with the keys near the prisoners."

"They might have heard us," Rudi said.

Fuentes didn't think so. "Maybe. But these walls, man, are thick." He looked at Amelia. "Three years I didn't hear nothing in there until they open the cell. Now you're ready?"

Amelia nodded and Fuentes stared at her a few moments before turning and going out.

Yaro had the horses across the yard and was through the archway before they reached it. Fuentes told him to get the Mausers from the room of the domino players, cover them with something. Yaro nodded. Now he pressed one finger to his lips and Amelia saw the blood on his hands.

They moved along this roadway through the fortress until they came to the first corridor and looked down the length of it, dimly lit with coal oil lanterns every ten meters or so. Fuentes motioned and they followed him, Amelia holding the grip of the big revolver in both hands. They came to doors that stood open and looked into bare rooms. At the first closed door Rudi pressed the latch and inched the door open enough to see a man asleep on a cot with an iron frame, the man lying on his back, his mouth open. Amelia, close to one side of the doorway, could hear him snoring. She watched Rudi ease the door open a little more, raise the machete in front of him and go in.

Fuentes stood on the other side of the doorway looking at her and she stared back at him waiting for the sound that would come, Amelia knowing the sound of a man being hacked with a machete, Fuentes holding her eyes she believed to test her, see how she accepted this. So when the sound came, the solid hacking, smacking sound of the blade striking a man's body, the gasp, the muffled cry cut off, she stepped into the doorway and watched Rudi Calvo raise the machete and hack down with it, the blade rising, falling, the man twisting in the bed, arms raised to protect himself, the metal frame scraping on the stone floor, Rudi grunting with the effort. When he had finished the Guardia and searched him for keys, he came toward them shaking his head.

Amelia said to Fuentes, "Two left," and saw in his eyes an expression she thought of as love.

They moved past the iron doors of cells and found the Guardia with the keys in an office no bigger than a closet, at the end of the corridor. Rudi put his revolver on the man and asked him to step out.

THE CANVAS CHAIR TAVALERA HAD SAT IN was still in the cell; but since it was the only chair neither one would take it while the other had to sit on the damp floor. Tyler would say, "Go on, sit in it." And Virgil would say, "No, you." They had become good friends since their meeting in El Morro, having no choice but to be together. They sat against the same blackened stone wall, legs stretched out, watching spiders and sometimes roaches appear and scurry around, the two patient in front of each other, waiting for whatever would happen next. They talked all the time, Tyler asking Virgil now if he'd ever shot a man.

Virgil said no, but there were some at home he'd like to have. He said, "But not ever having done the deed doesn't mean I don't know how to shoot. I'm a U.S. Marine and have been trained as a marksman. My shooting rule of thumb is, if I can see it, I can hit it. I also know semaphore, the use of flags to send messages, a skill I learnt aboard the *Maine*." Virgil got to his feet, like at attention. He stuck his right arm straight out, his left arm down at his side. Now he stuck his left arm straight out with the right one straight down, then stuck both arms down at an angle and said, "That's your name in semaphore, B-E-N." He sat down again, saying, "I know you've shot men, but I can tell by looking at you there was no pleasure taken in it. Was there?"

Tyler didn't get to answer. They both heard the key scrape in the lock and looked up to see the big iron door swinging open and a Guardia stumbling into the cell like he'd been pushed—the Guardia in uniform and now a man in town clothes coming in

to give him a shove and wave a pistol, telling the
Guardia to go over there against the wall, the one to
Tyler and Virgil's right. No sooner had the Guardia
stepped over and turned around in a pose, hands on
his hips, this Cuban in a dark suit and hat raised his
revolver and shot the Guardia through the heart—
Jesus Christ, *bang,* no warning, no ceremony or last
words—and the Guardia fell dead. Now Fuentes
was in the cell and right behind him came Amelia
Brown, both holding pistols, Tyler and Virgil so surprised they sat there without moving.

Fuentes said, "Come on, let's go. Quickly."

Virgil got up and then Tyler, still looking at
Amelia Brown, this girl with no business being here
saving his life. Now she came over, her eyes locked
on his and it was strange, this being only the third
time they'd seen each other, that taking her in his
arms, holding her, seemed the natural thing to do.
But that's what he did, opened his arms and felt her
press against him like they were long-lost sweethearts. It made him wonder who was saving who,
but felt so good he didn't make a fuss, ask her what
was going on. Now she was looking up at him again,
worry in her eyes. What she said, close between
them, was "Tyler, I hope to God you're glad to see
me."

Fuentes, at the cell door, waved them to come
on, hurry. Once they were in the corridor Rudi said,
"There's another guard?" looking at Tyler and
Virgil in their filthy clothes for help.

"We've seen four different ones," Tyler said, "two this morning and the big cheese himself, Tavalera."

"He left," Rudi said. "The rest are dead, unless there is the one more."

Fuentes, still anxious, said, "You want to stand here and talk about it?" He started back along the corridor followed now by Rudi and Virgil, Amelia and Tyler bringing up the rear.

She was holding his arm and said, "You smell awful, but it's all right. I brought soap."

That was fine, but what he wanted to know: "You killed all the guards?"

"They did."

"Walked in and started shooting?"

"Rudi used a machete."

"You saw it?"

"Yes—and Yaro, another policeman, he used one."

Tyler said, "I know Rudi," but then couldn't think of what to ask her; there was so much he didn't know.

They came to the roadway that tunneled through the fortress, followed it and soon they could see Yaro Ruiz and the horses, one with the bedroll, one with the Mausers rolled into a hammock, daylight showing above them in the entrance arch.

"Yours is the horse with the bedroll," Fuentes said, half turning to speak to Tyler as they kept moving. "Your clothes are in it." He said, "Listen, I'm sorry about Charlie Burke, but we can't talk now. We go south from here fast as we can to Ciénaga, where we have good friends with a place to rest. We go on and stop at San Antonio de los Baños, where there is a house we can stay for the night. Tomorrow we go all the way to Batabano, on the coast."

They were approaching the horses, Yaro ready to hand them their reins.

"From Batabano you go on a lighter to Cienfuegos," Fuentes said, "and catch a British steamboat to Jamaica, quick, before America declares war. Your consulate people and all the correspondents have already left."

Virgil said, "If the war's gonna be in Cuba, what do I want to leave for? I'm here."

Tyler said, "And I have business to take care of." Only that with Fuentes telling them to hurry and mount the horses that were skittish now, throwing their heads, ready to run. Yaro handed reins to Virgil and then to Tyler. Fuentes stepped into the saddle with the Mausers tied behind it and nudged his horse from shade into the bright sunlight of the parade grounds. Now Yaro and Virgil were mounted and joined him, looking back, Fuentes waving his hand again, telling them to come on.

Tyler stepped into the saddle and yelled at them to go and looked down at Amelia opening the saddlebag as her horse moved from the dim roadway into the sun.

"What're you doing?"

"Putting the gun in here," Amelia said, having trouble with the horse moving away from her.

It was Tyler who saw the Guardia step out of the doorway that was along the wall of doors and arched windows to their right. A Guardia raising a carbine, aiming at the three riders crossing the grounds toward the gate.

Tyler yelled at them, "Behind you!" and saw Fuentes and the others turn in their saddles, Rudi and Yaro reining their horses halfway around and raising their revolvers, the Guardia in that moment firing, throwing the bolt of his Mauser carbine and firing again. Tyler saw Yaro sit straight up in the saddle and then sink forward to hunch over his horse and seem to become part of it. Rudi and Fuentes, their pistols extended, their horses sidestepping. He saw the Guardia throw the bolt and raise the carbine and Tyler heard a gunshot in his ears it was so loud, saw the Guardia hit and sink back against the door frame and saw Amelia now, looking down at her, Amelia thumbing the hammer of her revolver and firing across her saddle, the butt of the big pistol in both hands resting on the seat, Amelia cocking and firing again and the Guardia dropped the Mauser and fell into the doorway.

Tyler kept watching her now, Amelia swinging up into the saddle, glancing at him as she said,

"Let's go," and they followed the three horses across the parade and through the sally port, Rudi with the reins of Yaro's horse, leading it as they crossed the drawbridge at a dead run and were out of the fortress of Atarés.

# 14

FUENTES BROUGHT THEM to the caves near San Antonio de los Baños: caves, he told them, that were like being inside a cathedral they were so big. Full of bats, of course, millions of them, and dung beetles eating the guano and newborn bats that sometimes fell from the ceiling. So the caves were not a good place to stay, to make camp. They rode past the black openings in the hillsides to a farmhouse sitting at the mouth of an arroyo, a house made of boards and adobe, wooden bars on the open windows, a thatched roof, a chicken pen in the yard but no chickens, or people living here, the house empty. Fuentes said the family, to their misfortune, were *pacíficos;* they tried to be neutral and that was impossible. A scouting party from Islero's army had raided the farm and taken food, and when the Volunteers in San Antonio de los Baños learned of it, they came and killed the family for giving aid to the enemy. Shot the father, his younger brother, his mother, his wife and his four children. "All the way here," Fuentes said, "you see what General Weyler left before he went home. Nothing. Like your General Sherman when he marched across Georgia to the sea. Listen, battles are fought over the capture of food, the hope that to win will mean something to eat."

They found field corn they could roast, squash and plantains. Fuentes had brought candles to light the house when it was dark. Now he'd ride into San Antonio, see what he could buy, maybe have chicken for supper. Then when he returned they could discuss this business of who was leaving and who was staying. He said to Amelia, "Imagine being a hostage and think what to write to Mr. Boudreaux, how hungry you are, how sure you believe they going to kill you if he refuse to send the money. Find out, uh, how much he loves you."

He was their leader and could speak to her this way if he wanted.

The two policemen were no longer on this trip. Rudi, less than a mile from Atarés and leading Yaro, had gone off in the direction of Cerro, on the edge of Havana, Yaro needing a doctor before he bled to death.

Virgil walked the perimeter of the farmyard with a Mauser cradled in his arm, the marine peering through the dusk at silent hills and pastures, came back to the house and sat on the doorstoop to eat plantains.

Tyler put the horses out to graze, their forelegs hobbled. Amelia strolled out, the sky dark now. She said she had never seen so many empty homes, all the poor people killed or imprisoned in those camps. She asked Tyler where his family had lived in New Orleans and they talked a little about the city he had left as a boy, polite with each other, Tyler sensing that they were both holding back, alone for the first time and feeling what it was like. He said well, it was time he washed the prison off him, bathe in one of those rock pools by the caves. Amelia gave him a bar of soap with lilac scent.

HE SAT IN COLD WATER in the dark, the rock tub shallow. It was strange, but smelling the soap made him think of Camille, back home with a husband now, the railroad dick. He hadn't thought of her once since turning his head to see Amelia Brown in that hotel dining room, and now Amelia's soap reminded him of an old girl he'd been fond of, a whore who never pretended to be anything else. He wondered how Amelia Brown saw herself. If being the pleasure of one man instead of anybody that came along made a difference. He dried himself with his blanket, spread it over a rock and put on a pair of canvas pants and a shirt he'd bought in Havana, and his old hat Fuentes had stuck in the bedroll. It felt good to be wearing a hat again. His new boots were about broken in. A guard at the Morro had wanted to take them off him; Tyler told the man he'd have to kill him first, and if he did he'd never get the boots off.

He started back and came to Amelia waiting for him in the dark, a few yards from the rock pool.

"What were you doing, watching me?"

"If I was," she said, "I didn't see much."

Already they were closer to knowing each other. He could feel it.

She said, "I want to ask you something, why you're staying."

It surprised him. He told her Boudreaux still owed him for the horses, forty-five hundred and forty-five dollars. Watched her nod, saying that's what she thought, and watched her draw on the cigarette she was smoking, the tip glowing in the dark. Now she offered him one from the pack and held her cigarette up to give him a light.

"They're Sweet Caps."

Tyler exhaled a stream of smoke and looked at the cigarette. He said, "You know I've never had a tailor-made before?"

She said, "I'd believe there all kinds of things you haven't tried yet. I imagine, though, mostly by choice. A man who robs banks must do just about whatever he wants."

This girl was closing in fast, still polite but having fun with him now. Tyler said, "Why does robbing banks seem to appeal to you?"

"I wondered what it was like."

"Why?"

"I'm curious, that's all."

"I can tell you in one word, it's scary."

"But you did it. Walked right in. . . . What did you say, Give me all your money?"

Yeah, she was having fun was all. He said, "I wasn't greedy, I only asked for *some* of the money, took it and left." He said, "What's the worst thing you've ever done," and watched her expression change.

"I killed a man today."

"You made a good shot too. You hadn't, Fuentes and those two policemen'd be dead. If you're gonna be in it, you have to be in all the way."

She said, still with her somber expression, "You sound like Victor. Do you know much about this war?"

"I just spent two months with a bunch of old patriots. I heard all the stories and I can be inspired by them," Tyler said, "or by Charlie Burke. Charlie, standing before that firing squad, turning his head to spit."

"To show his contempt," Amelia said.

"No, it was so he wouldn't be lying there dead with tobacco juice dribbled down his chin. Charlie Burke had more sand than any man I know. Or outside of those old patriots."

"Did you know Victor was one of them?"

"Charlie never told me, but I figured it out."

"Do you see a change in him?"

"You mean now he isn't your servant anymore?"

"He never was," Amelia said. "We're friends."

"Then what's bothering you?"

Something was, and she took her time now.

"I think of the way he used to speak to me, even telling about awful things, the Volunteers murdering people, firing into a theater. . . ."

"The Villanueva," Tyler said.

"Yes, and Victor was there, he saw it. But whatever he told me, it was always in a quiet tone of voice, never sounding mean or vengeful. So I believed, yes, this is his manner."

"But now," Tyler said.

"He's changed. Not a lot, but I can tell."

Tyler drew on the cigarette, giving himself time, not understanding why she didn't see it. He said, "You're used to him looking at the ground when he speaks. Maybe not to you but to most people and that's how you think of him, that nice old man. But see, now he doesn't have to act nice if he doesn't feel like it, same as you and me. He's joined to fight the war again, picked up a gun and it makes him a different person."

"I understand that," Amelia said. "I feel I know the man, but for some reason I'm not as sure of him as I was. It was a year ago he asked me, 'What's the point of you?' He saw me as a lady of leisure, not doing a damn thing with my life, and he must've thought hmmmm, maybe I can use this girl."

"You felt that?"

"Of course I did, I'm not dumb. I *let* him use me. I'd listen to Rollie and his buddies talking about the situation—it was always the way the Spanish saw it. Or it was about things people in the government told Rollie they were going to do. Rollie always saw General Weyler when we came to Havana. The general talked about the honor of retaking a town in the east, Victoria de las Tunas, no matter how many men it cost. Victor said, 'Las Tunas? Who cares about that place?' I never had much to tell that I felt helped the cause. But living here, I see what's happening to the people. I saw two men murdered. I did, I saw that Guardia, Tavalera, shoot them both in cold blood. And I began to think, what can I do? You must've felt the same way to bring in guns, risk your life for people you don't even know. I wanted to do something with *my* life. I mean short of losing it; I'm not a martyr."

Tyler liked the way she talked about how she felt, serious but showing she was human.

"Then when you were put in prison I thought, that's it, get you out. I talked to Victor about it for weeks and finally he said the time was right."

"Bless your heart," Tyler said. "You know I'm in your debt forever."

She was done with her somber mood, getting a keen look in her eyes as she said, "You mean it?"

"I'm here," Tyler said. "I have to collect from Boudreaux before I ever think of leaving."

"We do too," Amelia said. "I'm talking about the hostage money. We tell Rollie I'm being held by insurgents. He pays it or he never sees me again."

"I wondered about that. How much you asking?"

"Eighty thousand dollars."

Tyler took a moment to wonder what it would look like, all that money in stacks of U.S. scrip, before he said, "You think he'll pay?"

Not a question she seemed to expect. But then got that keen look in her eyes again and said, "Wouldn't you, if you had it?"

Showing a good deal of confidence in herself.

"I don't know," Tyler said. "Maybe."

Right there, she lost some of her spunk and gave him a shrug. "It doesn't matter."

"But if I didn't pay," Tyler said, "I'd never know what I'd be missing, would I? Was me, sure, I'd pay."

It put a nice smile on her face, a child getting what she wanted. She said, "I'll tell you this, Rollie knows what he'd be missing."

"He'll do what you want, huh?"

"He generally does."

Like she had gentled him, this millionaire, slipped a hackamore over his wavy hair and led him around by it.

"He pays," Tyler said, "and the revolutionary army gets the money. If that's the plan, I'll help you any way I can."

"Later on, after Victor gets back," Amelia said, "we'll write the letter. If you have any doubts about it, let me know, all right?"

Walking back to the farmhouse she took his arm, though he didn't offer it, the blanket folded over his other shoulder. Like they were coming back from having fun. Along the way she handed Tyler her revolver, saying she was better with a rifle, if he wanted it. Tyler stuck the .44 in his waist. Neither one spoke after that until the house came into view, candlelight showing in the barred windows. Tyler said, "Victor came to Charlie Burke for horses. Even though it's his boss buying them, Victor wanted five hundred dollars for his part. Charlie Burke said it was the way it's done here, like in Old Mexico, you set up the deal you expect a cut. See, what I'm wondering, if the hostage idea is Victor's, maybe that's why you feel different about him. Something tells you not to trust him."

She said, "I hadn't thought of that, Victor wanting some of it for himself."

"Or all of it."

She shook her head. "I can't imagine that."

They walked toward the lighted windows, the land beyond shapes against the night sky, empty and desolate.

"It was Victor's idea, wasn't it?"

She said, "No, I thought of it myself."

———

VIRGIL BELIEVED HE MIGHT'VE EATEN too many of those
goddamn black bananas, he didn't feel so good, but
said he'd better go clean himself up. He spoke in a
loud young voice, though sounded shy asking
Amelia was it all right he used her soap. Tyler
handed him the bar of lilac. Virgil stepped outside,
stood listening a few moments and came back inside.

"Somebody's coming."

The weapons they'd brought from Atarés were
on the table: the Mausers and a matched pair of .44
Smith & Wesson Russians. Amelia handed Virgil a
carbine and picked one up for herself. She said to
Tyler, in the doorway now, "Can you tell how
many?"

He said, "Three," looking out at the dark, waiting for them to come into view. Virgil, close by,
threw the bolt on the carbine as Tyler said, "It's
Fuentes," and there he was.

Fuentes in his town clothes and two riders trailing close behind who could be farmers in their white
cotton, but farmers with rifles, cartridge belts across
the chest, the brim of their big straws turned up in
front, Fuentes telling the house, "Friends coming!"
Shouting it out and saying it again as they appeared
out of the dark. In the yard he stepped down from
his horse and stretched and then gestured for them
to come out of the house.

"Please, my friends want to see what you look
like. They come from Islero." He gestured again.

"We meet on the road back there. Come on, we friends."

Tyler and Virgil stepped out to the yard, Virgil turning his head to Tyler as he said in a raspy whisper, "They're Negroes," maybe a little surprised. Amelia stayed in the doorway. They watched Fuentes untie a gunnysack from his saddle and turn to them, shaking out two lifeless chickens, their necks wrung. The mambís sat their horses without moving or saying a word, rifles across their laps, looking this way but mostly, Tyler believed, at Amelia in her blue bandanna.

"I meet these old friends," Fuentes said, "and they tell me where to steal the chickens." Fuentes in a good mood, not showing any wear.

Amelia said, "Are they staying for supper?" Asking the question, nothing more.

"No, they riding to scout to find cane fields to burn, ones as close as ten miles from Havana, so people in the city see smoke in the sky." He said, "Girl, you want to cook for them? Maybe in two days when we visit the general." He turned to speak to the men of Islero, finally raised his hand to them and waved as they reined their horses and rode out.

Amelia was waiting for him.

"Are you expecting me to cook?"

"I was thinking of chicken fricassee," Fuentes said, "and a nice plantain soup? Or, if you rather, you can pluck the chickens."

Amelia stared at him in silence.

Virgil said, "Hell, gimme the birds. Boil some water to stick 'em in and we'll get her done."

"I don't cook," Amelia said to Fuentes. "Let's understand that right now." She turned and was in the house.

Fuentes shrugged, acting innocent.

Now Tyler went inside.

"Amelia?"

It was the first time he'd said her name aloud. She had laid the Mauser on the table and stood with her back to him.

"He was kidding with you."

She turned now and seemed tired, nodding her head, not looking directly at him. "I know, I just . . . I felt he was making fun of me."

Now Tyler nodded, as though he understood, and said, "You don't ever cook, huh?" and saw her eyes flash, looking right at him.

"Don't you start."

They could hear a pump working around back, Virgil drawing water, the only sound.

LATER ON, Fuentes gave Amelia the pencil stub and sheets of tablet paper he'd brought folded in his suit pocket. Amelia, at the table, a candle burning, got ready to write and looked up.

"Should I say Dear Rollie or just Rollie?"

"Either one," Fuentes said.

"But if I'm being forced to write this and I'm petrified, would I think to call him Dear?"

"Is how you start a letter," Fuentes said. "You don't think, you write it the way you write a letter to anyone, from the habit of it. You say Dear or you say My Dear, My Dear Rollie . . . No, what you say is My Dearest Rollie, so he knows you have affection for him and it moves his heart to have you back in his bed."

Amelia made a face, frowning, and looked up at Tyler, watching her. "What do you think?"

He thought a moment. "I'd say, 'Dear Rollie, you wavy-haired tinhorn son of a bitch, send eighty thousand dollars quick or these boys are gonna put me under.'"

Amelia didn't smile.

Fuentes didn't either, but was nodding. "Yes, something like that; but we have to think some more about the amount we ask for. Listen, to me you worth a million dollars if I had it. But Mr. Boudreaux is a businessman, very practical, also not a generous man. We want his heart to tell him, make the payment, and his business mind to look at the amount and say, yes, I can do that to save the life of my sweetheart."

Amelia tapped the pencil on the table.

"Get to the point, Victor. How much?"

"Let me think a minute. Maybe you write down figures and we see how they look."

"Have you thought of the way he delivers it?"

"I have an idea for that," Fuentes said, "but we need Islero to help. I have to speak to him."

"He gets the money?" Amelia said, and looked at Tyler.

"Islero is the one receive the guns and bullets this man brought. He's going to attack Matanzas, blow up the fort and free the city. But to do it he needs money for his soldiers, four thousand in his army. They been in the field more than a year, no pay to give their families."

Tyler said, "You trust him?"

"Islero? Yes, of course. He's my little brother."

That stopped Amelia for a moment. "But he's Negro."

"Yes, and half of me is also," Fuentes said. "We have the same mother, but different fathers sired us. Listen, if you accept me, then I know you going to like Islero, a true patriot. He lives only to see freedom for our people."

Amelia said, "And that's why he's called the Black Plague?"

Fuentes shrugged. "What does that mean, a name the panchos gave him, the Spanish? He was a slave, he ran away and was a *cimarron*. When he was caught they cut the tendons in his legs so he can't run no more." Fuentes paused. "Oh, when you see him, don't say nothing as how he walks. . . . So they bring him back and make him a cook in a regiment of the Spanish army. This was in the Ten Years War. He always cooks very good," Fuentes said to

Amelia, smiling a little. "So good that pretty soon he was made the cook in the home of a general name Alvarez. He cook for him I think maybe a year. Until one night the general invite his staff and some good friend, all officers, to dinner, Alvarez telling them, 'Wait until you taste the yanyó,' like a very spicy gumbo. It so spicy they eating they don't taste the snake poison Islero put in it. Pretty soon they can't move, they paralyzed from the venom. Then, all of them watching him, he took a butcher knife and cut the throat of each one. Someone said, to see the bodies, it was like a plague had enter the room as they dined. A black one. Islero himself thinks of it as the Last Supper." Fuentes looked from Amelia to Tyler and back again, his old, brown-stained eyes gleaming. He said, "Now, how much do we ask of Mr. Boudreaux?"

# 15

GUARDIAS HAD BEEN WATCHING the doctor's home in Cerro, the doctor a Creole, on the side of the insurrection. They came in while the doctor was examining Yaro Ruiz's gunshot wound. They shot the doctor and took Yaro, bleeding, by this time unconscious, and Rudi Calvo to the old prison, Recogidas, where they questioned Rudi.

"Who was with you at Atarés this morning?"

"I wasn't there."

They broke his right leg beneath the knee with a baseball bat.

"Who was with you at Atarés this morning?"

"I wasn't there."

They broke his left leg the same way.

Rudi listened to them talking. One of them saying, "Yaro Ruiz is of no use to us, he's close to death." And another one said, "Leave him."

The next part was very painful, riding in the military ambulance and trying not to scream, loaded and unloaded and dragged between two Guardias into a building that smelled like a hospital, then seeing enough of it to know it was, it was San Ambrosio. Rudi was brought to a room and heaved onto a cot. A doctor came in, he looked at Rudi and asked if he had suffered an accident. One of the Guardia said yes, he fell down. The Guardia told the doctor not to be concerned with this one, he would be cared for.

A man was brought into the room and dropped on another cot. After a little while the Guardias left. Rudi heard the man groaning, turned his head and saw it was Lieutenant Molina from the Morro, his face and clothes covered with blood. Rudi asked what they did to him. Lieutenant Molina said they came in his cell to question him about the cowboy and the marine: Who was it helped them escape, the ones who visited them in the Morro? What was their plan? Where did they go? Questions he could not answer since he didn't know, so they beat him with chains. He said when he spoke it was very hard to breathe. He said, "They bring me here to mend my broken bones so they can send me to Africa. I'm sure of it."

Rudi said, "I don't think I'm going anywhere."

The Guardias who brought them here returned with Lionel Tavalera. He approached Rudi Calvo drawing his saber and touched Rudi's right leg with the point. Rudi gasped.

"Oh, does that hurt? It must be gangrene has already set in." He poked the left leg with the saber and when Rudi cried out, Tavalera said, "Oh, in that leg too. I think both your legs will have to be amputated."

As he was touching Rudi's legs and saying this, two doctors in white coats came in the room, the one who was here before and another doctor, this one with an air of authority as he said to Tavalera, "Excuse me, are you a doctor? What are you talking about, amputate the legs? Anyone can see the legs are fractured and need to be set."

Tavalera turned to the doctors with his saber, not in a threatening way; still, it was in his hand. He said, "We won't bother you, sir. The surgeon of my corps is on his way. These men will be in his care."

The doctor with the air of authority said, "There is no need for amputation. When your surgeon arrives, have him see me."

Tavalera said, "Of course," nodding. As soon as the doctors were out of the room he turned again to Rudi, Rudi looking up at him from the hospital cot.

"Eight of my men were murdered, two of them cut down with the machete. I would point out the one taken from you in Cerro has fresh blood on it, the blood of at least one of my men. I know you were at Atarés. Now tell me who was with you."

Rudi closed his eyes.

Tavalera pressed the point of his saber against Rudi's leg and Rudi gasped, trying hard not to cry out.

"Right there is where they would cut. Who was with you? Tell me and your legs will be set and placed in casts. Refuse, your legs will be chopped off with your own machete, the weapon of peasants, without anesthetic, without a stick to bite on, without hope for the rest of your life. Does that tempt you to speak?"

Rudi saw himself on a street in Old Havana, a legless beggar sitting against the wall of a building. Now he saw his son with him, people walking by, his little son offering a cup. He was thinking, No, his son wouldn't be there. . . .

As Tavalera was saying, "We could be wrong about you. Perhaps the idea of rebellion runs in your family and it was your son who was at Atarés."

Rudi felt himself trying to push up on his hands, his elbows, the shock of this man's words lifting him, the man a sorcerer who could see into his mind, the man raising the saber to rest the point against Rudi's breastbone and he sank back on the cot.

"What do you call the boy," Tavalera said, "Tonio? What if little Tonio falls down and breaks his legs and they have to be amputated? Where is he, still with your sister?"

Rudi felt his strength drain, all of it; he was unable to move. He stared up at this Guardia with

the sword and the mustache covering his mouth, his
expression, a man made of stone with marble eyes.

Tavalera raised the saber and touched the point
to the tip of Rudi's nose in almost a playful gesture.

"Rudi? Who was with you at Atarés this morning?"


NOVIS CROWE DIDN'T KNOW where he was till he heard
that tinny band music playing and realized, hell, he
was back in Havana, not too far from the park that
ran past the hotel. The greasers had brought him in
a wagon lying under a pile of sacks that smelled of
coffee, his head in a sack and his hands tied behind
him with twine—hours under there till the greasers
stopped and hauled him off the wagon. He said to
them, "Where'n the hell am I?" They didn't tell him
nothing, not a word, and left him there, the wagon
moving off. Pretty soon he heard voices, he believed
people talking about him. Novis said, "Will somebody cut me loose?" and they stopped talking. But
then the band started up, not too far away, and it
gave him an idea where he was. He started toward
the sound, walking on cobblestones, then must've
got off course, for he banged into a chair, heard it
scrape on the pavement and could see light now
through the gunnysack. Somebody with nerve—it
turned out to be a waiter—pulled the sack from his
head and Novis was looking at an outdoor café full
of empty tables. He said to the waiter, "Well, now

you had a good look, how about cutting me loose?"
Jesus Christ, but greasers were slow to move.

Something was different. It was the same soldier
band playing, but there were hardly any people here
listening, the rows of chairs empty. The people he
did see all looked to be in a hurry, wherever they
were going, people coming out of the hotel with
their grips and getting into coaches. In the Inglaterra
lobby it looked like the same confusion, people
bumping into each other, Novis not sure if they
were checking in or out, grips and steamer trunks
lined up by the entrance.

Upstairs he had to bang on the door a half dozen
times before Mr. Boudreaux opened it, his boss in
shirtsleeves holding a pair of binoculars. The first
thing he said, right away, was "Where's Amelia?"

"They got her, the mambís."

"Where?"

"I don't know where. They held me a couple of
days and turned me loose."

"You were with her?"

"You mean after?"

"For Christ sake, tell me what happened."

"They waylaid us—from then on I had a sack
over my head except when I et." Mr. Boudreaux
turned away from him and crossed the room to a
window where the drapes were pulled back and the
shutters open. Novis said after him, "What in the
hell's going on?"

Mr. Boudreaux stood at the window now looking off through the binoculars as Novis approached him.

"Sir, what's going on?"

"The U.S. fleet's out there," Boudreaux said, "blockading the harbor. You see the crowds, people on the streets? They're scared to death, don't know which way to run. All day they were taking guns off the *Alfonso XII*—her boiler's out of order—and mounting them ashore, on El Morro. God Almighty, the fleet could've sent the marines in today and taken Havana. The city's in total confusion. People are running like rats from the hotel, afraid it'll be shelled. I said to the manager, 'The Inglaterra? Our fleet wouldn't dare. Too many officers have gotten drunk here.' " He said this without taking the binoculars from his eyes. It was not until he said, "Tell me what happened to Amelia. Where was Victor?" that Novis remembered, Jesus Christ, they'd given him a letter to deliver.

He got it out and said, "Mr. Boudreaux?" and had to wait. You always had to ask a question more than one time to get an answer. "Mr. Boudreaux, they gave me a letter for you."

That got him around from the window in a hurry and got Novis an evil look, hell in the man's eyes, as Mr. Boudreaux took the letter from him and tore it open. The first thing he said was *"What?"*

It wasn't a question. Novis said, "Is Miss Brown all right?"

He had to wait then while Boudreaux read the letter and maybe read it again, he took so long.

"Sir, is it about Miss Brown?"

Boudreaux finished and stared straight into Novis's eyes from only a few feet away.

"They're holding her hostage."

"They are?"

"I have to pay forty thousand dollars, American currency, to get her back."

Novis said, "Forty thousand," and almost said, hell, send to Newerleans for another woman'd be cheaper. And was glad he didn't, seeing the way Mr. Boudreaux was looking at him.

"She was in your care, boy."

"Sir, I got hit from behind with a sack of coffee."

"I told you to watch out for her."

That evil look still in his eyes.

"Sir, they never gimme a chance. Was a whole bunch of 'em."

"Wearing uniforms?"

"Not as I recall."

Now he was reading the letter again.

"Sir, you gonna pay it?"

Still reading.

"They say how you're suppose to pay 'em?"

He must have been at that part in the letter, for he read aloud, " 'They said you are to put the money in a pillowcase wrapped in a hammock with rope around it securely tied. On a tag attached to it write: To Amelia Brown, for Cuba Libre. On April 27, five days from this date, put it on the morning train to Matanzas in the care of Novis Crowe.' "

"Me?"

Boudreaux was staring again, giving him the evil eye. He said, "Yes, but why you?"

"I reckon," Novis said, " 'cause you trust me. Could that be it?"

Mr. Boudreaux never said.

It was later on the bellboy knocked on the door and handed Novis a calling card for Mr. Boudreaux. It had a lot of printing on the front with *Mayor* and a Spanish name, big. TAVALERA. And with a note on the back that looked like it said this fella was waiting downstairs in the bar.


EARLIER THIS DAY, Andres Palenzuela received a telephone call from a Guardia officer informing him that one of his men, Yaro Ruiz, had been shot and died of the wound. Another one, Rudi Calvo, was in San Ambrosio being treated for an injury. The Guardia officer would not give details; the chief of municipal police would have to come to the hospital.

The telephone call was made after Lionel Tavalera had had time to think about the murder of his men by two policemen and that the next step would be to speak to their chief.

Lieutenant Molina had been removed.

Palenzuela entered the hospital room to find

Rudi on the cot with both of his legs in plaster casts. Major Tavalera was seated next to him in a straight chair. Palenzuela appeared genuinely astonished.

"My God, what happened?"

Tavalera said to Rudi, "Tell him what you told me. All of it."

Palenzuela stood with his back against the wall listening to Rudi's confession, looking from Rudi's face drained of color to the clean tubes of plaster encasing his legs. Rudi spoke for several minutes, Tavalera now and again prompting him. When Rudi finished and the room was quiet, Tavalera said, "You didn't say why the woman of Boudreaux was with you at Atarés."

Rudi said he believed she wanted to be celebrated as a heroine of the revolution.

"Go on."

And pose as a hostage to receive money from Boudreaux. He didn't know how much; the amount had not yet been decided.

This time when Rudi finished Tavalera looked at Palenzuela standing against the wall—though not the kind of wall he should be standing against—and said, "You don't tell Boudreaux any of this. You leave that to me. You understand? You don't speak to him; you're too busy inspecting buildings, or whatever you do." Tavalera rose from the chair. "I leave you alone, if you wish to say something to Rudi."

He watched the chief of municipal police

straighten, bringing himself to attention before shaking his head.

"To a traitor? I have nothing to say."

IN THE COACH on the way to the hotel and now in the bar with a glass of sherry, Tavalera had time to plan, a step at a time, how much of Rudi Calvo's confession he would tell. Not all of it, no. Not a word about the business of the hostage being a hoax. There would be satisfaction in telling it, that his woman had walked out and was now planning to rob him; but much more to be gained in the long run if he didn't tell it.

It would be far better to see the American so aroused with pity for poor Amelia that he pays the ransom to get her back. How much? It would have to be a fortune. Why ask a millionaire for anything less?

Tavalera was confident the amount would be enough—once the money was confiscated and disappeared, the tricky part—to buy land, a home, several homes if he wished. One here, one on the peninsula of Varadero . . . There seemed always to be ways to supplement a lean military income. In the penal colonies of Africa they would write to the families of convicts, tell them a donation would buy needed food and clothes for their unfortunate loved ones. Pesetas arrived and the miserable inmates continued to starve and die of disease. Why not? It was their due.

What Tavalera saw now, Boudreaux entering, coming to the table, was far more than a few pesetas; he was looking at his retirement after the war.

A drink arrived for Boudreaux as he sat down, whiskey with crushed ice. He said not a word to the waiter, his gaze holding on the Guardia major.

"Yes?"

"Two of Andres Palenzuela's men, it turns out, are traitors."

"You telling me this because Andres is a friend of mine?"

"Andres is a friend of everyone. I tell you because one of the traitors is a friend of your man Victor Fuentes. They are the ones to consider, not our friend Andres."

Boudreaux remained silent as Tavalera told of the murder of his eight men in the escape of the cowboy and the marine, and told of Amelia Brown's presence as a hostage. When he had finished Boudreaux said, "She went riding with Novis and Victor and never came back." He reached into his coat for the note and handed it to Tavalera.

"Ah, I wondered," he said, unfolding the sheet of paper, stained and creased, and read, " 'My dearest Rollie,' " aloud. He looked at Boudreaux and went back to the note, reading the rest of it in silence. He finished, but continued to look at the note as he said, "The poor girl, she seem very frighten."

"I would imagine," Boudreaux said, "she's scared to death."

"Why do you think they want Novis to bring the money?"

"I wondered the same thing."

"He could be with them, uh? They offer him some of it?"

"He's stupid enough. By the same token Novis is dumb loyal. I tell him to stick his hand in the fire, he'll do it."

Tavalera looked at the note again. "Deliver to Matanzas . . . April twenty-seventh . . . I'm going to be in Matanzas at that time."

"So am I," Boudreaux said. "I'm going tomorrow. I still have a mill to run. I'm in business as long as I can keep my fields from getting burned."

"You have your *guerrilleros* for that, good men; I know many of them."

"They're capable, yeah, but you have to keep after them."

"Like any soldiers," Tavalera said, wanting to be agreeable, and paused before asking the important question. "So, you're going to pay the ransom?"

Then had to wait while Boudreaux sipped his whiskey, the American showing no emotion, nothing.

He said, "Do I have a choice?"

Tavalera eased back in his chair. He said, "You can at least appear to pay it."

"Give them what, my dirty laundry?"

"I mean if you don't have the money."

"That's not a problem."

They were getting to the tricky part.

"I'll be in Matanzas and a squad of my men will be on the train, but not in uniform, as men on business. I have to think how to do it, how to place my men to meet various situations. The details I can tell you in Matanzas. But to answer your question, no, don't send your laundry. Place the money in the pack, all of it, forty thousand dollars in American currency. What will you do, draw it from the bank here?"

"Yeah, but why, if you're gonna be there to arrest them?"

"In case we fail. In case they have a plan so good they get away with it. They have the money, they give back your sweetheart, that lovely girl. But if you try to fool them, well, maybe they kill her."

Boudreaux took a sip of whiskey. He said, "There's something I don't understand," getting out his tailor-made cigarettes. "Why they risked their lives to save this Tyler and the marine." He lit a Sweet Cap and put them away without offering the Guardia one. "There's no news value in those two anymore; all the correspondents have gone home."

"What was the risk? They come to Atarés intending to murder my people, took them by surprise. They did that to *me,* not to you. Tomorrow it will be announced, three thousand pesos reward for Tyler, as a fugitive dead or alive, and the same for the marine, Virgil Webster, an *indio* but he looks to be American."

"Part *indio,* I'm told," Boudreaux said. "I don't care what you do to them. What I want is Miss Brown back safe and sound. I'm telling you, Lionel, because I'm going to speak to the captain-general, see what he'll do about it."

"I can tell you," Tavalera said. "Blanco will point to the American fleet blockading the harbor, so scared he can hardly speak, and ask you to please don't bother him. No—listen, Rollie, what you do, leave this in my hands. I have eight dead men, a personal reason to do this for you. Trust me."

# 16

NEELY TUCKER WAS NEVER SURE when Islero told him something if it was the truth or if the old warrior was kidding with him.

He said they had a game called "the cracker" and asked Neely if he'd like to play. He said you put four or five hard salted crackers on a board and you hit them with your *miembro viril*—honest to God, your peter—and the one who broke the most crackers was the winner. One evening Neely did see the game played, the contestants betting money on their prowess, but that didn't make whatever else Islero said true.

He said they never took prisoners. Oh, they kept them a few minutes, until they made them kneel down and chopped their heads off with a machete, one blow, his people experts at this. Neely hadn't seen it done and didn't want to, either.

Islero said his father was Lucumí, originally from western Sudan in Africa. But could he actually know this? He said Lucumí was born rascals, the most rebellious of the people brought here as slaves, and the bravest.

The old man's ebony face always bore a gray stubble, about a week's growth of whiskers; he always wore a panama on the back of his head and a sagging, threadbare white suit. The only thing military about him were his boots and a pistol he wore on his hip. Sometimes the old man cooked. His men all cooked for themselves or in small groups, two meals a day. Whenever Islero invited a few of them to dine with him, they'd jump at the chance. All except Neely. He'd suffer from indigestion any time he ate yanyó, Islero's red-hot gumbo, or obatalá, the black-eyed pea stew. Islero would say don't worry, the *curandera* will make you a remedy from cow patties. You boil the dry patty and strain it through a fine cloth. Two dozen will fix you up. And Neely would say cow shit as a remedy? Thanks anyway.

Islero told him he had over four thousand men. Neely had never seen more than a few hundred in camp at one time. It was an orderly, fairly military camp—which surprised Neely—with a bugler to wake the boys up and sound retreat in the evening; silence after 9:00 P.M. The boys slept in hammocks in their drawers; whereas the dons slept fully clothed and with their horses saddled. Neely had observed this firsthand.

The old warrior said he kept his people here and there out in the country, most of them off burning cane fields, but all would return in time for the attack on Matanzas. Neely said, "Matanzas—you're joking." The old man said no, it was true, the time had come.

If it was and it came off, an insurgent offensive against the second largest city in Cuba, the event would give Neely the biggest story of the war, an exclusive for sure—if he could get his report to Key West and from there by wire to Chicago.

He would not only scoop the big New York papers, there would be an ironic twist to his eyewitness account: the armored cruiser *New York* taking a vital part in the offensive. The ship, already in Cuban waters, was on its way to Matanzas to blockade the port and shell San Severino, the old fort protecting the harbor. The way this information reached Islero: some of his scouts had made contact with an American gunboat prowling the north shoreline, its mission, to locate any Spanish warships U.S. Naval Intelligence might have missed. They believed that by now most of the Spanish fleet, outgunned and in hiding out at Santiago de Cuba, was way off on the southeastern edge of the island.

Islero's plan: Wait for the American fleet to shell the fort, blow it to dust with its big guns, and when the Spanish came pouring out, Islero's people would cut them down. He had an old Krupp fieldpiece in this camp—in the wooded hills south of the rail line,

between the villages of Ceiba Mocha and Benavides
—only ten miles from Matanzas. He had his scouts
spotted along the coast, waiting to report the coming
of the big American cruiser bristling with guns. He
told Neely to be ready, the *New York* should be off
the coast by April 27.

WAS HE READY to scoop the world and make a name
for himself? He'd better be. Neely sat beneath a
shade tree on the edge of Islero's camp to study his
notes, see what he had on Matanzas he could use to
open the piece. His long-range description wasn't
bad:

*The city enclosed by verdant hills on three sides, the
open view a prospect of the lush, emerald (?) countryside that seemed an abode of pastoral well-being.*

Features of the city in a closer look. He had
those notes somewhere. Don't panic. The popula-
tion figure he remembered, fifty-four thousand. A
center of commerce, but a shallow harbor. Lighters
used to unload ships.

*Has become known as the Birthplace of Indepen-
dence.* That was better than calling it a *Nest of Rebellion.*

War comes. *A prosperous metropolis is rendered
helpless, infirm (?). Sapped of its life by the cruel dom-
ination of Spanish rule.*

Get to the policy of reconcentrating the popula-
tion. *Thousands brought to Matanzas from the country-*

*side died: 10,000 in a period of only two months,
23,000 all told. Many starved to death. No money, no
way to earn it. Rice, their staple, sold for 75 cents a
pound. Bodies taken to San Severino's infamous "shark
hole," where the victims of Spanish malevolence were
fed each night to the ravenous sharks.*

A transition here might be from the sharks in the
water to the armored cruiser *New York* steaming
toward the port, its screws churning the water—
what he needed were the horsepower figures—
churning the water and creating, even for sharks, a
terrifying disturbance the likes of which . . .

This thought was in his mind, hearing the word
*disturbance,* in the same moment he heard gunfire
and voices raised—amazing, the coincidence—and
saw a number of Islero's boys running through the
trees toward the south side of the camp, a couple of
them firing their weapons in the air.

TYLER, BRINGING UP THE REAR, had a good seat for their
reception at the camp. Four mounted insurgents had
met them on the road below. Once they'd greeted
Fuentes, one of them led the parade up a switchback
trail worn into the slope and across a high meadow
toward a stand of trees on the other side. Now figures in white began to appear, coming out of the
gloom. One of them raised a pistol, fired into the air
and pretty soon others were shooting, giving them a
loud welcome. Now Fuentes was off his horse

embracing an old man in black riding boots, the two of them grinning, patting each other, Tyler taking the one in boots to be Islero. He sure didn't look like any kind of plague. Jesus, and there was Neely Tucker waving a notebook, running to Amelia, hugging her as soon as she was down. Now Virgil had dismounted and was stretching as he looked around at the commotion, all the little fellas in white making a to-do over their arrival. Tyler stepped down and looked off to the south at the patchwork of fields he'd studied all the way up the switchbacks: too far off to make out the crops, some burned black, but something familiar about the lay of the land, soft and warm in the glow of late afternoon.

THERE WAS SO MUCH to talk about. Neely hoped they'd all sit down together so he could ask questions and take notes; but having them all in one place didn't happen until suppertime.

Islero took Fuentes off to the big shebang he used as his headquarters: a roof of palm fronds over a wood framework and canvas sheets that rolled down to keep out the weather.

He did get Amelia aside long enough to hear about their visit to Atarés—my God, Amelia relating the gruesome details so calmly she seemed like a different person. Not so animated. And she *looked* different. She'd cut her lovely auburn hair, hacked it off so short it barely covered her delicate little ears.

*Why?* She said, fluffing what was left up there with her fingers, a drawing room hairdo was too much trouble out here, adding, "Ben likes it"—Ben Tyler —which struck deeply into Neely's heart. He watched her stroll off with Tyler to the south edge of the camp where they stood talking, Tyler pointing into the distance.

Virgil Webster, meanwhile, was telling some of Islero's boys—one of them interpreting—about the *Maine* and how she blew up. It gave Neely an idea. As soon as Virgil noticed him Neely said, "Ever been aboard the *New York?*" Virgil said one time off Norfolk for a prizefighting event, the fleet anchored out in the Roads. "Would you happen to know anything about her armament and engines?" Would he. Neely began writing as fast as he could. Six 8-inch rifles, a dozen 4-inchers, up to ten inches of armor around her turrets and barbettes. Her engines put out over seventeen thousand horsepower, giving the *New York* a top speed of twenty-one knots. Virgil was serious as he said, "What else you want to know?"

FINALLY THEY GATHERED at a board table under the trees, right outside Islero's hut, for a dinner prepared by the *curandera;* Islero saying if her food poisoned anyone she would prepare a remedy. The food was served on banana leaves: *sesos,* which was sheep brains fricasseed, a hash of rabbit and tomatoes, rice, beans and of course fried plantains. Thank God no yanyó or other dishes from Islero's days as a slave. He talked through the meal and when he paused, Fuentes would pick it up, the two of them telling stories about the Ten Years War, most of it in English, though words and phrases of Spanish would slip in as they drank clay cups of wine and then brandy.

Tyler finally got a word in, asking Islero if he knew of a sugar estate called Sagrada Familia. It was the *central* his father had managed.

Fuentes said, "Why you never ask that before? Sure, is one of the estates Boudreaux bought and added to his land. He had the house and the *central* torn down, they had been burned beyond use, and the ground turned for the planting of cane."

Tyler said the reason he asked, the country to the south, the fields and the hills beyond looked familiar.

Fuentes said, "Yes, Sagrada Familia was only a few miles south of here. And the next estate to the east—follow the railroad tracks you come to—is Boudreaux's."

Islero said, "Where he is now, since yesterday. My scouts learn he left the train at Limonar, the way he does, and rode to the estate surrounded by his *guerrilleros*." Islero said he hoped the war lasted long enough they could burn that place to the ground.

Neely had the feeling Tyler wanted to say something else, maybe ask another question, but didn't plan the taking of the train," smiling at Amelia, who was smoking a cigarette, her food barely touched.

Neely got in one question. "What train?"

"She didn't tell you?" Fuentes said. "The one bringing the ransom for Amelia, our hostage."

Neely said, "Now wait a minute," but didn't learn much more about it at the table: Fuentes and Islero at either end, Neely and Amelia on a bench across from Tyler and Virgil, Virgil's head lowered, the marine eating like it was his last meal. Now Fuentes was saying, "You can pay your men with the ransom as much as ten dollars each."

Islero eating, drinking, saying, "Yes, but they not use to having money. Some would put it in their pocket and leave the army."

Fuentes saying, "You tell them they have to give it to their families."

Tyler was staring at Amelia. Neely turned his head to see Amelia staring back at Tyler. The cowboy had been eating slowly, listening to the two old warriors, but still putting away the chuck, not passing up any of the dishes. He wasn't eating now, though, watching Amelia smoking her cigarette. She offered him one from the pack. He took it and slipped it in his shirt pocket. Islero saying, "What we might do is save the money, put it in a safe place and to distribute at the end of the war, when they would begin planting and need it the most. This is something we can talk about."

Now, as Fuentes was saying, "First, of course,

we have to remove the money from the train and from the hands of Boudreaux's man, Novis Crowe." Amelia got up from the table and walked away. Tyler watching her. Neely didn't miss that, Tyler's gaze following her until she was off through the trees.

And now Islero was saying, "There is nothing to stopping a train. Tomorrow I show you the bridge we blow up, a little way past Benavides, a small bridge, but enough for the purpose. What day is it coming?"

"The one after tomorrow," Fuentes said, "the twenty-seventh."

Neely got to say, "Wait a minute," but that was all. Virgil, looking up for the first time, beat him. He said, "You gonna blow her with dynamite, huh?"

"We use hollow bamboo," Islero said, "put the dynamite sticks in there and fix to it the cap and the electric wire."

Virgil nodded, chewing. "Good idea."

Finally Neely got to say, "But what about the assault on Matanzas?"

"Matanzas," Islero said, "will be there."

"But the *New York*'s coming on the twenty-seventh to shell the fort. Did you forget?"

Fuentes said, "An American warship?"

Islero was shaking his head. "We haven't been told without a doubt of it the exact day when it comes. It could be the next day or the one after. Who knows?"

"You told me," Neely said, "it was a sure thing, April twenty-seventh."

"Yes, as sure as one can be," Islero said, "knowing that nothing is certain."

"Will you tell me, please," Fuentes said, "what this is about?"

They began speaking in Spanish to one another, Neely listening hard but catching only a word here and there. Virgil continued eating. Tyler got up from the table and walked away. In the direction, Neely noticed, Amelia had taken.

THEY STOOD AT THE EDGE of pine trees close to each other, almost touching, both watching the sky going dark before their eyes. While they were out here before supper he told her about visiting the estate his father had managed, coming with his mother and sisters when he was nine. Today he had looked out at the pattern of fields and hills and believed he'd found it again.

"Now Boudreaux owns it."

She said, "You're going to see him, aren't you?"

"I have to collect what he owes."

"He won't pay you."

"Why not?"

"He'll have a reason. Even if he doesn't, how can you make him?"

"I can tell him why he should."

"He'll know you're a fugitive. By now you might even have a price on your head."

Tyler took off his hat and let it drop. He turned, putting a hand on her shoulder, saying, "Amelia?" and she looked up at him. He took her in his arms, felt her press against him and there was no more holding back. They started kissing each other, making sounds, their lips smacking till their mouths found the right fit and they stayed with it, making up for lost time. Finally when they took a breath she said, "Oh my." She said, "I didn't know if I'd have to hit you over the head and jump on you or what."

His hands kept moving around on her back, feeling delicate bones. He said, "You know how long I've wanted to hug and kiss you? Since the hotel. I kept looking at you."

"We couldn't have then, Rollie watching."

"When I was in the Morro and you came to visit?"

"Yeah, I thought we might, alone in that office."

"The time I almost did was in the cell at Atarés."

"I wanted you to. Didn't you know that?"

"All those people were there, and Victor was in a hurry."

"You sure could've kissed me before this."

"Most of the time I was awful smelly; I didn't want you to gag the first time we kissed. Then the other night I almost did."

"When I saw you naked. I thought that might break the ice."

"But you wanted to talk, worried about old Victor."

Amelia raised her face and they started kissing again, getting as much of each other as they could, Tyler, his eyes closed, floating in air with the feel and smell of this young girl. Was he finally doing this? His mouth brushed her cheek and he heard her sigh.

"Now it's his brother I'm worried about," Amelia said. "You heard him. He's not gonna pay his men."

"He said not right away."

"You believe that?"

"Well, not if you don't." At this point Tyler was not getting into any kind of argument with this girl.

She said, "I *know* he'll keep it for himself. I've known it since Victor told us about him. It's his way, the man was a bandit. The war ends, you think the Black Plague is gonna settle down and farm? What I have to do now, when the money's delivered, get hold of it before Islero hides it away."

"Then what?"

"I don't know. Run, I guess. What would you do?"

It reminded Tyler of Charlie Burke saying why he wanted him along: a partner who knew what it was like to ride the high country, have a price on his head. As Charlie Burke put it, "Somebody that's et the cake." Tyler kissed this sweet girl again, thoughts in his head, ones he'd had since the other night but wasn't sure how to word them. He had to try, though, and said, "The ransom being your idea . . . You did worry about Victor taking it, now you're sure Islero wants it. Did you ever have the idea, knowing all that, you ought to keep it for yourself?"

Amelia smiled at him in the dark. He saw her eyes shine before taking on a serious look.

She said, "Ben, I have to tell you the truth; I knew I would sooner or later, so I may as well tell you now. The whole idea of my being a hostage? The reason I thought of it was so I could get my hands on the money. Keep it for myself."

It stopped him cold.

She said, "You're ashamed of me."

He wasn't thinking that, not at all; he wanted to ask if she was serious.

But now Amelia was saying, "Ben, I came here seeking my fortune, the same as you, to be able to leave here with something worth the trip. I thought of the idea and I said, Oh my God, it's possible, it can happen. And the more I thought about it the more certain I was it could be done. That is," she said, and hesitated, "if I can get this bank robber I know to help me."

She looked up at him with that gleam in her eyes and Tyler couldn't help but smile. She meant it. Wanted him to help her steal forty thousand dollars. That's what she was saying. But if it was stealing, who were they stealing it *from*? Boudreaux? No, he was giving it away. Islero? He didn't have a claim to the money; giving it to him would be an act of charity. Forty thousand dollars, Jesus, if there was a way to do it . . . Why not? Take it off the train, from Novis? The idea, she said, get hold of it before Islero hid it away. But how? He said, "I have to ask you something."

"How we're gonna do it?"

"Well, that, yeah. No, I wondered what I'm suppose to get out of it, as your little helper."

"Half, twenty thousand."

"You're serious, aren't you?"

"You bet I am. It's gonna happen too."

"You have it worked out?"

"So far so good," Amelia said. "The only thing I didn't plan on was falling in love with the bank robber."

FUENTES AND ISLERO WERE STILL at the table, a kerosene lamp between them. Fuentes motioned to Tyler, coming from the tent where they kept their stores, Tyler with a rolled-up hammock and blanket under each arm. "You keeping house with her now?" Tyler didn't answer and Fuentes said, "Never mind, it's your business. But listen, we want to know, you going to see Boudreaux, uh?"

"First thing tomorrow."

"He won't pay you."

"Maybe."

"I tell you, he won't."

"All right, what do you advise?"

"Don't go. But you will, uh? So Islero wants me to tell you something. You have trouble with him and somehow you escape, his guerrillas chasing you, don't come back here. You understand? Don't come near this place."

Tyler left them. He came to Virgil's hootch, Virgil in a hammock beneath a shelter of palm fronds. Tyler stopped as Virgil said, "Hey, partner? You gonna see that man owes you money, I'm going with you."

"You want to?"

"I need to."

Tyler reached the shelter where Amelia stood waiting. He dropped the hammocks and she said, "We have to sleep in those?"

"Or on the ground."

She said, "What's wrong with that?"

# 17

SIX A.M. VIRGIL FOLLOWED TYLER down the narrow switchbacks, their horses brushing vegetation still wet with dew. They were up with the bugle call, had coffee and checked their weapons; then Virgil had to wait as Tyler and Amelia stood talking before kissing good-bye. Virgil asked Tyler since he'd been with her all night what could they have left to talk about. He could kid Tyler, but knew better than to make a crude remark. Tyler said he would tell him on the way. Not kidding, making it sound mysterious.

Virgil had traded a Mauser carbine for a Krag-Jorgensen five-shot magazine rifle, the one the U.S. Army was now using. He carried it straight up, the stock resting on his thigh, and a bandoleer holding sixty cartridges. Islero told him a Remington did more damage, accounting for more kills and requiring more amputations; but Virgil liked the Krag on account of it firing a smokeless round. Tyler was armed with the matched pair of Smith & Wesson .44 Russians, one in a holster butt forward beneath his black suit coat and the other in his saddlebag. He had taken good care of that coat, not wearing it much while they were locked up. Virgil was still wearing the blue uniform pants Molina had given him at the Morro, now raggedy and filthy, and a Spanish military straw with the insignia torn off. He needed some fresh duds, but there weren't any clothes among the camp stores. Islero's crew looked mostly like beggars, some even without shoes or sandals, though every single one of them carried a machete, you could bet on that, and were armed to the teeth.

Once down that high slope they struck out east, the sun showing now in a dip between the range of hills. They kept single file along a row of palm trees Virgil recognized as date palms, a kind he had seen before in his travels with the fleet. The trees divided burned-out cane fields on both sides, brittle stalks creaking as the wind stirred. They climbed a defile, the dip between the hills, and found the railroad tracks down the other side, the tracks and a telephone line showing the way. Riding south now, side by side, Tyler looked over. "Amelia says Boudreaux has a horse saddled every morning by seven and goes for a ride."

"By himself?"

"With some of his army along."

"They the enemy?"

"They are if they shoot at us."

Fuentes had told them it was about four kilometers from here to the estate. They rode along in silence until Tyler looked over again.

"Amelia doesn't trust Islero. She says he's gonna keep the forty thousand dollars."

"I thought that was the idea."

"For himself, not give it up."

"Yeah?"

"She wants me to help her grab it and make a run."

"Yeah?"

"The war's almost over. . . ."

"You mean steal it?"

"Amelia says it'll have her name on it, so it must be hers. Or you can look at it as not belonging to anyone, there for the taking."

"That the way you see it?"

"Like the spoils of war. Why not?"

"You want me along? Is that what we're talking about here?"

"You and I'd draw ten thousand apiece. Amelia gets the whole other half account of she's the reason Boudreaux's paying and it's her idea. What do you say?"

"Well, I'd sure never pass up a chance to get rich. It's lucky me and you are the only white boys around, huh?"

Tyler jumped on that. "She's got other friends."

"Like who, that squirt Neely? Listen, I ain't arguing with you. Whatever her reason she wants us, it's fine with me."

LAST NIGHT TYLER AND AMELIA brought their hammocks and blankets to the trees along the edge of the slope to make a bed on the pine needles, Tyler putting off what he wanted to tell her until, finally, he couldn't keep it to himself.

"You didn't have to say you love me."

The words came out of a silence and he was sorry as he heard them, sounding so serious. Amelia, on her knees spreading a blanket, looked up at him.

"I didn't?"

"Just so I'd go with you."

She rose and kept looking at him as she undid the skirt she wore over the pair of trousers, let the skirt slip to her feet and stepped out of it. All she said was "My, my."

"I couldn't help but think it."

"I see myself as trade goods. Is that what you're saying?"

"What'd you tell Boudreaux?"

She said, "Ah, it's not as simple as you make it sound. Did I tell Rollie I love him? We could discuss what I did with him, and maybe with others you don't know about? That could take a while and you might be more confused than you are now." Amelia began unbuttoning her shirt. "Why don't we keep it simple and get undressed. You don't sleep in your clothes, do you, Ben? Let's wait till we're in bed, bare naked, then decide if you want to talk or what."

THEY SAW SMOKE RISING in clouds and pretty soon a pair of tall chimneys and Virgil said, "That must be it."

"The mill," Tyler said. "And there's the house." A plain, two-story structure made of stone, a fort with verandas. He had expected the house to be painted a bright color, more dressed up, flower gardens close around it. He couldn't see Amelia tending a garden, but she might've had it done. He realized he was looking for signs of her.

She had told him to sit down and she'd pull off his boots, saying she didn't want to get spurred and asked why he wore those big rowels. He told her he liked the sound they made, the *ching*, when he walked.

Virgil said, "I don't see nobody around."

When he and Amelia were undressed and before they got under the blanket, he knew that first sight of her naked would be with him the rest of his life. She asked if he still wanted to talk. Saying it now, she was having fun with him and he didn't have to answer. He remembered wanting to see her like that in daylight, though what he saw under the moon and stars would be enough.

The railroad tracks and telephone line were taking them through a field of scrub now, curving toward the mill, the chimneys rising above the main works, a factory stretching out into farmland with wings and sheds and stables part of it, the mill structures covering a good acre. They could make out oxcarts loaded with cane stalks in the yard close to the mill, a gang of workers pulling stalks from a cart and feeding them on to a conveyor that took the cane into the works.

They came to a dirt road where an oxcart, an old one missing a wheel, had been left there to rot. Tyler pulled up.

"How far to the house, couple hundred yards?"

"About." Virgil squinted. "Or a speck less."

"How about if you stay here and cover me?"

"I can do that."

"If I come running . . ."

"I'll be right here," Virgil said.

Tyler watched him get down and lay the Krag across the tilted-up side of the oxcart, the barrel aimed at the mill. At sunup this morning Virgil had tested the Krag, firing a magazine of five rounds to see how the rifle behaved and another five to see how fast he could fire and throw the bolt, Tyler watching him. Virgil said he had the eyesight for this work, he could see a mile and find his way in the dark.

Tyler nudged his mount to a trot, toward the mill and the house centered within a sweep of cane fields north to south, streets of workers' living quarters off beyond the mill. He kept his gaze on the house where several horses, four of them, were tied to a hitch rail near the side entrance. Reaching the mill yard he slowed to a walk, then dismounted among the workers pausing to look him over and led his mount toward an open section of the mill. He stood looking in, images of Amelia flashing in the gloom; he could not stop thinking about her—touching her lying beneath the blanket, her eyes closed and then opening, Amelia looking at him as she said, "Do you love me, Ben?"

He stepped into the gloom to look at the machinery pounding, grinding away, the sound of it bringing back the steps he remembered of the process: the shredder tearing the stalks apart, the crusher squeezing out the sweet juice they called *guarapo*—surprised he remembered that—the husks going into the furnace to make steam, while the juice flowed into the centrifuge to be refined, lime added to produce granulation, the liquid molasses drained off. . . . A man's voice in English said, "You have business here?"

Coming toward him, a man who'd be in his fifties, bearded, reserved, sounding more curious than here to stand in Tyler's way. One of the engineers.

"I'm in the horse business," Tyler said, "but my dad ran a *central* twenty years ago and I visited once. The noise is the same, but I don't recognize much of the machinery." He didn't want to stand here talking and said, "I'm looking for Boudreaux."

The engineer's gaze moved past Tyler to the house. "Mr. Boudreaux's home. I saw him ride in a little while ago." He looked at Tyler again. "I assume you're not one of the lawless liberators we have around here, though plenty Americans will be joining them now war's been declared."

Even knowing it was coming the man's words surprised him. Tyler said, "When was this?"

"Two days ago, the twenty-fourth. It's going to be interesting. American boys here making war against people we consider our friends. I say that even knowing they represent a medieval autocracy. I'm surprised you hadn't heard."

"I've been on the road," Tyler said, a strange feeling of relief coming over him: the war had begun and he was in it because he was American and he was here. It seemed to simplify his understanding of his role, knowing he liked the idea of being in a real war. He wouldn't have to wonder anymore what he was doing here.

He asked the engineer, "What will happen to this estate?"

The engineer said, "What will *happen* to it?" Sounding surprised. Maybe not understanding what Tyler meant. He said, "Nothing," still with that tone of surprise.

What Tyler wanted to ask was what side he was

on; but then realized this engineer was in his own world and it had nothing to do with war.

"I better go see Boudreaux," Tyler said, and moved off, led his mount through the congestion of workers and oxcarts and piles of cane stalks toward the house, looking at the four horses now tied to the rail.

One of them was his dun mare.

At the house Tyler dismounted, looking at the open double doors of the side entrance. He took off the dun's saddle and hung it on the rail, loosened the reins, tied them to his saddle horn and looped the reins of the horse that had brought him over the tie rail.

He walked through the open side doors to see three men in gray uniforms, their hats on, two with crossed cartridge belts, at a plain wood table having coffee. They stared at him. A colored woman appeared, skin and bones, wearing a turban, looking at him scared. He said, "I'm here to see Mr. Boudreaux," and that did the trick.

She took him up a staircase that turned once to reach the second floor, through a doorway and there he was at a polished dining table, a bowl of fruit sitting on it, with coffee and a copy of *Harper's Weekly* open in front of him. He looked up at Tyler's sound, the *ching . . . ching*, and they were once again face-to-face. Tyler started right in.

"I'm here to collect what you owe me, and I'll take my mare since she's right outside and wasn't part of the deal. I'll forget wharfage and feed in Havana to keep it simple; so all you owe is one-fifty for thirty mounts, or forty-five hundred dollars. That sound right to you?"

Boudreaux took time to ease back in his chair, still looking at Tyler. He hadn't taken his eyes from him, Rollie sitting there in a tan suit that looked like a hunting outfit, bullet loops in the pockets. What he said was "You know you're a wanted outlaw."

"Not anymore; we're at war. What do you think of it?"

"What do I *think*?"

He sounded like the mill engineer.

"I'll ask it another way. What side are you on?"

Boudreaux raised his eyebrows, like this was something he hadn't thought of till now. He said, "I'm not at war with anyone," with that soft accent of his.

"If I'd known you before," Tyler said, "I never would've agreed to sell you the string. I don't do business with tinhorns. But since I have, I expect you to pay what you owe, forty-five hundred."

"Your horses were taken by the Spanish Army."

"You mean *your* horses."

"In any case," Boudreaux said, gesturing with open hands, "they're not here."

"You still owe me," Tyler said. "You buy horses, you have to pay for them. It's how it works in business."

Boudreaux kept staring at him until, out of

nowhere, he said, "And where's my dear friend Amelia Brown?"

It caught Tyler by surprise. He said, "I came here to talk about your debt and that's all."

"Where is she?"

"She isn't any of my business."

"No, you're wrong," Boudreaux said. "If you don't tell *me* where she is, my men will hand you over to the Guardia and you'll have to tell *them*. Else they'll break some of your bones, cut off your hands. . . ." Boudreaux gave a little shrug in his neat hunting suit. "They're mean boys."

The smug son of a bitch.

The smug wavy-haired son of a bitch.

Tyler stepped up to the table wanting to hit him, but would have to go over it to reach him sitting back in his chair. He leaned over it, planting his hands on the polished surface to get as close to Boudreaux as he could.

"You're gonna pay me."

"How, write you a check? Say you put a gun to my head to make me. Where're you going to find a bank to cash the check? You're going back to Havana? No, our business is finished. I'll get to the people holding Amelia. Your purpose now—you walked in here, let's see if you can walk out."

In that quiet, reasonable tone of voice.

Tyler pushed up from the table, nothing left to say that wouldn't sound dumb, a wasted threat. He turned and walked off, got to the doorway before he looked back. There was a fact he ought to mention.

"You call your dogs, somebody'll get killed."

Boudreaux said, "I imagine that's so."

The son of a bitch.

Tyler went down the staircase. The three soldiers were no longer at the table. And their horses, he saw from the doorway, were gone from the tie rail. His horse was there, the dun's reins tied to the saddle horn. Maybe with luck . . . But in that moment heard Boudreaux's voice, Boudreaux yelling "Get him!" from the upstairs veranda. And saw the three soldiers then, off past the back of the house, walking their horses toward the rows of living quarters, those stone houses back there, the three of them coming around at the sound of Boudreaux's voice. Tyler mounted and got out of there, leading the dun.


THE KRAG WAS HEAVIER than the Mauser carbine, weighed nine pounds and had a kick, but felt good, Virgil's cheek to the stock, and had that clean smell of oil. He had spotted riders way off at the edge of cane, four hundred yards, who appeared military the way they rode single file, seven of them. They didn't look this way, which was a good thing, as he'd tried with no luck to get his horse to lie down.

Once Tyler had crossed from the mill to the house Virgil kept his front sight on it, watching from

behind the Krag balanced on the side of the tipped
oxcart. He watched the three fellas in uniform come
out and look at the horse Tyler had taken the saddle
from. Having a discussion in their fairly smart gray
uniforms. Virgil said, "And look at you in your old
hand-me-downs." The blue officer pants and pair of
sandals coming apart he'd got from the camp stores.
The three looked up at the second floor of the house,
but then must've decided the bareback horse wasn't
any of their business. They mounted and moved off
toward the back of the house.

It wasn't half a minute later a man in a light-
colored suit, maybe a uniform, appeared on the
veranda up there and began yelling *Get him!* Now
Tyler was back outside and in a hurry to mount and
leave whatever kind of rumpus he'd started.

Virgil sighted on Tyler coming this way, Tyler
and the bareback horse running with him shielding
the three coming hard behind him. He must've realized it, for he swerved, cutting off at an angle and
there they were. Virgil took his breath in and fired,
*bam,* and a horse tumbled headfirst and landed on
top of its rider. Damn. He wasn't aiming at the
horse. Virgil threw the bolt, put his sights on
another one, *bam,* and it took the rider out of his
saddle, the horse running free. Tyler was cutting
back toward him now, fast—Jesus, reining in and
swinging down as the horse was still moving, the
bareback one too. Tyler yanked on the reins and
brought them around. Looking back then he yelled,

"Shoot him!" But Virgil waited, his sights on the third one coming like a racehorse, the rider shooting a revolver as fast as he could thumb the hammer and fire, a brave man, set on riding right over them, twenty yards away when Virgil blew him out of his saddle. Now Tyler was yelling, "Where you going?" to Virgil running out to this third one he'd shot in the face and was lying dead. The man looked to be an officer by his uniform, taller than most, Virgil hoping to hell he was the right size and saw he was wearing boots, black ones. Virgil worked them from the man's feet, undid his belt and pulled his pants off, plain gray ones that could've been washed and ironed this morning. Way better than these fancy blue officer pants he'd been wearing what seemed half his life. Virgil switched hats with the soldier, putting on a gray felt that fit okay.

Tyler was standing there watching, not saying a word as Virgil came running back with his new pants and boots. He said to Tyler, "We best scoot for cover. There some other of those fellas around."

They rode hard following the train tracks till they came to the dip in the hills lying to the west, the way back to Islero's camp. Tyler reined in and said to Virgil, "War's been declared; it's official."

Virgil would've jumped up in the air if he wasn't mounted, excited, but still wanting to be sure. "How do you know?"

"Take my word," Tyler said, "it's finally happened. Go on back and tell them. I'm gonna keep north, toward Matanzas."

"What for?"

"I have to go to the bank."

# 18

TAVALERA WOULD LEAVE HAVANA for Matanzas on the twenty-sixth with a picked squad of men. Boudreaux's rustic bodyguard, Novis Crowe, would leave the next day with the bundle of money. Guardias in plainclothes would be aboard the train to keep an eye on him, see he didn't get off somewhere along the line.

That was the plan.

But then orders were received: Take the 2d Corps to Matanzas on the twenty-sixth. Yes? That part was all right. To reinforce the 12th Battalion de Asuntas at San Severino, the old fortress. That part was not all right, but had to be. Ships of the American fleet were lying six miles off the coast and our troops were working night and day to build earthworks along the Punta, the high ground, for the placement of artillery outside the fortress. Inside the historic walls were sixty-nine cannon, nearly all from an earlier period, big cumbersome pieces. Tavalera wanted to say to his commandant, "We're cavalry, not artillery. How are we expected to man those relics?" But of course he didn't. Tavalera never questioned his orders.

The problem it presented: How could he be at the station to greet Novis, and confiscate the bundle of money, if he was at San Severino, under fire from American ships? With war declared they were sure to attack.


VIRGIL RETURNED to Islero's camp leading Tyler's dun. Barely off his horse, there was Amelia Brown looking scared to death seeing him alone.

"I left him he was alive and full of spunk," Virgil said, to put her mind at ease. "But the man wouldn't pay him, so Tyler went to Matanzas."

It only settled her a little. She said, "Oh, my God, he's gonna rob the bank," knowing Tyler pretty well, it seemed, for having spent one night with him.

"He said to tell you he'll be back in plenty of time for the train business tomorrow."

When he let the others know what happened Fuentes shook his head, saying, "I told him the man wouldn't pay." He did not think they would ever see Tyler again. Virgil let him think what he wanted. He announced America was now at war with the dons and that stirred everybody up, got them firing their weapons into the air.

After that, Islero's fellas sat down to clean and reload their pieces, and sharpen their machetes. They had long ones for when they charged on horseback, short ones for close-in fighting and some machetes that looked like meat cleavers. Islero and some others were fixing dynamite charges, dropping the sticks into three-foot sections of bamboo, then sealing them up with a primer inside attached to a roll of electric wire.

Virgil heard that during the night Islero had moved his Krupp fieldpiece to bear on a Spanish blockhouse guarding the approach to a place called Guanabana, a few miles east of here. Virgil asked Islero how come and Islero said, "To draw flies." Which didn't make sense to Virgil.

Dinner being over, the *curandera,* a woman who looked about a hundred years old, fixed Virgil a plate at Islero's table: calalú, which was cornmeal and pork, and masango, boiled corn. She liked Virgil and would pat his shoulder acting motherly, saying what sounded like "Good boy," when he cleaned his plate. Neely Tucker came over while he was eating.

Neely agitated, sitting down on the bench across from Virgil and then getting up to pace back and forth by the table. What was upsetting him: "First Islero says he's gonna attack Matanzas, time it for when the *New York* starts shelling the fort."

"Yeah . . . ?"

"Now he says they can't count on the fort being shelled. And if it isn't, his men will be at the mercy of a superior force and get cut to pieces. But the real reason, he wants that hostage money more'n he wants glory. So he's playing the sure thing; and maybe for his own benefit, if you know what I mean."

This was something Virgil already knew, what Amelia Brown suspected and Tyler had mentioned to him. So he said, "Yeah . . . ?" not yet seeing the point. "What do you want me to do about it?"

"Go to Matanzas with me," Neely said. "Help me cover the biggest engagement of the war."

"It only started two days ago."

"And already we're in action," Neely said. "The *New York* will have gunboats with her, most likely a torpedo boat, maybe even a monitor. I need to witness the event from shore, see what the Spanish do. And then I'll have to leave Cuba in order to file my story."

"How you gonna do that?"

"Signal a gunboat to pick me up. Tyler was telling me you know semaphore, how to wave flags to send a message?"

"He told you that?"

"Said in prison you spelled his name for him."

"Yeah, but what you're talking about—Jesus Christ, a battle's going on. You think a ship'll come in under enemy fire to pick you up?"

"An American on Cuban soil," Neely said,

"with a story to tell the people back home. How our navy, our fighting marines, are on the attack and by God nothing's gonna stop them. Isn't that worth a try, Virgil?"

BY MID-AFTERNOON of the twenty-sixth, Tavalera's 2d Corps was manning the San Severino ramparts facing the American ships: three of them now, one identified as the armored cruiser *New York*, another said to be the *Puritan*, a monitor with a giant smokestack and four 12-inch rifles. The ships were somewhat east of the fortress, lying off the Punta, where artillery was still being moved into place.

Late that evening Tavalera left the fortress and rode a short distance to a cottage only a few blocks from the south shore in a poor section of Matanzas known as Pueblo Nuevo. A mulatta he called Isabela Católica, his black queen, lived here awaiting his visits to the city, to pour his whiskey, to make love to him, to listen as he told her secrets from his soul he told no one else.

"In the morning an emissary of the governor will take a launch out to the American flagship to ask if they intend to bombard the city. If it is their intention, the emissary will ask for time to evacuate noncombatants, the terror-stricken people hiding inside their homes. The American commander will say no, no, we only intend to destroy your fucking gun emplacements and your fucking historic fortress and kill as many of your fucking soldiers as we can." He said to his mistress, "So in the morning, early, leave here."

The mulatta asked when she would see him again and he said perhaps never.

"We are certain to lose this war, one I've been waiting for; and yet I don't want to go to the fortress tomorrow. I'm not afraid to die; understand that. But I don't want to be killed by a gun fired at me from six thousand meters. When I die I want the opportunity first to kill the one who kills me and when I fail, I fail and that's the end of it. So I have a choice to make."

The mulatta caressed him in her arms and tried to soothe him saying he should close his eyes and sleep, not drink more of the whiskey.

He said, "The train coming here stopped at Benavides and I saw an American I know, a very rich planter. He told me the captain of his Volunteers, a fine young man named Rafi Vasquez, was killed this morning by an American cowboy who took the boots and pants from Rafi's dead body and also killed two of his men. He shot the horse of one that fell on its rider and crushed him to death. I know this American who killed them, his name is Tyler. He and others killed eight of my men escaping from prison." Tavalera said to the mulatta, "Do you know what I think? It would be better to find this Tyler and kill him than to be killed myself at San Severino by sailors I would never see. I think this cowboy is going to be waiting for a train tomorrow." He took a sip of whiskey and said, "Find your brother for me."

Her brother Osma, who in another time was a hunter of runaway slaves; now he hunted mambís.

"Tell him to come here tomorrow, early."

TYLER'S PROBLEM, he couldn't find a bank.

He spent half the day working his way down through the range of hills south of Matanzas. From up there it looked like it would be easy to find his way around. There it was, laid out in a grid of streets, two rivers, the Yurumí and the San Juan, running through the city to the harbor. But once he was down there it became narrow little streets one after another, and Tyler had no idea where he was going. He didn't expect the city to be this big, even though some of the old patriots at the Morro were from here and loved to talk about their city, how beautiful it was. If he'd known then, he could've asked them where a goddamn bank was. Another problem was keeping out of the way of Spanish soldiers, though most of them seemed in a hurry with a lot on their mind. From up in the hills he had noticed the road lined with trees that went along the east side of the harbor to a fort like the Morro, out on a point of land. Down closer he saw troops and equipment moving up the road, horses pulling artillery, everybody going to the fort and nobody coming back. Tyler came down through outcrops of rock to a limestone quarry, deserted, and rode past farmhouses made of palm bark without seeing anybody around. Finally when he got to the Yurumí River he asked an old man scraping the bottom of his skiff where he could find a bank, a *banco*. The old man said he didn't know. Tyler asked another man down the way who said he didn't know of any banks. Not, he didn't know where one was, he didn't know if there even *was* a bank. Tyler felt people watching him. Not any he saw, but knew there had to be people in these houses and stores, and if they heard him clopping along the street would look out the window. What he'd better do, Tyler decided, go back to the quarry, about a mile up the hill, and hide out there till dark. Then come down and roam the streets till he found a bank, get one located, and come back in the morning.

That's what he did. Sat waiting for dark in an empty office down in the quarry, thinking about his night with Amelia Brown, hearing her say, "Do you love me, Ben?" And his own voice in the dark saying, "Yes, I do." And then Amelia asking, "Can you say it?" Something he'd never done in the thirty-one years of his life. He had shot four men—no, five—had taken their lives, but had never said "I love you" to a girl. Or to anyone.

"Do you love me, Ben?"

"Yes, I do. Very much."

"Can you say it?"

He whispered it against her cheek. "I love you."

Hearing it again in his thoughts it didn't sound too bad.

THE MULATTA SERVED THEM coffee in the early morning of the twenty-seventh, the two leaning on the table to conspire: her lover in his uniform talking, talking —it was what he did—and her brother listening, Osma the slave hunter resting on his thick arms, Osma nodding, Osma raising the cup to sip coffee through his beard. The mulatta hated her brother. No longer a hunter he murdered people for the Guardia, performed whatever obscene work they gave him. She listened, refilling their cups, to her lover telling about a train coming from Havana. Mambís wanting to stop it. Perhaps blow up the tracks. Her lover asking Osma to follow the tracks this afternoon and find this place where it could happen. With luck be a witness to the assault, and if the mambís are successful, follow them. Look for something wrapped in a hammock. Look for an American, a cowboy. Perhaps a woman will be there, too, and perhaps Victor Fuentes.

"They have something you want?"

"Why else do I tell you this?"

Osma left and the mulatta watched her lover button the neck of his tunic and strap on his pistol. She said, "You've changed your mind. You're going to the fortress to die."

"I have to see for myself," Tavalera said, "if American gunners are able to kill me."

NOVIS CROWE BOARDED THE 8:30 TRAIN to Matanzas at the Regla station, took his seat in the first-class coach and sat with the rolled hammock across his lap, his hands folded on it. He hadn't actually seen Mr. Boudreaux put money inside, but believed he must've; he'd gone to the bank the day before yesterday with a briefcase and was in the office of the bank president a long time. Men coming along the aisle would look at Novis like they knew what he had. He could tell the businessmen. Some others he could tell by their mustaches and the way they carried themselves were Guardia Civil, even though they weren't in uniform. A couple, he noticed, brought leather gun cases aboard. Oh, going out for some bird shooting? Bullshit, these boys only shot people. Novis had a Colt revolver on him. He wouldn't mind if there was trouble. Hell, 'specially if he was the one caused it. The cane seat was comfortable enough. The windows had shutters on them you could raise or lower to keep out the sun. He sat on the side of the train that would face north this trip, out of the sun. He was sweating in his wool suit. One thing you could say for the greasers, they knew how to dress for this weather, damper'n Newerleans. About 8:45 he said to the conductor going by in his white coat, "Hey, what're we waiting on?" The conductor said the train would be delayed an hour, perhaps for repair of the tracks, the usual reason.

It gave Novis some more time to look at his situation. There was no way he could have a plan. Not with those Guardia people in the same car. But if something *did* happen—six Guardias and he had six rounds in his Colt, didn't he—he'd have to be ready to take it. Walk off with forty thousand smackers.

Yeah, if that's what was in here.

THE BANK TYLER LOCATED was on Salamanca, three blocks from the Yurumí River and across the street from a park full of palm trees—one old man sitting on a bench. Tyler stepped from his horse and dallied the reins to a young tree at the street edge of the park, across from the Banco de Comercio. Tyler remembered Fuentes in Galveston saying the name of Boudreaux's bank in Havana, so this was a branch of it. Fine. He crossed the street with saddlebags over his shoulder and entered the bank, the place quiet and dim, the only sound coming from a ceiling fan, no lights on, no customers either. Tyler crossed the marble floor to a teller's window in a partition of dark wood and ornamental glass. He said good day to the teller, lifted the saddlebags from his shoulder and shoved one of them across the counter. The teller, a little bald-headed gink, looked at it and then up at Tyler.

"Yes, may I help you?"

Tyler said, "I'm withdrawing forty-five hundred dollars from Mr. Roland Boudreaux's account," and waited as the teller looked at the saddlebag again, his expression pleasant enough.

He said, "You have authorization?"

Tyler said, "Right here," and produced a .44 Russian he pointed at the teller, the butt resting upright on the counter.

The teller, the poor guy, looked like he couldn't believe his eyes.

"You robbing the bank?"

Tyler shook his head. "I'm robbing Mr. Boudreaux. Debit his account and tell him the next time he's in."

The teller stood so still he appeared dipped in starch.

Tyler asked him, "What're you waiting for?"

The teller answered, "I don't have American money here. I have to get it."

He was lying. Tyler saw his eyes shift and heard a voice behind him say in Spanish, "Close the bank." Tyler holstered the revolver, lifted the saddlebags and hung them over his left shoulder. He turned to see two Guardias with carbines as one of them was saying, again, "Close the bank. The Americans are coming."

The second Guardia said, "One is already here."

Tyler understood them. He said, "I'm not a soldier."

The second Guardia said, "What are you?"

The teller answered, calling to them, "He's robbing the bank!"

Now the first Guardia approached Tyler, looking him in the face, holding his gaze as he pulled Tyler's revolver from its holster and stepped back, the second Guardia saying, "I ask you again, what are you?"

Tyler hooked a thumb over his shoulder, in the direction of the teller. "He doesn't comprehend what I want. There is no problem here, no *problema*. Here, let me show you," Tyler said, with his left hand lifting the flap of the saddlebag hanging in front of him. "No, I didn't take anything from him." Now he slipped his right hand into the bag saying, "Here, look," and brought out the matching .44 Russian, cocking it in the first Guardia's face, giving the man no chance to use the revolver he had taken. Tyler put his hand out and the Guardia returned the revolver. Now with a .44 in each hand Tyler told them to unload their weapons and throw them out the door. When this was done Tyler told them if they came outside he'd shoot them. He walked out of the bank past the two carbines lying in the street, telling himself they weren't armed now, they weren't carrying pistols, so he could mount and ride out maybe with the two shouting after him, but that'd be all. . . . Unless there was a gun in the bank, and in that moment thinking it became sure there was.

Almost to the other side of the street he turned

to see the Guardia in the bank doorway aiming a
pistol at him, firing as Tyler fired, hit him with a .44
round and the Guardia went down. But now the second Guardia was taking the pistol from the first
one's hand. Watching him Tyler thought the man
must be crazy. Why would he think he had time?
Tyler yelled at him, "Put it down!" knowing he
wouldn't, saw the pistol come up and fired twice this
time, blowing the man back into the bank, leaving
the two lying dead.

He rode north on Salamanca, a deserted street,
no one watching or yelling after him, no sounds
from anywhere, the green range of hills waiting for
him, and the explosions began. Loud and not far
away. Tyler looked back knowing it was artillery
fire, and the answering thunder broadsides from the
American ships, the war creeping up behind him.

NEELY GOT ONE of Islero's scouts, a kid named Emilio,
to act as their guide and take them to the coast just
west of Matanzas. Virgil thought the squirt looked
about twelve, his rifle way too big for him, and
asked how old he was. Emilio said sixteen.

"What do you know," Virgil said, "my same age
when I joined the Marines."

In sight of the coast they left their horses in a
thicket and struck out afoot, Virgil carrying his Krag
and semaphore flags he'd made tying cloth from
wornout clothing to a couple of cane stalks three feet

long, the flags rolled together and stuck in his belt. He said if he got hungry he could eat them.

Neely was puffing to keep up with their kid guide. Once they reached the shore Emilio scooted through sea grape and palmetto, all kinds of vegetation, no trouble at all. He'd stop now and again to hack a path with his machete and it would give Neely a chance to catch his breath. He never complained though, Virgil would give him that. They were in the scrub when the firing commenced, that *ka-boom* of long guns opening up, giving Virgil a thrill knowing it was the U.S. Navy, here to settle the dons' hash.

They crept up to an open view, on the west side of where the harbor narrowed and met the sea. There was the mighty fortress across the way and, through a haze of smoke, American warships no more than two miles out in the stream. Busy, their long guns blazing away with port broadsides, fire shooting out of their big muzzles to raise a wall of smoke. Virgil, Neely and Emilio lay on their stomachs watching the guns making direct hits on the fortress, chunks of it blowing up in the air, and on the earthworks, mounds of sand they could see on the high ground just beyond.

"Them're ships of the North Atlantic Squadron under Admiral Sampson," Virgil said, pride in his voice. "The one in the middle's the *New York*, the flagship. The one with the rigging? It should be the *Cincinnati*, another cruiser. And the one leading the parade is the *Puritan,* the biggest monitor in the fleet with four 12-inch rifles. You punch an electric firing key and"—just then one of its guns fired—"*ka-boom!* You ever hear anything like that in your life, Emilio?" The kid shook his head, too intent on the fireworks to speak. Virgil was grinning. "Give 'em hell, boys. Those 12-inch rifles, each one's throwing seven hundred fifty pounds of metal at the dons. Look at that, pounding the shit out of the fort. There'll be a hot time in the old town tonight, boys. Now the *Puritan*'s coming over this way."

A Spanish battery dug in on this side of the narrows—only a couple hundred yards from the three lying there in the brush—opened up on the monitor, the cannon firing one after the other. The *Puritan* turned her forward turret on the site. Flame and smoke shot out of her rifles and the dug-in battery was blown to pieces. "Gone from this earth," Virgil said.

Neely, watching the monitor, said, "She sure is low to the water," thinking: *A raft whose guns belch fire and white-hot hell to bring death to the Spaniard.*

"Her deck's barely three feet above the waterline, but her stack towers, don't it? She's sweet-looking, but don't give me no part of monitor duty in a high sea."

"She's coming in," Neely said. "Taking rifle fire now, from the fortress. Watch yourselves, lads, don't get too close."

The *Puritan* let go with one of her long guns,

threw a shell into the fort, exploding, and the rifle fire stopped.

Virgil said, "Boy, I wouldn't want to be in there. Would you, Emilio?"

The kid said, "*¿Cómo?*"

Neely's gaze was still on the monitor. "She's coming in awfully close."

"Looking for targets," Virgil said.

Neely pushed up to his knees. "What's the matter with me—I said don't come too close? What is she now, about two hundred yards out?"

"Less," Virgil said.

Neely reached over to pat Virgil's shoulder. "Get out your flags. That's the ship will take me home."

"What do I say?"

"Welcome to Cuba. From Neely Tucker of the Chicago *Times*."

THERE WAS NOTHING to shoot at but smoke, that was the trouble. Once the ships began firing, where were they? They hid.

Tavalera estimated it had taken the Americans twenty minutes to destroy the interior of the fortress, the artillery earthworks and kill—how many? The 12th Asuntas were forming on the parade when a shell came down on them and they were no longer a battalion. A third of them killed outright, mutilated, blown to pieces; the rest, more than seventy, were now on the ground screaming—the ones he could hear—missing arms, legs, some already dying, Tavalera thinking: The war is over before it begins, but no one knows it.

He was bleeding from a head wound, cut by shrapnel. He could go to the military hospital and be out of action for a day or so. Or he could go to the mulatta's house. She made her own clothes, she could sew up the wound in his head. What was the hour?

This was done and there was time before the Havana train arrived.

AMELIA WATCHED through binoculars the tall rider and the short rider in white, two horses trailing behind. A few minutes passed before she became certain the tall one was Tyler and lowered the binoculars, relieved, feeling her body begin to relax. Gone more than a day to rob a bank, twenty-eight hours, and he was back. She stood at the edge of the trees where they had spent the night together and raised the binoculars again, putting them on the two figures far below, coming along the line of date palms now that separated burned-out cane fields. Soon they'd be out of sight, climbing the switchbacks to come out on the other side of the camp. Amelia walked back through the trees and came to Fuentes, the old man having coffee at Islero's table.

"He's back. Emilio's with him."

Fuentes, his cup raised, had to think about it. "Only the boy? Where is Virgil?"

"We'll know when they get here," Amelia said. "Come with me."

They walked through the camp—only a few of Islero's men around—to the pasture where the switchback trail topped the slope.

"Islero's moving his dynamite down the hill to plant it," Fuentes said. "Set it off as the train comes. In the smoke and confusion find Novis and take whatever it is he brings."

Amelia said without hesitating, "Do you want your brother to have it?"

"My half brother. No, I change my mind."

"Why?"

"He ask me if I want to share it with him. I said no, it isn't for you. But I can see he believes it is."

Amelia said, "Will you share it with me?" and saw the old man begin to smile.

"How long you been thinking about it? No, don't tell me, it doesn't matter. But listen, we have to get our hands on it before Islero. Even so, it could be an embarrassment. Open the hammock and find nothing there. You ever think about that?"

"Rollie'll pay."

"I don't know, maybe. If he loves you enough."

"I'm sure he will," Amelia said. "If for no other reason than to show he can bet forty thousand and risk losing it. He does it all the time and he's used to winning."

"But when it comes, how do we get it? We don't have much time to think."

"I have an idea that might work," Amelia said. "I'll tell you when we see Ben."

"He's with you on this?"

"Of course he is. Ben's my love."

THEY HAD A FEW MINUTES TOGETHER at Islero's table, talking, touching each other's hands. Fuentes spoke to Emilio, then came over to sit down.

"What he told me, Virgil use sticks with cloth tied to them he waved to a ship?"

"He knows semaphore," Tyler said. "I understand that much. Then a boat came from the ship?"

"Yes, to get the correspondent, Neely Tucker. But then soldiers in San Severino were shooting at them, at the boat, the sailors rowing, and at Neely and Virgil, so the sailors bring Virgil in the boat with Neely so he don't get shot and took them to the ship and it went away. Emilio say Virgil don't want to go but they make him. Then Emilio say he's coming back he sees you."

"He caught up to me," Tyler said, "in those hills above Matanzas. I thought he meant to shoot me."

"His bank robbery," Amelia said to Fuentes, "didn't come off. Ben's thinking of giving it up to rob trains. Ones that carry forty thousand dollars." She saw Tyler's gaze take on a frown and said, "Victor's with us, Ben. It's us three against this world. Now then, what I was thinking: For us to win the prize before Islero does, we're gonna have to get on that train."

Tyler thought about it, staring at her.

"As it's going by?"

"Unh-unh, when it stops at Benavides."

# 19

ISLERO WAS GIVEN the Krupp fieldpiece in
Oriente, August of last year, for aiding Garcia in the
assault on Victoria de las Tunas.

This was a major engagement against a heavily
fortified city defended by eight hundred Spanish
regulars. With them were forty-seven loyalist Volunteers who for the past year had been raiding
insurgent hospital camps and murdering the
wounded. For artillery they had a pair of German-
made Krupp fieldpieces, old ones—a puff of white
smoke, Islero said, and you could see the projectile
coming; but since it was in no hurry there was time
to move out of the way. The city's outer strong
points were connected by a system of trenches
banked with sandbags and protected in front by a
tangle of barbed wire.

To make sure there would be no relief columns

from either Bayamo or Holguin, both Spanish strongholds, Garcia sealed off each road with two thousand troops. For once, he was in a position to outgun the dons, and he attacked Las Tunas with another two thousand veteran troops and a battery of artillery; Hotchkiss 12-pounders and a Sims-Dudley dynamite gun, these directed by an American artillerist named Frederick Funston.

Islero loved that dynamite gun—oh, the explosions it made were something to hear, firing a brass cylinder loaded with five pounds of nitroglycerine. It wasn't so effective against heavy fortifications, thick walls, but tore trench lines to pieces, the sound of its eruptions enough to shatter the nerves of defenders. The cannoneers under the American gunner knocked out the buildings and blockhouses along the edge of Las Tunas and the *insurrectos* stormed into the city to attack fortified barracks of both infantry and cavalry. When the soldiers inside these places refused to surrender, one of the Hotchkiss 12-pounders and the dynamite gun were moved to within a few yards of the front doors. The American artillerist, Funston, walked out in the open, stood before these strongholds and called for the Spanish soldiers to come out and give themselves up. The Spanish regulars were allowed to surrender with honor and leave the city. The loyalist Volunteers who came out were hacked to death with machetes, their due, where they stood in the road.

For his part in the taking of Las Tunas, and

despite his fondness for the dynamite gun, Islero was rewarded with one of the Krupp fieldpieces.

The gun that now, from twelve hundred meters, was trained on the Spanish blockhouse guarding the approach to Guanabana. The train from Havana would pass this point at approximately 3:00 P.M. Islero's gunners were instructed to open fire on the blockhouse at 2:45; the purpose, to draw whatever Spanish troops might be in the neighborhood, keep them away from where Islero, several miles to the west, had planted his dynamite charges. The site: Near a small bridge the Havana train would approach shortly after leaving the station at Benavides.

It wasn't much of a bridge, made entirely of wood planks and beams to span a dry wash that came down from the hills above Matanzas; it would be nothing to blow up the bridge. What prevented him was Islero's agreement with the railroad company. Ferro Carriles Unidos paid him not to destroy their bridges; they paid him considerably less than it would cost to restore a bridge, but it was enough to satisfy Islero and Ferro Carriles accepted it as an operating expense.

So Islero planted his charges in the crushed-rock ballast of the roadbed some two hundred meters from the bridge, and let out his spool of electric wire across open ground and into the trees below his camp. They would wait here until the train was in sight and press the electrical connection to explode the charge. Once the train came to a stop, Islero would attack.

FUENTES RETURNED from his scout of Benavides to the yard of the deserted farmhouse where Tyler and Amelia waited in the trees. He had learned at the station that the train from Havana would be as much as an hour late. Amelia said, "After we break our necks to get here." They had no choice but to remain where they were, not approach the station until they saw the train pulling in. What they would do after that had finally been discussed, argued about and decided.

Fuentes would board the train, Fuentes the only one of the three who would draw little notice: an old Cuban in a limp white suit and panama. With two pistols beneath his coat he would enter at the rear of the first-class coach and wait there. Once the train was rolling he would have maybe two minutes to locate Novis and whatever Guardias or Volunteers were aboard. Tyler and Amelia would be in the stock car with the horses.

"Picture it," Fuentes said. "The explosion, the train comes to a stop. Islero's horsemen attack, surely coming from the trees to the side of the train facing them. You come out of the stock car with the horses on the opposite side and ride up to the first-class coach, where I'm inside. The guards have their backs to me, shooting at the horsemen coming toward them. What is Novis doing? I don't know. I take whatever he's carrying and throw it out the window to you. I deal with Novis. Maybe with others if I have to and leave the train."

Amelia said, "You deal with the others?"

"I don't know what I have to do," Fuentes said, "until I'm there. We leave the train. As we leave, we keep the train between us and Islero's people. It means we ride straight north from there into the hills above Matanzas. Maybe we have time then to look around, see if anyone is coming. We stay in the hills, as you did," he said to Tyler, "when you went to find the bank. Then we move east to go around the city." He said to Amelia, "You know that way, how Mr. Boudreaux's own railroad goes up to Varadero and that finger of land sticking out into the sea. Matanzas on one side, Cárdenas on the other. You go up that way to the summerhouse, six miles. You remember? Don't worry, you find it. You go to the summerhouse and wait for me there. I go to Cárdenas and find a man has a coastal boat and wants to be rich: a dollar for every mile on the way to Key West, or, one hundred American dollars."

Amelia said, "If we have the money."

Fuentes said, "Yes, and if we make it that far. Tonight I come from Cárdenas in the boat. You look for a signal, I swing a lantern back and forth. If you don't see me . . . well, you better go away from there quick."

WHEN IT WAS TIME, a train with six cars waiting at the station, the locomotive hissing, sounding anxious to leave, they left the tree shade and crossed a street of stone houses to the back end of the train standing by a water tower. The doors on both sides of the stock car were open. Tyler and Fuentes dismounted to pull the ramp out of the car and Tyler brought their horses aboard. He watched Amelia give Fuentes a kiss on the cheek. They both watched her lead her mount up the ramp; she was good with horses, Tyler believing she could walk down mustangs. Once they were aboard, he lifted the inside edge of the ramp, heavier'n hell, gave it a shove and let it fall to the cinders. Fuentes looked up at them for a moment, not giving any kind of sign, turned and moved off.

There were six horses besides their own in the stock car, the six tethered to ropes that extended from one side of the car to the other: the six horses, pretty fair looking, already saddled.

"We go down a slight grade," Amelia said, "the train will pick up speed and be roaring by the time it gets near the bridge." She looked at the horses. "And who do you suppose they belong to?"

She knew as well as he did.

Tyler said, "When we leave, they do too."

FUENTES WAITED as he said he would at the rear of the first-class coach; he saw cane seats and the backs of

heads and shoulders, most of the heads covered. All
men, no women aboard, at least not in first class.
They were businessmen and some who could be
businessmen, though Fuentes was sure these men
were something else, together in pairs along the
right side of the aisle, six of them. Maybe there were
more, but at least six to go with the six horses in the
stock car with Amelia and Ben Tyler. Yes, and there
was Novis, the back of his reddish hair, only a short
way up on the left side of the aisle, where most of
the passengers sat, out of the sun. The six on the
other side didn't care about the sun, their business
was to keep looking out the windows. Fuentes had
to stoop to look out—shutters covering the top half
of the windows—to see open land and the wooded
slope a few hundred meters beyond. They were
coming to it now. He stood holding on to the back
of an empty seat with one hand. No sitting down
with only a minute or so left. He could feel the
revolvers beneath his coat, .44s of the kind Tyler
preferred and recommended, stuck in the waist of
his trousers and pressing hard against his groin.
There would be the explosion of dynamite. Not
loud, the engineer would see the smoke in time to
begin stopping the train. Fuentes was ready, holding
on tight so he wouldn't be thrown down in the aisle
with the jolt of the train braking and the scream of
metal scraping metal. He wished he could see what
Novis had on his lap, Novis sitting against the window, alone, Novis's hand going to the seat in front

of him and now he was turning to look this way along the aisle, over his shoulder. *Why?* Who knows —but that's what he was doing, and now they were looking at each other, Novis's face showing dumb surprise, and Fuentes had no choice but to move up the aisle, quick, and slide in next to him, Novis scowling.

"How'n the hell'd you get here?"

As stupid as ever—thank God.

Fuentes used his right hand to draw a revolver and stick the barrel into Novis's side, Novis saying, "Ow," as he looked down and saw the gun. The hammock was on his lap, rolled and tied with rope. The tag fixed to it, cut out of cardboard, was blank. Or the writing was on the other side. Fuentes raised his left hand to turn it over and saw in block letters:

AMELIA BROWN
FOR CUBA LIBRE

"As soon as I tell you," Fuentes said, "pick that up and throw it out the window."

Novis said, "Are you crazy?" his eyes moving, head turning to the pairs of men in seats across the aisle and up a ways, Novis not knowing what to do.

Fuentes jabbed him again with the revolver. "Don't speak. Don't look over there. Pull your gun and drop it out the window."

THE STOCK CAR WAS like a cattle pen with a roof, the sides made of rails spaced a good foot apart; it was airy in here, a steady wind blowing through to stir the rich odor of manure. Tyler would look out through the rails, turn and see Amelia, close by, looking at him. He'd catch her like that and she'd smile, her teeth so white and perfect Tyler was embarrassed to open his mouth.

She said, "I haven't asked, what did Rollie have to say?"

They hadn't spoken about it since Tyler got back, not in any detail.

"The gist of it—he says he isn't gonna pay me."

"You expected him to?"

"Not after you told me he wouldn't, you and Victor, but I had to hear the tinhorn say it."

"Did he mention me?"

"He asked where you were."

"That's all?"

Tyler paused, looking away then, listening.

"Did you hear it?" He saw her shake her head, told her, "Hang on," and the jolt and the sound of couplings banging together came almost as he said it, throwing Amelia against him. He held on to her as the train continued to make a racket, steam hissing, wheels screeching, and now the horses were starting a commotion, pulling on the lines holding them.

By the time the train ground to a stop Tyler had the six horses free and was crowding them toward the left-side doorway, talking to them, swatting their rumps, the horses forcing each other out through the opening to jump for it and skid down the gravel pitch of the roadbed, none of them liking it, but all were out there running now, on their own and heading for the hills.

Tyler asked Amelia if she was ready. She didn't look it, but nodded her head, got her reins in her hand and mounted the sorrel she'd been riding. Tyler used his reins to swat her horse and she was out the door, nothing to it, reined a tight turn in the scrub and pulled up to sit waiting for him in that blue bandanna. Now he sent out Fuentes's horse and watched Amelia go after it, reach down and catch it by the reins.

Tyler said in the dun's ear, "Mind how you land. Don't make me look dumb in front of this girl." He heard gunfire off on the yon side of the train as he and the dun went flying out the door.


WHEN THE SHOOTING BEGAN it took the passengers a few moments to realize bullets were breaking windows, coming through the coach. There they were, all those heads and hats in front of Fuentes and then gone, the passengers flat on the floor by their seats now, some facedown in the aisle. Only the six Guardias or whoever they were in their business suits were in view, firing revolvers, two with rifles, firing out the windows at the horsemen coming across the open land—not many of them, maybe ten or so mounted—with horses scarce, don't waste them—but a swarm of mambís afoot coming behind, firing as they appeared out of the trees. Fuentes felt Novis pressing against him, Novis trying to hunch himself in a ball around the rolled hammock. Fuentes said, "Here, get up." Novis wouldn't do it, so Fuentes took a handful of red hair, raised his face and saw the terror in his eyes, this *yanqui* who would tell you how he fought a hundred times in the prize ring and beat up strikers with a pick handle.

"Man, throw the bundle out the window. Do it!"

The window was open. Fuentes looked out and there was Amelia riding up, leading his horse, and Ben Tyler, the cowboy coming close to the train, his hand reaching out. Fuentes's hand, still clutching red hair, turned Novis's face to the window, saying, "Give it to him," and Novis shoved the bundle through the opening. Fuentes didn't see if Tyler received it, but heard him shout "Come on! Run!" and Fuentes let go of the red hair, feeling his hand sticky, and rose from the seat, the revolver still in his right hand.

It was the heft of it, and the feel of the second revolver digging into his groin, that caused Fuentes to pause and look toward the six Guardias firing out the windows, none aware of him standing in the aisle, or that he was pointing a .44 at them now, moving it to the ones farthest up the aisle, Fuentes seeing his chance to shoot Guardias and that was what he did, opened fire, shooting as fast as he could, in a hurry and not making sure, seeing only one of them go down as he emptied the gun. But now the nearest one was aware of him. Fuentes saw the nearest one turn and extend his revolver; Fuentes saw the man's face with no expression, saw the face and the muzzle of the revolver, saw the Guardia's hand squeeze the trigger. And heard the *click*. In all that gunfire heard it again, the *click*, and again, the Guardia not wanting his gun to be empty, still holding it extended as Fuentes dropped the .44 in his hand and pulled the one digging into his groin. He said, "Thank you, God," believing in Him again, promising to always believe in Him, and shot the Guardia twice through his business suit.

# 20

OSMA WATCHED THE ATTACK on the train from a high vantage, an outcropping of limestone in the hills north of the railroad tracks. Osma, who used to hunt runaway slaves, watched through a pair of binoculars Tavalera had given him to aid in the hunting of mambís.

These were attacking from trees on the other side of the open land, shooting as they came, wanting something that was on that train, willing to die for it, two of the horses without riders, two of the infantry also on the ground, dead or wounded. In this part of the province they would be men of Islero.

What was it the old bandit wanted that Tavalera also wanted?

This morning Osma had waited for Tavalera to leave his sister's house. As soon as he was gone,

Osma went in again and asked his sister what this was about. What was on the train? She said she didn't know. He hit her in the stomach with his fist, but she still didn't know.

Tavalera had said follow the railroad tracks to look for this ambush. The easy part. When he came to the cannon firing on the Guanabana blockhouse, Osma couldn't see a good reason for it, so he believed it was only to draw the Spanish if they were near. He asked himself, Where would you stop a train around here? At a bridge, of course, the one near Benavides. Islero with his dynamite would think of that. Blow it up. Unless he was paid by the railroad not to destroy its bridges. If that was the case he would think of a good place not far from the bridge. Right here, where Osma had been waiting. And the ones out there—they must be Islero's men, his *macheteros*.

He had to think now of what else Tavalera had said.

Look for an American, a cowboy?

That's what he said, a cowboy. And perhaps a woman . . .

But now horses were coming out of the stock car, six of them, with saddles but no riders: horses jumping out of the train, smart ones, uh, not wanting to be shot. Now a rider, already mounted, came out of the car. A woman. And now another horse. And another one with a rider who could be a cowboy. That was what he looked like. Osma had seen

pictures of American cowboys. Now he listened to
Tavalera's words again in his mind. Look for a cowboy, an American, and perhaps a woman and there
she was, a blue scarf covering her hair. They were
on this side of the train and he could see them
clearly through the binoculars, trailing a horse as
they rode past the coaches, the cowboy so close to
the train he could touch it; stopping now. What was
he doing? Receiving something through the window, a bundle?

Look for something, Tavalera said, in a hammock, and that could be a hammock, white canvas
rolled up. It *was,* it was a hammock tied up with
rope, the cowboy carrying it across his pommel.
Now a figure in white appeared, coming out the
door of the coach, hurrying to mount the horse the
woman held for him.

And Osma remembered Tavalera saying, "And
perhaps Victor Fuentes," Tavalera knowing more
than he realized. If this one was Fuentes.

The three were coming away from the train now
in this direction, giving Osma the opportunity to see
their faces and the one in the white suit, *yes,* was
Victor Fuentes, the old patriot. Tavalera must have
remembered from some other time that Osma knew
him and would recognize him if he was here. Years
ago between wars Osma had said to Fuentes, "It was
good you ran away before I became a hunter, or I
would have caught you and sliced your legs." Like
his brother's. But now . . .

Why was Fuentes running from his brother's men if they were sympathetic to each other? But that's what he and the two Americans looked like they were doing, running for their lives.

Look—being chased by three of the horsemen who had come around to this side of the train. To get that hammock? To get whatever was in it, Osma thinking it would have to be something of great value. There were four men of Islero on the ground who appeared to be dead and perhaps more dead inside the train. No more white puffs of smoke or the popping sounds of gunfire. Mambís were entering the coaches.

And now Fuentes and the cowboy and the woman were approaching the wooded slope, several hundred feet below Osma, where he squatted with his glasses on a shelf of rock. He wondered if they knew where they were going or only running away.

There were trails through these hills that used to be roads, if you knew how to find them: a road that led north to Matanzas, and a road that went northeast in the direction of Cárdenas. Osma didn't believe Fuentes and his companions would be heading for Matanzas, a war going on there this morning, the city full of Spanish soldiers. No, they would have to go more to the east.

He believed the three men of Islero, approaching the trees now, riding hard, would catch up to them and kill them for whatever was inside the hammock.

Money. It would have to be money.

Osma lowered the glasses and half closed his eyes in the hot glare of the sky. He was bareheaded on this rock shelf, squatting, arms resting on his heavy round thighs. He thought of times he used to watch for runaways like this, from high ground. Or wait by water. Easier than tracking through *maniguas,* the thickets they would find to hide in. He was thinking now, Would it be easier to take the valuable hammock from the mambís, after they got hold of it, or from Fuentes and his companions? That was an easy one to decide. Fuentes and his companions might not even be armed.

So he knew what to do.

Osma rose from his perch, made his way through rocks and brush to where his horse waited, his panama resting on the saddle horn.

TYLER STOPPED THEM. He said, "Hold it," and pulled up in the pines to look back along the ruts of the narrow road. He listened but didn't hear a sound until Fuentes told him to come on.

"Y'all keep going. I'll wait for them."

"To do what," Fuentes said, "shoot them? They our friends."

"I can stop them and take their horses, run 'em off."

"You think, with what Islero knows we have, only those three are coming? Wait, you only waste time. We have to keep going, but not to Varadero, the trail north is too slow. So we change the plan and go east, it's better. Leave these hills soon and ride as fast as we can, get some distance on them. All right? So quit looking back."

"Ben doesn't like people chasing him," Amelia said. "What do you call it when you're on the dodge? Riding the owl hoot trail?"

Tyler looked at her, wondering how she knew that, and saw a smile in her eyes, having time for him in a spot like this. He said to her, "I'll ride with you anywhere. But I'd like to know what's east."

"More of Cuba," Fuentes said. "You be good, I'll show you."

OSMA MOVED THROUGH TIMBER and now a scattering of rock formations along the spine of the ridge, not bothering to watch below. The ruts of the trail east were down there out of view, but clear in his memory and wouldn't change. He lived in this country since the days of slaves; he knew where he was going and where he would see Fuentes and his companions again. If he didn't see them, then they were foolish and had gone north over the hills toward Matanzas. But he didn't think Victor Fuentes, in his old age, had become a fool. Osma came to the place where he would expect to see them and looked down through a wide gash in the trees, an arroyo strewn with rocks and dead foliage, young trees that had been uprooted, the wash dry this time of year.

Down there where it became as wide as the Imperial Road, that was the place where the trail crossed. If he was wrong he would have to go north and find them.

But in only a few minutes learned he wasn't wrong.

There they were—Osma put his glasses on them —Fuentes and his companions crossing the arroyo east, the old man taking them—where? It was something Osma would find out in time.

Now he had to wait again, but not long. He heard the three peasant soldiers, the *macheteros*, coming before he saw them, calling to each other.

The first one appeared in the arroyo.

Then the other two, twenty meters or so down the chute. They came up to join the first one and Osma put his glasses on them.

Boys, grown ones but still boys. Excited. Look at their faces. Up the other side now to follow the trail.

Osma gave them time to move off and set their minds on what they were doing, concentrate, look for those hoofprints in the road ruts, look for fresh manure, Osma wanting the horses of Fuentes and his companions to have been fed and watered sometime today. He nudged his horse, a buckskin gelding, and took the animal carefully down through the rocks and debris scattered over the wash. He pictured the three mambís coming in a short time to a glen, a clearing in the trees. Osma wanted to come on them as they reached the clearing, not bumping

into each other on the trail, but where they would
have room to turn and face him when he called.

There they were, the three in white, crossed
belts of bullets, machetes hanging from their saddles, hurrying. They didn't hear him coming behind
them. Osma pulled his Colt revolver and kicked the
buckskin.

They were in the clearing now.

He called out to them, "Wait! Wait for me!"

And they did. Good boys. They reined their
horses to see who this was coming, this stout man
with a beard. They sat motionless waiting, Osma
close enough to see their young faces, their open,
curious expressions as he rode up and shot each one
of them once, emptying their saddles. He shot two
of them again where they lay on the ground,
reloaded his revolver and shot the third one looking
up at him.

What did the old bandit teach these boys? Nothing?


THEY PAUSED hearing the gunfire, its echoes singing
off the high reaches, Tyler looking up, listening.
Five shots . . . and then another one. Too far
away to be meant for them. Pistol shots, he believed
all from the same gun, and told them so. Fired by a
man who carried an empty chamber. Tyler said he
believed the three mambís chasing them could be
dead. It was a feeling he had.

Fuentes shrugged at the idea. "So we have nothing to worry about?" He said they could talk about it when they were out of these hills.

"Don't you want to know," Tyler said, "who's following us?"

"I want to stay alive," Fuentes said. "That's all I know. And to stay alive we have to run as fast as we can."

Amelia put her hand on Tyler's arm but didn't say anything. She looked worn-out. Nobody so far had mentioned opening the hammock, even just to take a peek, see if they had the money. Tyler imagined Amelia and Fuentes were thinking about it the same as he was. Were they staking their lives on a pile of money being inside? Or a note in there from Rollie saying, in so many words, "You want her? Keep her."

They came out of the hills—by Fuentes's reckoning—eight miles southeast of Matanzas and rode past cultivated fields and rows of royal palms; they came to a banana plantation and followed aisles through the thick leaves brushing them, the grove opening onto graze, an empty pasture turning to scrub; they crossed shallow streams choked with lily pads, came to a mill that had been destroyed and saw stone houses in the near distance: a water tower, a train station with a loading platform, double tracks curving toward it from the north.

"Ibarra," Fuentes said. "A stop on the Matanzas Railroad line, but no trains this time of day."

They moved to high ground with tree cover, a ridge that was only a short run from the station. From here, Fuentes said, they could look back to see if anybody was coming and decide what to do.

Tyler kept watch, staring in late afternoon light in the direction of the mill, what was left of it. He heard Amelia: "Let's open it."

And Fuentes say, "If you wish."

Tyler was about to turn to them, but kept staring at the mill, over there across empty fields. He thought for a minute it was still burning. Then realized, no, the smoke was from a train, still off beyond the mill but coming this way toward the Ibarra station. He could hear it. And so could Fuentes, the old man next to him now, looking off at the smoke coming closer. He said, "But there is no train at this time."

"Maybe," Tyler said, "it's a troop train; they don't run on a schedule. Except if it is, it's going the wrong way. Matanzas is where all the soldiers are."

"We still have people following us. Stay here and keep watching," Fuentes said, "while I have a look at this train." He paused to say, "It's slowing down," then moved off through the trees to where the roadbed cut through the ridge. There, he could look down at the double tracks from no more than twenty feet and wait for the train to pass.

Tyler glanced around at Amelia, expecting to see her untying the hammock. No, she was stretched out on the ground staring at the sky, using the hammock as a pillow.

"What's wrong?"

"I don't feel good."

He wanted to go over to her, but stayed where he was, the sound of the train getting louder.

"You have the trots?"

"Neely would call it indelicate to ask me that."

"Do you?"

"Not so far. I feel kind of dizzy, like I might have a temperature."

Now all Tyler could see of the train was thick smoke filling the sky close to them, the engine and cars going past below the ridge, making that braking sound, slowing to a crawl as it approached the station.

Fuentes was back, hunching down next to Tyler.

"The train's empty, not a person in any of the cars. I think it deliver soldiers and now is going back to get some more."

"Going back where?"

"Las Villas, in the next province. The reason it stop here must be to take on coal or water, the Matanzas yard too busy. I think what we have to do is get on that train."

They both looked over as Amelia said, "Ben?" On her hands and knees now. "Help me, will you?"

OSMA HAD REACHED the blackened shell of the mill in time to see them cross the open ground to the ridge. He watched through his glasses, noticing the woman acting strange, holding on to her saddle horn, letting her head bounce with the horse's gait. Not used to this travel, or was she sick, wanting the ride to be over?

"I'll help you end your trip," Osma said to her.

Now they were in the trees up on that ridge.

"You feel safe, uh?"

He waited for them to come out and continue toward the station. But they remained in the trees. They liked feeling safe. They would watch now to see who was coming. Like little animals peeking out of burrows. Osma was becoming more certain they didn't have weapons. Or maybe only Fuentes.

Osma was aware of the train approaching from behind him; he could hear it and knew what the train was: the one that arrived from Las Villas today with soldiers for San Severino, to fight the Americans if they landed there. The train, he believed, was returning empty to gather more soldiers. When the war came he would sit back and watch it; it wasn't his war. This business, though, was different. With signs that it was something he should do.

Was it luck that put him here? Or his god, Changó, smiling at him, saying, Here, let me help you. Changó, or St. Barbara interceding. Either one. He would kill these people in their honor, offering them to the god and the saint for giving him the valuable hammock.

And for sending the train that would give him a way to cross the open ground without being seen. As it rolled by he would wait for the last car to pass, then ride the buckskin along the off side of the train, staying close to the coaches, out of sight of Fuentes and his companions, and be at Ibarra waiting for them.

On the train.

Osma certain they saw it as their escape.

THERE WERE STOCK CARS for horses on the tail end of a half dozen coaches. Tyler got busy loading their mounts while Fuentes put Amelia aboard and tried to make her comfortable. She looked to be in agony coming here, her face flushed, her forehead hot to the touch. There was no stationmaster about, so Fuentes spoke to the engineer, told him they had a sick woman who needed to get home to Las Villas. It made little difference to the engineer; he said they would leave in a few minutes, as soon as they topped off the boiler.

Tyler came in with their saddlebags. He dropped them across the aisle and turned to Amelia and Fuentes, in seats facing each other, Amelia with her eyes closed. She was holding the blue bandanna, touching her face with it. Tyler saw her hair damp and mussed, sticking to her scalp. Without opening her eyes she said to him, "Please don't look at me." Then opened them partway in a painful expression. "I look awful, don't I?"

"You look sick, that's all."

"My hair," she said, touching it. "I'm a mess. I think I have yellow fever."

Fuentes, sitting with the rolled hammock on his lap, said, "Don't talk like that."

"Well, I have *something* terrible, I *know*. Look at me." She said, "No, don't," and closed her eyes again. "I brought a bottle of quinine. It's with all my earthly possessions stuffed in saddlebags. Quinine and a bottle of Ayer's pills I've had over a year, Lorraine told me to bring."

"Your bags are right here," Fuentes said, and motioned with his head.

Tyler went through one and then the other, feeling what he believed was silk underwear among items of clothing he couldn't identify but didn't believe he should look at. He found hand towels, soap, bath powder, baking soda, a toothbrush, nail files, safety pins, matches, Sweet Caporal cigarettes, bottles of Ayer's pills, Lydia E. Pinkham's Vegetable Compound, Sherman's Papillary Oil, and a half pint of quinine. He turned as he heard Amelia.

"I'm gonna die, aren't I?"

Fuentes was shaking his head. "No, you not going to die. We won't let you."

"But I might," Amelia said. "While I'm still here on this earth I'd like to know if Rollie cared enough to pay the ransom. Open the hammock, Victor, if you would, please."

Tyler had the feeling she was making the most of being sick. She seemed to like putting on acts. Which was fine with him, he liked watching her. He couldn't look at Amelia without wanting to touch her so gently she would barely feel it. He said, "Here, take a swig of your medicine," handing Amelia the bottle.

She took it, but as she did her sad eyes looked past him and came to life. Tyler half turned, looked over his shoulder to see a bearded man in a panama coming along the aisle, the bearded man raising his eyebrows as he said, "Fuentes, is that you?"

Too much at ease, Tyler felt, for that look of surprise. Tyler glanced at Fuentes, whose back was to the man and had to turn all the way around. The look Fuentes showed was honest, more startled than just surprised, not liking what he saw; but gathered himself and said, "Osma, the slave hunter, how are you?" Then said in English, for Tyler, "You still kiss Tavalera's ass when he wants?"

It was all Tyler had to hear. He pulled a .44 Russian and put it in the bearded face.

"What do you want done with him?"

"Shoot him," Fuentes said, "what do you think?"

Tyler took a step toward the man and felt the train begin to roll, felt that jolt and heard couplings bang together. Two more steps, holding the man's

gaze, Tyler pressed the muzzle of the .44 into the
man's belly.

"You're getting off," Tyler said.

The man still seemed at ease. He gestured. "The
train is moving."

"Get off or get shot, partner."

"What are you, a cowboy?"

Tyler hit him across the jaw with his gun barrel.
No warning, whacked Osma to let him know there
was nothing to talk about, and again put the muzzle
against his belly. Now he reached into the man's
coat and lifted his Colt revolver. It had an ivory
grip. Tyler handed it behind him and Fuentes
reached out to take it, Fuentes saying, "Why don't
you shoot him? Then put him off?"

Osma had a hand to his face, touching his jaw.
He looked at the blood on his thick palm and then at
Tyler.

Tyler cocked the .44.

Osma turned and walked down the aisle to the
end of the car, Tyler a step behind him. Osma
opened the door and the sound of the train picking
up speed came in loud. Tyler gave him a shove, not
hard, but it was enough to send him out the door.
Osma grabbed the platform railing in one hand—
couplings below him, between the cars—and came
around to Tyler with a short-barrel pistol in his
hand, firing as Tyler slashed the man's arm with his
gun barrel, firing again as he went off the side of the
platform, Tyler firing now, snapping two shots into

the dusk, and knew he'd hit the man in midair before the man hit the ground.

Tyler leaned out to see Osma lying back there in the cinders and weeds; he looked done.

AN OIL LAMP HUNG at the end of the car. Tyler brought it to where they were seated, hung it from a coat hook and used Amelia's matches to light it. He sat with her legs on his lap, his hand on a boot feeling her slender ankle in there. Tyler watched her, flushed and sick as she was, puffing on a Sweet Cap, the smoke rising to hang about the lamp that moved with the sway of the train. Fuentes was taking forever to undo the rope around the hammock.

There was worry in his voice as he spoke about Osma. Was he dead? The man deserved to be. Tyler said if he wasn't dead he was likely on his way. Fuentes said he should have shot him as he stood there, through the heart and be sure. Saying he hoped to God never to see Osma again. Tyler thinking if Osma was dead, my God, that would be how many? Eight men dead by his gun and he wasn't even a shootist, had never sought a man to kill him and never would. Shooting men was not something to be known for, not even in the Wild West anymore. Though Tavalera would come to mind whenever he thought of Charlie Burke, killed by that firing squad. Be best to have all this over with and get back to raising stock. Maybe right here. It was something he thought about now and again, the idea of staying on after, wondering each time why this country seemed so familiar to him, like home.

Fuentes kept talking about Osma, telling how he had hunted runaway slaves, until Amelia said to him, "Victor, can't you untie that thing and talk at the same time?"

"I'm afraid of what we might find," Fuentes said, pulling the rope loose and laying the hammock on the seat next to him. "Or what we won't find." He let half the canvas unroll to the floor, felt in the part still on the seat and pulled out a pillowcase that had weight to it, irregular shapes inside, corners pressing against the cloth. He held up the pillowcase like a sack of—what?

"For God's sake, Victor, will you please open it?" Amelia's spunk letting her say this in her weakened condition, barely moving her mouth.

Fuentes turned the pillowcase upside down and bank notes bound in money straps poured out to pile on the seat next to him. Fuentes grinning, and yet seemed surprised.

"Count it," Amelia said.

Tyler watched her eyes hold on Fuentes as he riffled through several of the packets, counted to himself as he stacked them on the seat and said, "What you ask for, forty thousand American dollars, all there."

Tyler looked from the bank notes to Amelia, the flush of fever on her face, and saw her eyes shining.

———

THE MULATTA HE CALLED Isabela Católica worked on Tavalera's wound for two hours, first cutting and shaving hair matted with blood to see the wound clearly, then cleansing it with diluted carbolic acid. She closed the wound with needle and thread in twelve individual stitches as he lay facedown across her bed. She asked why the wound was in the back of his head if he had been facing the enemy. She could ask him that in his weakened state, but got no answer. She finished her sewing before discovering he had passed out sometime while she worked, from the pain or loss of blood. The bed looked as though a woman had given birth in it. She put ice in a towel and placed it against his wound while he slept through the day. In the evening, when he opened his eyes and knew the day was gone, he said, "I failed."

She didn't know what he meant—failed at what? —but didn't ask. He wanted to know if Osma had returned and she shook her head. Now he was angry, wanting to blame her because Osma hadn't returned. She brought him whiskey. He sat up to drink it, but soon closed his eyes, telling her his head was spinning. She left him alone and he again fell asleep.

Isabela sat in the front room, leaving him alone in the bed, and fell asleep with her head resting on her arms on the surface of the table. Sometime during the night she awoke to the sound of a horse outside, approaching the house. She waited, but now there were no sounds, nothing. Finally she went to the door and opened it.

In the dark a man was sitting his horse as though asleep, his back bent, head lowered, hands resting on the horn in front of him. She recognized the buckskin gelding and called in a low voice, "Osma?" She had to help him down and into the house. In the light of the lamp she saw his clothes, his face, his hands covered with blood. The sight lifted her spirit and she smiled.

Now she helped him into the bedroom, bringing the lamp and placed it on a stand next to Tavalera sitting up in bed asleep. She blew her breath in his face and he opened his eyes. It took him several moments to recognize the man standing by the bed. He said, "Osma?"

Osma's head came up. He said, "They went to Las Villas."

THEY KEPT THEIR VOICES LOW, barely above a whisper, while Amelia slept, lulled by the sound and sway of the train. Tyler had removed her boots and stockings and held her warm bare feet in his hands. He wanted to know if the quinine was working yet. Fuentes said it would take time. If she had yellow fever they would give her citrate of magnesia, castor oil in lime juice and the milk of green coconuts.

He said, "Is strange, but where we going the people don't get yellow fever. Perhaps because the city is on higher land than along the coast, and the air and the soil are dry." He said, "They suffer, of course, from consumption, malaria, dysentery, as people everywhere do, but not yellow fever. Or is because the water is clean. So we lucky to be going there—if that's what she has." He said, "The province is name Santa Clara and the city is Santa Clara, but everyone calls it Villa Clara or Las Villas."

Fuentes said this leaning toward Tyler in the seat across from him.

"Have you heard it call that?"

Tyler said, "Victor? Why don't you tell me where exactly we're going?"

"I just told you, Las Villas."

"We get off the train—what if there're soldiers around?"

"We come there it's still dark. Nobody see us."

"We're in Las Villas," Tyler said, "then where do we go?"

"We take Amelia to see this doctor."

Jesus Christ. "Why didn't you say so? He's a friend of yours?"

"I don't know him, but I have an old friend there, a woman name Lourdes. She can take care of Amelia and make her better." He said then, "Listen, you know what Las Villas is known for? Two things especially: its wide streets for one, and its beautiful women. You may not have interest in that, but is true." He said, "Why do you think it happens, one place having more beautiful women than another?"

"When we get there," Tyler said, "we leave the train, I get the horses—"

"Yes, I'm sure we come to Las Villas before the sunrise. It's dark by the railroad station, nobody sees us. You bring the horses for us, we ride a short distance on the Imperial Road and we there."

"You're sure," Tyler said, "this place'll be safe."

Fuentes reached over to pat Tyler's knee.

"I swear it."


APPROACHING LAS VILLAS they passed through an open gate in the barbed wire enclosing the city, a remnant of reconcentration, and rolled into the railyard. Tyler said to Fuentes, "Still dark, huh? I wonder what that is lighting up the sky over there."

All Fuentes could do was act like it didn't matter, daylight about to expose them to a few hundred Spanish soldiers up there by the station, where troops and supplies were loading. But what all the activity did, it held up their train while tracks were cleared; it allowed them to get off a good distance from the station.

"You have to trust me," Fuentes said, taking credit for the traffic.

He was right about how far they would travel from here. No more than a mile up the road they came to an open gate with a decorative wood-carved arch over it. They entered and walked their horses along a lane that cut through acres of banana trees.

The lane brought them to a wide one-story house made of stone, weathered and crumbling in places, with a porch across the front and a red tile roof with hardly any pitch to it. Cottonwoods shaded the house; the inside, through the windows, looked dark. They dismounted at the porch, no one around. Fuentes told Tyler to wait, keep an eye on the road, while he took Amelia inside.

She seemed worse than she was yesterday, with barely the strength to move. From the porch she looked at Tyler with the saddest eyes he'd ever seen.

"Will you stay here with me?"

"You know I will."

She said, "Guard the money with your life." Then, with a vague look: "No, not with your life. But guard it." She went inside with Fuentes.

Tyler got one of her Sweet Caps from the saddlebag and stood smoking in the shade, looking at clusters of green bananas. He turned, hearing the screen door. A woman with a clean white apron over her shirtwaist and gray skirt, and a straw sun hat low on her head, stood facing him on the porch.

She said, "You're with that darling girl?"

The woman was American, at most only a few years older than Amelia, and very pretty. Tyler said yes, he was, thinking it strange to see a woman wearing an apron with a sun hat, just the edge of the straw brim turned up in front.

The woman said, "Hello, I'm Mary Lou Janes. I assist Dr. Henriquez. He's with her now."

"Amelia thinks she has yellow fever."

The woman looked surprised. "She does?"

"Or some kind of fever."

"Why on earth did you bring her here? San Lázaro is a home for lepers."

# 21

NEARLY TWO WEEKS PASSED before Novis got up the nerve to report to Mr. Boudreaux, expecting to be cursed up and down and fired before he opened his mouth.

But that wasn't the man's way, was it? To act like a normal person. No, he was calm as could be, upstairs on the veranda in his starched white Cuban shirt, a guayabara he wore once in a while when he was in the country. A pistol that looked like a Mauser and a pair of binoculars lay on the porch railing. No doubt the man had watched him coming.

What he did first was talk about himself, telling where he was at in this situation, how he didn't hear a word until one of his guerrillas rode up from Benavides and told him about the attack on the train.

"He said three Guardias aboard at the time were killed. I said well, there must have been more than just three on the train. What happened to the others? He said he didn't know. I asked if he had seen my bodyguard."

"I went back to Havana."

Mr. Boudreaux stared and Novis stopped right there.

"I asked if he had seen you. He said no, he had not. I asked if anything had been taken from the train. He said he didn't know. He said he believed the mambís destroyed the tracks to get money from the railroad, not to stop the train." Mr. Boudreaux paused. "My hunch, Novis—no, my conviction—is that a number of individuals know exactly what happened but are reluctant to come forth. Why is that?"

"Sir, you want me to tell you what happened?"

"Is there a conspiracy? All of you in cahoots to steal the ransom money?"

"Sir, I went back to Havana 'cause I thought that's where you were at."

"But I told you I'd be here."

"You did?"

"Do you think I'm lying?"

Shit. Calm as swamp water.

"No sir, I don't think that at all. I musta forgot your telling me. So I hung around waiting to see if you'd show up."

"You're saying it was my fault I wasn't there?"

Jesus Christ.

"No sir, I'm not saying that. I got shot at coming

here to tell you what happened on that train and you won't let me."

Whether he liked it or not it seemed to satisfy him. Mr. Boudreaux nodded like he was giving his blessing.

"All right, Novis, tell me what happened."

He told about the dynamite going off, the mambís coming out of the trees shooting and the guards on the train shooting back, six of them.

Mr. Boudreaux stared, not saying a word.

Novis told about Fuentes being on the train, appearing from nowhere and thought Mr. Boudreaux would jump on that. No, he just kept staring.

He told how Fuentes put a gun on him and made him throw the hammock out the window. And how the cowboy, Tyler, was there to get it.

The man kept on staring, Jesus, like he was casting a spell, hypnotizing him so he'd tell the truth. And he *had,* everything he said was the way it happened. But then hesitated about Amelia being with them—something Novis could hardly believe himself. He waited too long and Mr. Boudreaux finally spoke.

"There's something you're not telling me."

You bet, and the reason was that fucking pistol sitting there on the rail. Boudreaux blamed him anyway for Amelia being taken. If he told she was with them, either Boudreaux would say he was lying or it would set him off and Novis saw himself getting shot between the eyes. What he said was "Fuentes shot one of the guards." Like that was the thing he didn't want to tell. "Him and Tyler rode off with the hammock. The guards stayed with the train and I spent the night at Benavides to get on the Havana train the next day."

"You didn't want to tell me about this, did you?"

"No sir, I wasn't anxious to."

"So you wasted precious time in Havana. What did you do, visit your whores?"

"Tell you the truth, I didn't see none around. People in Havana are going crazy, scared of the U.S. Army coming."

Mr. Boudreaux waited now, giving Novis his famous stare. "During the attack on the train, did you fire your gun?"

"I forgot to mention, Victor made me drop it out the window."

"You say he and Tyler rode off."

"Yes, sir, with some mambíses coming behind."

"You mean chasing them?"

Novis had to stop and think. "My recollection, the mambíses were bringing up the rear."

Now he was getting the stare again.

"Novis, are you part of this scheme?"

"No, sir, I'll swear to it."

Without a pause Mr. Boudreaux said, "Do you know where the Philippines are?"

"Sir?"

"I asked, Do you know where the Philippines are? That's a fairly simple question, isn't it?"

"The Philippine Islands? When I was working on the docks in Newerleans there was some ships come from there with timber. I think it's over by China?"

"Would you say the Philippines are at least ten thousand miles away?"

"Yes, sir, I would imagine."

"You're sure?"

Novis thought of hitting Mr. Boudreaux right in his fucking mouth. Hit him and walk out. But he stood there and said, "Yes, sir, I'm fairly sure."

Mr. Boudreaux said, "I've been sitting here in the dark, Novis, with barely a word from the outside world since the blockade. Then, lo and behold, a British acquaintance of mine sent over a number of New York papers he'd picked up in Jamaica. It seems that our Asiatic fleet, under a Commodore George Dewey, caught the Spanish fleet in Manila Bay. You've heard of Manila, Novis?"

"Yes sir, it's over in the Philippine Islands."

"Which you tell me is at least ten thousand miles away. Dewey's flagship, the *Olympia*, led the fleet to within twelve hundred yards of the Spanish ships, a bold move, and at this point Dewey said to the *Olympia*'s captain, a man named Charles Gridley, he said, 'You may fire when you are ready, Gridley,' and the American fleet launched its attack. They made five passes, swinging their turrets from port to starboard, starboard to port; they destroyed the entire Spanish fleet and not until then did they stop for breakfast. That, Novis, is determination. In this one battle the sinking of the *Maine* was avenged. There is no doubt in my mind we are going to win this war, and I don't think with much loss of life, no more than say five to ten thousand. That's inevitable, you can't fight a war and not expect casualties. But when it's over, Novis, we're going to see millions of acres of Cuban land, previously owned by the Spanish, up for sale."

Boudreaux continued to stare at Novis.

"So the future looks fairly promising."

Boudreaux put on a smile—so Novis did too—then turned it off.

"Dewey went all the way to the Philippines, a distance you tell me of ten thousand miles, to protect our interests in the Far East and did a bang-up job, got it done in less than a day, a few hours' work. Think of it, Novis."

"Yes sir?"

"All you had to do was go fifty-four miles with a hammock under your protection and you failed, miserably. What I'd like you to tell me, Novis, is what you're going to do to make up for it."

Novis said, "You think I'm ignorant, don't you?"

Boudreaux paused only a moment, maybe reading the remark, then shrugged in his tailored guayabara shirt. "Being ignorant, Novis, is nothing to be ashamed of. It merely indicates a lack of formal education. There are certain things I'm ignorant of myself."

Like he was saying, even if that might be hard to believe.

Facing Boudreaux, Novis could see out the corner of his eye the Mauser pistol sitting on the railing. Take one step to brush it off the rail. Take another step to pick Boudreaux up and chuck him off this upstairs porch on his head. Do it, Novis thought.

What stopped him was the look that came into Boudreaux's eyes, like the man saw it coming, about to die or suffer terrible injuries and there was nothing he could do about it. Novis had just a glimpse of the man's helpless fear, but enough to see him in that moment as an ordinary person, Jesus Christ, no better'n anybody else. Shit, all he was, he was rich.

"You know why I come here," Novis said, and waited. "Do you?"

"No, I don't."

"On account of you trusted me. If I don't show up here then you might think I took the money, which I didn't. Hell, there could've been dog shit in that hammock for all I knew. I did what I was told and that old man stuck a gun in my side. I told you I got shot at coming here from Benavides? People shooting at me from the hills and I don't even know who they are. I don't know one side from the other —they all look alike to me anyway, greasers do. I think you know, but you don't give a shit who's who or who wins. Is that true?"

Boudreaux didn't say anything.

"I asked you a question."

"Do I care who wins the war?" Boudreaux said. "Of course I care. I want *us* to win."

"Who do you mean by us, you and your buddies? That's what your lady friend calls 'em, your sugar buddies."

"She does?"

"Answer my question. Who's us?"

"America. We're Americans, aren't we, Novis?" The man getting some of his cocksure manner back.

"I think you say that on account of us whipping the dons' ass over in the Philippine Islands, and if it's that easy the war's good as done."

"You make a keen observation," Boudreaux said.

"Well, I get here, I see you got your gorillas all around the cane fields like they're expecting the mambíses to come riding down on them with torches. Well, the mambíses I'm told are on our side. So if you're fighting them, what side does that put you on?"

"Novis, it's not as simple as whose side you're on."

"The hell it ain't."

Boudreaux moved for the first time, turned to the railing and looked out at his estate.

"Novis, you want to know how I see this situation?"

He waited, but didn't prompt when Novis didn't say anything.

"I want us to win," Boudreaux said, "*us,* our side, and I know it will happen. But if by some act of God we *don't* win, a simple fact remains, Novis, and that is, I can't lose." He turned to Novis and said, "I'll tell you what: Why don't we go back to Havana and sit it out?"

# 22

AMELIA WOULD OPEN HER EYES and see faces looking at her. Sometimes she'd know the faces and sometimes she wouldn't. Most of the time she knew when it was Ben and when it was Victor. She knew Dr. Henriquez; he was handsome and wore a beard. She didn't know the woman who would stand by the cot with an anguished expression and wore a sun hat, always wore the hat, a straw with the edge of the brim turned up in front. Just the edge. Often she saw a Negro face, a woman who was skin and bones named Lourdes. The woman would lean over in her sack dress and Amelia would see the woman's breasts, flat as leather pancakes, or like the flaps on saddlebags, and Amelia would think of the money and want to tell Ben to take it out of the hammock and put it in saddlebags, in case they had to leave in a hurry. She could never remember if she told him.

Sometimes she would see a face that was deformed, the face lacking most of its nose. Once while Lourdes was feeding her, Amelia looked over and saw a man in the doorway with enormous legs, like the trunks of mahogany trees. Lourdes said he was her husband, he suffered from the disease elephantiasis. Amelia would burn with fever and lift her head to sip white, watery liquids or feel a spoon pour a bitter drug into her mouth. She would rest her head on the pillow again and see Lourdes's face looking at her, dry patches that were almost white on Lourdes's skin. Amelia had no sense of time. She saw a face she thought was Dr. Henriquez and it confused her, because the anguished woman had told her Dr. Henriquez was gone, taken from her, conscripted into the army of Spain. Now the bearded face came closer and it was Tyler: growing a beard and wearing the clothes of the country, an off-white shapeless suit that belonged to the doctor. Ben seemed different each time she saw him, the beard filling out on his gaunt face, but she knew his eyes; she loved his eyes. He told her he was going native, see if he could look like he belonged. She liked his beard, and when he kissed her forehead, her cheek and then her mouth she knew it was Ben, even if she didn't see his eyes. Ben always close whenever she woke up. She asked about the faces she saw with deformed features; were they real or did she dream them. He told her they were lepers and this was their home, San Lázaro, and she remembered Victor a

year ago as they sat astride horses telling about a
leper home in Las Villas where he knew a woman.
Ben told her there were three small houses behind
the main building in the grove of banana trees: the
houses, stone with thatched roofs and dirt floors,
were for married couples and this one wasn't being
used. He told her he stayed with her here, slept in a
hammock. Not the hammock full of money; that one
was hidden in the thatch of the ceiling. It was
Lourdes who cooked and attended her, gave Amelia
her quinine and green coconut milk, bathed her each
day and helped her manage the chamber pot and
into bed again to lie helpless, drained of all her
strength. She asked who the white woman was. Ben
said her name was Mary Lou but everyone called her
Miss Janes. She had come here to help Luis Henriquez, but now he was gone and she didn't know
what would happen to her. She wanted to go home,
but didn't see how that was possible with the blockade, no ships going to American ports. There were
words Amelia heard but didn't always understand,
or know if the words were spoken to her or if she
heard them in her mind. She would tell Ben she
wanted to die and he would put his mouth on hers,
and then—so close that she could see only his eyes,
his beard—he would whisper things to her, saying
he loved her, saying she would be his girl forever.
She would hear Ben and Victor talking, Victor telling how to find the drug shop, the one he had gone
to for quinine. Ben saying nothing was going to hap-

pen to him, not now, after all they'd been through. Victor saying yes, but just in case, one day I don't come back. Victor saying the Guardias were in Las Villas everywhere you look. Saying he had not seen Tavalera—thank you, God—but was sure he had seen Osma. Ben telling Victor he must be wrong; how could the man still be alive. Victor saying who knows, but when you see him, you know it.

A morning came and Amelia knew she was recovering, that she could get up from this cot and pretty soon would be herself again. She asked Tyler, "How long have I been lying here?"

He said, "Just over a month."

She said, "My God, that long?" And said, "I think in a day or so we'll be able to leave."

Tyler shook his head. "They're still looking for us."

She said, "You told me you love me."

He said, "I give you my word, I do."

OSMA WONDERED if the woman they were looking for could be among the women who bathed in the stream.

It served as a public bath for the poor, a time reserved for men and another for women. From the stone bridge on the Imperial Road, Osma would observe the women through binoculars, searching for pale skin and finding most of it as dark as his own. A few women stripped to the waist to bathe;

the rest removed almost none of their clothes,
allowing parts of their bodies to remain filthy. Some
would do their laundry along the edge of the stream;
some would sun themselves on the rocks, like liz-
ards. If it was the men's turn Osma would take one
look and leave to ride up and down the streets of Las
Villas or sit with Tavalera, who said they had to be
here still. But where? They had searched the hospital—Osma believing the woman to be ill—
churches, a girls' school, hotels, inns, the homes of
people suspected of being mambí sympathizers, and
several estates close to the city.

The Guardias Civiles stood in pairs in the shade
of porticoes and galleries, inspecting all who passed.
Osma saw this as no different than what Guardias
always did. They stood about to be looked at, but no
one dared look at them except Osma. He would
walk up to a pair and see them shuffle in their boots
or cock a hip to one side as he came, getting ready
for him. He'd ask them, "Have you seen any gringo
cowboys today? One tried to put a hole in me"—
Osma touching his side—"but his bullet only took
off some fat, here, that I don't need."

Tavalera was seldom found at the Guardia Civil
barracks, on the property of the governor's palace.
Word had come from Havana ordering him to bring
his corps back to the capital. He wired his reply saying a spy had informed him of a mambí plan to
attack Las Villas and he insisted on being here when
they came. It could be true. At any rate it was the

story he used to remain here and search for the old man, the woman and the cowboy. He had moved into a house that suited him, keeping on the retired couple who lived there as his servants. In the evening he would sit in the garden and drink whiskey, sometimes with Osma, the major no longer wearing the bandage around his head. Some of the things he said while drinking:

"When we find them, they'll be right under our nose all the time. We'll wonder why we didn't think to look there as soon as we came."

"We should look for the dun horse. Perhaps he sold it to someone here."

"When we think we see him, look again, because he will have changed his appearance."

"Look for the spurs he wears. Or listen for them."

"He could be posing as someone else, not American, perhaps *Inglés*. But he won't speak the same as the *Inglés*."

Tavalera was no longer eager to talk about the war or to find his place in it. He said there had been a naval engagement in the Philippines and a small one off Cienfuegos. He said it required months of planning to assemble an army. Spies had reported ships waiting at Port of Tampa and the movement of troops there from other parts of America. He said there was still time before an army came.

"But how long can these three hide and not be seen by anyone? Seven weeks now."

ONE EVENING HE SPENT with Tavalera, Osma drank too much whiskey listening to him. The next day he went to a drug shop for a bottle of Bromo-Seltzer or some stomach bitters. He stood waiting in the shop as the young clerk in a smock told a male customer about an old man who had come in twice to buy Lydia Pinkham medicine. Twice, the only times in the history of the drug shop a man had asked for Lydia Pinkham. The clerk said he wanted to ask the old man if it was for him. It would be funny, but the druggist would say he was disrespectful, even though the old man was mulatto. Several other times, the clerk said, the old man came in to buy quinine.

Osma said to the clerk, "Several times, uh?" thinking of the woman he had thought was ill by the way she rode her horse—weeks ago, but a picture of it still clear in his mind: her head lolling up and down with the horse's gait. "What was the quinine for, malaria?"

The clerk said, "No, yellow fever."

"I heard you don't have yellow fever here."

"Not many cases, no."

"Do you know him, this old mulatto?"

The clerk said he didn't, and Osma asked when he was in last. The clerk said oh, perhaps two weeks ago. He came in three times for the quinine and each time was two weeks from the time before. "One of the times," the clerk said, "he wanted another medicine also, but now I can't remember what it was."

Osma said, "So you think it's time for him to come in again?"

"It would seem so."

"All that quinine, the patient must be better by now. Wouldn't you think?"

"He should continue to take it," the clerk said, "to make sure. And if I think of the other medicine he bought, I'll tell you."

"That's all right," Osma said, and went to find Tavalera.

# 23

THE LEPER HOME SAT in a jungle of banana trees: an acre of trees ten feet high fronting on the Imperial Road by several acres deep, extending back to a creek where a rickety structure stood among cottonwoods, an old hay barn from another time. They stabled the horses here, water and graze close to the shelter. Every day Tyler would go back there to look at the horses, once in a while rubbed them down and gave them a hunk of sugarcane to chew on. They kept their tack in the shelter, ready to throw on saddles and ride out if the search for them ever came too close.

Tyler was with the horses when Fuentes appeared, the old man dressed for town, wearing a necktie with his coat and hat, saddlebags over his shoulder. "One last trip to the drug shop," Fuentes said, taking his revolver from his waist and slipping it into a saddlebag.

"Amelia looks to be out of the woods," Tyler said. "Why take the chance if she doesn't need anything?"

"Yes, she's been helping the woman this morning, that Miss Janes, and appears well, but you can't be sure. Listen, I hear the troops in Las Villas are going to Oriente, where they expect your army to come. So now the risk is nothing to speak of. If we going to leave soon I should get more quinine."

"You're tired of sitting around, that's all."

"Maybe that's it, tired of doing nothing after doing so much, uh?" He slipped the bridle over his horse's muzzle. "Did you think we would make it through all that?"

"I thought I came here to sell horses."

"And some guns," Fuentes said, "that put you in prison and what happens, a pretty girl gets you out. When Amelia told you of the money, did you think she wanted to steal it?"

"We don't see it as stealing."

"Whatever pleases you to call it. But were you surprised?"

"At first, but not once I got to know her. She wanted to, I believe Amelia could rob banks and make a good living."

"She's young," Fuentes said, "as you are. The two of you have fifty years to do what you want. I look in the future, is not so clear. Oh, I see a nice house, a garden. I see a woman who's not old but not young either, one who's just right for me. I sit down in my house and for the rest of my life the woman waits on me and I don't move."

"I can't see you sitting still."

"Well, once in a while I think of it and take the woman to bed. That's what I'm going to do with my life after this, nothing."

Fuentes saddled the horse as he spoke, Tyler watching him pull up on the cinch strap and loop it through the ring. He said, "Did you ever think I might run off with the money, being a bank robber at one time?"

Fuentes looked at him now. "You? Of course not, you are a man of honor. And you have Amelia. Could you think of leaving her? You be crazy."

"I've wondered if she'll leave me."

"You *are* crazy, I mean to think that. You going to get married and be together always forever."

"I don't know about that."

"She think so, she told me."

"She did?"

"Why you so surprised?"

"I haven't asked her."

"What is that? Some things you know without asking. I would know it even if she don't tell me."

"That we'll get married?"

"Yes, of course." Fuentes glanced over. "It's nothing to be afraid of."

Tyler watched him throw on the saddlebags,

more of a bulge to them than that Colt that he'd slipped into one side. "What've you got in there, clothes?"

"A poncho for the rain."

"The sky's clear blue, all the way up."

"You don't know Cuba, not yet."

"The way you're talking," Tyler said, "you make it sound like this business is over with and there's nothing to worry about."

"We close to it. Listen, yesterday I saw a man on the road I know from old times. He tells me of an American ship, the *Eagle*, not a big one but I don't know what kind, I think has a 6-pound gun. The ship is blockading the harbor of Cienfuegos off Colorados Point. A Spanish torpedo boat, the *Galicia*, goes out to fight it and the *Eagle* blows the smoke pipe from the *Galicia* and destroys its boiler. Listen, whenever the panchos try to stand before the Americans they can't do it. It will happen that way when your army comes—my friend say on the south coast of Oriente, near Santiago de Cuba. They don't have time for us here no more, even the Guardias of Tavalera will be going."

"But you saw Osma."

"That was some time ago. Listen, I know him. If Osma don't have to fight, why should he?"

They walked back through the banana forest, Fuentes leading his horse, to the house where Amelia stayed.

"I could grow this fruit," Fuentes said. "That

doctor say they ready to pick in eight months from the time you plant, and you can make as much as fifteen hundred dollars an acre."

"You said you were gonna just sit."

"Yes, I have my woman pick the bananas."

Amelia came out, a hand raised to shield her eyes from the sun: Amelia looking pale and scrawny in a faded blue dress too big for her. Fuentes told her she never looked more beautiful and she touched her crop of short hair and seemed to pose to show them her profile, a woman in an advertisement, her slender nose in the air. Amelia almost herself again.

Tyler watched them together, Fuentes giving Amelia a hug and kissing her cheek.

Tyler watched the old man step into his saddle, and as he rode out past the main house toward the road, raise his hand to wave.

Amelia came over to take Tyler's arm and press herself against him. They watched Fuentes turn into the road.

"That's the first time he's ever waved," Tyler said. "It's like he's saying good-bye."

"Victor sometimes shows a sense of drama," Amelia said. "He offers a fond farewell on the chance that, I guess after all we've been through together, we might not see him again."

"Or he doesn't expect us to."

"Why wouldn't he?"

Tyler stared at the road, empty now.

"He's an old patriot, and he left here armed. I

think he has some kind of scheme in mind, maybe even thinking to shoot somebody."

"A last desperate act in the name of freedom," Amelia said, sounding sad. "I hope you're wrong."

THE CAFÉ WHERE Tavalera and Osma waited was on a corner, on the opposite side of the street from the drug shop halfway down the block. They sat outside beneath the portico, behind the rows of Greek columns that extended along the curb. This was the third day of observing the drug shop, most of the time Osma standing watch, dedicated to the task, anxious to meet that cowboy again face-to-face. Tavalera would send Guardias to relieve him and stop by himself from time to time, Tavalera as anxious as Osma, wanting with all his heart the old man who came in to buy the Lydia Pinkham and quinine would turn out to be Victor Fuentes.

"Once," Osma said, "the old man bought a third medicine, but the clerk couldn't remember what it was. I could go ask, see if it returned to his memory."

"Do you think it matters?"

"I doubt it."

They watched the drug shop hoping to see the clerk come out to lower the awning over the front windows, the signal that would tell them the old man had returned and was inside. This morning they were distracted by the noise of people cheering,

illegal guns going off all over the city—though not
on this street with Guardias waiting in doorways,
horses tethered on the side street around the corner
from the café.

Tavalera took a sip of his cold coffee.

"This is my last day."

"You said that yesterday."

"Now it's true. I can't stay here."

"You like Santiago? That's where you'll go."

"Now my orders are return to Havana."

"So you can protect the captain-general. Blanco
must be shitting his pants by now."

"Mariel is still believed to be an invasion point.
Land there and take Havana."

They sat in silence for several minutes, staring.

"When you were on the train," Tavalera said,
"you don't know if they had opened the hammock.
But what about their faces? Did they express a particular kind of feeling to you? Their attitude, their
state of mind?"

"You want to know," Osma said, "were they
joyous or were they depressed, their faces hanging?
This cowboy has a gun in my belly. You think I'm
making a study of their faces?"

Tavalera said nothing and they were silent again,
Osma staring at the drug shop. Now Tavalera closed
his eyes.

He sat without moving, hands folded in his lap.
He heard in his mind the words: *Oh God . . . Listen, if You let this man be Victor Fuentes and he takes*

*me to the hammock and inside is forty thousand dollars, American funds . . . if in Your divine generosity You make this happen, I will give to the Church that portion of the money I was going to give Osma, who is an athe-ist with the manners of a fucking goat and is unworthy.*

Though he had not yet decided how much he'd give Osma, he realized the amount wouldn't seem enough to pledge to Holy Mother Church. No, he would have to give something else. Perhaps offer an act of mortification. He thought about it and when he continued to pray said:

*Oh God, grant my petition and whenever I go to Mass, I promise to fall on my knees at the Consecration and remain there until after the Communion, which I will receive, after I go to Confession.*

He saw himself at Mass, perhaps the only man on his knees in the entire Havana cathedral, his head bowed in supplication.

Osma turned to look at him.

"What are you doing, sleeping?"

TYLER DECIDED AGAINST riding the dun. He saddled Amelia's sorrel and brought it through the grove of broad green leaves to the yard behind the main house.

Miss Janes in her sun hat was there, and Amelia, at a wooden table where the twelve lepers who lived here stood in line and Miss Janes, from Gretna, Lou-isiana, would speak to each one in turn, touching them, applying medication, passing them on to Amelia, who bandaged the ones with open sores. The lepers with missing toes hobbled off. The man with elephantiasis moved past on his enormous legs and Tyler saw Amelia looking at him. She said something to Miss Janes, rose from the table and came over.

"You've made up your mind."

"He's been gone too long."

"You said yourself he was up to something. Whatever it is, there's nothing we can do about it. Is there?"

"You can tell me whatever you want to say and I'll listen," Tyler said, "but I'm going. I'll ask at the drug shop if he was there. Victor told me how to find it. I'll look around, stick my head in a café— he's got friends here, you know—and if I don't see him I'll come right back."

She said, "I don't want to lose you."

Looking up at him with her sad, moist eyes, this adorable girl. He said, "I want so bad to pick up and take you in the house."

"Why don't you?"

It made him smile because he believed she meant it. "When you get your strength. I don't want you going around with bruises all over you."

"You promise?"

"I'm yours, girl, from now on."

She said, "I've never wanted anybody so bad in my whole life. You promise you'll always love me?"

"Wherever we are."

She said, "That's something we'll have to talk about, huh?" Beginning to sound her normal self again.

"You want to stay here?"

*"Here?"*

"In Cuba."

"And do what?"

"Run a cow outfit, a horse ranch. It's all I know how to do."

He watched the tip of her tongue play against her upper lip, back and forth, Amelia picturing things. He said, "Think about it while I'm gone. I won't be long."

He saw the woman in the sun hat watching them. She called out, "Amelia?"

Amelia glanced over her shoulder and then looked up at Tyler. "I almost forgot—we need chaulmoogra oil. Should I write it down?"

THERE WAS A SAMENESS about these city streets in Cuba, lined with one- and two-story buildings, stone and concrete, weathered facades wearing away, big windows with wood shutters open. Tyler found the street he wanted and came to the drug shop in the middle of the block. He heard people some distance away yelling, and gunfire that sounded more in celebration than serious. He wondered if today was some kind of national holiday.

Spotting a pair of Guardias in a doorway didn't seem cause for alarm; that's what they did, they stood around.

The drug shop was dim inside, rows of drawers on the wall behind the counter. The druggist, an elderly man in a white doctor's smock, asked to help him. Tyler gestured toward the street. "What's all the yelling and shooting about?"

The druggist's eyes came open behind his pinch-nose glasses on a black ribbon. "You don't hear? The Americans have come with their army. Two days ago in Oriente. You don't know about it?"

"Where did they land?"

"Two places, Siboney and Daiquirí, to march on Santiago de Cuba. Also I think Guantánamo. You know where those places are?"

"I don't care," Tyler said, wanting to hug the man, "long as they're in Cuba. Have you heard they've had a battle?"

"I only know the American army is here, thousands of soldiers, thank God, finally."

"How did you hear?"

"It came to the train station, on the telegraph."

All kinds of questions were popping in Tyler's head, but now he was anxious to get back and let Amelia know. He told the druggist he needed a bottle of quinine, then brought a note out of his coat pocket and glanced at it. "And chaulmoogra oil, if you have any." He looked up to see a younger man in a white doctor's smock appear through a doorway from the back of the shop.

Right away this one, this clerk, staring hard at Tyler, said, "chaulmoogra—that was it, what the old man wanted I couldn't think of. Are you with the old man?"

"I might know him," Tyler said. "Have you seen him today?"

"You are with him, yes?"

"What old man you talking about?"

"You buy quinine and chaulmoogra as he did. Yes, you're with him, I know you are."

"Just tell me, was he here today?"

The druggist, looking confused, began speaking to his clerk in Spanish, Tyler not able to catch any of it except *qué pasa,* the druggist wanting to know what was going on. His clerk didn't even look at him. He said to Tyler, "Not today, yesterday. And you know where I saw him?" This young know-it-all looking down his nose at Tyler. "On the road talking to another old one like him, on the road by the banana trees. You one of the Americans they looking for, and you live at the leper house, don't you?"

He didn't stay for an answer or even hesitate as the druggist was questioning him, excited now, raising his voice. By now the clerk was around the end of the counter and running out to the street yelling, *"¡Está aquí! ¡Está aquí!"* Telling anyone who could hear him, "He's here!" as he yanked on a rope and an awning came down across the front of the shop.

Tyler got his horse from under it, slapped its rump and swung up on the saddle as the horse bolted, stretching its head to run. Behind him he could hear the clerk yelling, *"¡Chaulmoogra para los lazarinos!"*

"I THOUGHT I'D DIE once Dr. Henriquez was gone. I said, 'How can they take you? You're not even Spanish.' It didn't seem to matter. When I think about it, it was only four months ago, during Mardi Gras when we met. Luis had been visiting the hospital at Carville? It's up above New Orleans—I'd heard of it, but of course I've never been there. Dr. Henriquez told me about his work here and I said, 'Oh, Luis, please take me with you.' I was prepared that moment to dedicate the rest of my life to these people."

They sat at the table in the yard cutting up squash and yucca for soup, both in sun hats and aprons, Miss Janes' hands in white gloves. She spoke in quiet tones, unhurried by her anguish. "Do you think I was foolish? My mother does. She can't believe I'm here. At least I keep busy—thank God for small blessings. I keep hoping I'll hear from Luis. I don't even know what I'd do. I can't just leave. Until you came I had no one at all to talk to. While you were ill Victor provided *some* company.

You're so fortunate to have Ben. Do I envy you. I think, my Lord, just a few months ago my only concern, would my carnival gown be ready in time. This country, it's so . . . primitive. I don't think I can stay much longer."

"I love it," Amelia said.

"It is pretty."

"It's beautiful," Amelia said.

"You're so lucky. How long, if I may ask, have you known Ben?"

It was the first time the woman had asked Amelia anything about herself.

"I've known him all my life," Amelia said.

It was a few minutes later the woman straightened, cocking her head in the sun hat, listening.

"What was that?"

Amelia was up from the table. She said, "Gunshots," running to the house where she stayed.

# 24

THEY SAW HIM. They ran out to the street and saw the awning down and saw him swinging up on the horse and riding away from them. Tavalera looked toward the side street, waving for the horses.

Osma, his gaze holding on the horseman in white, was shaking his head.

"It's not the old one."

Now Tavalera was studying the figure becoming smaller up the street.

"Not Fuentes, no. It's the cowboy."

"That one rides a dun."

"It's the cowboy," Tavalera said. "Believe me."

Four Guardias came running with the horses and now Tavalera was deliberate in the way he mounted, careful not to appear eager. His troop behind him, he rode to the drug shop, where the clerk was in the street with his arms raised calling for them to stop. It

slowed them to a dogtrot and now the clerk ran
along close to the riders, pointing, telling them to go
to San Lázaro, the home of the lepers on the Imperial Road, two kilometers past the bridge, the clerk
calling, repeating, "San Lázaro!" as they rode away
from him, Tavalera raising his voice to Osma:
"What did I tell you. Under our nose."

So they would go to the leper home, not have to
waste time looking up and down streets. They kept
to a good pace and were coming onto the stone
bridge when they saw him, the cowboy not more
than a few blocks ahead of them. Osma pulled his
pistol, a Broomhandle Mauser, extended it as he
rode and began firing at the cowboy. He had little
chance of hitting him, but it satisfied Osma to pull
the trigger and hear the reports. Now they appeared
to be gaining on him; he was looking back.

*Saying follow me*, Tavalera thought. *Follow me
and don't go to the leper home.*

Now the cowboy was running hard again, con-
tinuing up the road past the grove of banana trees.
Tavalera brought his troop to a halt at the entrance
to the property, the leper home in there at the end of
the lane.

He said to Osma, "You see what he's doing? He
wants us to follow him, not go in this place. They're
in there because no one searched it. Isn't that true?"

"I didn't search it," Osma said. "Did you?"

"If I had known it was here," Tavalera said.
"What is it, you're afraid to go in there?"

"It's not that I'm afraid," Osma said, "it's because I know better than to be among lepers. You have enough men, you can go in without me."

"Or I bring them out," Tavalera said, already knowing what he would do, certain the cowboy was close by and would try to come to the house. He might run away leaving Fuentes—what was Fuentes to him?—but he wouldn't leave Amelia and that hammock they risked their lives to steal. He said to Osma, "The cowboy will find a way to come around behind the property and approach the house from back there. I give you two men, you go in the banana trees and wait for him."

"I can shoot him?"

"Of course, shoot him. Go on, while I speak to someone at the house. Negotiate," Tavalera said. "Offer them a way to remain alive."

AMELIA, HOLDING A CARBINE, watched from a front window of the main house, her view: through the shaded porch to the lane that reached some fifty meters to the road. Miss Janes, behind Amelia and across the room, stood at the dining table where they had gathered the lepers.

Now Tavalera appeared in the lane, two Guardias with Mausers behind him. He came halfway to the house, stopped and called in English, "Send the lepers out!"

Amelia turned her head. "Did you hear him?"

Miss Janes said, "But why?" with that tone of anguish in her voice again.

"I suppose he'd like them out of the way."

"But what does he *want*?"

"*Me.*" Amelia's voice trailing off as she said, "And Ben and Victor . . . wherever they are."

She heard the woman ask, "How does he know you're here?"

And then Tavalera again: "Are they coming or not?"

Amelia turned to Mary Lou. "We have to do it," and said to the frail black woman who had fed and nursed her, "Lourdes, take everyone outside."

For the twelve to get up from the table and file through the door took several minutes: Lourdes with a hand on her husband's arm leading them, her husband lifting his tree-trunk legs one and then the other, the lepers creeping along behind them, across the porch.

Amelia watched Tavalera wave at them to come on, hurry up. She raised the carbine and put the front sight on his chest, Tavalera standing in full view, hands now on his hips. She hesitated and now the twelve were in the lane, coming between Tavalera and the front sight. She could see him gesturing again, separating the lepers, some of them to one side of the lane, the rest to the other side, getting them out of the way—all but Lourdes's husband. Tavalera took him by the arm, pushing Lourdes away, and turned him to face the house.

Now the front sight was on Tavalera again as he called to the house in English, "Amelia? Come out now, dear, or I begin to shoot these poor people."

She kept the carbine steady as she aimed, the oiled-wood smell of the stock against her cheek, and his voice called out again:

"Do you believe me? If you don't, I show you."

Tavalera drew his pistol and, still holding the man with elephantiasis by the arm, shot him through the head. Amelia saw the man fall and saw Lourdes, crying out, try to throw herself on his body, but Tavalera caught her by the arm, pulled her over to him and placed his pistol at her head. This time there was a singsong air to his voice as he called:

"Amelia, dear, I don't see you."

She stepped out to the porch, unarmed. Tavalera released the black woman and came toward the house.

"Let them go," Amelia said.

Tavalera gestured with his hands. "Of course."


TYLER WAS BACK in the cottonwoods, at the hay barn they used for a stable. He was putting Amelia's saddle on the dun when he heard the pistol shot, that hard thin *pop* coming from the direction of the leper house. Tyler stood listening. He saw Amelia pull a gun out of her skirt and one of them shoot her. But then thought, No, she did that they'd all let go at her. Or she would've got one before they got her and that still would've been more than one shot.

He had recognized Lionel and the one called Osma, looking back to see the little drug clerk son of a bitch running along by their horses. Then on the road he was able to count six of them. Now some were at the leper house and some would've followed him. . . . Unless Lionel looked at it, couldn't see him leaving Amelia and Victor, and all that money, and knew he'd come sneaking back. So Lionel— wouldn't he put some of his men in the grove to wait?

He might already have Victor.

But that little clerk son of a bitch said he saw Victor yesterday talking to another old man. It could've been some fella from the old days, up on what was going on. Tyler wondered if Victor might not've found out then the American army was in Cuba. But if he did, and that's why he acted like this business was about over . . . Yeah? Why didn't he mention it?

Tyler told himself that was enough thinking for one day. He slipped a sixth cartridge into each of his .44 Russians. He had two horses ready. But should he bring both of them? No, not with what he had to do. There'd be horses, all kinds of horses, if he did this right and didn't get shot first. This time he led his cutting horse, the dun, out of the shelter and mounted.

AMELIA WAITED on the porch, the carbine inside the house. Tavalera came up, seemed to study her and said, "I understand you've been ill. I believe it, you don't look so good. But, I have to say, you don't look so bad either. Where is Victor?"

It caught Amelia by surprise. He had to notice it, the change in her expression.

"You don't know where he is?"

"He left this morning."

"To go where?"

"He didn't say."

"You such good friends—he rides off, he doesn't tell you where he's going?"

Amelia didn't answer.

Tavalera stepped closer to the window to look in the house. "Who is that woman?"

"She manages the home."

"Lives with lepers—I have to admire her. Do you think she might know where Victor is?"

"She doesn't know anything about us. Miss Janes has her own problems."

"Yes, I would think so, living here. You didn't show her what you carry in the hammock? I was thinking perhaps you opened it to give her something."

Amelia said nothing.

"This hammock you have hidden someplace? Perhaps where you sleep?"

Amelia remained silent.

"You don't tell me there is no money. You don't say go ahead and search for it. Listen, what I'm thinking, you and I could share it. All you been through, you work so hard to get it. . . . I would be willing to give you some. Uh, what do you think?"

Amelia said, "Do you have Tyler?"

"The cowboy? We know where he is. Pretty soon you hear some guns? It means he's no more."

Amelia shook her head very slowly from side to side.

"You don't believe me?"

"If you don't have him now you never will."

"I don't care about the cowboy. I'm thinking of my life, what happens to me after this war. And you must have been thinking what happens to you—am I right? The reason you took the money? Get it, Amelia, and we leave right now, go back to Havana."

She said, "Or what?"

"You mean if you refuse? Then I shoot another leper—take your pick. If they don't mean anything to you, that's all right, then I shoot that woman in the house."

LOURDES REMAINED with her husband, kneeling over him, praying to Almighty God to take his soul, praying to St. Barbara to give her strength. Two frail women, mulattas, stood in the lane watching her. By the time Lourdes rose all the lepers had wandered off, all but these two women, waiting; and when Lourdes made the sign of the cross over her husband, the two women went into the house. Lourdes followed, walking past the two Guardias on the porch without looking at them. These were the two who had remained with Tavalera; they had brought all six horses to the porch rail and tied them there.

In the main house Miss Janes sat at the dining table with her hands folded. Lourdes thought she looked to be asleep with her eyes open. Or in a trance, having seen a man put to death.

One of the women who had waited brought a machete from the folds of her skirt. She told Lourdes that Amelia had taken the officer back to the house she was using. The second woman came out of the kitchen with a machete in one hand, a butcher knife in the other. Lourdes was fifty-two and loved her dead husband. She chose the machete.

She looked out the window to see the two Guardias on the porch undoing the front of their trousers. Now both were pissing from the end of the porch into a flower bed.

OSMA, WELL INTO THE GROVE now with the two Guardias Tavalera had given him, stopped to speak to them for the first time. He said, "The cowboy is close enough that he heard the shot. He doesn't know what it means, but it will make him more anxious to reach the house, from wherever he is back there."

The Guardias looked around them as Osma spoke, maybe listening to him, maybe not. They were both veterans of three years fighting mambís, their eyes dull, their full mustaches covering their mouths. One said to the other, "Who did he shoot, a leper?"

The other one said, "Of course. He won't shoot the woman. Maybe the old one, but not the woman. Would you shoot her?"

"I don't think so, but I know I would fuck her," the first one said.

"Listen to me," Osma said. He waited for these veterans to look at him with their weary eyes, tired and red perhaps from drink. "This one, this cowboy, he makes up his mind, he doesn't wait, he does it. He wants to be a hero and save his companions. But he knows he has to be careful and creep through these trees like a cat. But look at this growth." They weren't looking, they were gazing about. So Osma kicked at the weeds and dry dead leaves with his boot. "You see? They don't clear between the rows. That's good, so we can hear him coming. We spread out and wait. You over there," Osma pointing, "and you over that way, thirty, forty meters between us, and we wait. Like waiting for deer. We don't move. You understand? We don't want to shoot each other, so we only shoot at whoever is moving, and that will be the cowboy. My friends, we have the best part of this game."

"You know," one of the Guardias said, "we have had nothing to eat today. You think there's food in that house?"

The other one said, "Are you crazy? You want to eat food prepared by lepers?"

They moved off together talking of food, the one asking the other, "What do lepers eat? I wonder, because I've never seen a fat leper."

Osma hissed at them, "We have to separate, spread out!" But they continued walking away, paying no attention to him, and now they were hidden among the trees. Osma moved off in the other direction, not far, took out his Broomhandle Mauser and squatted down among the hanging fronds to sit on his heels. He could still hear the Guardias moving in the leaves. That kind—they didn't argue or even speak to him, because he was mulatto. It was the way it was, here and even with Americans. He had heard that they blew up their own ship, the *Maine*, so they could blame the panchos and have reason to declare war on them; and it was all right to destroy the ship because most of the crew were Negroes and all the officers, who were of course white, had gone ashore. From his own experience Osma believed it could be true. He checked the Broomhandle Mauser now, feeling the weight of it, twenty rounds in the magazine that extended down from in front of the trigger guard. He loved this gun Tavalera had got for him. You could shoot this beauty all day without having to reload.

He heard something and got to his feet.

Not the Guardias, not from that direction.

It sounded like . . . It *was,* a horse coming, Christ, running hard, cutting through the trees, those big leaves waving, breaking and there he was, the cowboy on the dun coming right at him. Osma extended the Mauser, wanting so bad to shoot him, but in that moment saw the revolver pointing at him, saw the smoke burst from the muzzle as it fired and felt himself punched in the chest so hard he took a step back, still on his feet as the dun rode him down, slammed him flat on his back to lie in the dead leaves. Now he was looking at green ones hanging over him and part of the sky, not knowing how this could have happened. He said to himself, I was ready. Wasn't I ready? I was watching. . . . Osma had time to think this before he saw the cowboy standing over him blocking the sky. He tasted blood in his mouth but couldn't swallow and felt it warm on his cheek. He saw the cowboy—his face with a beard he didn't have before, on the train, and a different hat—come closer to him to say in a voice he could barely hear, "This one's gonna do it, partner. Your luck's run out."

THE TWO GUARDIAS SQUATTING in the shade looked at each other, waiting to hear the mulatto call out that

he got him. One shot. He had spoken forever about
the Broomhandle and the twenty rounds it held and
now he would boast of having to use only one to kill
the cowboy. They rose, pushing up on their carbines. Now, waiting in the silence that hung over the
grove, the two Guardias looked at each other again.
One of them shrugged and called out, "Osma?"

They waited, beginning to look about them.

AMELIA AND TAVALERA HAD COME to the one-room house
where she stayed. Both were looking at the thatched
ceiling that began low on the wall and rose to a
peak. Tavalera, holding his hat in one hand, pointed
with the other.

"There?"

"Higher."

Amelia saying no more than she had to, and even
this required an effort.

"I need something to stand on," Tavalera said,
still looking at the ceiling as the sound of a gunshot
came from out in the grove.

Amelia turned to the window facing the wall of
trees and stood waiting.

Tavalera didn't move, his face still raised, listening now. Finally he said, "Only one shot," and
looked at Amelia. "One or a dozen, uh? It makes no
difference. Your cowboy is no more to be." For several moments he held his hat to his chest; but when

Amelia failed to turn around he threw his hat on the cot and began looking around the room again.

"What can I stand on? Not the cot—what else?"

Amelia offered no help. She turned to see him walk to the door, look toward the main house and call out a man's name, and then another. He waited and called the names again and waited a few moments before turning from the doorway. "I think they with the horses. I know they won't go in that house with the lepers. No, they would choose to be with horses." He looked around again. "You don't have a chair in here?" He said, "Excuse me, I have to get the one outside, by the table."

He left and Amelia turned to the window again, to the wall of trees, their broad leaves hanging motionless, then beginning to stir as a breeze came through the grove. She heard him in the house again, and when he said, "Here?" turned to see Tavalera standing on the chair, reaching up to pull out clumps of straw. She said, "How do you know the shot was for Tyler and not one of your men?"

He didn't answer, busy pulling out straw, tearing at it until the rolled, rope-tied hammock appeared, part of it hanging out of the thatch. He tugged at it, leaned aside, and the hammock dropped to the floor.

Amelia stood watching as Tavalera came off the chair saying, "All that work, uh?" and went to his knees on the floor. Untying the rope, he said, "I trust Rollie sent the money and not played a joke."

And said, "What's the matter with me? Of course it's money, or you wouldn't hide it."

Amelia looked up to see Lourdes watching from the doorway.

THE DUN BEGAN SNIFFING at Osma, and Tyler led her off through the rows of trees to what he believed was the middle of the grove, those broad leaves close around him. He looked up at the sky to make sure he knew which way he was facing: due south, the way back to the cottonwoods and the hay barn.

All he'd heard was the one voice call out to Osma, coming from over on his left, which was east, the voice coming just the one time and getting no answer or encouragement. There could be more than one Guardia over there, or they could be spread out. But Lionel only came with five and had four left. He'd keep at least a couple for himself, wouldn't he, to back him up? And send Osma out here with the other two to lie doggo and kill him unawares.

Tyler thought about it as he checked his .44s, the one and then the other, spinning the cylinders and replacing the round he'd fired. He could go directly to the house, but would be leaving one or two here to come up behind him. He could turn it around, wait for them to get tired and start moving around. But that bushwhacking was a bunch of shit; he could sit here all day waiting. Hell, flush 'em, same as you drive strays from a brush thicket. Tyler rubbed the dun's nose, saying, "Mind me now, honey, what I tell you." And stepped into the saddle thinking, as the realization came to him: You call this animal a sweet name but've never called Amelia honey or dear or sweetheart. What's wrong with you? Are you scared of her or what?

It helped sometimes not to know too much, how things would come out—Tyler thinking this as he whistled a quick sharp note, nudged the dun and they took off in a hurry up a narrow space through the tree rows, covered about the length of a square acre when he nudged the dun again, laid the reins across her and she answered, cutting left to go brushing through those big leaves, nudged her again and the dun swerved at the touch, cut back north stretching to run and there was one of them right in front of him raising up with a carbine at his shoulder, firing, but in too much of a hurry and was throwing the bolt as the dun came past, Tyler putting his .44 on the Guardia and *bam*, took the man's hat off with a good part of his skull. Tyler kept on straight ahead, the dun digging in, and a carbine discharged behind him, the report singing off in the air to let Tyler know there was another one. He got the dun to cut left, the tree fronds whipping him, and left again, bringing him back to mid-grove—Tyler telling himself the live Guardia right now would be checking on the dead Guardia, occupied. Tyler came around in a tight circle through the trees, back to

where he hoped to see the dead one and, sure
enough, there was the live one stooped over him—
live for a few more seconds as Tyler came down on
the Guardia bringing up his carbine, Tyler pointing
a .44 at the carbine pointing at him, fired and fired
again and fired again and saw the carbine fly up in
the air. This time Tyler kept going all the way to the
road before he pulled up, took time now to breathe
and reload.

HE SAW THE HORSES in cottonwood shade, four of
them at the porch rail, tails shooing flies, and
Lourdes there in the deeper shade of the porch. She
raised her arm, motioning for him to come and he
walked the dun out of the grove, trusting the
woman, all the way to the house.

Tyler stepped off the dun and let the reins trail
on the ground. Coming up on the porch then he saw
the board floor wet, drying in places, and a mop
sticking out of a bucket of pale-pink dirty water, the
handle leaned against the wall by the window. He
looked in to see Miss Janes seated at the table staring
—not at him, he realized—at nothing. He turned to
Lourdes.

"Amelia?"

"I tell you about her," Lourdes said, and
motioned him to come with her. He took her arm as
she started into the house.

"The Guardias Civiles."

She said, with an accent like Victor's, "Two of them are in hell as we speak," pointing a finger straight down. She said then, "Come with me," and he followed her inside, pausing to look at Miss Janes again.

"She saw terrible things happen she not use to," Lourdes said. "She saw the officer shoot my husband and she saw the two Guardias Civiles put to death."

"Where are they?"

"You don't have to know. Or be concern about this woman. I get some whiskey for her, she be all right. Come, please."

He followed her through the kitchen and across the yard to the stone house where he had lived with Amelia during the past two months. He didn't want to see her lying on the cot again. There had been six horses and two were gone. . . . He didn't know what to expect. Lourdes entered and then Tyler.

He didn't look at the cot. The first thing he saw was the hammock lying open on the floor, empty. His first thought: it was the one he'd been sleeping in. But then looked up and saw where the thatch had been torn open. Lourdes had begun speaking as they entered.

Telling him, "The one who kill my husband, the officer of the Guardias Civiles, he say to Amelia he going to take her to Havana with him. I like to send him to hell with the two soldiers, but he took out his pistol when he saw me here and there was no way I

have to go near him. You understand? He hears the
guns and then he don't hear nothing. He call to his
men and still he don't hear nothing. Then he seem to
want to leave, not stay here longer but go right
away."

"And he took Amelia."

"Yes, he tell Amelia he going to give her back to
a man—I think his name is Rollie. Amelia, she don't
want to go, so he use the rope from the *hamaca* to tie
her, and then pull her with the rope to go with him."

Tyler listened, seeing Amelia with Lionel
Tavalera. He was taking her back. . . . But something didn't make sense and he wanted to be sure he
had heard it right.

"He's taking Amelia and the money to Havana,
to give to Rollie."

Lourdes shook her head. "No money. He is taking Amelia only."

"But it was in the hammock. What happened to
it?"

Lourdes said, "Oh, you talking about that
money. No, your friend Victor took that money.
Yes, in those saddlebags he bring to put it in. Was
this morning and then he left. You don't know that?
Sure, your friend Victor. I know him a long time ago
when I, and also two other women here, we were
*amazonas* during the time of Paulina Gonzales. It
was when we were with Gómez, before our affliction
and we have to come here."

"He tell you where he was going?"

"Victor? I ask him. He say, 'Oh, someplace I can grow bananas.' He say he give me a hundred dollars if I put the *hamaca* up there again, make it look like nobody ever touch it. I say, 'You mean it, a hundred dollars?' He say, 'Sure, why not? I got a lot of money.' " Lourdes smiled. "That Victor, uh?"

# 25

ONCE IT WAS DECIDED Guantánamo Bay would make a dandy coaling station, Huntington's marines were sent in to secure the area. The battalion boarded the steamer *Panther* in Key West and arrived off Guantánamo June 10, their objective: occupy a Spanish blockhouse that sat on a round, green-covered hill on the east side of the bay inlet.

Corporal Virgil Webster stood at the rail of the *Panther* looking at the hill, which did not appear to be much of a climb, only about a hundred and fifty feet, but that green cover was a dense growth of brush and dwarf trees. This time Virgil didn't have a career marine who happened to be the captain's orderly to ask what in the hell are we doing here, so he asked Lieutenant-Colonel Huntington himself, who seemed to admire Virgil for having been blown off the *Maine* and could be spoken to as a man.

"Why here? Why that hill? Virgil, you know the difficulty of laying a collier alongside a battleship in the open sea?"

Yes, he did; it was always a tricky maneuver.

And especially difficult, Huntington said, on this south coast of Cuba with its easterly winds. What they needed was a coaling station in a sheltered area not far from Santiago, where they had the Spanish fleet blockaded, and even closer to where American troops would come ashore to engage the enemy, and Guantánamo Bay filled the bill. There were six thousand Spanish troops fifteen miles away in the city of Guantánamo, but insurgents were up there keeping them busy. They also had a fort up the bay at Caimanera; but the *Marblehead* and the *Texas* would cruise up there and pound it to hell. So once the high ground around here was secured they'd have a coaling station: the reason for starting the war here.

Virgil, with Huntington's marines, went ashore on the tenth. First thing, they burned the Spanish barracks and huts on the beach, in case they were contaminated by yellow fever. Then they looked up at that blockhouse on the hill. It had been shelled good by the cruiser *Yankee*, which had run the dons out of there. But they were still around in force, so holding the blockhouse would not be a picnic.

Which turned out to be the case, mainly on account of the dense green cover on this hill and the ones nearby. Once the dons began to skirmish they kept at it three days and nights, laying down fire on the blockhouse and outposts that had been set up. Virgil and his mates kept waiting for an all-out assault that never came, the dons not anxious to charge the marines' automatic Colt machine guns or the Hotchkiss 3-inchers. But they sure raised hell firing Mausers from cover, with their smokeless rounds that never told where the shooter was. Soon they were sniping from up on nearby hills that were higher than the blockhouse hill and gave the snipers a bird's-eye view of the marines. Any time the fleet turned its big rifles on the hills it would clear them out for a time, then pretty soon they'd come sneaking back. These dons did not lack for courage, regulars in their pinstripe uniforms and funny-looking straw hats. Virgil wished they were Volunteers or Guardias, ones he had reason to hate. Huntington got tired of staying put and sent two companies of marines and about fifty insurgents to Cuzco, six miles east, where there was a heliograph station they used to blink messages to Caimanera, also a well that supplied the dons with their drinking water and five hundred dug-in Spanish troops. Virgil and his mates laid down fire with their Lee rifles, taking trenches and a blockhouse, fought the dons from eleven in the morning till mid-afternoon, finally to drive them off and blow up the well, losing two marines killed and six wounded. Virgil's first sergeant, a man name of Rawley, tallied the enemy casualties and came up with "Sixty-two garlics killed and a hunnert and fifty put on stretchers."

It sure amazed Virgil. He said, "They had position on us, they had numbers—how'd we beat 'em so lopsided?"

" 'Cause we're fucking marines," Rawley said. "Why do you think?"

Maybe it was true.

Later on Rawley sent Virgil to flush out a sniper up on high ground giving them trouble and said, "Take these niggers with you." Three mambís they were using as scouts. "They ain't worth a shit as soldiers, but they're all I can spare."

"They've been fighting a war," Virgil said, "for three years."

The sergeant said, "Yeah? And they didn't win, did they?"

Virgil went up the hill thinking of things to say to Rawley. The hell do you know about it? Shit, you've only been in Cuba five days. You don't even know what you're talking about to say something like that. What—they're not soldiers 'cause they don't wear fancy uniforms? You ever fight with nothing but a machete? In your bare feet? Virgil, thinking instead of paying attention, was hit before he heard that keening whine of a gunshot from way off and went down with a Mauser round, goddamn it, through his side.

The mambís carried him back. Colonel Huntington gave Virgil a pat on the shoulder, telling him, "Hang on, son, it missed your vitals and you are going to make it." That night Virgil was aboard the hospital ship *Solace*, his war over.

# 26

"IN ALL THE ROUSING ACCOUNTS you read in the newspapers," Neely said to Rollie Boudreaux, in the bar of the Hotel Inglaterra, "and in the illustrations of the glorious charge, Teddy is leading his Rough Riders up San Juan Hill. In some accounts they're even on horseback. But there was no mounted cavalry during the campaign; all the horses had been left at Port Tampa, though some staff and division officers had horses. Teddy, as a matter of fact, brought along two, one called Little Texas and another, Rain-in-the-Face, named for an Indian Chief. Teddy did take Kettle Hill, but by the time he got to the San Juan Heights the battle was almost over."

Boudreaux appeared, in his usual calm manner, to be less than interested. He looked not at Neely but across the formal garden in the center of the room, to the arched entrance and an area of the lobby beyond, polished tiles in Moorish patterns halfway up the walls. So far this morning they had the barroom to themselves. Boudreaux had mentioned that Spanish officers, now with the war over, came by in the afternoon.

Neely swirled the ice in his whiskey, staring at it.

"I have nothing against Teddy Roosevelt personally, you understand. He was an inspiring leader once in the fight, truly a brave man. What I resent is his getting all the glory, much of it thanks to Harding Davis, whom you'd think was Teddy's personal press agent. That Eastern Old School crowd hung together in ways you'd have thought the war was staged for their benefit and Teddy won it almost single-handedly." Neely paused. "I take it you understand the significance of San Juan Hill."

He waited.

Boudreaux turned his head now to look at him and it was encouraging, even though the man said nothing.

"San Juan," Neely went on, because he wanted to tell it, present this man with the facts, "was part of the outer defense of Santiago, the port where the Spanish fleet was bottled up, the objective of the campaign." Neely paused again. "I take it you're expecting someone."

Boudreaux raised his eyebrows. "Well, now, that's observant of you, Mr. Tucker."

"If I'm boring you, please tell me."

"Don't worry, I will," Boudreaux said, and then shrugged. "You can continue, if you want."

Neely hung on to his composure. He said, "Thank you," and cleared his throat. "I saw it as ironic that regular-army Negro soldiers, members of the 9th and 10th Colored Cavalry, were made to unload the Rough Riders' gear from the ship while Teddy and his volunteers, amateurs, really, marched off to meet the enemy. And when they walked into an ambush, at Las Guasimas, it was the colored boys along with the 71st Infantry who came along to prevent Teddy's boys from being wiped out. How could something like this happen? Incompetent leadership. Remember 'Fighting Joe' Wheeler, the Confederate general? He was in charge of cavalry, an old man with a white beard. At Las Guasimas, as the dons finally retreated, 'Fighting Joe,' living in the past, was heard to say, 'Boys, we got the Yankees on the run!' American soldiers won this war, Mr. Boudreaux, despite the incompetence of their leaders, especially General Shafter, who was in command. He did suffer from gout and a touch of malaria; all the same even Teddy thought him utterly inefficient. The food was awful or nonexistent. The supply line from Siboney to the front never better than a trickle of whatever was needed to fight a war. Medical facilities were a joke—though not to the wounded lying out in the sun. We lost over two hundred men killed and another twelve hundred wounded. All abdominal wounds were fatal."

"That's interesting," Boudreaux said.

The only rise Neely was able to get from him.

"Why did our army and our navy appear to have separate goals? Why didn't Sampson's fleet bombard San Juan Heights before the assault?"

Boudreaux said, "You're not asking *me*, are you?"

"We had seventeen thousand troops in the campaign. A third of them were sent to take a village called El Caney, defended by five hundred Spanish soldiers. Our boys spent nine hours at the task, when they could've been used in the assault on San Juan Heights."

Boudreaux yawned.

He actually did, yawned in Neely's face. It did not deter the Chicago *Times* correspondent.

"The brigade under General Hawkins was to lead the assault, but due to mix-ups and misgivings —again, poor leadership—it was delayed, the troops pinned down. But then a hero emerged, the brigade quartermaster, of all people, a Lieutenant Jules Ord, jumped up to lead the charge, inspiring men of the 6th and 16th Regiments, yelling, 'Come on, you fellows! Come on! We can't stop here!' They charged into the withering fire of Spanish Mausers and took the hill. This day to mark in our memories, July first, 1898."

Boudreaux raised his glass.

"To our boys."

"Many of them now down with yellow fever."

Boudreaux sipped his drink, then shook his head. "A shame."

"We were poorly armed," Neely said, "compared to the dons. Their Mausers fired smokeless rounds; the Springfields most of our boys had gave off plumes of white smoke when fired, revealing the rifleman's position."

Boudreaux was looking toward the arched entrance again.

"Clara Barton came to the field."

Boudreaux said, "Good old Clara," and glanced at Neely. "Can you guess who's coming here, to see me?"

The man so confident, more relaxed than he had any right to be. Neely was going to say "Amelia," but changed his mind and shook his head.

"I give up."

"Lionel Tavalera," Boudreaux said, "the Guardia major, and if he finds you here . . . If you haven't heard, Spain still runs Havana and American correspondents are not allowed in the city."

"They are," Neely said, "if you have a Double Eagle for the harbor police. I got here on a Norwegian cattle boat out of Santiago. It happened to pull in there looking for coal." He paused to sip his drink before bringing up what was foremost on his mind.

"I spoke to Amelia. She's in the lobby."

"Sitting there for a couple of days now," Boudreaux said, "waiting for someone, but won't tell me who. Did she happened to mention what she's up to?"

Neely shook his head. "But I think she looks—I was going to say no worse for wear, but actually she looks better than ever. Don't you agree?"

"Other than the hair, yes, still quite lovely."

"I understand you met with her. And got on your knees begging her to come back."

"I'm sure you recognized that as a figure of speech," Boudreaux said. "Our relationship, at the moment, is in negotiation. After all, I did put up a great deal of money when her life was at stake. She respects that."

"You make it sound like a business arrangement."

"It does have that tenor, doesn't it?"

"You think you'll get back together?"

"I think Amelia will always go to the highest bidder."

"She seems quite self-sufficient to me."

"Or, as you were going to say, no worse for wear," Boudreaux said. "The sunburn and callused hands might indicate a spirit of enterprise, but what did she get for her effort? Has she told you about it?"

"You know I was with her out in the country."

"With that bandit, Islero. But that was the last you saw of her."

"I got a ride to Key West on a monitor and went

on to Tampa, where the troops were assembling. I can't tell you what a mess that was. Confusion reigned, trains backed up all the way to Columbia, South Carolina."

"You're full of war stories, aren't you, Neely?"

"Once I get talking about it. I'm sorry, I interrupted you."

"Amelia hasn't told you of her adventures?"

"She told me she was ill for quite some time."

"That's all?"

"We only spoke for a few minutes. She seemed to want to be by herself."

"You don't want to betray her confidence," Boudreaux said, "as I trust you will keep what I tell you in confidence. Is it agreed?"

"Of course."

"You can give me your views after. So, who should come to see me but Lionel Tavalera. He's not out in Oriente defending his country's honor, no, he comes to deliver Amelia—not as a courtesy, mind you, but expecting a reward. It's the reason he wants to meet this morning, I'm sure, to badger me again. He arrives with Amelia in tow, I thank him for rescuing the dear girl, and he tells me, no, he didn't save her, he captured her. He tells me it was her scheme from the beginning to get hold of the ransom money and she got the cowboy and my *segundo* to help her. I asked him, what about Novis? He said no, they used Novis."

Neely interrupted. "I haven't seen him around."

"I fired him."

"I'm sorry, go on."

"I asked Tavalera, where's the money now? You understand, since Amelia obviously doesn't have it. Lionel said he didn't know. I asked him when it was he became aware of this conspiracy. On that score he's vague or makes no sense. I think he found out about it early on and planned to grab the loot for himself. Why not? So I asked Amelia. I said tell the truth and all will be forgiven, a lesson learned with relatively little harm done."

"Business is business."

Boudreaux shrugged. "If you like. I asked Amelia what happened to the money, and you know what she told me? Victor has it, my *segundo. Victor?* If it's true and you appreciate irony, then you must see this as a glaring example, the humble servant rides off with forty thousand dollars of his master's hard-earned cash."

Neely couldn't help but smile.

Boudreaux accepted it with a weary expression. "I thought you'd like that, a happy ending for the poor Cuban. Meanwhile, I have no idea what's happened to the cowboy. Amelia doesn't seem to know either. She resides in her own room here at the Inglaterra, under what Tavalera calls 'house arrest.' That applies to me, also. I can't leave the premises until he decides how much of a reward he wants. He claims he could even have us, as he puts it, 'jailed with every courtesy.' I mentioned that Spain still rules here, under the temporary articles of surrender, but with no advice from Madrid. So, I bide my time."

"Knowing," Neely said, "you'll be back in business before too long."

"If not sooner," Boudreaux said.

"But did Amelia actually admit she planned the whole thing, to run off with the money?"

"She did, while looking me straight in the eye."

"Contrite about it?"

"If she were, she wouldn't be Amelia, would she?" Boudreaux smiling just a little. "And I doubt if either of us would hold her in such high esteem."

"You respect her effort?"

"She saw the opportunity and took it."

"But, Rollie, she tried to swindle you out of forty thousand dollars."

"Bless her heart," Boudreaux said, "she's quite an astonishing girl."

Neely had to agree. He said, "I've been wanting to do a feature story about Amelia since the day I met her."

"If you ever do," Boudreaux said, "leave this business out of it, or I'll bring suit against you and your newspaper, whatever it is. And you know I'll win."

THREE DAYS AGO in the dining room having coffee, Amelia looked up to see Rudi Calvo approaching through the tables, Rudi with a stout cane in each hand, hobbling, throwing one leg out with an effort and then the other. Amelia hadn't seen him since Atarés. She rose to put her arms around him and heard him say, close to her, "I told Tavalera." So ashamed, but had to tell who was at the fortress with him and what they were doing there, or they would have cut off his son's legs. Amelia kept him in her arms—people watching, it didn't matter—telling Rudi no one could blame him, don't think about it, she would have done the same, consoling, mothering, getting him to join her at the table. As soon as they were seated he said to her, "The cowboy is near Jovellanos. He's going to be coming here soon. Two more days."

Amelia wanted to pull Rudi over and kiss him, but sat there as he explained how the cowboy was seen, how Tyler was hard to miss even trying to appear Cuban. "He was seen and spoken to by some of our people," Rudi said, "and the news about him came to me because they knew of Atarés." The cowboy, Rudi said, had been looking for the old man, Fuentes, but no one has seen him, not a soul, like he was disappeared. So they kept Tyler hidden until the war ended and now he was coming; but it would be two more days because there was no train he could take. "When I learn you were here, I knew I should tell you. Also that I confessed to the Guardia."

"He has me in prison now, so to speak," Amelia

said. "I'm not allowed to leave the hotel without his permission."

"You mean Lionel Tavalera?"

Amelia, that morning in the dining room, nodded and said, "I just hope he's not here when Ben comes."

THIS MORNING SHE WAS in the lobby and held the door for Rudi as he came in with his canes.

"He's in Regla. He said tell you to sit tight."

"Why didn't he come with you?"

"I took the ferry. He has his horse he rode all this way and won't leave her there. Listen, I'm going outside. It was almost an hour ago I walk from the dock, so he's going to be here soon. Come around by way of Atarés."

Rudi left. Amelia sat in a wicker chair in her white tea dress and made herself wait, glancing at the clock in the lobby, a half hour before she got up and went outside to stand beneath the portico, the outside tables empty except for one, where Rudi sat, away from the entrance. Rudi pointed and she turned to look in the other direction, east along the street past the Tacon Theatre, next to the hotel. There was a horseman way down the street. She looked at Rudi again and saw him nod and turned to watch the horseman.

He was coming. Walking the dun after that long, long ride.

Now she heard horses' hooves on the pavement close to her, a coach pulling up to the entrance, and then her name, "Amelia?" and turned to see Tavalera getting out, the Guardia major in a gray business suit this morning. Smiling at her as he took off his hat.

"Come in, dear, and have a coffee with me."

"Rollie's waiting for you in the bar."

"Then have a glass of wine with us."

"I can't think of a reason I'd want to drink with you," Amelia said, and turned away.

It was Tyler, for sure. She watched him take off his hat, a Cuban straw, and throw it up in the air as he came to the Tacon, the theater. She wanted to run to him and heard Tavalera again:

"Well, if you get thirsty."

He passed behind her entering the hotel.

And she ran to Tyler, holding up her skirts as Tyler was stepping down from the dun, went into his arms and got her mouth on his hard, smelling him, feeling his beard and not wanting to let go, but dying to look at him, too, his face so close and there it was, grinning at her. He said, "Well, you sure look sweet and wholesome. I can fix that in no time. You have a room or you hang out in the street?"

She got her arms under his arms and held on tight feeling hard shapes, his guns, one against her arm and one pressed between them against her bosom.

"You must have your strength back."

Amelia held on to him.

"Don't you talk anymore?"

She said, "God," looking up at him again.

"I may eat you up," Tyler said. They began kissing again. This time as they paused to breathe he said, "How about old Rollie, is he around?"

"He's in the bar."

"I'll get that done and then you and I can go play."

Amelia hesitated.

"Lionel's with him."

Tyler didn't say anything. Amelia watched a kid pick up Tyler's hat from the street and run off with it.

"Lionel brought you here?"

"On the train."

"He behave himself?"

"He bored me to death, that's all, talking."

"Well, I don't have any business with him, unless he messes with my gentle nature."

"You promise?"

He smiled again, running a hand through his hair. "I wondered, did you think I might've taken the money?"

"Of course not."

"Come on, tell me the truth."

"Maybe just for a second. But I knew it was Victor."

"You care?"

She said, "He took forty thousand *dollars*," making a face like she was in pain.

There were kids watching them. Tyler gave his reins to one of them to hold and came back to her saying, "I know where we can get some more. Come on."

NEELY HAD GOT UP from the table as Tavalera entered and came over, the Guardia officer in mufti this morning, paying no attention to him. Neely felt the need to say something.

"So your war's over, Major."

Tavalera gave Neely a moment, looking at him to say, "This one. I plan to stay to see how the Cubans fight you Americans," and sat down with Rollie.

Neely went to the bar to pay for the drinks they'd had, waited for the barman who appeared finally with a bucket of ice, settled the bill, and when he turned saw Amelia entering the bar with Tyler.

It *was* Tyler, though for a moment Neely wasn't sure. He walked back toward the table as Tavalera saw them and rose. Boudreaux remained seated. Now Tyler was looking this way, his set expression relaxing in a smile. He said, "Neely?" sounding glad to see him. They shook hands, exchanging a few words, Neely saying he was dying to hear his story —maybe later sometime? He wanted to hang around without being in the way, a fly on the wall, hear what Tyler and Tavalera would say to each other.

Neely moved off a few steps as though to leave. He saw the way Boudreaux was looking at Amelia and Tyler, the two of them as one—that was the feeling.

He saw Tavalera offer his hand to Tyler, saying, "We fought honorably and now it's over."

Tyler did not take the major's hand, though looked straight at him as he said, "I have no respect for you as a man. You say another word about honor, you son of a bitch, I'll shoot you, even if I have to go back to the Morro. You understand how I feel?"

Neely watched Tavalera consider this with hard eyes, maybe recalling what happened to that hussar officer, Teo Barbón, standing in almost the exact spot. All Tavalera did was shrug, though not without a certain amount of grace. Neely watched Tyler then turn to the table and say to Boudreaux: "I have no respect for you either, Mr. Tinhorn. We'll leave when I have your check for forty-five hundred and forty-five dollars."

Neely caught the *we* in "we'll leave," and he'd bet Boudreaux did too. He would describe the wealthy grower as sitting erect, facing Tyler with a bland expression, about to—what?—turn him down with wit? Logic? Confuse Tyler with demurring rationalizations? No, he reached into his suit coat, brought out his checkbook and then a fountain pen.

His gaze moved to Amelia with what Neely would describe as a look of melancholy transforming the man's bland expression, a sadness in his eyes. A glance at Amelia saw her own eyes as cold as the barman's ice.

Boudreaux became his old self again, filling in the check without hesitation. Extending it to Tyler, he said, "You withhold respect," and seemed to shrug. "I wonder, though, if I could buy just enough of it for you to stay on and run my horse farm?"

It was Amelia who answered, raising her voice to give him a resounding "No!"

Neely heard it as quite final and, it would appear, so did Boudreaux, who raised his glass—Neely thought for a moment to offer them luck. But no, he took quite a big drink of whiskey and put the glass down again.

It would seem to be over.

Until Neely noticed a somewhat familiar face. Yes, it was the municipal police investigator, Rudi Calvo, hobbling in with the support of a hickory cane in each hand. He moved past Amelia and Tyler and now they saw him. Tyler said, "Rudi?" and Amelia reached out to him, but too late. He didn't pause or even look at them, he walked up behind Tavalera, who was about to join Boudreaux at the table.

As Neely saw what happened:

There was Tavalera with his hand on the back of the chair to pull it out.

Rudi Calvo lifting the cane in his right hand to hook it on his left forearm. His hand then went inside his coat, Rudi saying, "Major?"

Tavalera turned.

Rudi's hand come out holding a pistol.

The room silent. Not a sound.

Tavalera seemed about to speak, raising his hand as Rudi raised the pistol and shot the Guardia squarely between the eyes.

The report filled the room and no doubt the ground floor of the hotel.

Tavalera fell dead.

Rudi tossed the pistol on the table, picked up his cane from his arm and hobbled out.


AMELIA WALKED with him through the lobby and held the door open, Tyler a few steps behind, people watching them. Outside, Amelia held on to Rudi's arm, asking him what he would do now, where was he going, if he had a place to hide, telling him to please take care of himself.

"I have a good friend, so don't worry about me."

It was all he said. Rudi walked from the portico to the edge of the street and raised one of his canes in the air.

There were coaches in line waiting. But the one that came was drawn by a matched pair of palominos. Rudi handed his canes to someone inside and pulled himself aboard. The door closed and the coach drove off.

Tyler raised his arm and placed it around Amelia's shoulder.

He said to her, "Man, this Cuba."

She turned her head. "Yeah?"

"It's gonna take some getting used to."